The Iron Curtain

The Iron Curtain

Robert Vaughan

© Copyright 1994 by Robert Vaughan
First e-reads publication 1999
www.e-reads.com
ISBN 1-58586-638-5

This book is dedicated to
my parents,
Richard and Aline Vaughan.
They not only lived this story,
they introduced me to it.

The Iron Curtain

1

JULY 26, 1945, THE MARIANA ISLANDS

A sign just over the door of the flight operations building read: WEL-COME TO NORTH FIELD, TINIAN, THE WORLD'S BUSIEST AIRPORT.

A sprawling complex of barracks and maintenance hangars, several hundred P-51's and B-29's, and four parallel ten-thousand-foot paved runways tended to support the sign's claim. At that very moment three of the runways were active with landing traffic.

On the remaining runway a B-29 was starting its takeoff roll, and the quartet of twenty-two-hundred-horsepower engines with their seventeen-foot, four-bladed props flailing at the warm Pacific air emitted a throaty roar. The glistening giant moved down the runway on its tricycle landing gear, gathering momentum as it passed row upon row of parked fighters, bombers, reconnaissance, and cargo planes until it was a speeding silver streak. As all men everywhere who love airplanes will do, several mechanics from the 315th Bomb Wing stopped their softball game long enough to watch the takeoff.

Three quarters of the way down the runway the bomber rotated, and its nose came up as it broke free of the ground, a graceful bird in flight. But almost immediately a brilliant flash of light came from the left inboard engine, followed seconds later by a heavy, stomach-jarring explosion.

"*Oh, shit!*" one of the mechanics shouted. As everyone watched in dumb-struck horror, the plane nosed back to the ground, then erupted in a huge ball of fire.

General William Canfield, just deplaned and heading for the headquarters building at the far end of the field, ordered his driver back to the crash site. He braced himself against the sway of the vehicle as the driver turned sharply onto the runway, then accelerated to seventy. At the end of the runway thick, oily smoke roiled up from the gasoline-fed flames of the crashed B-29.

"There may be survivors," Willie shouted over the scream of the jeep's engine and the roar of the wind. "It was a maintenance test flight, so there were only three on board."

"Jesus, General, there's no way anyone could lived through that!" Willie's driver, Sergeant Grega, shouted back. "It's burnin' like all hell."

"But it wasn't carrying a bomb load. There's at least a chance that there were survivors."

"Not much of one," Grega insisted.

By the time they arrived at the crash site, the fire trucks and ambulances that were on permanent standby at each end of the runway were already at work. The foam generators of the fire engines were spraying frothy suds into the fire while two asbestos-suited rescue workers dashed into the flames. After what seemed an agonizingly long time they reemerged, carrying one of the bomber crewmen with them. A stream of water was directed toward them as they broke out of the wall of fire.

"Over here! Get him over here!" a medic shouted, holding open the back door of the olive-drab three-quarter-ton truck marked with red crosses.

Struggling with their burden, the two rescuers started toward the waiting ambulance. As the medics loaded the injured crewman, Willie jumped from his jeep and hurried over. He recognized the victim as the flight engineer. The man was conscious but obviously in shock.

"Good work, men," Willie shouted encouragingly to the rescue workers. "What about the pilot and copilot?"

One of the rescuers took off his helmet and shroud, and when he did, Willie was struck by how young he was. He couldn't have been over eighteen. The young man looked at Willie with sad eyes and shook his head.

"Sorry, General. The other two was dead."

"Are you sure?" the noncommissioned officer in charge of the fire detail asked. "How do you know they were dead?"

2

"One of 'em didn't have no head," the young man answered flatly. "The other one had less 'n that."

"Okay, let's go!" one of the medics shouted to the ambulance driver, slapping his hand on the side of the truck. "Get him out of here!"

The ambulance raced off with its siren screaming.

"Did you know the two officers, General?" the noncom in charge asked.

"Yes, I knew them," Willie answered. "The pilot was Major Whittaker, the copilot was Captain Carlisle. They served with me in Germany, and I had lunch with them just a short while ago."

"I'm sorry," the NCOIC replied. "I knew 'em, too. They were fine men, both of them."

Willie sighed. "We've lost a lot of fine men in this war, Sergeant—so at least we know they're in good company."

"Yes, sir, that is a fact," the sergeant agreed. "That is truly a fact."

"General Canfield?" Sergeant Grega spoke up. "You ready to go back now? Don't forget, you got that meetin' with General LeMay."

"I haven't forgotten," Willie replied, walking back to the jeep. He sat in the right front seat with his foot propped up on the door sill and his arms folded across his chest. He stared at the fiery wreckage for a long moment, then said to his driver, "Okay, Sergeant, let's go."

As Grega put the jeep in gear and swung around, leaving the burning bomber behind them, Willie pulled his mind away from his dead comrades to his meeting with Curtis LeMay. He wondered what the general wanted to see him about—and whether his life would once again be irrevocably changed.

Though at five feet nine he was only of average height, Major General Willie Canfield was an imposing figure, a real man's man, with powerful shoulders and arms and a flat stomach, none of which he had to work at. His muscular conformation was just a part of him, like his hazel eyes, his auburn hair, and his stubborn determination. Thirty-seven and unmarried, he was the youngest son of Robert and Connie Canfield and the younger brother of John Canfield, once an adviser to President Franklin D. Roosevelt and now holding that same position of trust with President Harry S. Truman.

Willie wasn't a career Army officer and held his rank by direct congressional appointment. Shortly after the war had begun, President Roosevelt had prevailed upon him to accept the commission so that the War Department could utilize Willie's experience as president of a major airline. In creating and building World Air Transport, Willie had set up maintenance support bases and airline terminals and established worldwide airline routes; his experience with the movement of equipment and personnel and the demands placed on the support system by a large fleet of planes flying an intense schedule was an invaluable asset in helping the United States establish a bomber command in Europe.

Willie's World Air Transport venture was far from the Canfield family's conservative business roots. The family had made its fortune through landholdings and Canfield-Puritex International, a multinational food company headquartered in St. Louis that processed such things as cereals, baking products, canned meats, and animal feeds. The Canfields still owned vast tracts of land, including several thousand acres of farmland in southeast Missouri, a big ranch in Texas, and timberland in Washington and Oregon. Before the war Willie's name had kept popping up on lists of "America's most eligible bachelors." One of the few benefits of being in a war was that such foolish fluff seemed to have stopped—or at least Willie was no longer aware of it if it continued.

The jeep pulled to a stop in front of the 21st Bomber Command Headquarters Building, and a lieutenant colonel hurried out to meet Willie. He saluted crisply.

"General Canfield, I'm Colonel Hathaway of General LeMay's staff. Welcome to Tinian."

"Thank you," Willie replied.

"General LeMay is expecting you and asks that you come right in."

"That's Curt LeMay for you," Willie said as he climbed out of the jeep. "He never was one for wasting time."

The staff in the anteroom stood respectfully as Willie passed by. Colonel Hathaway, who was walking ahead, opened the door to Curtis LeMay's office, then closed it behind Willie as he stepped inside.

General LeMay was a big, broad-shouldered man with a square jaw, dark hair, and dark bushy eyebrows. He tended to walk and stand slightly hunched forward, as if rushing to the next event. A cigar firmly clenched in his teeth, he hurried around from behind his desk with his hand extended.

"Hello, Willie," he greeted. "How was your trip out here?"

"Impressive," Willie replied. "Very impressive. I came from the States by B-29. It was my first experience with the airplane. We caught the jet stream at thirty thousand feet, and that gave us better than a four-hundred-fifty-mile-per-hour ground speed."

"The B-29 is a wonderful airplane, now that we have all the bugs worked out," LeMay said. He walked over to his window and looked out across the field in the direction of the crash. "Of course, we still have our unfortunate incidents, as you no doubt just witnessed." He nodded toward the column of smoke. "General Powers said you knew those boys?"

Willie nodded. "Not intimately, but they were with me in Germany."

4

"That's too bad," LeMay said. "Any loss is bad enough, but it seems particularly hard to take when it's an accident that serves no useful purpose." He turned back toward Willie and changed the subject. "So, how were things in the ETO when you left?"

"Busy," Willie answered. "Everyone in the European Theater is getting ready to shift to the Pacific."

"How was it that you beat everyone else over here? Are you so anxious to get back into the war that you couldn't wait for everyone else to come? You had to get the jump on them?" LeMay teased.

Willie laughed. "I don't know. I think I may have stood up when I should have *shut* up," he said. "But for some reason the War Department seems to think that my being here might make the transfer of the Eighth Aircorps go a little easier."

"They've got good reason to think that," LeMay said. "There are some, myself included, who still remember what a brilliant job you did in getting our bombers moved into England." Noticing that his cigar had gone out, LeMay walked back over to his desk, picked up a lighter, and relit it. He waited until the tip was a red ember before he continued, waving it like a baton as he spoke. "But if we're lucky, Willie, we won't be needing your services here. The war will be over in a matter of days."

"A matter of *days*?" Willie asked, astonished. "Why would you say that? The latest intelligence reports I've heard give the Japanese a home-defense army of more than two million. . . and a kamikaze fleet of ten thousand suicide planes."

"Pretty formidable odds, wouldn't you say?" LeMay asked through a puff of cigar smoke.

"Formidable enough that the casualty figure estimates are running at better than one hundred thousand American dead in the initial attack waves," Willie replied.

"Yes, well"—LeMay pulled the cigar from his mouth and studied the end of it—"don't worry about it. I give you my word, we won"t have to invade Japan."

Willie looked at the general as if he were crazy. "Curt, do you know something that I don't know?" he asked.

LeMay smiled slyly. "As a matter of fact, I do."

"What?"

"I'm waiting right now for authorization to give you a full briefing. The problem is, it's the middle of the night in Washington, and I haven't gotten the okay yet. But I'll get it soon, and as soon as I do, I'll tell you everything."

"It must be something big."

"Big? Willie, it's the biggest damn secret of war in the history of our country. . . hell, probably in the history of the world."

5

"If that's the case, I may not even get a clearance," Willie said. "Don't forget, I'm really a civilian at heart. I'm an airline president, remember? I'm not a military strategist."

"You'll get clearance," LeMay said. "If we have to wake up the President himself to get the okay, you'll get clearance."

"And you feel that this secret—whatever it is—will eliminate the need for us to invade Japan?"

"It'll put the finishing touches on it, yes. But the truth is, we've already come a long way toward that goal. I suppose you've heard that I abandoned daylight precision bombing."

"Oh, I've heard," Willie answered with a little chuckle. "Believe me, I've heard."

"I guess the boys back in the old Eighth Aircorps feel like I've turned my back on everything we worked for in Europe," LeMay said. "Well, in Germany I went along with the idea because it was a valid concept. Germany had specific targets. . . factories, fuel dumps, and industrial areas that called for precision bombing. But Japan is different. Japan has what they call a shadow industry, consisting of thousands of tiny backyard manufacturing plants. We can't pinpoint them well enough to take them out with rapierlike thrusts—so I'm going after them with a sledgehammer. What's more, I'm going after them under the protection of darkness. To do that, I've stripped the planes of all their guns except the tail gun. Without the weight of the guns and ammunition and with a smaller crew, the planes can carry more bombs. And since January we've dropped fifty thousand tons in high explosives and twice that tonnage in incendiaries. We have been particularly effective over Tokyo."

"Yes," Willie said. "I've seen the figures on the firebomb raids on Tokyo. So far, I understand, fifty-six square miles have been gutted."

"It doesn't end with Tokyo. We're going to go after every city in Japan, one by one, until the Japs realize they can no longer resist. . . or until the entire country is turned into a smoldering cinder, whichever comes first."

The phone on his desk rang, and he picked it up.

"LeMay," he grunted. He listened for a moment, said, "Good," then replaced the receiver and looked at Willie. "You've been cleared by the War Department. Come with me now. There's something I want you to see."

KANOYA, KYUSHU, THE JAPANESE HOME ISLANDS

Though twenty-one-year-old Ensign Saburo Amano, a Navy fighter pilot, had never taken off from an aircraft carrier, he had flown his Raiden airplane valiantly against the repeated B-29 raids over his homeland. The name *Raiden* meant "thunderbolt." In this new airplane, which was larger than the Zero and equipped with a turbo-charged engine, more armor, and cannons instead of machine guns, Saburo had managed to shoot down two of the huge, swift American bombers. But there were far too few of the Raidens, and they had come much too late to turn the tide of war. As a result each B-29 raid was bigger and more devastating than the one before, and under the relentless firebombing more and more Japanese cities were being turned into burned-out wastelands.

Finally, in mid-July, Saburo had felt such impotent rage, coupled with burning hatred for the unreachable enemy who could attack with such impunity, that he had gone to see Vice-Admiral Matome Ugaki to volunteer for the Special Attack Corps.

The Special Attack Corps was the official name; most Japanese preferred to refer to it by the name the first attack group had taken: Kamikaze— "Divine Wind."

Vice-Admiral Ugaki had just been appointed commander of the final line of defense, a great kamikaze offensive code-named *Ten Go*, or "Heavenly Operation." This name, like Divine Wind, had been chosen to reflect the spiritual purity of those willing to make the supreme sacrifice.

"In order for Japan to survive," Vice-Admiral Ugaki told Saburo, looking up at the young officer from behind his desk, "we must depend upon the courage of our most courageous."

"I am honored to offer myself to such a glorious cause," Saburo replied, standing at rigid attention.

Vice-Admiral Ugaki got up and walked over to a beautifully lacquered cabinet. Taking out a bottle wrapped in red felt, he held it up for Saburo's inspection. "I was given this bottle of sake by Admiral Yamamoto," he explained. "I drink from it only on the most special occasions." He poured them each a glass. "And I would be deeply honored now," he continued, "if the son of an old friend would drink with me."

"Thank you, Admiral," Saburo said, accepting the glass, bowing, then drinking the liquor.

"I was, of course, extremely saddened to hear of the fate of your father, my good friend Hiroshi Amano," Ugaki said. "But I was filled with pride to learn that he was killed while flying Admiral Yamamoto. To die in such glorious company is indeed an honor."

"Yes. My mother and sister take great comfort in the glory of his death."

"Your mother and sister—they are still in Hiroshima?"

"Yes."

"Good, good. They are quite fortunate, you know. The bombers have not harmed Hiroshima, and the Americans have no intention of doing so."

"I am pleased that this is true," Saburo replied. "But I am puzzled as to why the Americans would spare the city."

Ugaki grunted contemptuously. "Well, of course, it is simply an example of the American arrogance. You see, they truly believe they can conquer Japan. And when they do, they will need an undamaged city from which to rule. They have chosen Hiroshima as that city."

"I would rather see Hiroshima destroyed than used in such a way!" Saburo said resolutely.

"Spoken like a true samurai," Ugaki responded with a chuckle. "But perhaps the Americans are a bit premature, eh? When they feel the full effects of our 'Heavenly Operation,' they will not think our homeland so easy to conquer.

"When I die," Saburo vowed, "I will take one thousand Americans with me."

Vice-Admiral Ugaki's eyes brimmed with tears, and he poured another glass of sake, then held it out in a stiff-armed salute toward Saburo. "I drink to you, Saburo, and one thousand like you. Together you will destroy one million Americans. . . and you *will* save Japan!"

As Saburo learned when he had reported to his barracks at the airfield near Kanoya, it hadn't been difficult to find volunteers for the Special Attack Corps. Like him, the other kamikaze pilots were convinced that they would not survive the war anyway and welcomed the opportunity for a patriotic suicide. They much preferred to die gloriously by crashing their bomb-laden planes into American ships than to bleed their lives away in some meaningless and obscure engagement.

Although Saburo had been under the impression that he'd be selected for the very next suicide mission, he soon found that wasn't the case. Each day when the rosters were posted, he hurried to the bulletin board with the other pilots to see if his name was there. Each day that it wasn't he turned away, deeply disappointed that his rendezvous with destiny was to be delayed a bit longer.

Those who did find their names on the board would laugh and pat each other on the back, proud of the selection that made them "Gods without earthly desires."

"We will wait for you," those who were chosen said to those who were left behind. "We will wait at the shrine of Yasukani until everyone else arrives."

Day after day Saburo would check the board looking for his name, only to come away disappointed that he hadn't yet been selected. Meanwhile, he settled into the routine of the Special Attack Corps.

To his surprise, the routine of the squadron was little different from that of any of the other units he had been assigned to. There was, however, a greater closeness among the men, with absolutely no bickering or jealousy or infighting. No brothers had ever been closer than these men were to each other, and Saburo's heart swelled with love and pride every time he passed his barracks' motto. One of the other pilots, skilled in the art of calligraphy, had made a beautiful brush-stroke rendering of the stirring words:

BORN APART, WE DIE TOGETHER.

Neither Saburo nor the others appeared to show any anxiety over their appointment with eternity. They read or played cards, and when there was someone among them who could play the piano, they would sing, generally picking folk songs or songs from their youth. Saburo had a fine, clear tenor voice, and he was often called upon to sing his favorite song:

> *Sakura, Sakura*
> *Yayoi no sora wa*
> *Miwatasu Kagiri*
> *Kasumika kumo ka*
> *Nioizo izuro*
> *Izaya, izaya*
> *Miniyou—kan.*

The song was an ancient Japanese folk song celebrating blue skies, cherry blossoms, and young love. Saburo knew about blue skies and cherry blossoms, but he knew nothing of young love, the love of a woman.

When Saburo told the others that he had never been with a woman and would die a virgin, he thought they might laugh at him. Instead they cried with him.

"It isn't fair. No one should be asked to sacrifice his life without having first known the pleasures of a woman," one of the others declared.

"I am prepared to give to the emperor whatever is asked of me," Saburo insisted.

"The emperor asks for your life and your soul. He does not demand that you die celibate."

That night as Saburo lay sleeping, a hand touched him lightly on the shoulder. He had been dreaming that there was no war, and he was home on his own sleeping mat. When he opened his eyes and saw it was a young woman who had awakened him, he thought it was his sister, Yukari, calling him to breakfast. Then he realized that he was not at home, and the young woman looking down at him was not his sister.

"Who are you?" he asked anxiously. "What do you want?"

"I am Sasi," the girl answered in a soft, lilting voice. "Your friends have brought me to you."

"My friends?" Saburo raised up on one elbow and looked around the barracks. To his surprise everyone was gone. He was alone with the girl. "Where is everyone?" he asked in alarm. He sat up quickly and reached for his clothes. "I must go!"

"No!" the girl cried. Gently but insistently, she pulled his hand back from his clothes. "Don't you understand? I am for you."

At first Saburo didn't understand. Then he realized what was happening. His friends, troubled by his confession that he had never known a woman, had arranged it so that he wouldn't have to die a virgin.

"What. . . what must I do?" he asked hesitantly.

Sasi smiled and brushed away a fall of hair. Her skin shone, and her eyes glistened in the ambient light coming through the barracks' door and windows. Saburo thought he had never seen a more beautiful woman.

"You don't have to do anything," Sasi said. Her voice was as musical as a wind chime. "I will do everything."

Her hands began their work then, gently massaging and kneading Saburo's body. He had never experienced anything like the sensations he was feeling now. He was hot and cold and shaky all at the same time, and he had a pounding erection. Sasi reached down to hold his penis, and he gasped in intense pleasure.

"Sasi," Saburo said, his voice breathless with passion. "Sasi, I love you."

Saburo knew that love was something that came later, after an arranged marriage and the long period of adjustment of a man and wife living together. It wasn't something one felt in the first few minutes of meeting someone, and certainly it wasn't something one felt for a comfort girl. But time and place had been altered for Saburo. This barracks, his sleeping mat, and Sasi made up his entire world, and time no longer had meaning. He was already standing at the portal of eternity; the few days he had left on earth were as decades; the hours, months. When he told Sasi he loved her, he meant it truly, and he gave her all that was his to give.

With a deft, lithe movement, Sasi threw one leg over Saburo's body, then very slowly made the connection. Saburo looked down at where they joined, watching in fascination as he disappeared inside her. She leaned forward across him and her breasts swung down, the nipples brushing across his chest. Her hair fell to either side of his face as she brought her own face down to his.

"And I love you, Saburo Amano-san," Sasi said, her sweet, minted breath caressing his lips. At that moment she meant it as much as he did.

10

The very next day, August 4, Saburo's name appeared on the roster.

He let out an elated yell, and the others whose names were also listed laughed and congratulated each other on their marvelous luck at being selected to die together.

"It will be glorious," one exclaimed. "I shall turn an American ship into a beautiful red rose of flame."

There was much celebration during the rest of the day. That evening, the pilots who had been chosen to fly the next day's mission went to the ready room to write letters and to sleep. Saburo's mother, grandmother, and sister didn't know that he had volunteered for the Special Attack Corps, so he had to choose the words of this, his last letter, very carefully.

Beloved Mother, Honorable Grandmother, and Esteemed Sister:

Tomorrow I am to be given the privilege of dying for the emperor. My death will be quick and clean, like the sudden shattering of crystal. It is my hope that by my death I will also cause the death of many Americans, thus exacting from them some measure of repayment for the evil they have visited upon our country.

As I am but twenty-one, I will be dying in the fullness of life; in that I will be like a cherry blossom, which drops from the tree when it is most beautiful. I do not fear death, for there is no reason to fear that which is part of the harmony of all things. As I believe that the soul of man survives, my soul shall join that of my father, and together we shall wait beyond death until our family is once more united.

Saburo put the pen down and looked at his letter. He hadn't been much of a letter writer since leaving home, and now he regretted it. There was more he wanted to say, much more, but he didn't know how. How could he express the feeling of warmth and contentment he had had as a child, waking up to the aromas of breakfast being cooked by his mother and grandmother? How could he put in writing the picture he had frozen in his mind of his father and mother on the last day he had seen them together? Could he make Yukari understand the pleasure he took in having someone so beautiful for his sister?

Finally he decided to end the letter in a way that was most fitting for the occasion. He added a finishing haiku.

When you feel a gentle
breeze in the night,
it is a kiss from my soul.

11

Afterward, Saburo lay with his head on the hard, round pillow, and though he sought sleep, it wouldn't come. He closed his eyes and tried to rest, listening to his pounding heart. Again he recalled the image he had fixed in his mind of his father and mother, and he smiled. At least he would soon see his father.

"Saburo?" one of the others whispered. "Saburo, are you awake?"

"Yes."

"Are you afraid?"

"No."

"Not even a little afraid?"

"No," Saburo said, and he realized then, with some surprise, that he really wasn't afraid. An inexplicable calm had come over him, and he thought of his impending death as no more than a journey.

"I'm afraid," the voice admitted.

"You don't have to go," Saburo said. "You can go to the squadron leader and tell him you don't wish to go."

"I won't do that. I'm afraid, but I will go."

"Think of our friends," Saburo said.

"I know. If I didn't go, they would all hate me."

"I don't mean our friends who are alive. I mean our friends who are dead. They are our friends again, for we have already left the world of the living and are halfway to the world of the immortal."

"Yes," the voice said, "yes, that's true, isn't it? Soon I will be with my brother. Thank you, Saburo. I'm not afraid anymore."

Saburo did finally manage to fall asleep, and he had to be awakened the next morning in time for the mission. He put on his uniform, then wrapped his *senninbari*, his "sash with the one thousand stitches," around his waist. The stitches had been gathered by Yukari, who had stood on the streets of Hiroshima with the sash, asking strangers to add their stitches to the others. Each stitch represented a prayer so that those who wore the sash went into battle armed with a thousand prayers from their countrymen. After Saburo was dressed, he walked out into the rising sun, and the beauty and symbolism of it brought tears of joy to his eyes.

A farewell party was held on the flight line, and the commander stopped in front of each man to pour a cup of sake for the pilot.

"I have only one final word of advice for you," the commander said. "Do not be in too much of a hurry to die. Make your deaths mean something. If you can't find a worthy target, turn back."

The pilots were fitted with their *hashamaki*, the rising-sun headbands; then they saluted their commander and walked to their planes. One of the Zeros was painted a bright red, meaning that until this mission it had been used as a trainer. The other pilots shied away from it, perhaps thinking the color would attract unwanted attention from the enemy. Saburo smiled and headed right for it. If it attracted attention, so be it. He was samurai. He welcomed the challenge.

Those several pilots not yet selected for a mission, along with the mechanics, were gathered alongside the parked airplanes, and they raised their arms in the banzai cheer as the kamikaze pilots climbed into their cockpits.

Saburo remembered the many times he had cheered the other kamikaze pilots when they had left, often wondering what they were thinking about. Now *he* was one of them, and he knew what he was thinking about: He was going out to do a job. It was as routine as that.

He climbed into his plane and started the engine, then taxied out onto the runway in line with the others. Finally the green flag went down, and Saburo opened the throttle and roared down the runway. A two-hundred-fifty-kilogram bomb was suspended beneath his plane, enough explosive force to sink the largest ship if he was able to deliver the blow.

Saburo suddenly felt the need to urinate, and he wished he had gone before he took off. Then he laughed and urinated in his pants. How simple life was when it was about to end.

JULY 29, ON BOARD THE CRUISER
U.S.S. BALTIMORE

Twenty-six-year-old Chief Petty Officer Kevin McKay stood leaning over the after rail, watching the wake boil up behind the old cruiser. They were three days out of Tinian, having delivered a cargo that was so secret no one on the ship had been allowed to handle it. Armed marines had come aboard with the cargo when they took it on at San Francisco, and an armed detail was posted around it for the entire voyage. No one could get into the cargo hold where the device was, not even to perform routine maintenance or hull integrity checks.

Though no one on board knew what they were carrying, everyone was aware that it was something extremely important because Captain Fitzhugh had told them they'd be able to take pride in the fact that by this one mission they had contributed significantly to the shortening of the war.

Whatever the device was that they'd delivered, a ship was being sent back to San Francisco for another one. Kevin wondered why they were moving the devices—whatever they were—one at a time. They could easily have accommodated more than one in the cargo hold.

"I'll tell you what I think," one of the other chiefs said. "I think it's some sort of secret weapon, so secret and so important that they don't want to take the chance of losing more than one at a time. I mean, think about it. Suppose we'd been attacked on the way to Tinian and went down, taking the device down with us. If we had more than one of them on board, then we'd have lost more than one. Makes sense, don't you think?"

Kevin agreed that the chief's reasoning did make sense. . . but the question still remained as to just what the hell it was that they had carried.

For the entire voyage rumors had circulated through the ship. Poison gas, some had said, though others pointed out that gas was outlawed by the rules of war. Some had suggested it might be a large canister of deadly germs that could be released over Japan to infect all its people. A seaman first-class who had had three years of schooling at the Missouri School of Mines had thought it might be some sort of bomb that used atomic energy, and he used one of the plotting boards to illustrate his point by drawing pictures of atoms, showing how energy would be released by splitting them.

At first Kevin had thought the seaman didn't know what he was talking about. Then he learned that the young seaman had been ordered to report to the captain. Ever since that visit the seaman had refused to take part in any more conjecture as to what they were carrying. Once when he was asked to explain his theory again, he mumbled that he'd just been shooting off his mouth and wished they'd leave him out of it. Now Kevin was absolutely convinced that the seaman was right, and they had carried something that had to do with splitting atoms.

They had spent no time in Tinian but left as soon as the device was unloaded, then went back to sea, this time to establish a "life station" position between Tinian and Japan. Their job would be to rescue any bomber crews who might have to ditch at sea on the way to or back from a raid against Japan.

It was a Sunday morning, and, as always, there'd been church services conducted on the fantail. The smoking lamp had been out until after the services were over, but now it was lit, and Kevin stood there enjoying his cigarette and watching the relaxed, lazy movement of sailors who were savoring the fact that there'd be no work before the noon meal.

When they were in San Francisco to load the secret weapon, they had picked up several new sailors. This was the first cruise for many of them, and several had still not gotten their sea legs. The small chop of the early morning sea increased to a rather rough swell, and the ship began plowing through it like a porpoise. The bow would lift high, shudder, then slam with a rolling, twisting motion back down into the waves. Though the bow wasn't actually coming out of the water, the pitch was so severe that every time it dropped back down, it sent sheets of spray flying back over the ship, drenching anyone on deck.

Kevin laughed at the green-faced young men who were "feeding the fish." He finished his cigarette, pinched out the flame, and put the butt in his pocket. It was forbidden to toss cigarette butts overboard on the theory that Japanese submarines might be able to pick up the *Baltimore* by following a trail of trash. Kevin was certain that a cigarette would come apart long before any sub ever saw it, but he reasoned that if everyone was careful about all the little things, none of the big things would get through, either.

Suddenly the bell started clanging, and a metallic voice blasted over the loudspeaker, "*All hands, all hands, man your battle stations! Man your battle stations!*"

Kevin ran quickly to his station as chief of antiaircraft gun tubs five and six. Even as his men were getting into position, Kevin smeared on his antiflash cream, donned the flak jacket and steel helmet, then put on the headset and collar.

"Five and six ready," he said into the mouthpiece that rose up from the collar, similar to those used by telephone operators. "What have we got, Talkie?"

"*CIC reports bogeys, bearing one-two-zero,*" came the voice through his earphones. "How many?"

"*We have multiple blips on the scope.*"

"We'll be ready," Kevin said. "All right, guys, listen up!" he shouted to his two gun crews. "We've got bogeys coming in from one hundred twenty degrees. Get ready for 'em."

"There they are!" one of the sharper-eyed sailors said, pointing. Kevin put his field glasses to his eyes and located them. There were at least six coming in low, determined and with no evasive maneuvering. He knew in the pit of his stomach what they had to be.

"Shit!" he said aloud.

"What is it, Chief?"

"Kamikazes."

"Kamikazes? Oh, my God!" one of the new men said. He began shaking uncontrollably.

"Hey!" Kevin called down to him. He forced himself to smile. "Take it easy, Wilkes. If those bastards *are* suicide pilots, they just make it easier for us to kill 'em, that's all."

"*Gun captains, get ready,*" the voice said in Kevin's ear.

"Get ready!" Kevin repeated. The gunners leaned into the half-circle armrests, then swung the guns free into the direction of the approaching planes.

"*Open fire at gunners' discretion,*" the voice said.

"Gunners, fire when you have a target!" Kevin shouted.

"Here comes one!"

The guns opened up, not only tubs five and six, but every gun on the ship. The noise was deafening, and the sky was filled with dirty black puffs from the exploding antiaircraft shells.

15

Kevin watched the balls of fire reaching out toward the attacking Zero. The gunners used the streams of fire to find their target. Like squirting water from a hose, they adjusted their guns so that two of the streams of fire converged on the attacking plane. The Zero flamed, tried to continue its attack, then suddenly tumbled forward and hit the water with a big explosion.

A couple of the new guys yelled victoriously, but the others were quiet, knowing that the attack had just started. Another kamikaze started toward them. Kevin often wondered why the suicide planes always came in one at a time, because that just made it easier for his gunners. Whatever the reason, he wasn't complaining.

The plane got closer and closer still, until Kevin could see the big five-hundred-pound bomb clutched underneath. If the pilot got through with that bomb, there'd be major damage to the *Baltimore.*

"Come on, come on!" Kevin shouted. "What the hell're you screwing around for? Get on his ass! Get on him, get on him, get on him!"

Suddenly the attacking airplane exploded into one big fireball.

"*Yeah!* Yeah, that's the way to do it!" Kevin yelled.

Three of the remaining four airplanes turned away, but one continued the attack. This one was painted fire-engine red, and it got so low to the water that its propeller was actually kicking up spray. It raced toward the *Baltimore.*

"Shit!" Kevin bellowed. "Stop that son of a bitch!"

"Chief, number five gun won't bear!" the gunner shouted, having discovered that the attacking plane was out of his field of fire. In fact, more than half the guns of the cruiser were unable to track the incoming Zero, and those that could found the red airplane an exceptionally difficult target. Kevin knew then that this one was going to get through.

The plane smashed into the hull of the cruiser amidships. There were two explosions, one when the plane first hit, then a second, much larger one deep in the bowels of the ship. The second explosion opened up the deck and spewed fire like a volcano, higher than the ship's stacks. When the fireball died away, Kevin saw that the bridge had sustained very heavy damage.

"Talkie! Talkie, what's the damage up there?" Kevin called into his mouthpiece.

Not only did he not get an answer, even the rushing tone was gone. His communications were completely dead.

Secondary explosions suddenly sounded from down inside, and now from the bridge forward the ship was a blazing inferno. Kevin could feel the stern lifting up out of the water, and he realized that the ship was going down by the bow—and it was going fast.

"Abandon ship! Abandon ship!" an officer shouted, coming aft and yelling through cupped hands. The officer's face was blackened with soot, and blood was running down his forehead.

16

"Has the captain ordered us over the side?" Kevin hollered.

"The captain?" the officer said. "The captain is dead. So is everyone else who was on the bridge. I'm in command now. Abandon ship!"

"Okay, men," Kevin said. "Into the water, let's go!"

Taking off his helmet and flak jacket, Kevin ran to the rail, then dived over. He was prepared for a long fall and was surprised at how quickly he hit the water. That meant that the ship was much lower than he'd thought, and he began swimming hard to get away from the suction. After several seconds he turned to see how far he had come and saw the stern of the *Baltimore* lift out of the water. It hung there for a long moment, the screws motionless and dripping; then it started sliding down. It sank out of sight, to be followed by a boiling caldron on the surface of the sea; after that, nothing.

Grasping hands pulled Kevin onto a life raft, and he thanked the men, then draped himself across the side and puked up the oil that he hadn't known he'd swallowed. Finally, when the vomiting stopped, he saw that there were only three rafts in the water, each completely jammed with survivors. Hanging on to the ropes of the rafts were perhaps two dozen more sailors. He didn't see anyone else.

"We had over twelve hundred men. I see less than a hundred. Is this it? Are we all that's left?" Kevin asked a seaman.

"We're it, Chief."

"Where's Mr. Abernathy?" That was the young jg who had ordered the ship abandoned.

"He ain't nowhere around."

"I seen 'im go into the water," another sailor said. "But I ain't seen 'im since then."

"There!" someone said. "Isn't that him back there?"

Kevin looked across a couple hundred yards of open water and saw a head bobbing in the waves. It was the jg. He was trying to swim toward the life rafts, but he was tiring quickly.

"I'm going after him," Kevin said, diving in before anyone could talk him out of it.

He swam hard, easing off when the swell was against him, using it to push him on when it was in his favor. It took him about five minutes to cover the distance.

"Mr. Abernathy!" Kevin called. "Mr. Abernathy, over here!"

The young officer looked toward Kevin, and the expression on Abernathy's face made Kevin's blood run cold.

"No leg," he said.

"What?"

"My leg is gone. Shark."

17

Suddenly Abernathy grunted; then his head disappeared, his body jerked down beneath the waves. There was a frenzied froth of water, then a spreading stain of red.

Kevin turned to start back toward the raft and saw that sharks had already attacked the men hanging on the raft ropes. A couple of the sailors in the rafts were trying to beat the sharks away with paddles—or maybe they were trying to beat the men away from the rafts to get rid of the sharks. Whatever they were doing was having no success, because the sharks were striking again and again.

Suddenly Kevin felt a blow to his back, as if someone had hit him in the spine with a baseball bat. It had hurt on impact, but almost instantly the pain went away. Then he felt something else, the most gentle pressure against his leg as if he were rising and falling in the swell. Then he saw a shark swimming away with a leg in its mouth—and he knew that it was *his* leg.

He felt no pain or fear, only a sense of irritation.

Four years of war and I get killed by a shark, he thought calmly. *Now, if this ain't a helluva note.*

2

AUGUST 6, 1945, TINIAN

Sergeant Grega could only take Willie Canfield as far as the brightly lighted barbed-wire fence surrounding the 509th Composite Group area. There Sergeant Grega was required to wait in the jeep. Willie got out and walked through the gate, showing his special pass to the half-dozen armed guards who didn't know themselves what they were guarding.

The B-29's of the 509th were parked on a large concrete apron just outside the security hangar. At first glance these B-29's seemed no different from any of the other B-29's on the field. A closer look revealed that the side gun blisters were masked, the ventral area was painted white to reflect a flash effect, and the airplanes had a distinctive tail marking so that they could be readily identified. On the towering vertical stabilizer of the 509th bombers was a large circle cut by an arrow, pointing forward.

Willie's clearance had allowed him to examine the airplanes more closely, so he knew there were even greater differences. The B-29's of the 509th were fitted with Curtiss Electric propellers, rather than the normal Hamilton Standard Hydromatics, which had reversible pitch to increase braking power and sported special blade cuffs that would increase airflow into the engines, aiding in the cooling. And inside each plane the bomb bay had been completely gutted of the normal racks and replaced with one large H-frame suspension mechanism—to accommodate the special bomb it would be carrying. The actual delivery of the weapon was called "Project Alberta."

The B-29 nearest the hangar was glistening brightly under the high-intensity lights. There was no nose art on the plane, just the name *Enola Gay* Willie had asked about it earlier and was told that Enola Gay was the name of Colonel Paul Tibbets's mother. As commanding officer of the 509th Composite Group, Colonel Tibbets could appoint anyone he wanted to fly history's first atomic bomb mission. He appointed himself.

Dr. W. W. "Dub" Wilkerson, one of the civilians who had been involved in developing the weapon and who had accompanied the device to Tinian, was standing in the door of the hangar looking out toward the airplane as Willie approached. Before the war Dr. Wilkerson had been a professor of physics at Jefferson University in St. Louis. Willie, his brother John, and his mother and father had all attended Jefferson University. In fact, the Canfield Foundation was one of the pillars of financial support for the private institution. As a result, Willie and Dr. Wilkerson had known each other for a long time.

"Good morning, Dub," Willie said.

"Hello, Willie."

"Is the crew on board?" Willie asked, pointing to the plane.

"No, they're still at breakfast. Captain Parsons is in there, though."

"The Navy ordnance man? What's he doing out there so early?"

"He's disarming the device," Dub explained. "He'll rearm it after they're airborne."

"Won't it be harder to do it then?"

"I'm sure it will be," Dub replied. "But as you know, in the last twenty-four hours four B-29's have crashed on takeoff. If this one were to crash with the bomb armed, there wouldn't be anything left of North Field."

"It seems incredible that one bomb could do that much damage."

Dub shook his head. "My boy, this bomb is just a popgun compared to the weapons that are to come. It is quite possible to build a device big enough to vaporize this entire island."

"It's a pretty frightening prospect to think of power like that in the hands of man," Willie observed.

"It isn't in our hands anymore, Willie," Dub replied. "It's in God's hands. Or Satan's," he added chillingly.

From out on the runway the sound of accelerating engines reached them, and Willie looked at his watch. It was 1:45 A.M.

"That's Major Weatherly in the weather recon plane," Willie said. "It won't be long now." He looked at Dub. "I'm going to grab some breakfast, then go down to the tower to watch Colonel Tibbets's takeoff. You want to come?"

"No," Dub said. "I've done my work. I'm going to rest now. I'm suddenly tired. Very, very tired. I think I'll go to bed." He turned and walked back into the hangar, and Willie watched until the professor was swallowed up by the shadows.

Wilkerson was one of the few men at Tinian who had also been a part of "Project Trinity," the code name given to the test blast. Willie found it amazing that Dr. Wilkerson, who had spent the last four years working on the atomic bomb, would not stay around to watch the takeoff.

Willie started back to his jeep just as the truck carrying the crew of the *Enola Gay* arrived. Another truck was there as well, loaded with several dozen newspaper reporters and photographers. The tight veil of secrecy had been lifted just enough for the press to record the beginning of this historic event, and as Willie returned to his jeep, the darkness around him was illuminated by the repeated popping of flashbulbs.

"Where to now, General?" Sergeant Grega asked as Willie slipped into the jeep's passenger seat.

"Let's go over to the crews' mess and see if they have anything left for breakfast," Willie suggested.

Grega started the jeep. "General, the announcement they released tonight said this airplane was carrying something called an atom bomb. Is that right?"

"Yes."

"Excuse my ignorance, General, but just what the hell is this atom bomb supposed to do?"

"It uses the same kind of energy that powers the sun," Willie replied.

"Sir, that still doesn't mean anything to me. Hell, the sun could be a big electric light bulb as far as I know."

Willie laughed. "Well, let me try it this way. We've hit Japan pretty hard, haven't we?"

"Yes, sir, I would say we have."

"Then maybe it'll help you to understand the power of atomic energy if I told you that just three of these atom bombs would equal all the high explosives we've dropped on Japan for this entire year."

"And we're going to unload all that on one city?"

"That's right."

"My God," Grega said quietly.

Willie didn't know if it was an oath or a prayer.

After a breakfast of creamed beef on toast, called SOS—shit on a shingle—by the GIs, Willie went to the tower to watch Colonel Tibbets take off.

He found that he had arrived just in time. The *Enola Gay* was calling for taxi and takeoff instructions.

"*North Tinian Tower, this is Dimples eight-two. Ready for taxi and takeoff instructions,*" came a voice over the tower loudspeaker. Willie recognized the voice as that of Captain Robert Lewis, Colonel Tibbets's copilot.

"Tower to Dimples eight-two," the man seated in front of Willie replied. "Clear to taxi. Take off on runway A for Able."

"*Dimples eight-two,*" Lewis replied.

"There they are," General Farrel pointed out, and Willie saw the three ships glistening in the darkness. They were accompanied by a lead jeep, whose headlights illuminated the special procedures put into effect for this takeoff, for there were ambulances and fire trucks parked every fifty feet down each side of the runway.

"*Dimples eight-two to Tower. Ready for takeoff.*" Willie thought that young Captain Lewis's laconic voice was amazingly calm, given the significance of the event.

"*Tower to Dimples eight-two, you are clear for takeoff.*"

"*Rolling,*" Lewis responded.

The three B-29's began their simultaneous take-off runs. *The Great Artiste* *and Number 91* left the ground at no more than half the length of their available runway, but the *Enola Gay* was burdened by its nine-thousand-pound load. It started slowly, then gradually began building speed, going faster and faster until it reached 180 miles an hour. And yet it was still on the ground.

Willie thought of the B-29 crash he had witnessed on the day he arrived on Tinian, and he couldn't help but worry about this one. Even though the bomb had been disarmed, would that really stop it from exploding if the plane crashed? He involuntarily held his breath and squeezed his hands into fists as he watched and willed the plane into the air.

Not until the airplane reached the short overrun and then the cliff at the very end of the runway did the *Enola Gay* rotate and climb up into the darkness where the other two B-29's were already waiting for it. Willie breathed a sigh of relief, then looked at his watch. It was exactly 2:45 A.M. on the sixth of August.

"Damn!" somebody said. "I was beginning to think he was going to *drive* that big sonofabitch to Japan."

It wasn't really that funny a remark, but it eased the tension, and everyone laughed.

HIROSHIMA

Yukari Amano was awakened by the clack of the noodle vendors' advertising blocks, and she yawned and stretched, then looked over at the clock.

It was after eight! She quickly wrapped herself in her kimono, then hurried out into the great room, where her mother and grandmother were busy rolling bandages.

"You should not have let me sleep so late," Yukari complained, and even the frown on her face didn't diminish the beauty of the twenty-six-year-old.

"Oh, but you were so tired when you returned home last night," Yukari's mother, Yuko, replied. "I fear you are doing too much."

"It is my duty to do all that I can for the emperor," Yukari answered. "Think of the sacrifice Father made. And think of Saburo, flying his airplane against the giant American bombers night after night. I would be unworthy if I didn't work."

"Dr. Nomura shouldn't work you so hard."

"He doesn't work me as hard as he works himself," Yukari said. "He is only one doctor, and he has forty patients in his hospital."

"Still, you will be no good to Dr. Nomura or to yourself if you get sick," Yuko scolded. "You must take better care of yourself. Will you have breakfast?"

"Yes, thank you," Yukari answered. "But I think I'll get some air for a moment."

She walked over to the sliding door and opened it, then stepped out onto the deck. Although the day was warm, it was not yet unbearably hot, and a gentle breeze was blowing from the nearest of the seven estuarine streams that branched out from the Ota River. The city, a kaleidoscope of color and pattern, was already about its daily commerce: Vendors were loudly hawking their various wares. Shopkeepers were sweeping the sidewalks in front of their stores. On the waterways the fiat boats glided effortlessly across the surface, the painted eyes on the bows staring back from their reflections as if keeping watch on the scene.

Then, for one long minute all the sounds of the city were masked by the mournful wail of the air raid siren. Yukari paid little attention to it—one long wail was only precautionary. If it had been an actual air raid, the siren would have emitted a series of short blasts. She looked up and saw only three American bombers, so high that there was scarcely a sound from their engines. She figured they were either weather planes or the propaganda planes that dropped leaflets. Such planes frequently flew over the city and represented no real danger to the populace below.

Hiroshima had been extremely fortunate, for although it was the eighth largest city in Japan, it had never been heavily bombed. There were all sorts of rumors as to why, from the ridiculous—*"The mother of the American President lives here"*—to the *hopeful*—*"For all their faults, the Americans do have an appreciation of beauty, and they believe Hiroshima is much too beautiful a city to destroy."*

Yukari preferred to believe the latter.

A not-unpleasant smell of fish carried up from the river, mingling with the smells of burning charcoal, steaming soup, and strong soap. Hiroshima, like all Japanese cities, did much of its food and grocery business in large, open marketplaces. In fact, just beside the Amano house and along the river was a wide area where fish, vegetables, and other produce were displayed. The war had brought severe shortages to the marketplace; Yukari could remember a time when it teemed with live chickens, ducks, pigs, and goats. There were very few chickens, ducks, pigs, or goats now, but fish was still in abundant supply, and every day the fish were laid out artfully, head to tail, glistening from the buckets of water the vendors frequently splashed over them.

The voices of two vendors competing with each other to make a sale to a woman shopper came floating up with the breeze.

"This looks like a nice fish," the woman said, pointing to a fish of one of the vendors.

"*That* fish?" the competitor scoffed. "Madam, I do not wish to alarm you, but I saw that same fish here yesterday. Would you not prefer one that is fresh?"

"It is not *this* fish you saw," the other vendor insisted. "It was his brother, and the lady who bought the fish returned to tell me it was the most delicious fish she had ever cooked. Madam, you have made an excellent choice. I was thinking of keeping this fish for my own meal, but I will sell it to you."

Suddenly Yuko called from inside the house. "Yukari, come and see if these bandages are good enough for Dr. Nomura."

Yukari turned from the deck railing. "Of course they will be," she replied as she started back into the house. "Dr. Nomura is always pleased with the bandages you roll."

Nearly six miles overhead the three B-29's that had gone practically unnoticed by the awakening city below continued on their mission. *The Great Artiste* opened its bomb bay doors to drop parachute-suspended gauges for monitoring the blast. Meanwhile, *Number 91* made a ninety-degree turn to get into position to take photographs.

At fifteen minutes and seventeen seconds after eight, the *Enola Gay's* bomb bay doors snapped open, and the bomb was released. The airplane, suddenly nine thousand pounds lighter, bounced straight up about ten feet.

A timer inside the bomb tripped the first of a series of switches in the firing circuit. The bomb continued to move horizontally for a moment just beneath the airplane, almost as if it were flying. Then its blunt nose tipped down, and it started its long plunge to earth.

Colonel Tibbets put the *Enola Gay* into a severe high-G diving turn to the right. The crew hung on at their flight stations as the blood rushed from their heads.

The bomb that had left the *Enola Gay* twenty seconds earlier flashed silver far below. The blast gauges dropped from *The Great Artiste* continued to drift down slowly under billowing parachutes. The *Enola Gay* came out of its breathtaking turn and began racing away from the city.

Inside the bomb, which had now fallen nearly five miles, a barometric-pressure device set to five thousand feet tripped the next-to-final switch in the sequence of arming mechanisms. Five seconds later, at exactly 8:16 A.M., the detonator activated, and the bomb exploded.

At that exact moment a light many times brighter than the sun, brighter than anything Yukari had ever seen or imagined, burst all around her. She was momentarily shocked into insensibility, but even if she had been able to reason, she could not have known what it was.

The flash had come from the detonation of a single bomb, dropped from one of the three airplanes she had just discounted as being nothing to worry about. It exploded 1,890 feet above the Gokoku Shrine and one and a half miles away from Yukari's house. It erupted into a brilliant fireball with a temperature at its core of twenty million degrees centigrade.

The Gokoku Shrine was completely vaporized in the first second. Spreading out from the shrine, the asphalt pavements were turned into flaming pools of oil, steel doors became molten, and stone and brick walls glowed red hot. Flash fires were instantly set within a one-mile radius.

Immediately after the heat came the blast, a shock wave that moved out concentrically to smash down walls and buildings; toss cars, trucks, and trolleys around like so much scrap paper; and rip up railroad tracks like matchsticks. Sixty-two thousand of the ninety thousand structures in Hiroshima were instantly flattened, and most of the rest were gutted. A billowing cloud of particulates—the pulverized and incinerated city—spread out for a diameter of three miles at the base, rushed five miles high, then formed a five-mile-wide mushroom cap across the top.

Yukari was walking into the house from the porch when the flash washed out everything with its blinding light. She saw her mother and grandmother looking toward her in openmouthed astonishment, and she started toward them when the shock wave hit. The floor was jerked out from under her feet just as if someone had snatched a rug out from under her. She was thrown down, and before she could grab anything, the house itself collapsed, toppling into the Ota River. Yukari opened her mouth to yell for her mother, only to have it filled with water, and she was surprised to find that she was submerged.

Fighting for breath, she came up from beneath the water to see what was left of the house swirling in bits and pieces in the river all around her. She looked for her mother and grandmother, but they were nowhere to be seen.

Yukari swam hard to get out of the river, and she pulled herself up onto the bank. Her immediate thought was that their house had suffered a direct hit from a bomb, perhaps dropped by one of the three airplanes she had seen. But her house, like all the other houses around, was gone. Frantic, Yukari looked toward the fish market; to her astonishment, all the fish were cooked, many still lying in the neat rows that the vendors had so carefully arranged. The woman shopper and the two competing fish vendors were dead.

In a daze, Yukari began wandering around. It was so dark now that she could almost believe night had fallen, and she wondered if it had. She lost all sense of time, and didn't know if she had been wandering around for seconds, minutes, or hours. She was aware of people coming out of the cloud, away from the center of the city. They were moving like sleepwalkers, devoid of expression and absolutely silent. Many had their hair burned off, and their skin was badly blistered and peeling.

An unusually large number of the people shuffling past her were naked, and Yukari wondered how that could be, until she realized that somehow their clothes had been burned off them. Most of the naked women had strange marks on their skin, and when Yukari looked closer, she saw that the marks were imprints of the patterns on the kimonos they had worn.

"Help me," a weak voice called. "Help me, please."

Yukari looked toward the voice and saw a man half buried in a pile of debris, his hand stretched out in supplication. She walked over to him and grabbed his hand. The skin slid off like a glove, and Yukari dropped it, then turned away, retching.

"Please forgive me," the man said calmly, as if he had offended her.

Yukari thought of Dr. Nomura and the hospital where she worked. All these people, so grievously injured, would be flocking to the hospitals for emergency treatment. Dr. Nomura would need her.

That worked a miracle in clearing Yukari's mind. She still didn't know what had happened, how so few airplanes had brought about so much destruction, or even how long ago it had happened, but she was no longer moving as if in a trance. She was fixated on getting to the hospital where she could be of some use to others, and that determination sustained her.

Yukari started toward the hospital, but it wasn't easy. It meant going against the stream of injured who were moving out of the city—people naked, burned, bleeding, and silent. And it meant passing by an even larger number of dead.

Yukari's route took her by a small hill; knowing that it afforded a very good view of the city, she climbed to the top to have a look around and see if she could gauge the extent of the damage. When she reached the summit she was struck dumb by what she saw. For as far as she could see, Hiroshima was covered with choking vapors, a thick and foul miasma. There were hundreds of fires—possibly thousands of fires. The whole city seemed to be burning, though there was no lake of fire such as she had heard described in the great Tokyo firebombing raids. In fact, the fires seemed to be so indiscriminately scattered that it was quite difficult to determine which direction offered the greatest danger.

Yukari retreated down the hill and continued her trek toward the hospital. A few moments later she saw an unbelievable sight. A horse was standing on the corner, looking at the passing throng through large, liquid-brown eyes, as if trying to understand what was happening.

The horse was pink!

For a moment Yukari couldn't believe her eyes, then she realized that the blast had burned off the poor animal's skin. Turning away from the horse, Yukari continued on to the hospital.

There was no hospital.

Only a smoldering pile of rubble remained where the hospital had been. However, she did see Dr. Nomura, and they greeted each other with a small shout of joy.

"Are you badly hurt?" Dr. Nomura asked.

"No, I don't think so," Yukari answered. "In fact, I think perhaps I am not hurt at all, though with so many injured and dead I don't know how this can be. I feel ashamed for being unhurt in the midst of such misery."

"Don't be foolish," Dr. Nomura said. It was then that Yukari realized that the doctor was bleeding. When she examined him, she saw that there were several pieces of glass embedded in his back and in the back of his neck.

"I was standing by the window," Dr. Nomura explained. "When that very bright flash happened, I looked away. The next thing I knew I was outside, and the window and the hospital were gone."

Yukari rumaged through the wreckage of the hospital. Almost miraculously, she found some undamaged medical equipment, including tweezers and bandages, and she began removing the bits of glass from the doctor's back and neck.

"What about our patients?" she asked. "The ones who were in the hospital."

"Dead. They are all dead," Dr. Nomura answered. He looked out with dazed eyes at the unending stream of grievously wounded wandering around insensibly and at the many dead who were lying in grotesque and sometimes charred and smoking piles amidst the rubble. "I think perhaps they are the lucky ones," he added.

"What was it, Doctor?" Yukari asked. "I saw only three airplanes. How could such terrible destruction come from an empty sky?"

27

"I don't know," Dr. Nomura said. "It is all a great puzzle. There was no sound. Only a flash of light. . . that terrible, terrible flash of light."

"But there *was* a sound," Yukari said, bewildered by the doctor's remark. "There was a roar greater than a thousand thunderclaps."

Dr. Nomura looked off into the distance. "Strange," he said. "I heard nothing."

By dusk the thousands of fires, having exhausted their supply of fuel, slowly began to die. When at last the smoke and dust had cleared, Yukari was able to see for the first time just how extensive the damage really was. Where once there had been a city, now there was a desert. Ironically, there was a strange and spectral peace to the scene, the more so because, high above, the stars seemed brighter and more beautiful than ever before.

Yukari and Dr. Nomura had worked all the first day and then all that night treating the wounded as best they could. Sometimes the treatment consisted of nothing more than bathing the wounds with water from one of the few taps that still worked. They still had no idea what had happened, but the next morning they got an account from someone who had been listening to Radio Tokyo.

The official word was that a terrible new kind of bomb had been used against the innocent people of Hiroshima—further proof, if proof were needed, of the inhumanity of the Americans. Exactly what kind of bomb was dropped was unknown, although, the radio said, "Details are still being investigated."

Over the next few days Yukari learned to gauge how far patients had been from what was now being called "Ground Zero," or the exact point where the bomb had exploded, just by the way they referred to it. Those who had been very close were aware only of the brilliant flash of light from the bomb's fireball. When they spoke of the bomb, they referred to it as lightning. Those who had been farther away spoke of the deafening roar of thunder that followed the flash of light.

On the ninth of August, Yukari learned that another of the terrible bombs had been dropped on Nagasaki. That was also the day that she received Saburo's letter, for although mail was not actually being delivered, a post office had been established in the railway station, and the people of Hiroshima could call and inquire if they had any mail.

Oddly enough, Yukari felt no emotion over Saburo's letter—neither sadness nor anger nor a sense of pride. Her mind was overloaded by too many dead to be moved by the poignant and poetic last words of another person about to die, even if that person happened to be her brother. She did realize, however, almost as if in passing, that she was probably now the only member of her family left alive.

28

Another B-29 flew over Hiroshima, and whereas before single airplanes hadn't created panic among the citizens, they now fled in terror from them. But this B-29 didn't drop another bomb. It dropped leaflets—thousands of them—and they fluttered down like multicolored snow on the vast wasteland that had been Hiroshima.

After her visit to the makeshift post office, Yukari had spent another unsuccessful day searching for some sign of her mother or grandmother. Exhausted, she was sitting on a stone in front of a shelter that had been hastily constructed from corrugated sheet metal, and when she saw the leaflets falling, she was able to reach up and grab one without having to leave her seat.

TO THE JAPANESE PEOPLE

America asks that you pay immediate and close attention to the contents of this leaflet.

We now possess the most destructive explosive ever devised by man. A single one of our newly developed atomic bombs is actually the equivalent in explosive power to what 2,000 of our giant B-29's can carry. We urge you to ponder this information, and we solemnly assure you that it is grimly accurate.

We have now begun to use this weapon against your homeland. If you still have any doubt, ask your officials what happened to Hiroshima when just one atomic bomb fell on that city.

We are prepared to use this bomb to destroy every resource of the military by which they are prolonging this useless war, but before we do so, we ask that you now petition the emperor to end the war. Our President has outlined for you the thirteen consequences of an honorable surrender. We urge that you accept these consequences and begin to build a new, better, and more peaceful Japan.

You must take immediate steps to cease all military resistance. If you do not do so, we shall resolutely employ this bomb and all our other superior weapons to end the war promptly and forcefully.

Evacuate your cities now!

On the morning of August 15, Yukari went to the wreckage of her house and prayed to the souls of her father, mother, grandmother, and brother that the war would soon end. When her prayers were finished, she went again to the railroad station—not for mail, but because Dr. Nomura told her that a relief train loaded with rice and medicines would be arriving that day. As she waited for the train she listened to the depot loudspeaker, which was connected to a radio broadcast. At exactly noon she heard the familiar voice of Chokugen Wada, a well-known radio announcer.

"This will be a broadcast of the gravest importance," Wada said. *"Will all listeners please rise? His Majesty Emperor Hirohito will now read his Imperial rescript to the people of Japan. We respectfully transmit his voice."*

The announcement was followed by the national anthem, and that was followed by a strange, high-pitched voice that brought chills to Yukari.

"To our good and loyal subjects: After pondering deeply the general trends of the world and the actual conditions obtaining in our empire today, we have decided to effect a settlement of the present situation by resorting to an extraordinary measure."

Suddenly everyone around Yukari began weeping. At first Yukari was puzzled; then, as she listened to the emperor's voice and the strange, archaic patterns of his speech, she realized what he was saying. Japan was surrendering!

"No!" someone shouted when the broadcast was over. "Hear me, everyone! We must stand together! We must send word to the emperor that we will never surrender! We must fight on to the end!"

Yukari turned and ran from the depot with her own eyes blinded by tears. Unlike so many of the others, however, her tears were not tears of remorse or shame. They were tears of joy. Her prayers had been answered. The war was over!

AUGUST 25, 1945

As the airplane circled Hiroshima, Dub Wilkerson looked through the window at the devastation below. He was nearly struck dumb by the scene.

"That's Hiroshima?" someone in the plane asked.

"My God," another breathed. "It looks like the surface of the moon."

Dub had seen pictures of cities laid to waste by bombing, and he was familiar with the blackened, skeletal remains of gutted buildings and rubble-filled streets. But what he was looking at now defied all the senses. There was no rubble. . . there weren't even any streets, There was nothing below them but a vast, lifeless desert. It was as barren as the Trinity test site had been after the detonation of the world's first A-bomb.

Dub wondered how the pilot could pick the airport out of the desert, but somehow he managed to do so, and the plane landed gently and rolled across a wide-open field.

"Has anyone gotten a radiation count?" someone asked anxiously. "Is it all right for us to get out?"

"It's been checked," another answered. "It's okay."

Okay? Dub thought. What was okay about this? From the field the destruction seemed even more complete, because here he was on ground level, and he still had a totally unobstructed view all the way across what had been a large city. He stepped out of the plane and took a long, painful look around.

Some survivors of the attack had gathered at the airport, pitiful groups of maimed and deformed people who sat around stoically, waiting to die.

An American major who was already on the scene saw that Dub's uniform had no insignia.

"Are you a reporter?" the major asked.

"No, I'm a scientist."

"A scientist, huh?" The major chuckled. "Well, if you're coming to see how good a job you boys did, I can tell you. You did one bang-up hell of a job."

"The total destruction," Dub said softly, "it's almost incomprehensible. My God, what have we done?"

"Hey, look, Doc, don't go blaming yourself for this," the major said. "As far as I'm concerned, the Japs brought it all on themselves. Besides, if we hadn't dropped this thing, we'd be mounting an all-out assault against the home islands by now, and I'd be writing my last will and testament. That is, if I was still around to write."

"I'm sure the weapon can be justified," Dub said. "I wouldn't have worked on it if I couldn't justify it. In fact, when some of my friends in the project began to question what we were doing, I was one of those who always defended it. But justifying it in theory and seeing the results of its actual use against human beings are very different things."

"Yeah, I know what you mean," the major replied.

Dub saw something that startled him, and he stared for a long moment, then pointed. "What on earth is that pink thing?"

"That is a horse," the major replied.

"A *what*?"

"A horse. He had all his skin burned off by the bomb. He shuffled in right after we got here. He lived for a couple of days, wandering around in a daze like he didn't know what happened to him; then this morning he just keeled over dead."

"Do you plan to just leave him there?"

"Doc, we still have tens of thousands of human corpses to get rid of," the major retorted. "I can't be worried about a horse."

"I'm sorry," Dub replied. "Of course you're right."

The major softened. "Look, it'll take you a while to adjust to everything you're going to see here," he said. "And then you won't adjust; you'll just find some way to put it out of your mind. You'll have to, or it'll drive you crazy. By the way, there's already some bigwig Japanese scientist here. A Dr. Shigita. Would you like to meet him?"

"Yes, I would. Dr. Shigita is a respected physicist. His preliminary findings will be invaluable to our study."

"Well, you'll probably find him over at the aid station," the major said. "The truth is, there's not very much anyone can do for any of these people now, but he stays over there all the time anyway."

"Thanks," Dub said.

He went back to the plane and took out a bag that contained a geiger counter and some medical supplies. Then he walked across the field to the aid station the major had pointed out. The facility had been thrown together from numerous pieces of corrugated tin. There were literally hundreds of patients inside, but as there were no beds, they were all lying on the ground. Most of them were moaning, though quietly, discreetly, as if their injuries were an embarrassment to them.

A pretty young Japanese woman was applying bandages and ointment to the patients. Dub watched her for a moment, moved by the tenderness and compassion she was showing. She didn't see him, and when she backed up, she backed into him. Startled, she turned around, then lowered her eyes in humility.

"Please excuse my clumsiness," she said in excellent English.

"No, no, it is I who should apologize," Dub said. "I just blundered into you."

"May I help you?"

"Uh, yes. I'm looking for Dr. Shigita."

"He is over there," she said, pointing.

"Thank you."

Dub recognized Dr. Shigita from pictures he had seen, and he walked toward him. Like the young woman, Dr. Shigita was applying bandages and ointment, though it seemed like a totally futile gesture.

"Dr. Shigita?"

The physicist looked up.

"Your assistant pointed you out," Dub said.

"My assistant?"

"That young woman."

Dr. Shigita smiled. "She is not my assistant. Her name is Yukari Amano. She is one of the victims."

"She is? She was here when the bomb went off?"

"Yes."

"But she's uninjured."

"That would seem to be the case," Dr. Shigita said. "But of course, we won't know for certain until we learn whether she has been affected by the radiation poisoning. Dr. Nomura, who built this aid shelter, was also uninjured. But he has since died of radiation sickness."

"Dr. Shigita, I am Dr. Wilkerson."

"Good, we have a great need for doctors."

"Oh, uh, I'm not a medical doctor," Dub apologized quickly. "I, too, am a physicist."

"Ah," Dr. Shigita said. "You are one of the men responsible for the bomb." It wasn't an accusation or even a denunciation. It was merely an observation.

"Yes," Dub replied. "God help me, I am."

"You should not feel too badly about it," Dr. Shigita said. "The blame is not yours alone. The blame lies with everyone whose action brought on this war. It is good the war is finally over, even if it did require the employment of such a ghastly weapon as the atom bomb."

Nearby, someone began retching, and Dub looked over at him with a sense of helplessness.

"Many who were uninjured by the blast have now begun to show symptoms of radiation sickness, such as epilation, petechi, nausea and vomiting, and diarrhea," Dr. Shigita explained. "They do not understand the disease and believe the Americans have spread a poison that will last for one hundred years. I have tried to calm them by telling them their fears are false."

"I *hope* their fears are false," Dub said. "I hope we haven't unleashed a lethal radiation that will linger for one hundred years."

"Your testing did not discern what the effects would be?" Dr. Shigita asked in surprise.

"No," Dub answered. He made an apologetic gesture. "I'm afraid we were so dedicated to making the bomb work that we paid no attention at all to the aftereffects."

"Then we will work on it together," Dr. Shigita suggested. "Come with me. I have found the epicenter. I will show you."

Dub followed Dr. Shigita away from the shelter and across the quiet, desolate plain that only weeks before had been a vibrant, beautiful city.

"The power of the bomb was such that it marked its place for us," Dr. Shigita explained after they had walked for some distance. "I was able to locate the epicenter by examining the pattern of scorching on the telephone poles and concrete walls. I used a method of triangulation, and it brought me here."

Dub looked around. He could see a graveyard nearby. Perhaps even those who had already lain there had been disturbed by the blast. He saw a number of chunks of glass on the ground, and he wondered what window could be so large as to leave so much. Then he remembered the scene at Trinity. Here in Hiroshima, as in the desert of New Mexico, the bomb had made glass of the sand in the earth. What must it have been like at the exact moment of detonation?

"What is this place?" Dub asked. "Or rather, perhaps I should ask what *was* it?"

"It was the Torii gateway of the Gokoku Shrine," Dr. Shigita said. "Notice, if you will, some of the oddities of the bomb." He pointed to a concrete building that was still standing, though it had been completely gutted. The building was of reinforced concrete, built to be earthquake resistant.

On the roof of the building Dub saw a permanent shadow of what had been a tower.

"It is as if a photograph were made," Dr. Shigita noted. "Such shadows are also found in other places." He pointed to the granite tombstones within the graveyard of the shrine, and Dub gasped, for on one he saw clearly the imprint of a man. The man must have died in that instant, but his picture stayed behind to tell his story.

"It's incredible," Dub murmured.

"Perhaps such scenes should be preserved," Dr. Shigita suggested. "In this way the world will not quickly forget."

"Dr. Shigita, I assure you, I will *never* forget what I have seen here for as long as I live," Dub said quietly. "And I intend to see to it that we fully document the horror of this place so we can let the world know what it was like. With God's help, mankind will understand the fullest ramifications of such a weapon, and never again will it be used as it was used here."

3

AUGUST 22, 1945, NEW YORK

S haylin McKay's bags were packed and piled up on the floor of her cabin on board the *U.S.S. Daniel S. Norton.* The *Norton,* carrying 4,390 returning servicemen, had docked approximately one hour earlier, and the celebration of the ship's arrival was still in full swing.

When the ship docked, Shaylin had been up on deck. She saw the large banner someone had stretched across the pier, welcoming home the HEROES OF THE WAR. She had also seen the bands and the huge crowd of people gathered on shore to wave and throw confetti at the disembarking soldiers. Not wanting to get involved in the celebration, Shaylin had returned to her cabin and lain down on her bed to wait until everything calmed down before going ashore.

Though she was not a member of the military, she was returning from the war, having spent most of the past five years in Europe as a foreign correspondent for the Petzold News Group. She had covered the Blitz in London, then the buildup of American troops, and finally the D-Day invasion, managing to convince General Eisenhower to allow her to cross the English

Channel on one of the invasion ships. Later, Shaylin had pushed across the continent with the American forces liberating occupied Europe.

Wanting to send back her dispatches from the most forward positions she could reach, she had stayed as close to the front lines as she could. As a result, she had found herself under enemy fire more than once. She was, however, a resourceful and self-sufficient woman who managed to move about with a minimum of trouble to the American commanders. Therefore, her presence, even under such extreme conditions, hadn't been resented. In fact, Shaylin, an attractive and fiery red-haired, green-eyed, Irish-American colleen of thirty-five, could give and take in practically any situation, and she had been extremely popular with the GIs. That same presence, though, had made it necessary for her to develop a sense of detachment from her stories. Otherwise she couldn't have written about a young soldier one day, only to see him killed the next.

She had suffered her own loss during the war; her English lover, Colonel Sir John Paul Chetwynd-Dunleigh of His Majesty's Forces, had been killed in the China-Burma theater. She had learned of his death on the eve of the Normandy invasion, but the tragic news hadn't stopped her from carrying on with her job.

Only once, in fact, had Shaylin's professional reserve almost crumbled. She had seen entire families killed in the Blitz. She had watched landing boats destroyed, tanks burned, and young men killed. She had thought she was immune to anything. . . until she had gone in with the American troops to rescue the prisoners of Buchenwald.

Instead of being greeted by cheering throngs, Shaylin and the American soldiers were met by the walking dead—those who could walk. Most of the prisoners couldn't even stand; they lay on their bunks, barely able to raise their heads, staring with vacant eyes and blank faces at their liberators. There was no flesh on any of them, only pale, yellow skin stretched over skeletal frames. They were covered with fleas and ticks, and maggots were nesting in the corners of their eyes.

Gradually the horror of the death camps became known as the prisoners came forth with horrifying stories of wholesale murder by firing squad, gas chambers, torture, and starvation. Shaylin had seen the huge brick ovens where the dead had been cremated and learned that they had run twenty-four hours a day to accomplish their grisly task.

Shaylin's article about those camps—*Open: The Gates of Hell*—had been her last report before coming home. The article, published by *Events Magazine,* had created a worldwide sensation, and Shaylin found herself being interviewed by reporters from other American news organizations and from other countries.

Making the news instead of reporting it was an uncomfortable change for Shaylin McKay, and for the first time in her career she found that she had developed an affinity for people who didn't want to be interviewed. It was this newfound desire for privacy that made her wait in the quiet of her stateroom until after the troops had debarked, the bands had gone, and the crowd had dissipated. Not until dusk was she ready to leave the ship.

"Miss McKay?"

Shaylin groaned. Who had waited this long for her? Someone must really want a story. She turned toward the sound of the voice and was surprised to see not a newspaper reporter, but a Navy officer.

"Are you Shaylin McKay?"

"Yes," Shaylin said. She shifted the duffel bag strap on her shoulder and cocked her head curiously. "I'm Shaylin McKay."

"Miss McKay, I'm Lieutenant Commander Gordon Beaman," the officer said. He cleared his throat. "According to our records, Chief Petty Officer Kevin McKay has you listed as his next of kin."

Shaylin smiled. "That's me, all right," she said. "Kevin's my younger brother. Did you say Chief Petty Officer?" She clucked her tongue. "I'm impressed. I keep telling Kevin, if he stays in long enough, he's going to make admiral yet."

"Miss McKay. . ." Beaman paused.

Suddenly Shaylin felt cold all over, and she began shivering uncontrollably. She felt a lump grow in her throat, and her eyes began to burn.

"He's. . . he's dead, isn't he?" she asked.

"I'm sorry, Miss McKay," the officer said. "He was on board the cruiser U.S.S. *Baltimore* when it was sunk by kamikaze airplanes. It may be of some interest for you to know that the *Baltimore* was the ship that delivered the atomic bomb."

"What about Kevin?" Shaylin asked.

"As I explained, the ship was sunk," Beaman said. "Some of the men got off, including your brother. But he left the safety of the raft and swam out to try and help a shipmate—an officer—make it to safety."

"And he drowned?" Shaylin asked. "How could that be? Kevin was a strong swimmer. A very strong swimmer. He wouldn't have gone so far that he couldn't get back."

"There were, uh"—Beaman cleared his throat—"unusual circumstances."

"Unusual circumstances?"

"I wish I didn't have to tell you this, Miss McKay, but you'll find out soon enough. Your brother, the officer he attempted to save, and more than eighty others from the *Baltimore* were attacked and killed by sharks."

"Oh, my God!" Shaylin said, putting her hand to her mouth. Tears began flowing down her cheeks.

"Miss McKay, I have a staff car and a driver here," the officer said. "I would be honored if you would let me drop you off somewhere. Do you have family or friends in New York?"

"No family. No friends."

"An apartment?"

"I gave it up when I went to Europe. Take me to a hotel."

"Yes, ma'am, it will be my privilege. What hotel would you like to go to?"

"I don't care, Commander," Shaylin said wearily. "As long as it has clean sheets and running water."

SEPTEMBER 2, 1945, ST. LOUIS, MISSOURI

Willie Canfield sat in the overstuffed leather chair tucked in the corner of the library in his parents' house. There was a comforting familiarity about the house, even about the room where he had once studied his lessons.

He scanned the bookshelves beside the chair. Even the books were the same. His gaze went to the second shelf, where he looked for and found the inverted copy of *The Pilgrim's Progress*. He smiled to himself. He had turned that book upside down when he was in the eighth grade, just to see how long it would be before anyone noticed it. That was twenty-four years ago; the book was still upside down.

But despite the familiarity with his surroundings, Willie was experiencing a disconnection from reality. Sometimes he thought he could hear the distinctive whine of a three-quarter-ton truck on its route around the airfield, picking up guards going off duty and dropping off their replacements. And earlier he was almost sure he had heard the cough and rumble of an aircraft engine being worked on at a maintenance hangar.

Willie felt a sense of uneasiness, of expectation, as if he were waiting for planes to return from a bombing mission. He wasn't, of course. That was all over now, and he was back in St. Louis, released early because the mission he had been sent to Tinian to perform—overseeing the transfer of the Eighth Aircorps from the European to the Pacific theater—had been canceled by subsequent events.

With no mission and no assignment, Willie was supernumerary to General LeMay's operations, so he was provided with a seat on a C-54 flight and sent back to the States. From San Francisco he flew to Washington, where he made a personal report to the Secretary of War. After that he expected to return to his old command at Waddlesfoot Air Base in England. Instead, he was discharged "with the appreciation of a grateful nation."

It had all happened so quickly that Willie couldn't get over the feeling that he should be somewhere else. Colonel Jimmy Blake, Willie's executive officer during most of his time in Europe, was still at Waddlesfoot as the acting commander. Actually, Willie suddenly realized, now that he wasn't there, Colonel Blake *was* the commander.

But if Willie wasn't in England, at least his presence might still be. He pictured his desk, with the In and Out baskets spilling over with paperwork. And the refrigerator in his room containing exactly eight bottles of beer (good American beer, Tannenhower, not that tasteless British ale), two Pepsis, and half a bottle of milk—though surely by now the milk was spoiled and had been poured out. Realistically, he didn't expect the beer or the Pepsis to be there either.

His mind toured the rest of the office. On one wall was a map, marked with all the missions flown by his command. On another was a dart board, with a photo of Hitler's face tacked to it. On the dresser in his quarters was an autographed picture of Demaris Hunter, given to him when the famous actress came to England to entertain the troops, inscribed: *"To Willie, from one St. Louisian to another. I'm tired of us Missourians saying 'show me.' Let's show them! Love, Demaris Hunter."* On the table beside his bed was a small photograph of Candy Keefer, taken by Jimmy Blake just before Willie and Candy went into London to do the town—the day before Candy, a ferry pilot who had brought a B-17 over, was killed when the plane taking the ferry pilots back to the States crashed in the Atlantic.

Candy was gone, like the 1,611 brave young men of Waddlesfoot who had been killed in the cold skies over Germany. Everything was gone— the whine of the trucks, the rumble of aircraft engines, the In and Out baskets, the beer, the Pepsis, the milk, the map, the pictures, Colonel Blake, Sergeant Grega, General LeMay. . . That was all part of another world, so distant and so different from this one that perhaps it had never existed at all.

Or perhaps *this* world didn't exist, except in a dream. Perhaps he was dreaming now, and at any moment the duty officer would shine a flashlight in his face and tell him that Waddlesfoot had a mission.

Willie's head started spinning, and he realized that he was having a problem with reality. He gripped the arms of the leather chair tightly. He could feel them under his hands. . . they were real. *This* was real. He wasn't dreaming. . . he really was in the library in his parents' house in St. Louis. He looked around the room to clear his mind of extraneous thoughts and to reorient himself.

The library was dark except for the little green "Magic Eye" light on the big console radio. Willie remembered then that he had come in here not only to get away from his mother's house guests, but to listen to the surrender ceremony on the radio. He looked at his watch. It was about to begin.

39

The Magic Eye indicated that the radio was perfectly tuned, but the signal was less than perfect because it was a short-wave broadcast from aboard the battleship U.S.S. Missouri in Tokyo Bay. Willie could hear the whistle and the fade of the carrier wave, but the announcer's words were clearly understandable.

"This is Floyd Stoner, ladies and gentlemen, broadcasting to you for the Affiliated Radio Network, from aboard the U.S.S. Missouri, where, in a short while, General Douglas MacArthur, in his capacity as Supreme Commander of all Allied Forces, will accept the surrender of Japan.

"It is fitting that the battleship Missouri be selected as the site for the surrender. Not only is it one of the four biggest battleships in the world, it is also named for the President's home state, and it was christened by his daughter, Margaret.

"A number of admirals and generals are already aboard, including Halsey, Helfrich, Turner, Percival, Stilwell, Wainwright, Spaatz, Kenney, and Eichelberger. And now Admiral Nimitz is being piped aboard. And here is General MacArthur.'

"Oh, here you are," a voice said from behind Willie. Bob Canfield stepped into the library and smiled at his son. "We've been wondering where you disappeared to. Everyone has left the dinner table, and they're gathered out in the summer house."

"Hi, Pop. I'm sorry I wandered off, but I was beginning to feel a little out of place with those people," Willie replied. "All that celebrating. . ."

"Out of place? Nonsense. 'Those people,' as you call them, are all your friends. As as for celebrating, well, of course they're celebrating. They're happy to see you back."

"Yeah, I know." Willie picked up his drink and looked into it for a moment. "I'm just not up to all the slapping on the back, the laughs and jokes about how we showed Hitler, Tojo, and the world."

Bob leaned against the fireplace mantel. He was sixty-two years old now, and though his once-dark hair was now white, his once-chiseled features had softened, and his once-lean runner's body had thickened, his eyes were as piercing a blue as they ever were.

"Don't you think pride over the outcome of the war is justifiable?" Bob asked.

"Sure it is, Pop. Don't get me wrong, I'm as full of pride as the next man. After all, I did everything I could to contribute to that victory. And we had to come out on top. If the other side had won, civilization would have been set back a thousand years."

"I hear an implied 'but' there," Bob said.

Willie sighed. "But. . . I flew missions against Hamburg and Nuremburg and Dresden, and I visited the ruins after Germany surrendered. And I studied the strike pictures of Tokyo, Hiroshima, and Nagasaki. I'm afraid I can find little stomach for the unbridled celebration of what we did there."

"If the Nazis and the Japanese had gotten their way, the cities lying in ruin today would be places like New York, Washington, Detroit, Los Angeles— and St. Louis," Willie's father reminded him.

"I know," Willie said. "That's what's so frightening. It couldn't be neither. . . it had to be either. Right now a war crimes tribunal is being put together in Nuremberg to try the Nazi leaders for their actions. If we were really going to be honest about it, we wouldn't indict the Nazis alone, we'd indict all mankind."

"That's not a very practical solution," Bob said.

"There is no solution."

"Maybe there'll be some hope in the United Nations."

"That's what they said about the League of Nations after the last war."

"True. But who knows? If Wilson had prevailed, if he'd been able to bring the United States into the League, perhaps history *would* have been different. We didn't belong to the League, so we took little interest in its affairs. But we *do* belong to the United Nations."

"Germany and Japan don't," Willie pointed out.

"For all practical purposes, Germany and Japan don't even exist any-more," Bob said. "When they are reorganized as nations—peaceful nations—I'm certain they'll be accepted as members. And if all the nations of the world are meeting in a common forum, differences of opinion can be worked out peacefully."

"I hope and pray you're right, Pop, 'cause with these new atomic bombs, it won't make any difference who wins the next war. Civilization won't survive."

"Willie, the entire world shares your hopes and prayers. That's the basis of the United Nations, and that's the one thing we have going for us. Now, why don't you try to put all of that behind you and come on out with the others? This welcome-home party is very important to your mother." Bob chuckled. "I think she began planning it the day you left."

"Just let me listen to the rest of this surrender broadcast," Willie said. "Then I'll come join everyone. I promise."

"All right," Bob agreed. He squeezed his son's shoulder and smiled at him. "It's good to have you back, Willie," he said softly, his voice choking. "I can't tell you how good it is." He turned away quickly, clearing his throat as he left the library.

Willie leaned his head back against the cushiony leather and listened to the continuation of the broadcast.

"The clouds have rolled away now, and the sun is shining brightly on these ceremonies. In the distance we can see beautiful Mount Fujiyama, said to be sacred to the Japanese, sparkling in the brilliant morning light. And now, General MacArthur has signaled to the first of the Japanese delegates that it is time to sign the surrender instrument. The first Japanese delegate to do so is Foreign Minister Shigemitsu. Mr. Shigemitsu lost his leg a few years ago in an

41

assassination attempt by an extremist who opposed his wanting to seek a peaceful end to the war. He is limping to the table on his artificial leg, and now he sits. He appears to be hesitating somewhat, as if confused about what to do. Ah, but General Sutherland is pointing out where he is to sign, and Mr. Shigemitsu does so without further ado.

"The next Japanese delegate to approach the table is General Umezu. Whereas the foreign minister signed willingly, we are informed that General Umezu is very much against this surrender. The fact that he is participating in the ceremony at all is significant, for it sends a message to other militarists that the war is truly over. General Umezu, perhaps showing his disdain for the proceedings, doesn't sit in the chair provided for him, but leans over to sign. He does so quickly, then withdraws to stand at attention with the remaining Japanese delegation.

"Now General MacArthur is signing as Supreme Commander of the Allied Forces. Oh, and here is a touching moment, ladies and gentlemen. General MacArthur has just given one of the pens he used to General Wainwright. General Wainwright, as all of you know, was captured by the Japanese at Bataan and spent the entire balance of the war as their prisoner. What a glorious moment this must be for him!

"And now the representatives of China, England, Australia, Canada, New Zealand, France, the Netherlands, and Russia are signing in turn."

In the background there was a low roar, which got louder and louder. Willie recognized the sound even before Floyd Stoner told his listening audience what it was.

"The sound you hear now, ladies and gentlemen, is the sound of hundreds, perhaps as many as a thousand, Navy carrier planes and Army bombers sweeping over Tokyo Bay. What an inspirational sight this is! And now General MacArthur is about to speak. Ladies and gentlemen, the next voice you hear will be that of the Supreme Commander of the Allied Forces."

There was a brief pause, and then another voice filled the airwaves.

"Today, the guns are silent. A great tragedy has ended. A great victory has been won. The skies no longer rain death. . . the seas bear only commerce. . . men everywhere walk upright in the sunlight. The entire world is quietly at peace. The holy mission has been completed. . ."

A shadow filled the library doorway, and Willie's older brother, John, came into the room. John had been active in President Roosevelt's administration and was among those who had recommended strongly that President Roosevelt put Senator Harry S Truman on the ticket for the election in 1944. When Roosevelt's death elevated Truman to the presidency, the new President had asked John to stay on, at least until the war was over. John had agreed to do so, but he had recently submitted his resignation and now planned to return to the family business in January of 1946.

"Hi, John," Willie greeted. "Did Pop call in reinforcements to get me to join the party?"

John chuckled. "If he had wanted reinforcements, he would have sent Faith. No one can hold out against her," he added, referring to his wife.

"Faith is pretty formidable, all right." Willie grinned. "You could say that since she's both pretty and formidable, she makes a pretty formidable combination."

John groaned dutifully at the bad pun. Then he turned his attention to the broadcast. "Who's that speaking? MacArthur?" he asked, pointing to the radio.

"Yes. The surrender documents have just been signed. The ceremony's about over."

They fell quiet as they listened to the general's concluding remarks.

". . . *The utter destructiveness of war now blots out this alternative. We have had our last chance. If we do not devise some greater and more equitable system, Armageddon will be at our door. . .*"

Abruptly, Willie reached over and snapped off the radio.

"He wasn't through yet, was he? Why did you shut him off?" John asked.

"I don't know. It sounded to me like he was about to warn us about the next war," Willie said. "I'd like to get this one behind us before I start listening to someone talk about future wars."

"Yeah," John agreed, "I know what you mean. This war is barely over, yet there are people in Washington who want us to keep the military at its current strength as a bulwark against the Russians. I have to tell you, people like that make my ass knit barbed wire. I'll be glad to get back into private business."

Willie laughed. "Are you sure? I believe you're going to miss Washington."

John smiled. "What are you suggesting? That I have Potomac fever?"

"Could be. You've been there a long time. To tell the truth, I thought maybe when Faith's father retired, you'd run for his seat in the Senate."

"Well, I did think about it," John admitted. "But FDR talked me out of it." His face grew sad, and he sighed. "It's still hard for me to realize that he's gone. He had such a huge impact on my life for so long—on *all* of our lives, really. I don't think there's an American alive who doesn't feel as if they almost knew Roosevelt, he was such an enormous presence and influence for so many years. It's such a damn shame that he didn't live to see the end of the war—that he couldn't have lived a few more months to see our victory." John was silent for a few moments, then went on, "Anyway, he said I'd make a bigger impact and have fewer frustrations if I stayed just where I was."

"He was probably right," Willie agreed.

"Oh, I know damn well he was right. The only advantage to being a senator would be if I wanted to run for a higher office someday."

"A higher office? What's higher than a. . . John! You don't mean president?"

"That's what I mean. But don't worry. I've decided that I don't have presidential aspirations. I won't deny that I considered it, but I decided that it just wasn't for me. The truth is, I'd have been back home running the business five years ago if it hadn't been for the war."

43

"I know Pop is glad you're coming home to take over," Willie said. "He says he's earned his retirement."

"I sure agree about that. Pop has had quite a career, when you think about it. First he drained all that worthless swampland down in the Bootheel and converted it into the best farmland this side of the Nile Delta. Then he took over a failed animal-feed company and turned it into one of the biggest food-processing companies in the world. . . What can I possibly do to top that?"

"You don't have to top it," Willie said with a laugh. "All you have to do is keep everything going."

"Ha! Easy for you to say. You've already made your mark with your airline."

"*Our* airline," Willie corrected.

"Ours in name and investment only," John countered. "You were the creative genius, the driving force that made it what it is today."

Willie shook his head. "I wish I could take the credit for that," he said. "But the truth is, the airline grew with events. We were in the right place at the right time, and as each new development in aviation occurred, we were in position to take advantage of it. Then the war came along, and air transportation became one of the most valuable commodities around. No, I'm hardly in the same league as Pop. He drained the swamps and built Canfield-Puritex with his brains and energy. I built the airline by luck."

"Still, you have something concrete to point to," John said. "What do I have?"

"Come on, John, don't give me that self-deprecating bullshit. You were one of the brightest young New Dealers in Washington. I might have helped build a company, but you helped save an entire nation. You helped pull the country out of the Depression. Not only our airline, but thousands of other businesses survived because of what you did. Who knows? Canfield-Puritex might have been one of them. Besides which, you haven't exactly been sitting on your thumbs in Washington during the war. You made a few pretty good decisions there, too, as I recall."

"If so, the best decision I ever made was to convince FDR to appoint you a general."

Willie laughed. "Yeah, I sometimes forget that I have you to blame for that. You know, I used to hear the GI's swear at the draft board that got them there, and I always wondered what they would think if they knew that in my case my own brother was my draft board. They even discussed the possibility of tarring and feathering the members of their draft board after the war. I have to admit that there were a few times when I thought that might not be a bad idea."

"What? Tar and feather *me?*"

"Yes, you."

44

John laughed. "You try it, and I'll tell Mom."

Willie grinned. It suddenly felt like old times. He looked at his glass. "Whaddya know? This thing is empty. Have any idea where we might get another?"

"I think we can find a bar somewhere," John said. "Come on, you've kept your adoring public waiting long enough."

The Canfield home was one of the extremely large and ornate homes St. Louisians called "Brewer's Baronial." The brewing industry had provided St. Louis with its earliest millionaires, and the homes the beer barons had built for themselves had provided the name for an entire school of architecture.

The Canfield home was a noteworthy example of its kind. It was situated on five rolling acres, complete with a formal garden that had been designed and was lovingly tended by Connie Canfield. In the spring the garden was dominated by pink and white dogwood trees and banks of colorful azaleas. During the summer, a host of various perennials took over, followed in the tall by dozens of chrysanthemums. In addition to the flowers, scores of deciduous and evergreen trees as well as sweet-smelling shrubs provided shade and various hues of green in the summertime and a blaze of autumn color in the fall.

A long sidewalk bordered by sculptured hedgerows led from the back of the house to the "summer house," an outbuilding that consisted of one large room appointed with several sofas and settees, a bar, a tiny kitchen, and a couple of bathrooms. As it lacked a bedroom to qualify it as a guest house, the primary function of the summer house was as a setting for garden parties. As Willie and John walked through the garden toward the summer house, they could hear the laughter and conversation of the guests.

Kendra Petzold, president of the Petzold News Group, was there. PNG consisted of the flagship newspaper in St. Louis, *The St. Louis Chronicle*, plus newspapers in twenty other cities as well as *Events*, a New York-based national news magazine that competed with *Time* and *Newsweek*. In addition to the print media, PNG owned KSTL radio station in St. Louis as well as radio stations in Atlanta, Baltimore, Louisville, Nashville, and Phoenix, and a television station was under construction in St. Louis but hadn't yet begun operation. PNG's biggest impact on radio, however, wasn't the stations it owned, but the influence it exerted through the Affiliated Radio Network. ARN produced and provided regularly scheduled news services, subscribed to by more than two hundred stations across the country.

Tanner Morrison was also there. Tanner's real name was Brunhilde Winifred, though no one ever called her that. Her maiden name had been Tannenhower, and her own mispronunciation of her surname had provided her nickname.

45

It was a close call as to whether Anheuser-Busch or Tannenhower was St. Louis's biggest brewery. Tannenhower was certainly large enough, and Tanner had inherited a total of fifty-three percent of the stock from her father and her uncle, passed down from their father, the founder of the company. She was chairman of the board, though her husband, Mitchell Morrison, was the chief executive officer and the one responsible for the actual management of the company.

Mitch was Tanner's second husband. Her first marriage had been to Eric Twainbough, a bigger-than-life novelist whose name and face were recognized far beyond the literary world. Tanner and Eric's son, Hamilton Twainbough, was an Army captain currently with the U.S. Occupation Forces in Germany.

Dr. Stacy Williams, the president of Jefferson University, was also present at Willie Canfield's welcome-home party. Willie's family had been closely associated with Jefferson for many years; a statue of Willie's maternal grandfather, William T. Bateman, graced the Statue Circle on the quadrangle, and the university library was named the William Canfield Library after Willie's uncle, Billy, an aviator who was killed in action during World War I. The student body of Jefferson U., in a mixture of affection and irreverence, called the library "Billy Books."

The guest Willie felt closest to was Rex "Rocky" Rockwell. Rocky had been a squadron mate and the best friend of Billy Canfield during the First World War. After the war Rocky had come to St. Louis to carry out Billy's dream of building airplanes, and with a loan (long ago repaid in full) from Bob Canfield, he had done just that. Rocky was the Rockwell of Rockwell-McPheeters Aviation, best known for the Windjammers, the great flying boats that along with the Pan American Clippers had pioneered the trans-Atlantic and trans-Pacific routes for commercial aircraft.

Despite the age difference, Rocky had transferred his friendship with Billy to Billy's nephew and namesake, young Willie Canfield. It was Rocky who had taught Willie how to fly. He had also invited Willie, while he was still in his teens, to be the copilot on the very first passenger-carrying commercial airliner to fly the Atlantic. Made within a few weeks of Charles Lindbergh's flight, that flight was actually much more important to the overall development of aviation, though it failed to capture the public imagination to the degree that did the heroic solo flight of the "Lone Eagle."

As Willie now approached the summer house, Rocky came out to greet him, meeting him at the fountain.

"I was beginning to think I was going to have to come into the library and drag you out," he teased.

"Not necessary," John interjected cheerfully. "He finally succumbed to the smell of liquor and the sound of tinkling glasses."

46

"Only partially true." Willie held up his empty glass. "I smelled the liquor; I'm afraid I don't hear well enough to hear the sound of tinkling glasses."

"Hell, what aviator can hear after more than two hundred hours?" Rocky cracked. He held out a bourbon and water to Willie. "Notice, if you will, that I didn't come empty-handed. You haven't changed your tastes in the last few years, have you? You haven't switched over to schnapps or sake or something foreign like that?"

"It's still bourbon and water," Willie said, taking the proffered drink. "Thanks."

"Are you through with your military obligation? I mean, you don't have to go to some Army post somewhere to muster out, do you?"

"No, that's the beauty of going in as a general rather than a private. I'm all through now and ready to get back to business."

"Good," Rocky said. "I hope your first order of business is to come out to the plant tomorrow. I have something I want you to see. Or do you plan on trying to operate your postwar airline with prewar airplanes?"

"Until something better comes along, I guess I'm going to have to," Willie replied.

Rocky's drink was gone but he raised the glass to his lips and sucked out a piece of ice. He crunched it loudly for a moment as he studied Willie; then he smiled. "My boy, something better *has* come along."

The Next Morning

Willie was riding in the passenger seat of the Lincoln Continental being driven by Rocky Rockwell. When they reached the Rockwell-McPheeters Aviation complex at the back of St. Louis's Lambert Field, he let out a low whistle. The complex was at least three times larger now than it had been the last time he had seen it.

"Holy smoke, would you look at all this!" Willie said admiringly. "I had no idea that you'd grown so large."

"We're larger than Martin and Grumann combined," Rocky said. "I'm just glad Bryan lived to see it come to this."

Bryan was the McPheeters of Rockwell-McPheeters. Of the two company founders, Rocky was the one who had the flying experience, and, as it developed, the one with the better business head. Bryan McPheeters had been the designing genius behind the airplanes, and before he died, he had earned a reputation as one of the top aircraft designers in the world. He had died of a heart attack just one month before the Japanese surrendered.

The flight line was crowded with the twin-engine, twin-boom, P-38 Lightnings that Rockwell-McPheeters was building under a subcontract to Lockheed.

47

"What happens to these now?" Willie said, pointing to the long row of warplanes.

"Well, the Army will take delivery of them because they've been paid for," Rocky explained. "But we'd already stopped production on them and begun work on the next generation of fighter aircraft. Take a look over there."

The airplane Rocky pointed to was low and sleek, poised on tricycle landing gear. The nose came to a tapered point and was conspicuous by the absence of a propeller.

"I knew the U.S. was building a new jet plane. I didn't know Rockwell-McPheeters was."

"Technically we're not. Like the P-38, that plane is also being built for Lockheed. It's the P-80 Shooting Star. My boy, you are looking at the future."

"What will it do?"

"Top speed is classified, you understand," Rocky said. "But I can tell you it'll do better than five hundred miles per hour."

Willie whistled. "That's faster than the Me-262's that the Germans sent up against us toward the end of the war."

"Of course it is. It is faster, more maneuverable, will carry a greater payload, and has a longer range than the Me-262."

"How many have you built?"

"Very few," Rocky said. "And the numbers have just been cut by an additional seventy-five percent." He made a sardonic face. "I'm very glad the war is over—but it does mean the end of all that wonderful contract money."

"You haven't overextended, have you?" Willie asked anxiously. "I mean, you aren't going to be hurt by losing the subcontracts?"

"We're going to have to lay off quite a few people because our production will be way down, but in the long run we'll be okay. The war's brought about a lot of changes in the way the world thinks about flying. The great flying boats—the Pan Am Clippers and our own Windjammers—beating through the air at one hundred fifty miles per hour just aren't going to be accepted anymore. People want bigger, faster, and more comfortable planes. You mark my words, Willie. The time is coming—and coming soon—when more people will be crossing the two great oceans by plane than by ship. And we are going to build the planes the people want."

"I hope you're right," Willie said. "I've got an airline to run—and the bottom-line figures always look better if there are a lot of people willing to pay to fly somewhere."

Rocky grinned. "Funny you should mention that, because now I want you to see the airplane that's going to do the job for you."

The Lincoln rolled around the corner of one of the buildings, and Rocky stopped, then pointed through the windshield at a huge four-engine plane.

48

Except for the experimental number on its nose and tail, it was unpainted, so it glistened a bright silver in the morning sunlight. A handful of workers were puttering around the craft, all wearing the light-blue, one-piece maintenance uniform that identified them as Rockwell-McPheeters personnel.

"Willie, I would like to introduce you to the RM-505, or, as we like to call it, the Moonraker. What do you think of it?"

"My God, it's the most beautiful thing I've ever seen," Willie said, awestruck.

Both men got out of the car to get a closer look at the giant aircraft. It was big, bigger even than the C-54. The wings were long, thin, and graceful, very similar in appearance to the wings of a B-29. But whereas the B-29 had a long, cigar-shaped fuselage, the fuselage of the RM-505 was much larger, deeper, and oval-shaped, as if two B-29 fuselages had been molded together. Rather than being ungainly, though, the result was a beautiful curving piece of sculpture.

"I can see that you're impressed," Rocky said dryly.

"Rocky, it's truly magnificent!"

"Would you like to go aboard and have a look around?"

"As if you have to ask."

At a signal from Rocky, one of the workers moved a big yellow boarding ladder up to the rear door. Because the aircraft sat high on its landing gear, the door was more than ten feet off the ground.

Willie climbed the boarding ladder, then stepped into the plane and looked up the aisle toward the front. "Holy shit! This thing is bigger than a barn."

The cabin configuration had four seats across, divided by a center aisle. The cabin seemed to stretch on forever, and Willie began a mental count.

Second-guessing him, Rocky said, "There are forty cabin-class seats and sixteen first class. But if you wanted to convert it to a shuttle with all cabin class, you could carry seventy-two paying passengers."

"What about the crew?"

"Pilot, copilot, flight engineer, and navigator up front. Three stewardesses, one for first class, two for the cabin."

Willie walked up the length of the airplane, letting his hands touch the backs of the beautifully upholstered, color-coordinated seats as he passed them. He opened the bulkhead door and looked into the flight deck. The panel was awash with instruments and dials and switches. They spilled over to each side and even above the windshield.

"It's fully pressurized," Rocky said, "so passengers can walk around in their shirtsleeves at thirty thousand feet. And those big R-3350 engines out there will haul this baby along at three hundred miles per hour nonstop for five thousand miles."

"I've got only one question," Willie said. "How soon can I take delivery?"

49

"Ah, yes, well, that's the sticky point," Rocky replied. "This prototype is the only one we have. And before we can make any more, we're going to have to shut down our wartime assembly lines, extricate ourselves from the remaining government contracts, retool, then get in the raw materials. Also, this plane is going to have to undergo a lot of flight testing. You see, this isn't a rehash job from some existing design; this is a one-hundred-percent new airplane."

"Yeah, yeah, I know all that," Willie said, waving his hand impatiently. "How long?" he asked again.

"Two years. That is, if we get the orders. This is going to be a very expensive airplane, Willie."

"How expensive?"

"Fully instrumented and equipped, I'd say in the neighborhood of a million dollars each."

Willie blinked. "That's a pretty classy neighborhood," he said. "That's seven or eight times more than we paid for the Windjammers."

"But you have *ten* times more airplane here. And don't forget, the Windjammer could only land in coastal cities where there was a protected waterway to receive it. The Moonraker can land anywhere there's an airport: London, Paris, Frankfurt, Rome. Passengers could board in inland American cities, like St. Louis, Chicago, or Denver, and fly to their overseas destination without having to change planes. Think of what that'll do for your marketing."

Willie laughed. "You can stop your sales pitch, Rocky. I'm sold."

"What about your board of directors? Will you have any trouble convincing them?"

"You forget, my father, my brother, and I make up three-fifths of the board," Willie said. "Start building your airplanes. We'll buy them."

OCTOBER 27, 1945, DELTA, MISSISSIPPI

Stump Pollard, Delta's chief of police, tuned in *The Grand Ole Opry* on the radio, then sat down at his desk to eat his supper. He took a big bite of the bologna sandwich Cora Jean had made for him, washing it down with a swallow of Spur Cola.

It was quiet for a Saturday night. Billy Ray, who was cruising around town in one of the two patrol cars, had only picked up two lawbreakers, both drunk and disorderly. Right now they were sleeping it off in their cells out back.

As Stump ate his supper, he thumbed through the October 15 issue of *LIFE* magazine. On the cover was a beautiful young model identified as Evelyn McBride. Truthfully, Stump thought that Cora Jean was just as pretty, but the girl on the magazine cover had a cool, sophisticated look about her, like a very wealthy northern girl. There was no way Cora Jean could compete with that, and it was unfair to even make the comparison.

The most interesting part of the magazine to Stump was an article about a new offensive formation that the New York Football Giants had developed called the "A Formation," which, according to the article, combined the power of the single wing with the deception of the "T."

Stump enjoyed the action sequence of pictures. Taken from the defensive backfield, the perspective put the viewer right in the play. He could almost feel the physical contact of a good, solid hit.

In his younger days, Stump had been an all-star football player for Ole Miss. In fact, it was a knee injury from that time that had kept Stump from serving in the Army.

When he first learned he was 4-F, he'd been very upset. He'd felt left out and guilty about not doing his part, though some of his friends had tried to convince him that he was doing his part just by staying on as police chief. And, as Cora Jean liked to remind him, if he had been in the Army, they'd never have met and gotten married.

The phone rang just as Stump took another bite of his sandwich, and he poked a dangling piece of bologna into his mouth as he reached for the receiver.

"Police station, Chief Pollard."

"Chief Pollard? This here's Officer Burns over at Hernando. We got a nigger belongs to you."

"What do you mean, he belongs to me?" Stump growled. "Surely you've heard of the Emancipation Proclamation."

"Say what?"

"Never mind. What's the charge, D and D?"

"Naw, hell, I wouldn't call you about drunk and disorderly. Niggers are just naturally goin' to get drunk on Saturday night; you know that. But this here nigger tried to buy hisself a hamburger down at the bus station. I mean, he walked up to the white lunch counter just as bold as you please and asked could he buy a hamburger."

"What do you mean 'white' lunch counter? As I recall, your bus station doesn't even have a colored counter, does it?"

"No, it don't."

"Then if a colored man is hungry, how the hell is he supposed to eat?"

"He could always ask a white man to buy somethin' for him."

"But if this man is from *my* town, like you say, he may not know any whites in *your* town."

"Yeah, well, that ain't the whole of it. This here nigger was dressed up like he's a Army officer. I mean can you imagine that? A nigger lettin' on like he's a officer?"

51

"Oh, damn," Stump said, sitting up straight in his chair. "What's the man's name?"

"Let me see here." There was a brief pause and the sound of papers being shuffled. "Jackson, I think it is. Yeah, Travis Jackson."

"He *is* an Army officer, you dumb shit. He's not only an officer, he's a bona fide war hero. He's an ace."

"He's a what?"

"An ace. He shot down fourteen German planes. And you threw him in jail? That's quite a welcome home, isn't it?"

"Well, how the hell was I supposed to know he's for real?" Burns complained. "I mean, I ain't never even heard of no nigger officer before, let alone a ace. 'Sides which, there's still that little matter of him tryin' to buy hisself a hamburger where he didn't have no business. What am I supposed to do about that?"

"I'll tell you what you do," Stump said. "You let me talk to him."

"This here is a long-distance call," Burns complained. "The law says I gotta give a prisoner one telephone call, but it don't say nothin' 'bout it bein' long distance."

"I'll get hold of the operator and have the charges reversed," Stump said angrily. "Now, you put Captain Jackson on the telephone."

"All right, all right, hold your horses," Burns grumbled.

Putting the telephone down, Burns looked across the room at the other police officer on duty. "Hey, Hodge, can you beat that? This here nigger really *is* a officer. I hope we don't get in no trouble with the Army over this."

"What do you mean, 'we'? You're the one what put him in jail, not me," Hodge said.

"Yeah, well, you're workin' tonight, same as me, so if any trouble comes down, it's goin' to come down on both of us," Burns muttered.

He walked back into the jail. There were four cells and three prisoners. A black man and a white man who were in adjacent cells for drunk and disorderly conduct were playing a game of checkers through the bars that separated them.

"You gots to take your jump, Mistah Ancel. That's the rules," the black prisoner was saying.

"Not if I don't see it, I don't have to take it," the white prisoner retorted.

"But you do see it. I'm showin' it to you."

"That don't count."

"Cap'n," the black prisoner said to Burns as he passed by, "you tell 'im. You tell Mistah Ancel he gots to take his jump."

"Poke is right, Ancel. You got to take your jump, even if he points it out to you."

52

"Goddammit, that don't seem right," Ancel complained, moving his piece.

"Now I gotcha!" Poke said, laughing as he made a triple jump.

Burns walked back to the rear cell where a young black man lay quietly on his bunk with his hands behind his head, staring up at the ceiling. He had removed his jacket, and it was hanging neatly at the back of the cell, the captain's bars and the wings shining silver, the U.S. and Air Corps insignia glistening gold. A rainbow of ribbons was displayed above the left pocket.

"Hey, you. Jackson," Burns called. "They's someone on the phone wantin' to talk to you."

Travis Jackson shifted his gaze toward the policeman standing by the cell door. "I made no calls," he replied.

"I called him. He's the chief of police over in the town you say you come from. Name's Pollard, and he tells me you're some kind of a hero or somethin'. It don't make me no never mind whether you talk to him or not, but he's wantin' to talk to you for some reason."

"I'll talk to him," Travis said. He got off the cot and reached for his uniform jacket.

"You don't need that on just to talk on the phone."

Travis just eyed him silently as he put on the jacket. Only when it was fully buttoned, belted, and his tie straightened did he present himself at the door of the cell.

"I'm ready," he said quietly.

"You are really somethin'," Burns said, half exasperated, half admiring. "You know that? You are really somethin'." He opened the cell door, then pointed toward the front of the jail. "The phone's in there."

Burns followed Travis as he left the cellblock. When Travis reached the small office, he looked around with distaste. The ashtrays were full, and the waste cans were running over. The desks were messy, the floor needed sweeping, and the windows looked as if they hadn't been cleaned since before the war. The bulletin board was so sloppy that it would be impossible to determine what information was new and important and what could be discarded. If he had ever caught the operations office looking like this, he would have chewed his sergeant up one side and down the other.

Travis walked over to Burns's desk and picked up the phone.

"This is Captain Jackson."

"Travis? Travis, is that you? This is Stump Pollard."

"Hello, Chief," Travis said.

Stump laughed. "Hot damn, it is you! Boy, you're quite a hero around here, did you know that? We've been reading all about you! Fact is, I've got an article about you pinned up on the wall in my office. I'm looking at it right now. When did you get home?"

Travis snickered. "Well, that's just the point, Chief," he said. "I'm *not* home. At least, not yet. I take it you know about the little problem I ran into over here in Hernando."

"Yeah, Burns told me about it," Stump said. "Well, listen, don't you worry. You just stay right there. I'm going to come over myself and get you. I'll drive you right on out to your pa's house. Man oh man, is Professor Jackson ever proud of you! Well, hell, for that matter, we all are."

"You don't need to come after me," Travis said. "There's a bus leaving in the morning."

"Bus? To hell with the bus. Look, it'll only take me an hour to get there and an hour to get you back. . . you can be with your family before midnight. Now, wouldn't you like that?"

"Yes," Travis said wearily. "Yes, I would."

"Well, okay then; nothing else needs to be said. So you just wait for me. Oh, is there anything you need?"

"Well, I'm a bit hungry. I haven't eaten since early this morning." Travis chuckled. "Trying to get something to eat is what got me in trouble in the first place."

"Listen, you put that goddamn shit-assed cop back on," Stump instructed.

Travis looked over at Burns, who while pretending to be interested in something Hodge was doing was actually trying to listen in on the conversation. Travis held the receiver out toward him.

"He wants to talk to you," he said.

Burns took the phone.

"Yeah, Chief?"

"Didn't you give this man his supper when you picked him up?" Stump asked.

"I didn't pick him up till nearly seven. We feed at five-thirty."

"Well, since you picked him up for trying to buy a hamburger, couldn't you figure out that he might be hungry?"

"That ain't none of my concern, Chief," Burns said huffily. "Like I said, we feed supper at five-thirty."

"Feed him now," Stump ordered.

"Can't do that, Chief. The woman we hire to do the cookin' for the jail has prob'ly already gone to bed."

"Isn't there anything open over there? A restaurant? Anything?"

"There's the café in the bus station. It stays open till midnight. 'Course, that's where he got into trouble to begin with."

"Find out what he wants and go over to the bus station and buy it for him," Stump demanded.

"There ain't nothin' says I got to feed a prisoner after five-thirty," Burns protested.

54

"Yes, by God, there is! *I'm* saying it, you worthless shit," Stump shouted, his voice rising with his anger. "Now, you find out what he wants, and you go get it for him, or so help me I'll personally break your goddamn arm! And then I'll file charges against you for mistreating prisoners!"

"Ha! There ain't no way you're goin' to make charges of mistreatin' a nigger prisoner stick."

"Then I won't bother with the charges, I'll just break your goddamn arm."

"All right, all right, don't get yourself all in a tizzy. I'll get 'im somethin' to eat," Burns groused. He hung up the phone and looked at Travis. "Whatcha want to eat, boy?"

"Hey, Burns, I'll bet he wants a RC and a Moon Pie," Deputy Hodge quipped; then he laughed.

"I would like a hamburger, fries, and a Coke, please," Travis said. "Mustard and onion on the hamburger. And try to get it here before it gets cold."

"Whaddya mean, try and get it here before it gets cold? What do I look like? A goddamn waiter?" Burns growled.

Travis smiled. "Since I can't get it for myself, I suppose you are," he said. "I'll be waiting in my cell."

"You might as well wait out here," Burns said, looking defeated. "Soon as Chief Pollard gets here, I'm goin' to let you go anyway."

"No, thank you," Travis replied. "I prefer the company in the cellblock."

"I was real sorry about your mama," Stump told Travis. The town of Hernando was just a memory as they sped back to Delta. There was very little traffic; virtually the only thing they passed were the white lines in the middle of the road that popped up out of the darkness, raced toward the car at nearly sixty miles per hour, then flashed by to disappear in the darkness behind them. "She was a real good woman."

"Pop wrote me how kind you were to her, how you drove her up to Memphis to the hospital," Travis said. "I thank you for that."

"Yeah, well, I wish it had done some good." Suddenly Stump smiled broadly. "Say, did you hear? I got married."

"Pop told me. Congratulations."

"Thanks. Of course, it's been nearly two years now. We've already got a kid. A boy."

"Well, congratulations again."

They fell silent for a while. Then Stump said, "Now, about the war. What was it like?"

"I'm not sure I can explain what it was like," Travis answered.

"Please try," Stump insisted. "Maybe you heard I was classified Four-F. I couldn't go. I wanted to, but I couldn't."

"Where do I start?"

"Tell me what it was like to be in a. . . what do they call them? A dogfight?"

"All right. To begin with, you fly all alone, connected with straps and hoses and wires to a plane that becomes your own little world. You move through time and space at better than four hundred miles per hour, so when you see the enemy, you and he close on each other at a combined eight hundred miles per hour. You touch the firing button on the stick—just a tick, you understand—and you see a few balls of fire racing ahead of you toward the German plane. Sometimes you miss. Sometimes you hit him, and he falls off on one wing and drops away. If you look around, you might see a long stream of smoke heading for the ground, but when you see that, there's a curious sort of detachment as if that crashing airplane has nothing to do with you. And even if the enemy plane blows up right before your eyes, it does so in silence. It's the silence, I think, that makes it all seem unreal. And because it's unreal we can accept it. If I'd seen just one of my victims burn. . . well, I'd never have been able to fly again."

"They were the enemies of our country, Travis," Stump said. "You not only had a right to shoot them down, you had an obligation to."

"That doesn't make it any easier to think about," Travis said quietly.

"No, I guess not." Stump fell briefly silent again, and then he asked in a lighter tone, "So, what are you going to do now?"

Travis chuckled.

"What is it?"

"You asked what I was going to do now. The truth is, I don't have the slightest idea. You see, I thought about this moment hundreds of times while I was over there. But it was always this moment. . . returning to Delta in triumph, wearing my uniform with all the medals. But I never thought *beyond* this moment. All my fantasies stopped right here." He laughed again. "I guess it's time I figured it out."

4

NOVEMBER 20, 1945, NUREMBERG, GERMANY

E ric Twainbough held his arms out to submit to the American military
policeman's search. It was the third time he'd been searched since
arriving at the prison.

        He had come to Nuremberg—or Nürnberg as the Germans
called it—to observe the war-crimes trials. The allies had specifically chosen this place to conduct the trials because of the city's significance to the
Nazi movement.

"You're all clear, sir," the MP said.

"I should hope so," Eric replied. "I was just searched three minutes ago. If
I'd managed to get hold of a weapon since then, your security would be terribly suspect."

"Yes, sir," the MP responded. "Would you wait here, sir? Major Quinn will
be with you in a moment." He pointed to a coffee urn. "You can help yourself
to a cup of coffee if you wish."

"Thanks, I'll do that," Eric replied.

When the MP left, Eric selected the cleanest of several heavy white porcelain cups, then drew himself some coffee. Taking the cup over to the window, he drank the hot brew as he looked out at the cold rain.

No matter which direction Eric looked in, his eyes fell upon piles of broken brick, twisted steel, and concrete rubble. Here and there empty shells of buildings stood alone, like tombstones high and gaunt against the cold, gray sky. Many were without roofs, windows, or floors. The cold rain not only added to the dreariness of the scene, but it was also, Eric knew, making life miserable for the tens of thousands who had little shelter and no heat.

Already the Germans had started rebuilding, and all day a gray pall of dust and smoke hung over the city from the dynamite charges used to bring down walls that couldn't be salvaged. Those sturdy enough to be used again were braced by weblike networks of cable and scaffolding until they were sufficiently strengthened to stand alone. Though incomplete, and in some cases still open to the elements, many of the buildings undergoing reconstruction were already occupied simply because there was nowhere else for the people of Nuremberg to go.

The door opened and closed behind Eric, and he turned to see an American major coming toward him, smiling broadly.

"Mr. Twainbough," he said. "I'm Major Quinn."

"It's good of you to see me, Major Quinn," Eric replied.

"Believe me, sir, it is an honor to meet you," Quinn said. Hesitantly he held up two books. "I hope you don't mind. I took the liberty of bringing a couple of your books. I'd like very much for you to autograph them."

"I'd be glad to," Eric said. He took the two books and read aloud the titles on the dust jackets. "*Confession at Linares* and *Fire on the Northern Ice.*" He smiled. "Are they your favorites? Or are they the only two you could come up with on such short notice?"

Major Quinn laughed. "You got me. These *were* the only two I could come up with. You're pretty astute. My favorite is *Stillness in the Line.*"

"Astuteness is as necessary a tool to the novelist as talent," Eric said as he took out his pen and began to inscribe the books.

"I had the pleasure of serving with your son," Major Quinn said.

"Yes, I know," Eric replied, looking up from his autographing. "He mentioned you. He said he served with you twice. Once with pleasure when you were in North Africa and once not so pleasurably when you were at Fort Benning, Georgia. There you were his—I believe he said 'TAC' officer, whatever that is."

"Tactical officer," Major Quinn explained. "That was when Ham was in Officer Candidate School. A TAC officer is like a glorified drill sergeant. And, by job description, TACs are supposed to be sonsabitches."

58

Eric signed the second book, then handed them both back, telling Quinn, "From what Ham tells me, you seemed to follow your job description with particular enthusiasm."

Both men laughed.

"But I'm glad," Eric continued. "Ham survived the war, and I credit people like you with giving him what he needed."

"Captain Twainbough developed into a very fine officer," Major Quinn remarked. He put the books down. "Now, as to the purpose of your visit. I believe you're here to see the prisoner Karl Tannenhower?"

"Yes."

"May I ask why?"

"There was a time when we were friends."

Quinn opened a folder and read from it. "'Karl Tannenhower, Oberreichsleiter of the Nazi party and Obergrupenführer in the SS.'" He looked up from the folder at Eric. "Every gauleiter in Germany was under his authority. The charges were read against all the defendants today. Your friend is charged with conspiring to make war, aiding the German war machine, and crimes against humanity. He is one of the prisoners we will be seeking the death penalty for."

"Yes, I know. I was in court today when the charges were read."

"Well, if you don't mind my saying so, Mr. Twainbough, you certainly do have a strange choice of friends."

"Is there a problem, Major Quinn? Because I was led to believe by General Eisenhower that I would be able to see him."

"No, no, there's no problem," Quinn said. "You can see him, all right. I just wanted you to be prepared for the tight security you might encounter, that's all."

"I've already seen an example of it. I was searched three times coming in here."

"And you'll be searched again before you go into the meeting room. Also, you will not be allowed to touch him. No shaking hands or anything like that."

Eric chuckled. "What's the matter? Do you think I could sneak a gun past all these searches, then somehow slip it to Karl?"

"Oh, we aren't looking for guns," Quinn said easily. "We're looking for cyanide capsules. We don't want anyone else to beat the hangman's rope the way Himmler did." Major Quinn made the motion of putting something in his mouth and biting down with his teeth.

"Oh, yes. I see what you mean."

"Well, come along. I'll take you to him."

Eric followed the major out of the small waiting room, through a long corridor, then down a flight of steps. At the bottom of the steps was a metal door guarded by two armed guards. At a signal from Major Quinn, one of the guards opened the door, then stepped aside to let the major and Eric pass through. The door slammed shut behind them, echoing loudly.

Now they were in another long and well-lighted corridor. As they walked their footfalls rang hollowly on the concrete floor. They passed at right angles to another corridor, and Eric looked down it and saw cells. But they weren't cells in the conventional sense, for instead of iron bars, the walls were constructed of solid steel. The only opening was an eighteen-inch-square barred window cut into a heavy oak door. A soldier stood outside each door, looking in through the window.

"Why are all the guards looking into the cells like that?" Eric asked, stopping for a moment to observe the strange sight.

"We have orders from the military tribunal to keep the prisoners under constant observation, twenty-four hours a day," the major explained. "They are not to have one second of privacy. As you may know, Robert Ley used a towel to hang himself in his own cell. We don't want to lose anyone else by suicide."

"How can you see them at night, after lights out?"

"There is no lights out," Quinn answered simply. "Come along. The visiting room is down this way."

They continued to walk down the long echo chamber of a corridor. The visiting room was at the far end of the hallway, and when they reached it, Eric was subjected to another search, this one more thorough than any of the others had been. His body was patted down, and then he was made to empty all his pockets and turn them inside out. When the guard was satisfied, he nodded to Major Quinn, then resumed his position beside the door.

"We can go in now," Quinn explained.

"Good," Eric said.

The meeting room was twelve feet by fifteen feet and divided in the middle by a solid half-wall topped by a heavy mesh screen. Chairs lined each side of the wall, facing each other through the screen.

"This is where the prisoners may see their families," Major Quinn said.

"It's not exactly a warm meeting area, is it?"

"No, it isn't. But these men have it a lot better than the prisoners in the concentration camps did. Don't you agree?"

"Yes," Eric answered softly. He had visited Dachau in the first weeks after the conclusion of the war, and the horror of what he had seen flashed into his mind. "Yes, I certainly have to concede that point."

"Have a seat," Major Quinn invited. He pointed to a door at the back of the room. "The prisoner will be coming through there."

"Are you going to stay?"

"No. You'll have him all to yourself. But, as you can guess, we'll be just out-side, watching. Please remember what I said about touching."

"Don't worry. I hardly think we could shake hands through a mesh fence," Eric replied.

Quinn left and Eric sat down. After a wait of a couple of minutes, he heard the distant slamming of a door, then the drumbeat of footfalls that grew louder as they approached. There was a loud clanking on the other side of the prisoners' door, and finally the door opened. An American guard pointed through the doorway, then stepped back. Karl Tannenhower came into the room. His hands were held together by man-acles that were attached by a length of chain to the shackles that bound his ankles.

Eric thought of one of the many times he had visited Karl Tannenhower. One particular time that came to mind was in the late twenties, when Eric and his then-wife, Tanner, had traveled to Germany to visit Karl and his wife, Uta. It was in the fall, and there were dozens of beer and wine festivals going on all over the country. They had chosen to go to one in the small Bavarian village of Wertheim.

Eric's first book had just made *The New York Times* Best-Seller List, and he was happy and Tanner was happy and Karl and Uta were happy, and it had been one of the most wonderful weeks of his entire life. If Eric could work magic, he would have frozen time so that one week would have continued forever.

That was a lifetime ago.

Eric stood up. He had always known Karl as handsome and muscular. Now he was haggard and thin. But it wasn't just Karl's complexion or physique that had changed. Something else about him had, too, and though it took Eric a moment to figure it out, he finally realized that it was the eyes. They were flat and lifeless, and Eric could almost believe he was looking into the eyes of a dead man.

"Hello, Karl," he said.

"You shouldn't have come," Karl replied. His voice was totally devoid of expression.

"You and I were very good friends once. I couldn't just ignore that. I had to come. Are you getting along all right?"

"Yes."

"Is there anything I can do for you? Anything I can get you?"

"No."

"How about your lawyer? Are you satisfied with him?"

"I am satisfied."

The two men sat in absolute silence for a long, awkward moment; then Eric spoke again.

"Karl, I know you. I was a guest in your home many times. And the Karl Tannenhower I know cannot be guilty of all the charges contained in the indictment they read today. The concentration camps. You didn't have any-thing to do with them, did you?"

"What do you want me to say to you?" Karl asked.

"I want you to tell me you are innocent."

"I cannot tell you that," Karl said. "I am *not* innocent. No one in Germany is innocent."

"My God. You. . . you *knew* about the camps?"

"Not at first. Very few knew about them at first. But I learned of them."

"And you did nothing?"

"What could I have done?"

"I don't know. Try and prevent it from happening, I guess. Make a protest, leave the country. Surely you could have found *some* way to express your disapproval."

"There was no way."

"You could have resigned. You were the Oberreichsleiter, Karl. As I under-stand it, that made you the governor-general over all other governors in the Reich. In addition, you were an Obergrupenführer in the SS. If you had resigned those posts in protest over Hitler's policies, it would have made a statement to the whole world."

"Yes, perhaps," Karl said. "But I didn't do it. Now I am prepared to face the consequences. . . as all Germany must be prepared."

"I wish there was something I could do for you," Eric said.

"There is nothing." Karl stood. "I must be returning now. Thank you for your visit."

Eric looked at him sadly. "Good-bye."

Karl started toward the exit, then stopped and looked back at Eric. "There is one thing. . . ." he said.

"Yes?"

"The football matches for Jefferson University. During the war I could not follow them. I would like to know how they have been doing."

Eric smiled. "They're six and one this season. Their only loss was to Illinois."

"Yes," Karl said, nodding, "Illinois always was difficult. Do they still play Washington U. on Thanksgiving?"

"Oh, yes."

"That will be soon, will it not?"

"Day after tomorrow."

"I wish them luck."

62

The rain ended in time for the prisoners to be turned out into the yard for their half hour of "exercise." Karl looked forward to this period because it allowed him a little more space to stroll than did the small cell he was confined in. Here, also, was the opportunity to speak with the other prisoners.

Hitler, Goebbels, Himmler, and Ley had all committed suicide. Martin Bormann had disappeared. Gustav Krupp, head of the mighty Krupp industries, was deemed too senile to stand trial. But what remained of the Third Reich's leadership was right there in that very prison garden.

As Karl looked at these drab, disheveled, frightened men, he had a difficult time accepting who they were. Now their clothes were black-dyed cotton fatigues, but once the military men had been resplendent in custom-tailored uniforms dripping with medals, while the civilians had worn elegant silk suits as befitted princes of state.

Karl called the roll silently. They were all here: Hermann Göring, Rudolf Hess, Joachim von Ribbentrop, Field Marshal Wilhelm Keitel, Alfred Rosenberg, Hans Frank, Julius Streicher, Walther Funk, Hjalmar Schacht, Admiral Karl Doenitz, Admiral Erich Raeder, Baldur von Schirach, Fritz Sauckel, General Alfred Jodl, Franz von Papen, Wilhelm Frick, Arthur Seyss-Inquart, Albert Speer, Constantin von Neurath, Hans Fritzsche, Ernst Kaltenbrunner, Paul Maas, and, of course, himself, Karl Tannenhower. All present, all accounted for—and all ready to face the judgment of the world.

Of all the prisoners, Paul Maas was the only one Karl could actually call his friend, and they had been for many years. It was Paul who had recruited Karl into the Nazi party in the first place, taking him to hear Hitler speak when National Socialism was in its infancy.

Paul came over to Karl. "I heard your door close this afternoon. You left your cell, didn't you?"

"Yes," Karl replied. "An old friend, an American, came to visit me."

"Was it someone you knew when you attended Jefferson University in St. Louis?"

"No. It was the man who was once married to my American cousin. He is a very famous novelist. I'm sure you've heard of him. Eric Twainbough."

"Yes, of course I've heard of him. I have even read one of his books, *Stillness in the Line.* That's a very good book for a soldier to read. You are fortunate that he came to visit you."

"I was ashamed to have him see me," Karl said. "The indictments they read today. . ." He shook his head slowly. "They are very damning."

"They are also very generalized," Paul noted. "Surely they don't expect to conduct this trial by charging all of us with the same crimes. They must assess specific guilt for specific crimes. That is the law."

63

"What law?" Karl asked, his tone sardonic.

"International law," Paul replied. "The law of justice and fair play."

"Paul, there are no laws for us," Karl said. "This entire trial is without precedence, therefore everything that takes place within the trial is also without
precedence. You know what our lawyers have told us: We will not be able to
use as a defense that the trial is illegal or the procedure incorrect. It is correct
simply because the four-power tribunal, the victors in this war, *say* it is correct."

"Being correct does not mean being right," Paul insisted. "I am going to say
as much from the docket tomorrow.

"They won't allow it. You can only plead guilty or not guilty."

"Why do they waste their time listening to our pleas?" Paul asked. "Is there
a man among us who would actually plead guilty?"

"None of us are innocent," Karl said.

"Wait a minute! What are you saying?"

"But not all of us are guilty," Karl added quickly.

Paul sighed. "It doesn't matter. We're all going to hang anyway," he
said gloomily.

"Yes, you're right. It's too bad you couldn't have been a bird watcher," Karl
said lightly.

"I beg your pardon?" Paul replied, looking confused.

"A bird watcher," Karl repeated. "If you had been as interested in bird
watching as you were in politics, you and I wouldn't be here now. You would
have recruited me for a bird-watching society instead of for the Nazis."

"I tried bird watching," Paul said, picking up on the banter, "but I couldn't
pass the bird identification test."

"Oh, well, then of course, the only alternative was to join the National
Socialists," Karl replied, and both men dissolved into laughter over the black humor.

"I must say, it's good to see that some among us have retained a sense of
humor," Hermann Göring said, coming over to join them. When Karl shared
the joke with him, he laughed with them.

Göring had been forcibly withdrawn from the drugs he had been addicted
to for twenty years. Additionally, he had lost almost one hundred pounds.
The change was dramatic. Instead of the perfumed, hair-netted, heavily
rouged clown the world had known for the past several years, Göring was
once again a bright, articulate, and dominating personality.

He looked toward the far end of the prison yard, the area prisoners
referred to as the "military garden." There, on the other side of a small
hedgerow, Generals Keitel and Jodl and Admirals Doenitz and Raeder paced,
keeping their distance from the other prisoners.

"There is our vaunted military," Göring sneered. "No doubt plotting how
to throw all the blame onto the statesmen."

"They have a point," Paul said. "I mean, it *is* all Hitler's fault, isn't it? He was the one who made all the decisions. The rest of us had no choice but to abide by those decisions."

"It would be a big mistake to try to paint Hitler as Satan come to life," Göring insisted.

"I agree," Karl said. "We must all accept responsibility. After all, if we had won the war, wouldn't we all be wanting to get our share of the fruits of victory? Instead we must take our share of the bitterness of defeat."

Göring nodded in approval. "My defense shall be that while some mistakes were made, we were, for the most part, motivated by a genuine desire to do what was right for Germany," he said.

"Surely you don't expect such a defense to save you from the gallows, do you?" Paul questioned.

Göring smiled patronizingly. "Of course not, dear boy. I will be hanged, as will we all. I have no intention of defending myself before this court. I'm defending myself before the judgment of history. And it is there that I shall win my case. By the year two thousand, my remains will be dug up and placed in a marble sarcophagus so that I may be honored by the German people as one of the genuine heroes of this century."

"Hermann," Karl said scornfully, "the Americans have a saying for someone like you."

"And just what would the Americans say?"

"You are as full of shit as a Christmas goose."

The trial was being conducted in the Palace of Justice, and when the defendants filed into court the next day to enter their pleas, the room was filled to capacity. In addition to the judges, prosecutors, clerks, and translators, there were also spectators, reporters, and newsreel cameramen.

The docket was a small area enclosed by a knee-high fence. A row of tall, expressionless military policemen stood like statues behind the docket. The defense lawyers sat at tables in front of it. Karl took all this in as he entered, blinking at the brightness of the high-intensity lights that remained on constantly, to accommodate motion- and still-picture photographers.

Karl reached for his headset, which was available at each seat within the docket. Headsets were also available for the judges, the prosecutors, and the defense attorneys, allowing for the simultaneous translation of everything that was being said. Though Karl didn't need it when either English or French was spoken, he did need it to understand Russian.

Göring was seated in the first chair in the docket, a position indicating that the Allies considered him the most important of all the defendants. It was an opinion that Göring shared, and he occupied that chair with great pride. Next to Göring was Rudolf Hess, and next to Hess was Karl Tannenhower.

When in their cells or the exercise yard, the prisoners were allowed to wear only the prison-issue black fatigues. When they were in court, however, they were given their choice of what among their old clothes they wished to wear. As might be expected, the military men chose uniforms, though their uniforms were stripped of rank insignia and devoid of any medals or decorations.

Göring had lost so much weight that none of his well-known lavender, sky-blue, or pink uniforms would fit him. As a result he was dressed in a very plain gray uniform lacking any distinguishing marks. Knowing Göring's penchant for the gaudy, Karl was certain that this enforced drabness was as great an affront to the Reichsmarshal as anything else that had been done to him.

When all the defendants were in position, the president of the court, Lord Justice Geoffrey Lawrence of Great Britain, banged his gavel and called the court to order.

"The defendants will now enter their pleas," Lord Justice Lawrence said. "Defendant Hermann Göring, how do you plead?"

Göring walked over to the microphone and raised a piece of paper.

"Before I enter my plea of guilty or not guilty, I wish to make a statement," Göring began.

Lawrence interrupted him with a bang of his gavel. "The court will not accept a statement at this time," he said. "The only thing you can do is enter your plea of guilty or not guilty."

Göring glared at the bench for a moment; then he leaned over to the microphone. "Not guilty."

"Defendant Rudolf Hess, how do you plead?"

Hess was not only not wearing his headset, he wasn't even paying attention to the proceedings. He was reading a book of Bavarian folk tales. Göring had to lean over and punch him and whisper into his ear. Hess nodded, put down his book, and walked over to the microphone.

"*Nein*," he said.

There was a beat of silence while Lawrence conferred with the others on the tribunal—Francis Biddle from the U.S., Donnedieu de Vabres from France, and I. T. Nikitchenko from the Soviet Union.

"The court will accept that as a plea of not guilty," Lawrence said. "Defendant Karl Tannenhower, how do you plead?"

Karl got up and walked over to the microphone. He and his lawyer had discussed this very moment many times. In the beginning Karl had wanted to plead guilty and accept the responsibility he believed was rightly his as one of the leaders of the country. But he hadn't participated in any of the concentration camp atrocities and in fact hadn't even known, except in the most general terms, what was going on there. He had heard that the concentration camps were extremely harsh prisons, but he had known nothing about the wholesale slaughter or the huge crematoria until after the war was over.

The films he and the other defendants had been forced to view had made him physically ill, and he had felt sick to his soul that he could have been a part of a regime capable of such heinous acts. He had repeatedly asked himself how such monstrous behavior could have taken place without his knowledge.

Then he recalled an inspection trip that he had made to Schweinfurt during the war, after an Allied air raid on the ball-bearing industry there. Paul Maas had made the trip with him, and on the flight back Paul had brought up the subject of the concentration camps.

"*Karl, my friend, have you toured any of the relocation centers?*" Paul had asked almost casually.

"*Relocation centers?*"

"*The concentration camps where we are shipping all the Jews.*"

"No," Karl had replied. "No, I haven't seen any of them. Why do you ask?"

Paul's eyes had grown flat and dead. "*Don't. Don't visit any of them.*"

"*Why not? Have you?*"

"*Yes,*" Paul had replied. "*I had to see for myself why the trains were being tied up transporting Jews instead of war matériel.*"

"*And?*" Karl had prodded when Paul hadn't continued his thought. "*What did you see?*"

"*I saw hell.*"

Karl hadn't pursued that conversation any further, and now he believed with all his being that his failure to investigate—or even to ask questions—constituted a guilt of omission. Given the magnitude of Germany's crimes against humanity, the guilt of omission was as great as the guilt of commission.

It was for this reason that Karl had wanted to plead guilty. His lawyer, however, managed to convince him that neither the court nor the world would recognize the subtlety of that plea unless he was afforded the opportunity to present his case. And a plea of guilty might preempt that opportunity.

"Defendant Tannenhower, please put on your headphones," Lord Justice Lawrence directed.

"I don't need them, Your Honor," Karl said, speaking in English and leaning down to the microphone. "I plead not guilty."

5

FEBRUARY 1946,
FROM "TRAILMARKERS"
IN EVENTS MAGAZINE:

NAMED: As Secretary-General of the United Nations, Trygve Lie, at the first session of the UN held in London. In welcoming the delegates of fifty-one nations (representing four fifths of the world's population), British Prime Minister Clement Attlee stated that this noble experiment in world diplomacy would be successful only if the nations involved would bring "the same sense of urgency, the same self-sacrifice, and the same willingness to subordinate self-interests that they bring to conducting a war.

CONTACTED: The moon, by radar signal from the United States Army Signal Corps. The signal was sent from a transmitter on Earth, hit the moon, then bounced back to be picked up as an "echo" on the receiver. This marks the first time in the history of mankind that anything generated by man has left the planet.

DEBUNKED: The myth that Emperor Hirohito is divine. In an Imperial decree, Hirohito declared his divinity a "false conception" founded in fiction. Until the proclamation, Japanese citizens believed the emperor was descended from the Sun Goddess Amaterasu. In the announcement the emperor stated that the Japanese people should build a new state based on democracy, peace, and rationalism.

AWARDED: National Journalists Award to Shaylin McKay, for her series *Open: The Gates of Hell*, about the concentration camps in Nazi-occupied Europe. Miss McKay, who began her career as a reporter for *The St. Louis Chronicle*, was a foreign correspondent for the Petzold News Group during the war. Though still accredited as a pool reporter by the PNG, Miss McKay is now an associate editor for this New York-based publication of the PNG, *Events Magazine*.

FEBRUARY 1946, NEAR CHEYENNE, WYOMING

Technical Sergeant Richard Edward Parker had received orders to return to the United States one month earlier than his scheduled date because he had been selected to accompany the remains of Sergeant Eddie Yamaguchi.

Though the decedent, a nisei, was originally from Los Angeles, and though his widow, also born in L.A., had returned there after being freed from internment at the detention camp at Heart Mountain, Wyoming—where she had met Eddie Yamaguchi—the HOR (home of record) on Sergeant Yamaguchi's 201 File was where he had entered the service: Heart Mountain. But since the camp was no longer in operation, the Army, in its sometimes convoluted wisdom, decreed that the remains of Sergeant Eddie Yamaguchi would be delivered to Cheyenne, Wyoming. His widow would have to meet the body there and make further arrangements for the final disposition.

Richard Edward had been somewhat surprised when orders were cut assigning him to escort duty, because not only had he never heard of Sergeant Yamaguchi, he and the sergeant hadn't even been in the same unit. Richard Edward was in the 3rd Infantry Division; Sergeant Yamaguchi had been a member of the 442nd Regimental Combat Team. But what made it really curious was the fact that Sergeant Yamguchi's family had specifically requested him.

Richard Edward was intrigued enough about the strange turn of events to want to investigate, but several of his friends convinced him to leave it alone.

"Look, you're going back a month early," one fellow soldier had told him as he prepared to board the troop ship that would take him to San Francisco, where he would then take a train to Wyoming. "What difference does it make if you're escorting someone you've never heard of? Don't look a gift horse in the mouth."

Richard Edward decided to take everyone's advice and ask no questions. The mystery was cleared up a couple of days later when he received a letter from his sister, Rubye Murtaugh:

Dear Richard Edward,

If you haven't already learned that you are going to accompany the body of Sergeant Eddie Yamaguchi back to America, then you will soon. I know it'll be a surprise to you, since you have no idea who Eddie Yamaguchi is, so I'm writing this letter to explain why you're being asked to be his escort.

Actually, neither Del nor I ever met Eddie Yamaguchi, but he was married to Yutake Saito's daughter, Miko, and that is good enough for us. If you remember, back in the thirties, Del and I would have been out on the street if it hadn't been for Mr. Saito. He was absolutely the only one who would give Del a job when we were so desperately in need of one. Mr. Saito ran a landscaping and lawn-care business, and from the very beginning he and Del got along really well. Del discovered that he truly loved that kind of work, and eventually he and Mr. Saito became business partners.

Then, just when things were going really good for everyone, the war started and the government moved all the Japanese out of Los Angeles. I suppose they thought it was necessary, fearing some of the Japanese really were spies, but it worked a great hardship on some very nice people. It absolutely broke my heart to see Mr. and Mrs. Saito have to sell everything they owned and leave with just what they could carry on their backs.

Of course, Mr. Saito has since come back to Los Angeles, and he and Del are in business again, just as if nothing had ever happened. But it will take quite a while before the Saitos will be able to buy another house as nice as the one they were forced to give up.

Anyway, while the Saito family was in the detention camp at Heart Mountain, Wyoming, their daughter, Miko, married a young man she met there—Eddie Yamaguchi, the man whose body you are going to escort home.

Interestingly enough, though neither Del nor I ever met Eddie, we had seen him play baseball. He was a pitcher for the USC Trojans, and according to Del—who was a pretty good baseball player himself, so he should know—Eddie was quite good.

We're told that Eddie won the Silver Star, and the Saito family is quite proud of him, though I'm sure they'd rather have him back than the medal. When the government informed Miko that his body would be returned and asked if she had anyone in mind she wanted to act as his escort, she had her mama and daddy come to me. You see, they knew that I had a brother over there, and they asked me if I thought you'd do their daughter this honor. Forgive me, Richard Edward, for answering for you, but I said yes. This is very important to them, and because it is, and because they've been so wonderful to Del and me, then it's important to us as well. I hope you understand.

Your loving sister,
Rubye

It was three A.M. and Alice Parker opened the vent window on the car to direct a blast of frigid air onto her face. Because it was nearly zero outside, and because she was driving at nearly sixty, the cold wind managed to wake her up, though it lowered the car temperature several degrees in the process.

Alice closed the wing, then looked over at seven-year-old Bobby, who was sleeping in the front seat beside her, his head on the pillow jammed up against the passenger window. Harry, who was five, and Freddie, three and a half, were sleeping in the back seat. She had made a bed of the back by piling up suitcases and cartons on the floorboard until they were even with the seat, then laying a baby-bed mattress across the top of everything.

Alice glanced at the lighted instrument panel of the '41 Ford. The gas needle was just on half, the temperature and oil pressure were good, and the battery was charging nicely. Before the war all she ever bothered to check was how fast she was going and whether or not she needed gas. But nearly four years without a husband around to take care of things had forced her to learn more about operating a car than just how to start it and make it go.

"Pile the kids in the car, and come to Cheyenne, Wyoming, to get me," Richard Edward's excited letter had told her. He had explained that his orders were to deliver Sergeant Yamaguchi's remains to his widow, then report to Jefferson Barracks in St. Louis for his discharge. *"And from there, it's home to Sikeston,"* the letter had continued. *"By this time next month I'll be sitting behind the wheel of my own truck again!"*

Getting in the car and going to Cheyenne wasn't as easy as Richard Edward made it sound. In the first place Alice would have to put together enough gas ration stamps to make the trip. Also, it was a long drive from Sikeston, Missouri, to Cheyenne, Wyoming, and the distance between tourist courts, restaurants, and gas stations grew longer the farther west one got. And last, it was the middle of winter, and though Alice hadn't yet encountered a

71

winter storm, she was terrified that she would, and she studied the sky anxiously, alert to the slightest cloud buildup. But despite the difficulties, there was no way she'd miss being there when Richard Edward stepped off his train.

It had been nearly an hour since Alice had seen another car, and she was lost in a void of darkness. There wasn't even a white line in the middle of the road. There was nothing but her own headlight glare immediately in front of the car, then gray, then black. The drone of the car's engine and the warmth of the heater combined to make her drowsy again, and she would've given anything if she could just sleep.

She had spent the first night in Kansas City. She planned to spend the second night in Denver, but when she got there the kids were sound asleep, and she wasn't feeling too tired, so she'd decided to go on through the night and get a place in Cheyenne. Besides, it was much easier driving at night, without complaining or crying kids to worry about.

But the long, monotonous hours were beginning to yank at her now, and she was starting to have second thoughts about the wisdom of her decision. If she could only pull over for a little while. An hour. . . just an hour. . . that's all she'd need.

But in an hour in this cold without the heater they could all freeze to death. And she was afraid to run the heater while the car was parked because she feared carbon monoxide poisoning. That meant there was nothing she could do but keep going.

Alice reached for the radio dial. She knew that she must be a very long way from any stations, but some of the major stations had really strong signals at night, so maybe she'd get lucky. After considerable twisting of the knob she found a good, clear station and began singing along with the song:

> *My mama done tol' me*
> *When I was in knee pants*
> *My mama done tol' me, son. . .*

Suddenly ahead she saw the lights of a town, and she felt almost euphoric. A large billboard advertised THE COFFEE CUP, THE ONLY ALL-NIGHT CAFÉ IN GREELEY, COLORADO.

"Greeley, Colorado," she said aloud. "Horace Greeley. Go West, young man, go West."

"What did you say, Mommy?" Bobby mumbled.

"Nothing, pumpkin. Go back to sleep," Alice said.

But Bobby sat up and rubbed his eyes. Spotting the lights of the town looming ahead of them, he asked, "Is that it? Is that where we're going to get Daddy?"

72

"No, but it won't be far now," Alice said. "Say, how would you like a little breakfast?"

"It's too early for breakfast. It's still dark."

"Yes, I suppose it is. But I've got to have some coffee to help keep me awake, so I'm going to stop there. And it's too cold to leave you and your brothers in the car, so you're all going to have to go in with me."

"I could have a Coke," Bobby said.

"A Coke? Don't be silly. It's too cold for a Coke."

"Cokes are supposed to be cold."

"That's true, I guess. Well, all right. If a Coke is what you want, a Coke is what you'll get."

A number of big trucks were stopped at the Coffee Cup. Alice's husband, Richard Edward, was a hauler who owned his own rig, and seeing the big trailer trucks reminded her again of why she was making this trip. She felt a flush of excitement so great that it nearly drove away the sleepiness.

Harry complained about having to wake up and get out in the cold. Freddie didn't even wake up, and Alice had to carry him inside. She found a booth near the back and she lay Freddie, still sleeping, down beside her. Bobby and Harry sat across the table from her, but Harry promptly put his head down on the table and went back to sleep. Bobby started examining the songs on the small remote jukebox that hung on the wall over the end of the table.

A waitress came over and smiled at Alice. "Oh, honey, it looks like you've got some sleepy kids on your hands."

"Well, that makes us even," Alice said, laughing, "because they have a sleepy mother on *their* hands. Would you bring me some coffee, please? And make it strong."

"Honey, I'll make it strong enough to melt the spoon," the waitress promised.

"And I want a Coke," Bobby said.

"In a bottle or a glass?"

"In a bottle, please. We're going to see my daddy," Bobby added.

"Are you, now?"

"We're not just going to see him," Alice explained. "We're going to Cheyenne to get him. He's coming back from the war today."

"Oh, how wonderful. How long's it been?"

"Almost four years. The children can't even remember him."

"I can remember him," Bobby insisted. "Freddie can't, of course. He wasn't even born. Harry says he can remember him, but I don't think he can."

"Can, too," Harry mumbled, though he didn't raise his head from his arms.

The waitress laughed. "Honey, you don't have to worry about remembering him. He'll remember all of you, and that's all that's important. I'll get the coffee and Coke now."

As the waitress started back to the counter, she stopped at another table and leaned over to say something to the man who was sitting there drinking a cup of coffee. The man, who was wearing a leather jacket and a cap like most truck drivers generally wore, looked at Alice and the children, then nodded. He stood up and walked over to Alice.

"Ma'am," he said, touching the bill of his cap, "Maggie tells me you're goin' to Cheyenne."

"That's right," Alice answered. "Oh!" she gasped. "Has there been a snowstorm? Is the road closed?"

The man chuckled. "No, ma'am, nothin' like that," he said. "But she said you were sleepy and havin' a pretty hard time of it. I just thought I'd let you know that I'm headed up that way, and if you'd like, you can follow along behind me. That way I can sort of keep an eye on you."

"Why, thank you," Alice said. "That's very kind. Yes, I'd appreciate that very much."

"I'm drivin' the green International," the man said, pointing through the window. "That's it over there. Just give me a nod when you're ready to go."

"Yes, I see it," Alice said.

"A REO is better," Bobby said.

The man grinned. "Is it, now?"

"Yep. That's what my daddy's truck is. It's a REO. A red one, with a red trailer."

"Oh, I agree, a REO is a good truck, all right," the driver said. "But I work for Rocky Mountain Express, and that means I have to drive what they give me."

"If you have a choice next time, tell them you want a REO," Bobby said earnestly.

"I'll try to remember that," the driver said, laughing as he returned to his own table.

Alice finished her first cup of coffee, then had a second. When she finished that cup, she signaled to the International driver that she was ready. Picking up Freddie, she left the café, piled the kids back into the car, and began the last leg of her journey.

The coffee helped her hold off sleep. After several hours the sun began to come up, and when the darkness rolled away, it was easier to stay awake. Finally it was bright enough for the truck driver ahead to turn off his lights, and Alice turned off her own lights. She cracked the wing just enough to direct a stream of air into her face, without making the car significantly colder. The sound woke Bobby, and he sat up again.

"How much farther?" he asked.

"Not too much," Alice said. "I saw a sign a few moments ago that said Cheyenne was only thirty more miles. That'd be like driving from Sikeston to Cape Girardeau. Now, that's not too far a drive, is it?"

74

"No," Bobby agreed. "Oh, there's another poem! Do you want me to read it?" The boy pointed at the series of Burma Shave signs looming just ahead, one of hundreds of the clever advertisements posted alongside highways throughout the country, each of which was part of a limerick that took about half a mile to complete.

"Sure, go ahead," Alice said.

"'There was a man,'" Bobby began. Then he waited for the next sign. ". . .'who was such a grouch. . . every time he shaved. . . he gave a big ouch. . . then along came Mary. . . to save the day. . . removing his beard. . . the Burma Shave way. Burma Shave,'" he completed, reading the last sign. He turned to watch it go by, then turned back to the front and stared out the windshield. "I'll be glad when we get there," he muttered.

Richard Edward Parker was asleep when the conductor put a hand on his shoulder to shake him gently awake.

"Soldier, we're coming into Cheyenne," the conductor said. "You wanted me to tell you so you could be in the baggage car with the coffin."

Richard Edward opened his eyes. "Yes, thanks," he said, stretching. He stood up and got his uniform jacket down from the overhead rack and put it on. Two rows of ribbons and a Combat Infantryman's Badge were above his left breast pocket, and above that was the wreathed-eagle insignia, indicating that he was on terminal orders and about to be discharged. Called the "ruptured duck" by every GI, it was the most prized decoration of them all because it meant that the wearer's service was finished.

Richard Edward walked through the train to the baggage car. Eddie Yamaguchi's coffin had been moved to the middle of the car, and a flag was draped over it.

"I see you've got the coffin ready," Richard Edward said to the baggage man.

"Yes, we've handled quite a few of these things in the last few years," the man said.

"Well, this is my first," Richard Edward said. "So maybe you can tell me what happens now."

"When we get there, the coffin will be the first thing we off-load. The only thing you have to do is stand by until someone comes for it."

"Then I salute them and present them with the flag and the condolences of a grateful nation," Richard Edward said, quoting the paragraph of instructions from his orders.

The train began to rumble and squeal, and Richard Edward had to reach out to brace himself as it slowed. In a moment they'd be in the station, and if Sergeant Yamaguchi's family was there, he would soon be performing his last official act for the United States Army. He was glad his service was almost over, but he wished his last act didn't have to be such a sad one.

As the train came to a halt Richard Edward looked out the open door to see Miko Yamaguchi waiting on the baggage platform. But before the coffin could be off-loaded, the Cheyenne stationmaster came forward to inform the baggage handlers that the coffin would stay on the train to continue its journey to California after all.

Richard Edward wasn't certain what his role should be under the circumstances, so he extemporized and quickly folded the flag into the prescribed tight little triangle, making certain that none of the red showed. Hopping down off the train, he then presented it to Miko, saluting as he did so.

"Mrs. Yamaguchi, on behalf of a grateful nation I present you with this flag and extend the condolences of the President and the United States Army."

"Thank you so much for your kindness," Miko said. She took the flag from him.

"Mrs. Yamaguchi, I didn't know your husband," Richard Edward admitted, "but I do know something about the 442nd Regimental Combat Team. They were a real bunch of heroes, every single one of them."

"They were all nisei," Miko said. "They felt they had to prove they were good Americans."

"From what I hear, they made their point."

"Yes, Sergeant, but at a price. A terrible price. But it's all over now, and it's time for happier things." Miko smiled. "Such as your own homecoming. Your wife and children are waiting for you in the depot."

Richard Edward grinned. "They made it, huh? Great. I started thinking about it on the way out here, and I realized that it had to be quite a trip for them. I probably shouldn't have asked her to do it."

Miko giggled. "I don't think you could have kept her away. Oh, and your sister sends her love. She wants you to bring your family to California for a visit sometime soon."

"'Board!" the conductor shouted. "All aboard!"

"I must go now," Miko said. "I'm taking this train back to California." She shook his hand, adding softly, "Thank you, Sergeant, for bringing my husband back to me. I will always be grateful."

Richard Edward watched her until she was on the train; then, as the engineer gave a toot on the whistle and the steam valve released a gush of vapor, he turned and headed toward the depot. Just on the other side of the accordion gate, a woman and three young boys were waiting for him, smiling shyly. The scene was just exactly how he had been picturing it for the last three years.

MARCH 5, 1946, ON THE ROAD
BETWEEN ST. LOUIS AND FULTON,
MISSOURI

"Westminster College. . ." Bob Canfield grumbled from the back seat. "Who would ever believe that Winston Churchill would come all the way to a sleepy little town like Fulton to make a speech at a college as small as Westminster? I mean, if he just wanted to make a speech at a college in Missouri, why didn't he go to Jefferson?"

John Canfield, who was driving, laughed. "Because Westminster asked, and Jefferson U. didn't," he explained. "And President Truman wrote his own endorsement on the letter of invitation. Anyway, I think it's a good thing for Missouri. And at least we were invited to come hear him speak, so we can't complain."

"That's true," Bob admitted. "It's just that I would think a city like St. Louis would be a better platform. I wonder if there'll be any press coverage."

"Oh, I'm sure there will be. He may not be prime minister anymore, but he's still a newsworthy figure. I know *The Chronicle* will be covering it, and I imagine other papers will, too. Particularly since the President is accompanying him."

"Well, I doubt Churchill will say much of importance," the elder Canfield remarked. "With the situation so fluid in Europe since the end of the war, he's going to have to be pretty low-key."

"Maybe so," Connie Canfield put in, taking her husband's arm and squeezing it. "But whatever he does say, I will love the way he says it."

Faith Canfield turned around in her seat and smiled at her mother-in-law. "Me, too. I just love to hear him talk. 'Umm, we will fight on the beaches. . . umm, we will fight in the towns. . . umm. . .'" she mimicked.

"Is that Winston Churchill or Jimmy Cagney?" John quipped. "Umm, you dirty rat."

"You're just jealous," Connie said. "I think she does a perfect Churchill."

"Yeah, you're right. I actually couldn't tell the difference," John said. "I mean, if I'd had my eyes closed, I would've thought it was Winnie himself."

"You don't have to be so sarcastic about it," Faith scolded.

"No, I'm serious. Pop, there's the answer. You were complaining because Churchill is going to speak at Westminster instead of Jefferson. . . .Heck, all we have to do is give Faith an umbrella to carry and have her put on a bowler hat and puff out her cheeks. Why, she'll have *everyone* convinced she's Churchill."

"Stop it," Faith said, laughing and hitting John on the shoulder.

The campus was already jammed by the time the Canfields arrived, and many of the streets were blocked off. Fortunately, they had been given a placard that would let them through the barricades. John placed it in the Cadillac's window, and the policemen moved the barriers and waved them through.

The speech was to be given in the gymnasium, so John parked the car across from the gym in one of the reserved spots by the columns. The columns were all that remained from a campus fire at the beginning of the century, and now they were one of the most honored symbols of the college.

The Canfields made their way inside the gym, which had been modified for the occasion with a dais banked with flowers and decorated with flags. On one wall was a painting of a large bluejay, reminding John that the Westminster athletic teams were known as the Bluejays. Their seat pass put them on the free-throw line, and he wondered with a smile if in the whole of Winston Churchill's illustrious career he had ever made a speech on a basketball court.

"How are you, Mr. Canfield?"

Both John and his father turned toward the sound of a voice. A white-haired, dignified-looking Negro man was standing there. A somewhat younger, very attractive Negro woman was with him.

"Dr. Booker," Bob Canfield responded, "it is so good to see you again."

Their formal miens abruptly slipped away, and both men laughed, then embraced each other. Connie, John, and Faith joined in the greetings.

"Della, how do you manage to stay looking so young?" Connie asked.

"She *is* young," Bob said. "Don't you remember? Dr. Booker robbed the cradle."

Della smiled. "Oh, it wasn't that bad. He's only ten years older than me." Her smile widened and she added dryly, "Of course, I have aged far better."

The friendship between Bob Canfield and Loomis Booker went back many years, to the dawn of the century, when Bob had been a student at then-Jefferson College and Loomis had been a janitor and handyman. Using salvaged books and a well-structured and rigorous self-study program, Loomis had managed to master every course and discipline offered by Jefferson.

Bob and Loomis had held many long philosophical discussions in those days, and they had developed a genuine affection for each other. Bob, perhaps to demonstrate the respect he had for Loomis, had always called him Mr. Booker rather than Loomis, and Loomis had reciprocated.

Though Negroes hadn't been allowed to attend Jefferson College, Loomis's studies were subsequently validated, largely due to Bob Canfield's efforts, and Loomis was awarded a Doctor of Humanities degree, making him the only Negro ever to graduate from Jefferson College, now Jefferson University. He had been serving for many years as chancellor of Lincoln University, an all-Negro university in Jefferson City, Missouri.

78

"By the way, I want to thank you for getting tickets to this event for me," Loomis said to Bob. "It's quite an honor to be here."

Bob looked surprised. "I didn't get those tickets for you. I wish I could take credit for them, but we didn't get tickets ourselves until two days ago."

"That's strange," Loomis said. He looked at the seating passes that had allowed Della and him in the gym. "I had assumed they were your doing. I wonder where they came from."

"Ladies and gentlemen," the moderator shouted loudly, "from our own state of Missouri, the Honorable Harry S Truman, President of the United States!"

Everyone in the gymnasium stood and applauded and cheered.

When the applause had died down, Winston Churchill was introduced. There was another outbreak of enthusiastic applause, and Churchill, round-faced, balding, and wearing a great flowing academic gown, stepped up to a garlanded podium. He pushed a few papers around, cleared his throat, then began speaking.

The Canfields, like most of those present, had never seen Churchill in person. All had heard his speeches over the radio or had seen him in newsreels, so the resonant, cultured tones that Faith had tried to imitate in the car were very familiar. Nevertheless, it was a thrill to be hearing the words coming from the mouth of the man himself.

"A shadow has fallen upon the scenes so lately lighted by the Allied victory," Churchill said. "Umm. . ."

At his "Umm," Faith grinned and reached over to lightly poke John.

"From Stettin in the Baltic to Trieste in the Adriatic, an iron curtain has descended across the Continent. Behind that line lie all the capitals of the ancient states of central and eastern Europe."

John sat forward in his chair, studying President Truman's face to see how he was reacting to Churchill's speech. This wasn't the soft pedal everyone was expecting. This was anti-Russian—and very provocative.

". . . all are subject in one form or another, umm, not only to Soviet influence, but to a very high and increasing measure of control from Moscow."

John looked over at his father to see if Bob realized the significance of Churchill's remarks. He was, in effect, throwing down the gauntlet to the Soviet Union. Of course, Churchill had no official function right now. But he was speaking as President Truman's guest, and the President was sharing the dais with him; therefore, his comments would appear to reflect approved U.S. policy. Bob returned his son's glance, and John knew that he, too, understood quite clearly what was happening here.

"Last time I saw it all coming," Churchill continued, "and cried aloud to my fellow countrymen and to the world. . . umm. . . but no one paid any attention. Up until the year 1933, or even 1935, Germany might have been saved from the awful fate which has overtaken her, and we might all have been spared the miseries Hitler let loose upon mankind. We surely must not let that happen again."

Churchill continued in that vein, pointing out that the Soviet Union was quickly moving into position to take Hitler's place as the number-one threat to peace in the world. It could only be prevented, he concluded, with a show of strength and solidarity by England and America.

At the reception following the speech, Harry Truman grinned broadly as John, Faith, Bob, and Connie Canfield moved toward him through the reception line. When John reached him, he shook his hand enthusiastically.

"Hello, John," he said. "It was good of you to come and to bring your family."

"It was good of you to see that we received an invitation, Mr. President," John replied.

"Well, there was an ulterior motive in that," Truman explained. "I just wanted you to get a taste of some of the things you're missing by leaving Washington." He laughed. "I'm trying to convince you to come back and work for me."

"It is tempting, I agree," John admitted. "But I was in Washington long enough. I've got family business to look after now."

Addressing Bob, Truman shook his hand and said, "Mr. Canfield, I know I'm not telling you anything new when I say that your son is one mighty fine young man."

"Thank you, Mr. President, and you're right—I am well aware of that. In fact, I have two mighty fine young men for sons."

"Yes, I've met Willie as well. It's people like you and your, sons that make me extremely proud to be a Missourian."

"Mr. President, if you would allow me, I'd like to introduce another fine Missourian to you," Bob said. Loomis Booker was in line behind him, and Bob put his hand on Loomis's arm. "This is —" Bob started.

"Dr. Loomis Booker," Truman finished. He smiled warmly and reached out to grab Loomis's hand. "I see that you got the tickets I sent you."

"I did receive the tickets, Mr. President, but I had no idea they came from you," Loomis replied.

Truman laughed at the bewildered expression on Loomis's face. "You don't remember me, do you?"

Loomis looked even more confused.

"Well, of course there's no reason you should," Truman said quickly. "I was just a captain in the Missouri National Guard then, but I had a job to do, and by golly, you helped me do it."

"I helped you, Mr. President?" Loomis asked, nonplussed.

"You certainly did. I was an artillery captain, you see, and I thought it might be nice if, when I reached France, my guns were with me. You were working in the same office as General Eisenhower at the time, although he was only a major then, and it was your job to make certain that men and equipment got on the right train at the right time."

"I *do* remember, Mr. President," Loomis said, recognition dawning. "I remember because, being from Missouri myself, I paid special attention to the needs of the Missouri National Guard. As I recall, we shipped your cannons by train from—let me see—I believe it was Wheeling, West Virginia, to the port of debarkation."

"Yes, it was indeed Wheeling, but please, Dr. Booker"—Truman sighed—"as an old artillery officer it pains me to hear those beautiful pieces referred to as 'cannons.'"

Loomis laughed. "Now that I recall, Major Eisenhower *did* once remind me that canons were church laws." Beaming with pleasure at his wife, Loomis put his hand on her shoulder. "You haven't met my wife, Della, Mr. President."

"I'm delighted to make your acquaintance, Mrs. Booker." Turning to Connie, he said, "And it's good to see you again, Mrs. Canfield." He then smiled at Faith. "*Both* Mrs. Canfields. Well, now that we've all reacquainted ourselves, I would like to introduce all of you to Prime Minister Churchill."

John suppressed a smile. It was Truman's habit, he knew, to continue to refer to Churchill as the prime minister, even though Churchill no longer held the job. That was a peculiarity of Truman's, for whenever he spoke with Herbert Hoover, which was quite often, he always referred to him as "Mr. President."

"Mr. Prime Minister," John said, taking his cue from the President, "that was quite an impressive speech you just gave.

"Thank you," Churchill replied. "I suspect that once it gets out, it's going to rattle a few china closets here and there."

"An iron curtain. . ." John said. "You've always had a reputation for coining a phrase, but that one is quite dramatic."

"Do you think so? I couldn't think of a better metaphor, though the term 'iron curtain' does seem to beg the issue a bit. No matter. I'm sure the term will soon be forgotten. It is the *content* of the speech that is important. I hope it is remembered. Umm. . . remembered and taken to heart."

As the Canfields drove back to St. Louis that night, they discussed the speech and the impact it might have on the rest of the world.

"If you ask me, it was damn foolish," Bob insisted. "Sure we have some differences of opinion with Russia, but we were able to put those differences aside and work together during the war. Why can't we do it during peace?"

"Because during the war we had a common interest," John replied. "That is no longer the case."

Bob shook his head angrily. "I'd like to see the world at peace for a while. I don't want another situation like the one we had after 1918, where there was just a realignment of partners before we were ready to go to war again."

"I'm afraid we're already in that position, and Churchill didn't cause it—he just recognized it and spoke it aloud," John said. "Russia is without doubt going to test us. Why, do you realize they have more troops in Eastern Europe now than they did at the end of the war? While we've been bringing our men back home as quickly as we can, they've been building up their forces."

"Good heavens, what if they decide to start something?" Faith asked. "If they have as many soldiers there as you say, there's no way we could stop them."

"Oh, yes, we could stop them all right," John said.

"How?"

John drummed on the steering wheel of the car for a moment, then let out a long sigh. "It's terrible to contemplate," he said, "but we do have one thing that will guarantee peace on our terms. . . at least for a little while longer."

"You're talking about the atom bomb, aren't you?" Bob asked.

"Yes, Pop, I am."

"You know how your brother feels about that thing."

"Yes, I do. And I don't blame him."

"My God, I'd hate to see that thing used again," Bob said softly.

"So would I. But, thank God, right now the U.S. is the only one who has it. And who knows, Pop? Maybe your faith in the concept of the United Nations will be justified. Maybe men will be able to get together and settle their differences without going to war. God knows we had better, because the next conflict might well be the end of us all."

JUNE 1946, LOS ANGELES, CALIFORNIA

"Ladies and gentlemen," the voice over the airplane's public address system announced, *"we are on final approach to Los Angeles. The captain has turned on the no-smoking lamp. Please extinguish all cigarettes, return your seat backs to the upright position, and fasten your seat belts. The temperature on the ground in Los Angeles is a very pleasant eighty-two degrees. We hope you enjoyed your trip, and we thank you for flying World Air Transport."*

The DC-4 banked to the left. Eric Twainbough, sitting next to the window on the left-hand side of the airplane, looked down over the top of the wing and across the two engine nacelles. For just a moment he had the odd sensation that he was hanging motionless while Los Angeles revolved slowly beneath him, as if the entire city were mounted on a lazy Susan.

82

The plane came out of its bank, then started its long, flat glide toward the airport. Eric heard a whirring sound and saw the flaps being lowered to their fullest extension. There was a rumble, then a loud thump.

"Oh!" the woman in the seat next to him exclaimed in alarm. Eric glanced over at her and saw that her head was hunched between her shoulders, and she was sitting very stiffly. She was clutching a rosary, and her lips were moving desperately.

"It's all right, ma'am," Eric said soothingly. "That was just the wheels going down."

"The wheels?" the woman replied in alarm. "Do you mean to tell me there were no wheels on this airplane while we were flying?"

"The airplane had wheels, but they were drawn up inside."

"Oh, my, I'm glad I didn't know that. That would have scared me to death! I mean, what if we had needed them very quickly? They certainly wouldn't have done us any good if they were drawn up inside, now, would they?"

Eric was about to explain it to her, then decided against it. Instead, he just smiled and answered, "No, ma'am, I don't suppose they would have."

"This is the first time I have ever flown," the woman said, somewhat unnecessarily.

"Is it? I never would have known. You handled it beautifully."

"Thank you," she said, smiling broadly. "I did, didn't I? You know, for this entire flight I've been wanting to tell you something."

"What's that?" Eric asked.

The woman pointed to Eric's beard. "With that gray beard and your size and everything. . . you look enough like Eric Twainbough to be his brother. Have you ever heard of him? He's a very famous novelist, you know."

Eric smiled. "I've heard of him, yes." He stroked his beard. "But I've always thought I looked more like Ernest Hemingway."

"Oh, heavens, no. You're much more handsome than Hemingway," the woman insisted.

"Thanks," Eric said, chuckling, savoring the idea of recounting the woman's comment to his old crony, Hem. It was also reassuring to hear that at fifty-six he was still considered handsome—by at least one woman, anyway.

The airplane touched down at the end of the runway, sending out little puffs of smoke from the tires with the instant acceleration of the wheels from zero to one hundred miles per hour.

"Oh, we're on the ground!" the woman said, visibly relieved.

"Yes, ma'am, I believe we are."

The airliner gradually decreased speed until it reached a place where it could turn off the runway and start toward the airport terminal. Through the window Eric could see a long, low, stucco-sided building with a red tile roof, separated from the tarmac by a chain-link fence. The terminal area was bustling with a dozen or more DC-3's, DC-4's, and a couple of the new triple-tailed Constellations parked alongside the fence. Eric's flight, World Air Transport Flight 91 from St. Louis, taxied into its assigned spot; then the pilot killed the engines.

The novelist exited the plane and climbed down the steps, and as he walked through the gate in the fence, he heard his name called.

"Eric, over here!"

Recognizing Guy Colby, Eric grinned and walked toward him with his hand extended.

"Hello, Guy, you old horse thief."

"Come on," Guy said, pumping Eric's hand, "we'll get your baggage, and then I'll take you out to the house. I've got a new place right on the beach. I think you'll like it."

"I'm sure I will," Eric said. "And I really appreciate your offer to put me up."

"I'm anxious to get your draft of the screenplay," Guy said. "And if it means I have to put you up and stand over you with a martini, then I'll do it."

Eric snickered. "I thought you were going to say stand over me with a whip."

"I've always believed you could get more with a carrot than a stick," Guy replied, laughing.

Guy Colby was one of Hollywood's best directors and had been for many years. He had directed all three of the pictures that had been made from Eric's books, and the screenplay he was talking about was for a new picture he planned to make from Eric's latest book, *Out of the Night.*

For the next few minutes conversation centered on retrieving Eric's baggage and then getting it loaded it into Guy's yellow Buick convertible. That done, the two men piled themselves into the car. As the director pulled away from the curb and out into traffic, he asked, "By the way, have you seen the latest best-seller list? *Out of the Night* is number one."

"Yes, I talked to Sam Hamilton just before I left St. Louis."

"Sam Hamilton?"

"He's the publisher—formerly my editor—at Pendarrow House."

"Oh, yeah, I remember."

"I have to admit I've been a little surprised at the acceptance of this book," Eric said.

"Why should you be surprised? People have been waiting a long time for another book from you."

"I wasn't sure how a story about a young white girl being raised by a Negro couple would go over."

"Listen, it's about time America took a good, long look at itself," Guy said. "We need to examine our attitudes about a lot of things. A country that can build the atomic bomb and fight a war across two oceans can do anything it

84

sets its mind to. We could eliminate poverty, see to it that all our citizens get a good education and have quality medical care. . . and we could eliminate racial hatred and prejudice."

Eric smiled ruefully. "You're asking a lot."

"I'm not asking for more than could be done," Guy insisted.

"Okay, you've convinced me," Eric said. "Now all you have to do is convince a hundred and forty million more people."

"It'll require some education of the masses, yes, but it must be done."

"Education of the masses? Quality medical care?" Eric laughed. "Come on, that's enough politics. Let's talk about something else."

"Fine with me," Guy replied. "How about sports? What did you think of the Louis-Conn fight?"

"A mismatch. Conn put up a real good fight in '41, but he had no business getting in the ring with Louis this time. He's right to call it quits."

"Maybe so, but he got paid pretty well for his twenty-two minutes of work. That's the fastest and easiest payday I ever saw."

"You think so, do you?" Eric asked. "Well, I did a little boxing in my younger days, and I can tell you, it's neither fast nor easy."

"Come to think of it, I guess it isn't very pleasant to get your head beaten in," Guy agreed, wincing at the thought.

They chatted on about sports and movies, and finally Guy turned off the coast highway, announcing, "Well, here it is—home sweet home." He drove up a long drive to a rather large, rambling house built with wings and porches and decks, all designed to take advantage of its beach location. "What do you say? I'll admit it doesn't have the same class as your place on Bimini, but it's pretty nice, don't you think?"

"It's *very* nice," Eric agreed.

"It better be, for what it cost me. Anyway, Demaris kept the Beverly Hills house. Of course, it was hers even before we were married, so she had the right to it when we were divorced."

"I was really sorry to hear about the divorce," Eric said. "I was hoping you two would make it."

Guy laughed. "Come on, Eric, don't be so naive. How could two people who live and work in Hollywood ever make a marriage last? It simply can't be done. I'm not sure, but I think it's even against city ordinances or something."

Eric laughed with him. "Nevertheless, I did have hopes for the two of you. I know how you used to feel about her."

"Oh, I still love her," Guy admitted. "I probably always will. And in her way I think she loves me. We just can't live together, that's all." He suddenly smiled. "At least I got a daughter out of the situation. Wait until you see her, Eric. Karen is absolutely beautiful."

"How old is she now?"

"She's three going on twenty-one. The most precocious child you ever saw." He stopped the car under one of the overhanging porches. "You know, I don't regret for one minute marrying Demaris to give that child a name. Because that made her mine. I don't give a damn who the biological father is or that some people snicker over a sixty-three-year-old man having a three-year-old daughter. Karen is mine and will be forever. It's a good feeling knowing that there's at least one person in the world who'll always belong to you." He suddenly laughed one of those edgy laughs that announce, "I'm embarrassed by having been so candid" and slapped the steering wheel. "But enough of all that. Come on inside and I'll show you where you'll be working. You've got a wonderful view of the ocean, a brand-new typewriter, a fresh ream of paper, and a refrigerator stocked with deli meats and cheeses and cold beer. It's Tannenhower," he added. "And out here that took some doing."

"You sound like you don't want me to ever leave the house," Eric said, narrowing his eyes suspiciously.

"Leave the house? Why would you want to? There's absolutely no need for that, my good man," Guy said. "This is Hollywood. You've got the world at your fingertips."

BEVERLY HILLS

Demaris Hunter had put a red light bulb in the lamp, and now, standing nude in its crimson glare, she looked as if she were an artistic creation from a master sculptor who had chosen pink marble as his medium.

She didn't look like an over-the-hill star—which was what the article in *Variety* called her:

> At this point it isn't known whom Guy Colby will select to play the role of Aletha Pitts in the movie version of Out *of the Night*. He has used his ex-wife Demaris Hunter in three previous movies based on Twainbough novels, but the over-the-hill star seems a bit too old for this role, even with the artistry of makeup and the wizardry of Hollywood special effects like soft-focus lenses.

An over-the-hill star? Demaris wished that whoever wrote that story could be here right now to check out Brick Taylor's condition. At twenty-three, Brick was twenty-one years younger than Demaris, but an ingenue of eighteen wouldn't have inspired an erection any harder than the one he now displayed. It was more than obvious that *he* didn't think of her as an over-the-hill star.

86

"Well," Demaris said in a low, throaty voice, "are we just going to stand here and model for each other? Or are we going to fuck?"

Brick didn't answer her with words, but, smiling, he reached for her and took her hand in his, then led her over to the bed. It was her bed in her bedroom in her house. But, of course, it would have to be. Brick didn't have a house; Demaris wasn't sure he even had a bed.

Demaris lay back with splayed legs, looking up at Brick. He was naturally large anyway, but from this angle his penis so commanded attention that it seemed obscenely huge, out of proportion with the rest of his body. He knelt on the bed between her legs and posed for her, displaying like a peacock and drawing his own degree of sexual excitement from her appreciation of his efforts.

Oh, my beautiful young lover, do you think you have the only penis in the world? Demaris thought. *It isn't the only penis I've ever seen—or even the largest. I have had. . . how many men have I had in this bed alone?*

Many, she answered herself. *Many, many, many. But right now you are the largest and the only one that I know.*

Brick had been with Demaris before, and he had learned well the lessons she'd taught him. He didn't rush. He knew what she desired and needed, and more than that he knew how to give without having to be led. He lay down on the bed with her, pressing his body against hers, caressing her breasts, kissing her all over. His tongue was both gentle and rough, tentative and demanding, enticing and frightening, and she sought it eagerly, lost in the sensations that were now overcoming her.

"Yes," Demaris whimpered. "Yes, you do know what to do for me, don't you?"

Brick continued to explore Demaris's body with patience and intensity, moving his fingers from her nipples down across her flat stomach to the center of all her pleasure. His hand rested there for just a moment, then she felt his fingers inside her, sending wonderful pulsing sensations through her body, like gentle electric shocks. Her blood turned to liquid fire, and her loins yearned for more.

"Now," Demaris groaned, pulling at him with her long, perfectly manicured fingernails. "Now, damn you! Don't you dare make me wait one second longer!"

Brick moved over her, and she opened to him, wanting nothing more than the feeling of him inside her. She gasped at the intense pleasure of their joining.

Brick began the slow, deep thrusts, his strong, young, muscular body moving steadily, unceasing, as if he could keep going for hours without tiring. Demaris quit trying to exercise control over him then—hell, she no longer even had control of herself—and abandoned herself to the moment.

87

Then she felt the beginnings of her orgasm. It started as a tiny, almost sub-liminal sensation deep inside, moving out slowly, broadcasting waves like radio signals as a presage of what was to come. The sensations moved with greater and greater urgency, drawing up tighter and tighter until a million small electric shocks rippled through her body.

Still vibrating with the force of it, Demaris was carried to a second peak even more intense than the first, and she threw herself into it, raking at his back with her nails, calling out her pleasure until finally it was over, and she floated like a feather down from that lofty peak, encountering several smaller but still pleasurable after-shocks along the way, rising a bit before slipping back down again. Finally, after there was nothing left but the warm, banked coals of the blazing fire, she held him, spent, in her arms and smiled.

An over-the-hill star, my ass, she thought.

SEPTEMBER 1946, A DISPLACED PERSONS CAMP IN AUSTRIA

The flickering candle projected outsized shadows of the two women and the girl on the bed onto the wall of the tiny room. Anna Gelbman, a woman of sixty, dipped her cloth into the basin of water, wrung it out, then draped it across the forehead of the feverish teenage girl. The girl's older sister leaned over the foot of the bed, looking on anxiously.

"She can't die," Esther Stein said softly. "Lily and I are all that is left of our family. I don't know what's wrong with her. She was fine this morning, then she began to feel poorly this afternoon, and tonight she has this terrible fever."

"I believe it's the flu," Anna said. "I think she will be all right, but in this place"—she shrugged eloquently—"even a cold can be dangerous, so we must be careful. Did you go to the camp authorities? Perhaps they have some medicine that can reduce her fever."

"I am frightened of the authorities," Esther admitted.

Anna looked up at her and smiled gently. *If Miriam is still alive*, Anna thought, *she would be about the age of this woman—in her midtwenties.* She suddenly shook her head and chided herself. *Foolish old woman. You are losing touch with reality. Miriam is some ten years older than Esther. If she is still alive.*

Anna had last seen her daughter at the railroad station in Vienna five years before, on the day the Nazis had rounded up all the remaining Viennese Jews and transported them to concentration camps. That was when Anna's cousin, Simon Blumberg, had announced that he wasn't going to go with the Nazis, he was going to escape —and he had offered to take Miriam with him. Anna had been frightened of the idea, but her husband, David, had encouraged Miriam to go.

Anna had agonized over it at the time, but her own experience in the concentration camps in the years that followed had convinced her that David had been correct in urging their daughter to flee.

Had Miriam made it? Anna didn't know, but she had never stopped trying to find out. Since the war ended, she had interviewed hundreds of prisoners from dozens of concentration camps, but none of them had known anything about Miriam or Simon.

Anna knew that they could very well have been among the multitudes of faceless, nameless Jews who were rounded up and killed so quickly that no one ever heard from them again or bothered to record their deaths. Or they could have been killed in their initial escape attempt. Anna was prepared for either eventuality, but until she had definite proof one way or the other, she would continue to hope that Miriam was still alive. She couldn't abandon that hope. It was what had gotten her this far. Particularly after David's death.

"I know you probably think I'm foolish to be frightened," Esther said, bringing Anna out of her reverie. "But I can't help it."

"Esther, these officials are not Nazis," Anna explained. "They are Americans. Do you really think they would harm your sister or refuse to help? I know Americans; they are good people. My David was an American."

"Americans, English, Austrian, German. . . it makes no difference. I am frightened of all gentiles," Esther confessed. "They all seem to hate us so."

Anna got up from the side of the bed and walked over to put her arm around the young woman. She pulled her close and patted her on the back as if she were her own Miriam.

"They hate us because they fear us," Anna explained.

Esther looked into Anna's face with an expression of surprise.

"They *fear* us?" she repeated. "Why would they fear us? How can they fear us? We are the ones who were put in concentration camps. . . we are the ones who were gassed and burned. . . we are the ones who now have no place to go, no place to live. But you know this. Were you not in a concentration camp? Did you not return to Vienna and find someone else living in your beautiful home? Is there not another name on the store that was once yours?"

"Yes," Anna said. "All that you say is true."

"Then how can you say that they fear us?"

"They fear us because we have kept our identity as a people. No matter where we are Austria, Russia, France, even in America—we are Jews. We kept our customs, our culture, our religion, and we did not assimilate. And though the Nazis tried for ten years to eliminate us, we would not be eliminated. Others fear our tenacity, because in our tenacity they see our strength."

"Strength? What strength?" Esther scoffed. "Perhaps we were not totally eliminated, but we were led like lambs to the slaughter. The Nazis killed millions of our people."

"Yes, that is true," Anna said. "I have been told that two thirds of all Jews in Europe were killed. But one third survived, and already those of us who survived are saying, 'Never again.' That is why all the Jews who are left in Europe must go to Palestine. We *must* have our own homeland."

"And how will we do that?" Esther asked. "There are millions of us. . . yet the British will allow only fifteen hundred per month to get in."

"We will put our faith in the Haganah," Anna reminded her. "The Haganah will help anyone who wants to come."

"The Haganah is an outlaw group," Esther replied. "If they continue with their illegal activities, they will so enflame the authorities that the concentration camps will be opened again."

Anna sat on the bed again and rewet the cloth, then put it back on Lily's forehead. She looked around the little room. "Esther, what do you call these displaced persons camps in which so many of our people are gathered? Are they not concentration camps?"

"No!" Esther replied resolutely. "There are no gas chambers here! There are no ovens here! We are not being beaten and starved!"

"Perhaps not. But there is such a thing as enslavement of the mind and soul," Anna said softly. "And that can be as brutal as enslavement of the body. I will not stay here. I am going to Palestine, with or without the approval of the British who control it. I think you and your sister should come with me."

"I don't know," Esther demurred. "I'm not brave like you. You are the one who escaped from the Nazis. Lily and I were still cowering in the concentration camps when the Allies came."

"And do you still want to be in this place one year from now? Two years? Three? Lily is sixteen. She has known nothing but concentration camps and D.P. camps since she was ten. Do you want her to reach adulthood in such a place?"

"No," Esther admitted.

"Then when I leave, you and Lily must come with me," Anna insisted.

"I'm frightened."

"What is there to fear, Esther?" Lily piped up in a small voice.

"Lily, dear, I thought you were sleeping," Esther replied. "How are you feeling? Are you all right?"

"I'll be fine," Lily answered. "Why are you frightened?" she repeated. "If we leave and are caught, the only thing that will happen is we'll be returned to this place. It isn't like it was when a fleeing Jew would be killed. And if we are returned to this place, we'd be no worse off than we are now."

"Your sister is right, you know," Anna said. "We have nothing to lose by trying."

"Frau Gelbman, tell us again about your escape from Auschwitz," Lily pleaded.

"Oh, I don't know," Anna replied. "Perhaps you should try to rest now."

"Please, tell us the story. It is such a wonderful story, and I know it will make me feel better."

Anna wet two more cloths and put one on the inside of each of Lily's wrists. Then she lay her hand on Lily's cheek to check her temperature. She wasn't sure whether or not the young girl's fever was coming down, but at least it didn't seem to be getting any worse. That was a good sign.

"I'll just keep my eyes closed," Lily said quietly. "But I'll be listening."

"All right," Anna agreed. "I'll tell you the story again." She paused, casting her mind back, then began her tale. "After we were taken to Auschwitz, for two years I didn't know whether my husband, David, was dead or alive. Then one day I saw him, and I learned that for an entire week the women from my barracks and the men from his barracks would be working at the railroad station at the same time, loading bundles of clothes taken from prisoners to be sent back to Germany. David and I could not speak to each other, for if the guards saw us speaking or even exchanging glances they would beat us unmercifully—probably kill us." Inexplicably, Anna's eyes were shining with joy. "But we didn't care," she continued. "We could see each other and we could feel our love and I was deliriously happy."

"It must have been wonderful to see him again," Esther said.

"Yes, it was. But David had clearly decided that that wasn't enough, because he devised an escape plan. It would be dangerous enough, but the most difficult part of the plan would be explaining it to me because he could only do it a few words at a time, and I had to be able to understand and react without question.

"The key part of his plan was to get me onto one of the outgoing cars. Once I was on board, he would load the clothing bundles in such a way as to make my presence undetectable.

"He managed to clue me to get into the clothing bin without being seen and hide under the bundles that had already been prepared for shipment. I waited and watched for my chance, and when one of the SS guards came over to the section where I was working and selected three women to go with him, I put down my bundle of clothes and started off with the others. The guard assigned to us hadn't noticed that I wasn't one of the women selected, and neither did he notice that four women, and not three, had left.

"I followed behind the guard and the other women until they reached the clothes bin; then, with a quick look around to make certain I wasn't being seen, I slipped into the bin and burrowed under the bundles.

91

"I waited huddled under the clothes for over an hour, terrified that at any moment I would be discovered or that something would happen to David. Then, after praying steadily for the entire time, I heard David's voice.

"'Anna, if you are in here, get into my wheelbarrow now!' he whispered to me.

"I climbed into the wheelbarrow, and David covered me with more bundles. He started pushing the wheelbarrow toward the railroad car, whispering to me that he had to time things exactly right. He had to be the last wheelbarrow to arrive at the car, for the door would be closed by whoever was last.

"I could tell that David was watching the other wheelbarrows because he sped up or slowed down as was necessary. I continued to pray that we would arrive at the car at the proper moment.

"Then I heard the SS man in charge of loading shout, 'Go to the next car!' At first I thought he had shouted this to David, and I resigned myself to getting caught; then David whispered that the guard was calling the person just behind us. We had made it! We were going to be the last wheelbarrow at this particular car!

"We reached the door, and David whispered that he would put me on the car, and that when the train left the camp, I should wait for a while, then jump off.

"'And you?' I whispered back to him.

"'I will find a way,' he told me. I almost cried aloud then, because it was not until that moment that I realized David had planned *my* escape, but he had no plan for himself.

"He picked up a bundle and me at the same time. The bundle was heavy and David was terribly malnourished, as of course we all were, so I know it must have been very difficult for him to make the lift and do it as easily and quickly as if he were lifting only the bundle of clothes and nothing more. But my David always was a man of great determination—and he did it!

"He set me down inside the car, then turned away to grab the next bundle. Within a moment he had his wheelbarrow empty, me hidden, and the door ready to be closed. He called softly that he was going to shut the door but not set the latch so that I would be able to open it from inside.

"'I love you,' I told him. My voice was choked with fear—not for myself, but for him.

"'Good-bye, my love,' David said. I heard him take a step away from the car, and I know now that he was telling me his final good-bye.

"He closed the door and turned the handle, making certain that the locking pins weren't really engaged. It was a long time before the train began to move. I had managed to position myself so that I could look through a small crack in the side wall of the car, and I was trying to see whether or not David had gotten on the train. To my horror I saw one of the camp guards looking very closely at each boxcar as the train rolled past. I knew that when my car drew even with him, he would see that the pins weren't set!"

Anna paused and looked at the sisters. They were watching her with rapt expressions.

"What happened?" Lily asked in a hushed voice, as if she had never heard the story before.

Anna smiled sadly. "Suddenly I saw David running directly toward the guard. I knew he was going to try to divert the guard's attention, but I knew also what that would mean for him. I held my breath and bit my lip until I drew blood to keep from calling out to him.

"I had no idea where David found the strength to run so far and so fast. I do know that when he was a student in college in America, he had run for the college running club. He had always been proud of that fact. On that day David ran like he was a young college boy, not an old man of sixty. He was faster than the wind, and he overtook the train. Then he. . ."

Anna stopped and closed her eyes. Tears began streaming down her face. After a few moments she regained her composure and continued.

"He threw himself at the guard, and he knocked him down. The guard, you must remember, was a big, strong, well-fed man who was thirty years younger than David. But my David knocked him down as if he were nothing more than a bowling pin. The guard regained his feet and got his gun out and shot at David, but he missed. Then David grabbed him, and they began struggling. The last thing I saw was the two of them rolling under the train and—"

Anna stopped again, only her expression wasn't one of sorrow, it was one of wonder. "Esther, Lily, I could see David's face," she said, in a voice little more than a whisper. "He was smiling from ear to ear! He was giving up his life to save me, and his face was filled with joy!"

"What happened then?" Esther asked, tears in her own eyes.

"After the train left the camp, I changed out of the prison clothes into a dress that I pulled from one of the bundles. I even managed to roll up a couple of extra dresses, and during the night when the train stopped to allow another train to pass, I slid the door open and slipped out into the darkness.

"I walked all night. I had no idea where I was or where I was going. I just wanted to get away from the railroad track and from where I had been. Finally, at sunrise, I saw a barn. I hid in the barn and fell asleep in a hayrack. That's where I was when Frau Papf found me."

"You must have been terrified," Esther said.

"Yes. I was. But thank God I had nothing to fear, because even though Frau Papf realized that I was an escaped Jew, she took me in. She passed me off to her neighbors as a cousin of her husband, telling them that my house had been bombed in an Allied air raid. I spent the rest of the war there, and when Frau Papfs husband failed to come back from the Russian front, I grieved with her, even though I had never met him."

"Where is Frau Papf now?"

"She is still on her farm in Germany, near Wildflecken," Anna replied. "She asked me to stay with her, and I nearly agreed to do so."

"Why didn't you? Surely the farm was better than this place."

"Yes, it was. But there are two things that made me leave. One is my anxiousness to find out what happened to my daughter and my cousin. And the other is my determination to reach Palestine."

"Is it beautiful, this Palestine?" Lily asked. "Is it a land of milk and honey?"

Anna laughed. "Yes, Lily, dear. For us, Palestine is a land of milk and honey."

"When will we go?"

"When the time is right," Anna said firmly, patting the girl's hand. "We will go when the time is right."

6

OCTOBER 1946, THE PALACE OF JUSTICE, NUREMBERG

As Karl Tannenhower and his fellow defendants filed into the courtroom, they took their seats in the docket for the final time. For the first time since the trials had begun the movie cameras were gone and the overbright lights extinguished. Their absence made the room much dimmer, almost foreboding, and Karl thought that the mood was especially appropriate since this was the day the verdicts were to be announced.

After the prisoners were seated in the docket, the judges entered, and defendants, lawyers, prosecutors, spectators, and press representatives stood. As had been his custom throughout, the presiding judge, Lord Lawrence, bowed to all sides, encompassing the defendants as well. After that he took his seat, the signal that everyone else could, too.

Then, in turn, each of the four judges read his individual report. The first part of each judicial report condemned the German leadership collectively for the war and for the evil the war had brought about. However, as they got further into their reports, the judges got away from collective accusations and assessed the specific guilt for specific crimes committed by individual defendants.

Karl had been Hitler's Oberreichsleiter, a job that, as Karl's lawyer had pointed out, had a lot more pomp and title than substance. His principal duty had been to tour the cities that had been bombed, providing moral support and assurance to the victims that their suffering was appreciated by the Reich. Because of that he was often in the public eye, and his picture frequently appeared in newsreels, newspapers, and magazines. The prosecutors made much of those photographs, using them to prove that Karl had filled an important post in Hitler's government.

Another specific charge against Karl was the fact that he held the rank of Obergrupenführer in the SS, equal, as the prosecutor had pointed out, to a general's rank in the Wehrmacht. However, Karl's rank was an administrative one only. He had been appointed to that position by Hitler so that he could draw the salary of a general in addition to his salary as Oberreichsleiter. It had been Hitler's way of seeing that Karl received more pay, since his salary as Oberreichsleiter was actually no more than that of a gauleiter. Ironically, Karl was found guilty of defrauding the German people by holding a paid position, Obergrupenführer of the SS, for which he performed no duties. And yet, had he actually performed any of the duties of an SS general, he would have undoubtedly been guilty of far worse crimes.

The most damning brick in the prosecution's case against Karl, however, was that he had participated in Hitler's abortive putsch in November of 1923. He had carried the flag during the march against the Army headquarters, and when the Army had opened fire and several of the marching Nazis were wounded, Karl had tended to them by using the flag he had carried to stem the flow of their blood. As a result, that flag became known as the "Blood Flag," without doubt the most sacred icon in all of Nazi ideology. As the flag bearer, Karl had become so associated with that symbol that his very existence had helped to perpetuate the Nazi party.

It was also pointed out that even on the last day of Hitler's life, Karl had visited him in his bunker. Albert Speer had established Karl's relationship with Hitler when, in his own testimony, he stated that "Hitler regarded very few men as personal friends, but I would certainly have to be one, and Karl Tannenhower would have to be another." Karl's own testimony confirmed Speer's statement.

Karl was a relative of the Tannenhower brewers in the United States, and as a young man he had attended Jefferson University in St. Louis. He had even played varsity football while he was enrolled, and in a sidebar story during the trial, an American reporter had discovered that Karl had been named to Jefferson's "All Decade" team for the period 1911 to 1920. In fact, Karl's name was inscribed along with ten others on a brass plaque still mounted on the wall in the locker room of the Jefferson University stadium.

Early in the trial the prosecutor had tried to use Karl's American experiences as an example of his ingratitude to the country that had temporarily taken him in. Realizing there was nothing to be gained from that tactic, however, he had dropped it and gone on to other things, it generally being accepted that Karl's "American connection" was, in fact, embarrassing to the Americans.

The one thing Karl seemed to have going in his favor was that no evidence existed to connect him to, and neither was he ever specifically charged with, any of the atrocities of the regime. Not only was Karl's name remarkably clean as regards any paperwork about the concentration camps, but not once during the entire trial was it ever suggested that he had even visited a camp.

Karl's friend Paul Maas's record was not so clean, however, and the trial hadn't gone well for him.

When certain specific accusations were first leveled against Paul, Karl hadn't believed them. Throughout the war Paul had held the position of Expediency Leader. His job was to make certain that critical materiel and critical labor—slave labor if necessary—be in the right place at the right time. Paul's efforts had contributed immeasurably to the German war machine, and his indirect involvement with slave labor was the reason his case was considered with those of other top-level Nazis rather than being relegated to one of the subsidary trials.

Karl knew that Paul's job in and of itself would probably not condemn him to the gallows. But when witness after witness testified, and as letters and orders bearing Paul's name began to surface, Karl learned that Paul had been involved in evil activities that went far beyond the scope of his job. But even then Karl had a difficult time accepting the evidence as the truth. How could a man he had known and trusted for so many years be capable of such despicable acts?

It was some weeks after Karl had learned of Paul's particular crimes before he could bring himself to talk to the man who had once been his closest friend. And then it was because Paul approached Karl and begged him to speak to him.

"I didn't kill anyone," Paul pleaded. "I didn't put anyone in the gas chambers, and I didn't light the ovens."

"Perhaps not. But you were quick to use the threat of the gas chambers to have your way with young female prisoners. You treated the concentration camps as if they were your personal whorehouses. You had young girls—very young girls—sent to you for your own perverted purposes. And always the girls were paralyzed with the fear that if they didn't please you, they would be sent immediately to the gas chambers."

"It wasn't like that," Paul insisted. "I thought I was doing them a favor. I thought I was keeping them from being killed."

"Don't give me that crap, Paul. After you used them and sent them back, they were killed just like the others. And you knew it."

"Even so, there was nothing I could have done to stop them from being killed," Paul argued. "I had no authority to prevent it."

"But you could have at least let them die in dignity. You didn't have to subject them to that one final degradation."

"Karl, please, do you think I haven't put myself through hell for the things I did? I am not strong like you. I never was. When the temptation was first put before me, I tried to resist. Honestly. But those Jewish girls. . . you know how they are. All those young girls, even the ones who were only ten, eleven, or twelve years old, thought that their bodies would be their salvation. They threw themselves at me. . . they were—"

"*Stop it!*" Karl demanded. "Stop it, damn you! Are you now going to blame your crimes on your victims?"

"But you don't understand. It's a sickness, this unholy desire to. . ."

Paul's words trailed off, and he stared at Karl in anguish, then broke down into sobs. The other prisoners in the exercise yard turned away in disgust, and though Karl wanted to turn away as well, he couldn't.

"Please, Karl. The whole world is against the few of us now. If you turn against me, too, if I don't have at least one friend, I will go insane. Please forgive me! I beg of you. You *must* forgive me."

"I will never be able to understand what made you do such a thing, Paul," Karl said. "And only God will be able to forgive you, for I cannot do that either." He sighed in resignation. "But then, God is going to be sorely tried to forgive any of us. I will be here, Paul, and I will be your friend for whatever time we have left."

A week had passed since that conversation. Today they would hear the verdicts. Tomorrow they would be sentenced. Their lawyers had already told them that after the sentencing, those who were receiving prison terms would be taken immediately to Spandau Prison to begin serving their time. Those who received the death penalty would stay there at Long Water Kasserne, isolated from the others, until their sentences were carried out.

The Soviet member of the Tribunal, Major General of Jurisprudence Nikitchenko, finished his report; then, laying his paper down, he glared at every man in the docket. Karl knew that Nikitchenko had dissented from the other judges on the charges against him because Nikitchenko wanted Karl's specific indictment to include crimes against humanity.

General Nikitchenko's judicial report was the last one given. All that remained was the rendering of the decrees.

"And now the verdicts," Sir Lawrence announced. The defendants who had not been wearing their headsets put them on to pay close attention. Karl didn't do so because the verdicts would be read in English.

"Hjalmar Schacht, not guilty."

Schacht, Karl knew, was the man who was most responsible for turning around Germany's economy. But he later broke with Hitler and finished the war in a concentration camp himself. His acquittal came as no surprise.

"Hans Fritzsche, not guilty."

Fritzsche was Goebbels's assistant. He had claimed that he was no more than an errand boy, and the court believed him. Karl had to admit that Fritzsche's acquittal surprised him a little.

"Franz von Papen, not guilty."

Von Papen was a career diplomat who was most responsible for Hitler's legitimacy, for he had persuaded von Hindenburg to appoint Hitler chancellor. His acquittal also surprised Karl.

That was the end of the surprises. All the other defendants, including Karl and Paul Maas, were found guilty.

After the final verdict was read, the defendants were dismissed and court was adjourned.

The next day the defendants saw each other for what they knew would be the last time as they gathered, not in the defendants' docket, but in the cellar of the Palace of Justice, to await pronouncement of their sentences. They had been told that they would enter the courtroom one at a time so that their sentences could be pronounced individually. From there they would be taken to their respective destinations, without rejoining the others.

"It seems strange to me," Paul complained to Karl, "that we were indicted together, we were tried together, and we were pronounced guilty together. But today we're to be sentenced separately."

"Perhaps the Tribunal has decided to grant us the dignity of privacy as one last concession," Karl suggested.

"Concession? You call this a concession? It is persecution," Paul protested. "I would rather face my fate with all of you." He turned away from Karl. "I'm afraid to go in there alone," he admitted quietly.

"You have more strength than you think," Karl remarked.

"That's easy for you to say. You aren't facing the death sentence. I am."

"Herr Göring," one of the guards abruptly called, interrupting the dozen or so quiet conversations, "it is time."

Göring looked at the other defendants. He had been the dominant personality of the entire trial, even gaining a measure of respect from the Allied reporters covering the proceedings. This was partly because, unlike so many of the other defendants, Göring hadn't attempted to place the entire blame on Hitler.

In the end, though, he, like everyone else, was subject to the will of the Tribunal. And despite Göring's prediction that fifty years hence he would be regarded a German hero, Karl knew—and he knew that Göring now knew as well—that such a thing would never happen.

Göring stepped into the small elevator with the American MPs who were escorting him and turned around to face front. Seeing Karl in the hallway, he smiled, and unexpectedly Karl felt a small twinge of melancholy. Of all the men in Hitler's immediate retinue, Karl had felt closest to Göring. He had always believed that while Göring had made no overt effort to stop the persecution of the Jews, it would never have been initiated had he been the driving force behind National Socialism instead of Hitler.

"Don't feel so bad, Karl," Göring said, as if reading Karl's mind. "I have no intention of dying on their schedule."

The door closed on a smiling Göring, and the elevator went up.

"What do you think he meant by that?" Paul asked.

"I have no idea," Karl answered. "Maybe he was just putting up a brave front."

"Or maybe he knows something," Paul said hopefully. "Maybe he's heard that none of us are to be executed. I mean, what would be the point? They've had their show trial, haven't they? They've held us up to the nation and to the world as criminals. And the worst of the lot—Hitler, Himmler, Goebbels—are already dead. They wouldn't gain anything by killing us. Maybe they told Göring that. He's been their prize catch ever since the trial began; he's the one they would tell."

"Maybe," Karl agreed, though he didn't for a moment believe it. In fact, he believed just the opposite. Karl thought the possibility was very strong that all of those who had been found guilty would now receive the death penalty.

"Hess," a guard called after a brief interval had elapsed, and Rudolf Hess walked over to the elevator. Now Karl began to prepare himself; he was next.

After an agonizing wait of several more minutes, he heard the elevator coming back down. When the doors opened, one of the two white-helmeted MPs called, "Tannenhower."

Karl took a deep breath, then stepped into the elevator for the ride up to the courtroom.

Neither of the MPs said a word as the elevator rose from the basement to the courtroom. The only sound was the whir of the lift mechanism—and the pounding of his own heart. When the elevator stopped, the door opened, and Karl found that everyone in the courtroom was looking in his direction. His legs felt like lead, and his heart was in his throat, but somehow he managed to force himself to move. He walked out into the courtroom, stepped up onto the low platform, and turned to face the four judges. He took a deep breath and waited.

"Karl Tannenhower, this Tribunal sentences you to twenty-five years."

Karl let his breath out in a long, slow sigh. He had been so convinced that he would be executed that he hadn't even thought out the ramifications of twenty-five years in prison. But, he told himself as he was led away from the courtroom, he would have twenty-five years to think about it.

Paul was the last prisoner to be taken up to the courtroom, and left alone in the basement he found the waiting almost unbearable. Finally his turn came, and when he stepped up onto the platform to receive the sentence, he put on the headset with trembling hands, then faced the four judges.

"Paul Maas, you are sentenced to death by hanging," the judge said.

Paul flinched once, as if he were dodging a blow, hung his head for a second, then removed his headset and walked back toward the MPs. The death wait had now begun.

OCTOBER 16

During Paul's waiting period he learned the fate of all the others who had been tried with him. Besides himself, the others who had received the death penalty were Reichsmarshal Ernst Göring; Field Marshal Wilhelm Keitel; Ernst Kaltenbrunner, Himmler's second-in-command; Alfred Rosenberg, publisher of the Nazi newspaper; Hans Frank, governor of occupied Poland; Wilhelm Frick, Minister of the Interior; Julius Streicher, the number-one Jew hater in all of Germany; Fritz Sauckel, head of slave labor; General Alfred Jodl, chief of the General Staff; and Arthur Seyss-Inquart, governor of the Netherlands.

Rudolf Hess, Admiral Raeder, and Walther Funk had received life imprisonment. Albert Speer and Baldur von Schirach had received twenty years, Constantin von Neurath fifteen years, and Admiral Karl Doenitz ten years.

At midnight on the night his execution was to take place, a team of guards suddenly showed up in Paul's cell. He was removed from his cell and held under very strict guard while the room was thoroughly searched; then he was brought back in and ordered to strip. His clothes were inspected and his naked body was physically searched, with no cavity left unexplored.

"What. . . what are you doing?" Paul protested as a rubber-gloved finger was thrust roughly into his rectum.

"We are making one last search for poison," one of the guards explained.

"This is crazy. Don't you think if I had any poison that you would have found it by now?"

"That's what we thought yesterday," one of the guards said. "But we didn't find the poison Göring had hidden."

"What? What do you mean?"

"Göring just cheated the gallows. He committed suicide."

Paul remembered Göring's boast—that he had no intention of dying on the Allies' schedule. It would seem that he had made good on his boast. He died on his own schedule.

Paul laughed.

"You think that's funny, do you, you baby-fucking kraut bastard?" one of the guards snapped angrily.

"That's enough!" the guard's superior sharply reprimanded.

Up until that moment the guards had been courteous to a fault, so coldly courteous, in fact, that Paul couldn't stand it. Now Göring, by cheating the hangman, had created a small chink in the demeanor of at least one guard, and, ironically, rather than feeling chastised by the guard's remarks, Paul was grateful to him. The anger and frustration he could understand. It meant that there was at least some human connection between himself and the ones who were taking him to the gallows.

As Paul had been the last to learn his fate, he now was the last to have his sentence carried out. That meant that through the window in the door of his cell, he could see each prisoner in turn being taken on his last walk and hear his final words.

Von Ribbentrop was first. He walked stiffly, staring straight ahead. As he was waiting to pass through the door at the far end of the corridor, he suddenly shouted, "God protect Germany!" A moment later the door was opened, and Von Ribbentrop was taken away.

He was followed by Field Marshal Keitel. Keitel seemed a little more relaxed, as if he were going to review his troops. And in a way he was, for more than two million of his soldiers had died before him. "I follow now my sons. . . all for Germany!" he said as he waited at the portal.

After Keitel came Ernst Kaltenbrunner. As Kaltenbrunner passed Paul's cell, Paul saw that he was wearing a sweater beneath his blue, double-breasted suit jacket. Kaltenbrunner almost gave a speech: "I have loved my German people and my fatherland with a warm heart. I have done my duty by the laws of my people, and I am sorry my people were led this time by men who were not soldiers, and that crimes were committed of which I had no knowledge."

Paul wanted to shout out that Kaltenbrunner was a liar, for he knew that under Kaltenbrunner's personal orders nearly three million human beings had been gassed at Auschwitz. But though he opened his mouth to shout, he could make no sound. It was as if his throat had swollen shut.

Rosenberg was next. His complexion was pasty, and he was sunken-checked, but he walked by Paul's cell with a steady step. Rosenberg stood in front of the door for only a few seconds, shrugged, then crossed over to the other side without saying a word.

Hans Frank walked by with a smile on his lips. Paul knew that Frank had converted to Roman Catholicism while in prison, and he looked almost as if he were relieved to be able to atone for his evil deeds. "I ask God to accept me with mercy," Frank said when he reached the door at the end of the corridor.

Wilhelm Frick followed Frank. Frick stumbled once as he walked down the corridor, and the guards had to grab hold of him to keep him from falling. As he waited at the door he shouted, "Long live eternal Germany!"

Julius Streicher, whom Paul remembered as an exceptionally flashy dresser during the halcyon years of National Socialism, was the most poorly dressed of any of them tonight. He was wearing a ragged suit and a well-worn blue shirt, buttoned at the neck, with no tie. Whereas everyone else had stared straight ahead as they walked down the corridor, Streicher kept glancing around, like a beady-eyed rat. His eyes fell on Paul, and, stricken, Paul stepped back from his cell-door window.

"Heil Hitler!" Streicher screamed at the top of his voice, and the words echoed up and down the length of the corridor. Then, a moment later he shouted, "Purimfest, 1946!"

Paul knew that Purim was a Jewish holiday commemorating the execution of Haman, an ancient persecutor of the Jews. Had he not heard it, he would not have thought Streicher capable of such irony.

Fritz Sauckel was wearing a sweater but no coat. Like Streicher, his wild-looking eyes darted about. But Paul pulled away from the window, not giving Sauckel the chance to look at him.

When Sauckel reached the end of the corridor, he yelled, "I am dying innocent! The sentence is wrong! God protect Germany and make Germany great again! Long live Germany! God protect my family!"

General Jodl was next. Jodl was wearing his Army uniform with the black collar half turned up in back, as if he had put it on hurriedly. When he stopped at the door, he said in a loud, calm voice, "My greetings to you, my Germany."

Suddenly Paul's own door was opened, and two military policemen stood there, waiting for him.

"No," Paul said. "Seyss-Inquart is next."

"He is going next," one of the guards said. "But we must have you ready to follow him."

Paul shrugged in resignation, then reached for his suit jacket. Then he pulled his hand back. "I guess I won't be needing my jacket," he said dryly. "I don't suppose it will be cold where I'm going."

103

"Please put out your hands," one of the guards ordered, speaking indifferently, not reacting to Paul's weak attempt at a joke. Paul put out his hands, and the MP snapped on a pair of handcuffs.

Seyss-Inquart passed Paul's cell just as Paul was being taken out into the corridor. Seyss-Inquart looked right into Paul's eyes, and Paul saw the fear from deep in his soul. He knew that his own eyes were probably reflecting the same fear.

When Seyss-Inquart reached the end of the corridor, he and his guards stopped for a moment, and Paul and his guards stopped right behind them.

"I hope that this is the last act of the tragedy of the Second World War," Seyss-Inquart said, "and that the lesson taken from this world war will be that peace and understanding should exist between peoples. I believe in Germany."

He passed through the doorway, and Paul remained outside, flanked by his two guards. Four or five minutes went by. Paul's stomach was churning and his knees were turning to water. He stayed on his feet only by a sheer effort of will.

Finally the door opened, and someone signaled to Paul's guards to bring him inside. This was Paul's first look at the execution room.

The room was actually a gymnasium, eighty feet by thirty-three feet, with markings on the floor and basketball goals on the wall. In the middle of the floor were three wooden scaffolds standing side by side. The platforms on the black-painted scaffolds were eight feet high, and they were mounted by thirteen steps. They were boarded up at the bottom on three sides, with a dark canvas covering the fourth side.

The most distant scaffold had no rope at all on the crossbeam; the one in the middle did have a rope, but it was hanging taut, extending down through an open trapdoor. Paul assumed that the rope was tight because Seyss-Inquart was hanging, just out of sight, on the other end.

One of the guards on duty inside the execution room removed Paul's handcuffs and replaced them with a leather strap. After that Paul was led to the bottom step. A chaplain and an American officer were standing at the foot of the steps.

"State your name," the American officer said.

"Paul Heinrich Maas."

"Climb the steps, please."

Oddly, Paul's stomach had stopped churning, and his knees no longer felt like water. He found a strength and calmness that he didn't know he possessed. He had the strangest sensation that he had already left his body and was now one of the witnesses.

"Do you have any final messages?" the officer asked.

Paul shrugged. "You aren't hanging me." He laughed. "You think you are, but you aren't. I have already left this body."

The officer nodded at the hangman, and a black hood was pulled down over Paul's face. A second later he felt the rope being placed around his neck. He suddenly remembered the teasing remark Karl had made to him several months ago, when they were first brought to Nuremberg: *"If you had been as interested in bird watching as you were politics, you and I wouldn't be here now."*

Recalling that he had joked that he had ended up by default with the National Socialists because he couldn't pass the bird identification test, Paul said aloud under his hood, "I think it was a warbler." Then he chuckled, because he knew the statement wouldn't make any sense to those who heard him.

Suddenly he felt the floor drop out from under his feet. His stomach come up to his throat, followed by a jarring thump at the base of his neck. . .

7

APRIL 30, 1947, BETWEEN TEL AVIV
AND HAIFA

Moshe Meir scrambled down from the railroad trestle, ran through the brush, then scooted quickly across the dry wadi, trailing out a length of electrical wire behind him. Two men and a woman were waiting for him in the rocks on the opposite side of the dry creek bed. The two men, each armed with a Sten submachine gun, stood careful watch for anyone who might be approaching. The woman was on her knees behind the rocks, holding a box and plunger-type generator.

"We're all ready," Moshe said. He handed the wire to the woman, and she separated the two leads, then began attaching them to the generator terminals.

The woman was in her midthirties, with black hair, dark, almost almond-shaped eyes, and an olive complexion. Like the men, she was wearing a khaki shirt and trousers. She and they were members of the Irgun.

Commanded by a refugee Polish Jew named Menachem Begin, the Irgun was an underground organization whose aim was the forcing of the British out of Palestine. It had brought the concept of guerrilla warfare to the cities, using hand grenades, mines, and bombs to get the point across. Its most dramatic action so far had been the bombing of the King David Hotel, in which ninety-one people were killed.

"The dynamite. Did you put down a big enough charge?" the woman asked.

"Six sticks. That's enough."

"Eight would be better."

Moshe raised his hand in frustration. "'Eight would be better,' she says, as if I had never done this before. Will you quit being a woman who questions everything and be a lieutenant who follows orders?"

The woman smiled, and when she did it softened the hard-shelled military visage so that it became evident that she was actually very pretty. "Now you want me to be a lieutenant. Last night you wanted me to be a woman," she said wryly.

"That was then, this is now," Moshe replied. "And I want you to be more than just a woman. I want you to be an honest woman. Miriam, when will you marry me?"

"You know my answer," she replied. "We will get married when we can get the license in our own country. To be given permission by the British to be married. . . that I will not do."

"You are a stubborn woman, Miriam Gelbman."

"That's because I am half-American," she countered. "Americans are stubborn people. And impatient. I am growing tired of waiting for the United Nations to tell us, yes, we can exist."

"Well, you can't say I'm not doing my part to hurry things along," Moshe said dryly, hefting his Sten.

A train whistle sounded in the distance, and Moshe stood up and shielded his eyes against the glare of the sun as he looked down the track beyond the high trestle. A pencil-line of smoke hung in the bright, blue air.

"We have about five minutes before the train gets here."

"You're sure it's a troop train?" Miriam asked. "It isn't the express from Cairo?"

"It is definitely the First Battalion of the Argyll and Sutherland Highlanders," Moshe replied. "Very British and very military, coming to prevent the *Let My People Go* from off-loading its passengers."

"Well, if they are so determined to keep the immigrants on the ship, then I suppose we must do this," Miriam said in a less-than-certain tone.

"Of course we must," Moshe said. "Why would you even question it? During the war we destroyed many troop trains. You never questioned it then."

"That was different," Miriam said simply. "Every dead German was a dead Nazi. But the British fought *against* the Germans."

"True, but now the British are fighting against us, and we have no choice but to fight back. Even your cousin, Simon, has left the Haganah and joined the Irgun."

107

"Moshe!" one of the other two men shouted. "Moshe, an airplane!"

"Get down!" Moshe ordered, and he, Miriam, and the two men dived for cover under the rocks. "Don't look up," Moshe warned. "Our faces will stand out against the rocks. They could see us."

It wasn't a fighter aircraft. It was a light, high-wing, single-engine plane that gave off more of a high-pitched snarl than a roar.

"He's scouting the railroad tracks ahead of the train," Moshe explained. "If he doesn't see us, we'll be all right."

The engine noise lowered in pitch and became louder as the airplane approached. Then when it had passed over them, the pitch rose again, and the sound became fainter.

Moshe waited a moment longer, then raised his head slightly and checked the sky. "All right, it's gone," he said. "Let's get ready." He reached for the generator.

"I'll do it," Miriam offered.

"No, you won't," Moshe replied. "They may be soldiers, but the Brits on that train are still human beings, and some of them are going to be killed. I can live with that. I don't know if you can."

"All right," Miriam agreed. "Have it your way."

Moshe rose on one knee to watch the approaching train. A flatcar was being pushed in front of the engine, and mounted on it was a machine gun shielded by sandbags. One soldier was standing behind the gun; another was sitting on top of the wall of sandbags.

The engineer blew his whistle as the train started out onto the trestle. Moshe pulled the plunger up on the generator and waited until the flatcar, the engine, and the tender were on the trestle. Then he pushed the plunger down.

Approximately one hundred feet in front of the train there was a brilliant flash of light. Bits and pieces of the trestle blew away from the center of the flash, tumbling through the air as if they had been caught by a slow-motion camera. As smoke billowed up, the heavy, jarring thump of the explosion rolled across the distance.

The engineer applied the brakes, and a shower of sparks spewed out from beneath the locked wheels as steel slid on steel. But the train was going too fast, and the explosion was too close for it to stop in time. The flatcar left the track first, thrusting out over the ten-foot hole the dynamite had just put in the trestle. The car hung there for just a moment as if making an effort to leap the gap, then it dropped, twisting away to the right as it did so. The sandbags, machine gun, and soldiers pitched down toward the rocky bottom of the dry wadi some twenty feet below the trestle.

The engine followed the flatcar down, and as it hit the rocks the boiler jacket burst open, releasing a huge, loud gush of steam. Crashing down behind the engine were the tender, two flatcars bearing machine guns, two flatcars carrying trucks, and one carrying two tanks.

The flatcar carrying the tanks broke its coupling and separated from the remainder of the train. Without the plunging engine pulling them down, the passenger cars simply rolled to a stop, just before they reached the abyss—sparing the several hundred soldiers riding in the cars.

The train tumbled down to the terrible banging, clanging cacophony of wood and steel crashing against itself. Trucks and tanks broke their moorings and slid forward to add to the general din of screeching metal and roaring steam. Then, when all the steam pressure was vented and the final car was still, the noise ceased.

It was deadly quiet for almost thirty seconds. But even before the dust settled, the first of the British soldiers started scurrying down the side of the gully to investigate.

"Bloody hell! What the hell happened?" one of the soldiers shouted in the distance.

Moshe got to his knees and looked over at the twisted pile of wreckage and at the shouting British soldiers who were climbing down toward it.

"Danny, Ben, Miriam," Moshe whispered. "On my signal, start shooting toward the soldiers. Give them an entire magazine, then get the hell back to the car. I want the Brits to know that this was no accident."

Miriam opened and closed the bolt on her submachine gun, peeling a round off the top of the magazine and sliding it into the chamber, then pointed the barrel in the general direction of the soldiers in the gully. Danny and Ben did the same. Moshe looked at them for a second.

"Now!" he shouted.

All four of them squeezed the triggers, and the rapid-firing Stens spat out volleys of bullets. Some of the bullets were tracer rounds, and Miriam watched the bright little fireballs as they flashed quickly across the distance, then hit the rocks and careened away with loud whines.

"Fall back! Fall back!" one of the British officers shouted. "Form a defensive position!"

The Brits who had started down into the wadi now turned and, alarmed, began scrambling back up to the top. A few dropped their weapons in the process, though many more hadn't bothered taking their weapons when starting down in the first place.

"Let's get out of here?" Moshe hissed loudly, and the four of them turned and ran, bending low, following an intersecting wadi back to where they had hidden the car.

109

MAY 2, 1947, ABOARD THE LET MY
PEOPLE GO AT HAIFA

Although the British had let the refugee ship *Let My People Go* dock, they hadn't let anyone leave the ship. A double row of concertina wire separated the pier from the rest of the port, and just behind the barbed wire armed British soldiers stood vigilant watch. The passengers had been refused permission to disembark, and the ship was given forty-eight hours to make ready for departure.

Anna Gelbman was standing at the railing of the ship on the afterdeck, looking toward the shore, when Lily Stein came up to join her.

"Why do you stand here looking at the barbed wire and the soldiers?" Lily asked. "That is too depressing."

Anna smiled and put her arm around Lily's shoulders.

"Oh, my child, it isn't the barbed wire I see or even the armed soldiers," she answered. "I'm looking at the hills beyond. And do you know what I see?"

"What?"

"I see towns and farms. . . and highways filled with cars and trucks and buses. I see schools and synagogues and libraries and concert halls. And I see marketplaces and theaters and long-winded politicians making speeches."

"You're talking about our own homeland, aren't you?" Lily sighed. "I wish I could see it, too, but I can't. I see only guns and barbed wire. . . the same things I've seen for most of my life."

"Well, that's the problem," Anna said, smiling gently. "You have never seen anything but guns and barbed wire, and I have never seen anything but a Jewish homeland. I'm one of those people that everyone used to call a radical. I'm an unreconstructed Zionist. I always have been, and I always will be."

At that moment there was an outbreak of excitement amidships, and several people hurried from all parts of the ship to see what was going on. Anna and Lily looked in that direction, curious as to the cause of the intense interest.

"What do you think it is?" Lily asked.

"I don't know," Anna answered. "But I think we should find out, don't you?"

They moved toward the center of the ship to join the scores of other passengers gathering there. When they reached the outer perimeter, they could hear loud talking, but because they couldn't hear the words distinctly, they began working their way toward the front. Finally they got close enough not only to hear, but to see.

The captain of the *Let My People Go* was in a heated discussion with an Arab merchant. The British had been allowing Arab merchants to come aboard to resupply the ship so that it would be able to make the return passage.

110

It quickly became clear, however, that this man was not an Arab, but a Jew dressed as an Arab.

"Do you think I would take such a risk if I wasn't absolutely sure?" the visitor asked the captain. "I mean, look at me, dressed like this. The British could throw me in jail; the Arabs, if they discovered me, would kill me; even some of our own people in the Irgun or the Stern Gang might mistake me for an Arab, and that could be just as dangerous. I'm telling you, this ship is not returning to Cyprus. . . it is going to Hamburg."

"Germany?" someone gasped. "No, surely not?"

"The English wouldn't do that!" another shouted.

"They wouldn't, would they? Then who are these soldiers who come into our homes in the middle of the night, breaking down the doors and pulling our people out of their beds before marching them off to prison? They are not the German SS. They are British soldiers."

"All right, suppose what you are telling me is true," the captain said. "What do you propose that I do about it? There is nothing I can do. If this ship is ordered to leave, I must leave. If it is ordered to Hamburg, then I must go to Hamburg."

"No," the visitor said. "That is what happened to us before. We meekly did what we were told to do. Never again."

"*Never again! Never again! Never again!*" several of the passengers shouted.

"Then what do you suggest?" the captain asked.

"We have learned that the harbormaster will come aboard this afternoon with new sailing orders. They will not make you leave tomorrow, for that's the Sabbath, but they will insist that you get under way by sunrise of the fourth. What you must do is find some way to delay that departure by at least twelve hours. We have an event planned for that day."

"What kind of event?" the captain asked.

The visitor shook his head. "That I cannot tell you," he said. "But I will tell you this: It will be significant enough to draw soldiers from all over Palestine, and that means many of the guards who are here as well. When the guards are gone, we will have some of our people come to help anyone who wishes to leave the ship."

"Surely all the guards won't go?"

"No. Some will remain," the visitor admitted. "So that means leaving the ship won't be without risk. My advice would be that you discuss this matter with all your passengers and let them examine their hearts. Only those who are willing to take the risk and who have a reasonable chance of success should try. There will be no dishonor attached to those who stay on board. In fact, it won't be possible for us to get everyone out, so some *must* stay."

"*I'm* going," someone insisted.

"Not I," another spoke up. "I haven't survived the Germans just to be shot by the British. I will do what I am told to do, and I advise everyone else to do the same. Even as we speak, the United Nations is considering our problem. What if we try to escape and are killed, then the United Nations rules in our favor next week, next month, or even next year? Would that not be a foolish move on the part of the ones who are killed?"

"That's the same attitude that allowed the Germans to imprison us," someone challenged.

"We were imprisoned, yes, but we are alive today, and we are on the threshold of having our own homeland. Don't you see? It is by reason and logic that the Jew has survived—not by foolish risk."

"Mr. Mayer is right," someone said. "There is nothing to be gained by risking our lives now. We should wait and cooperate. All will be put right in God's own time."

"God's time is eternal. My time is short. I can't wait for God's time," someone said, and many laughed.

"I must go now," the visitor said. He looked at the captain. "Remember, you must find some way to disable your ship. On Sunday, we will come."

"What will be the signal that you are here?" someone asked.

"Do you have any radios on board?"

"Yes, of course. We have a two-way radio."

"No, I mean commercial radio receivers."

"Yes, we have them as well."

"Listen to the radio on Sunday. When our event happens, you will know."

"I am definitely going," Anna Gelbman told Esther and Lily Stein as they gathered around Anna's bunk in the women's hold of the ship.

"Lily and I are, too," Esther replied. "We haven't come this far only to be turned away."

"We must be prepared to act quickly and—" Anna was interrupted by a shout from the hatch that led into the women's hold.

"The captain has called a meeting in the first hold! A meeting in the first hold!"

"I wonder what that is all about?" Esther mused.

"There is only one way to find out," Anna replied. "But I will tell you now, I don't like the sound of it."

The *Let My People Go* had been bought and supplied by a group of American Jews. It was very small, originally a Chesapeake Bay freighter with very few accommodations for passengers. Only by converting the cargo holds into dormitories could it carry a significant number of passengers, and even with the conversion, only about four hundred could actually be accommodated.

112

Judging from the press of people in the first hold, it looked as if all four hundred had gathered for the meeting.

As soon as everyone was gathered, the captain turned the meeting over to Isaac Schechter. When Anna saw that Schechter was actually conducting the meeting, she felt relieved, because he was the one who had been arguing with Solomon Mayer. However, Mayer was sitting very close by, as if he and Schechter had come to some kind of agreement.

"We have formed a committee," Schechter began. "The purpose of the committee is to make certain that those people who wish to go ashore when the time comes will have every possibility of success. Solomon Mayer has agreed to be on the committee."

"And so do you now wish to go ashore, Mr. Mayer?" someone asked.

Mayer stood up and ran his hand nervously through his hair.

"No," he said. "And I still feel that it is a foolish adventure. However, I also feel that I have no right to interfere with those who wish to go. . . just as those who wish to go have no right to increase the danger for those of us who wish to stay. Therefore, it is only logical that the best solution is to find a way to let the adventurous leave without increasing the danger for the more cautious. That is why I have agreed to serve on the committee."

"What's the purpose of the committee?"

"I can answer that question," Schechter replied. "We will organize everyone who wishes to leave so that when the time comes, there is no last-minute confusion. We must be able to move quickly and resolutely. And"—here he paused for a long moment, as if unwilling to continue—"we must also make the selection as to who can go. . . and who must be left behind."

"Who gave you that authority?" someone shouted angrily.

"Yes, who made you our leader?"

"I appointed myself," Schechter admitted, and when more protests were shouted, he held up his hands to call for quiet. "Please, listen to me for a moment and give me a chance to explain. After you have heard me, I will ask for a show of hands from those who support me. If a majority of you support me, I will continue in this position. If a majority of you oppose me, then I shall step down."

"That sounds fair enough," someone said.

"Let him continue," another insisted.

There were a few more shouts, though now most were of encouragement, until finally, with his hands upraised to call for quiet, Schechter began to speak again.

"Thank you," he said. "Now, let me begin by saying there is much wisdom to what my friend Solomon Mayer says. We all know that soon, very soon, the United Nations will partition Palestine, and we will have a homeland."

There was a scattering of applause and a few shouts of excitement, but Schechter just smiled and held his hands up again. Everyone quieted down, and he continued.

"Once this happens, immigration will be controlled by the Jewish people themselves, and we will open our borders to any Jew anywhere who wishes to come home. It is entirely possible that this could occur within days or weeks. Those of you who are forced to return to Germany now will be eligible to come back and join us. So, I say to you that there is no dishonor in taking the more prudent course.

"Now, I speak to those who will make the attempt to go ashore. You must be prepared to follow orders without question, for there are no individuals here; there is only the greater good for the greater number. Therefore, those of us on the committee must approve of everyone who plans to leave. If your escape does not serve the greater good, you will be made to stay on board."

There was a period of chatter as the passengers talked among themselves. Finally someone asked aloud the question that many of them had posed only to themselves.

"How do we know if our escape would serve the greater good?"

"I will answer that for you. As you can surely understand, our new country, once it's born, will need young, healthy, energetic citizens. Therefore, only those who meet those guidelines will be allowed off the ship. That means no men over the age of fifty and no women over the age of forty will be allowed to leave."

"No!" someone shouted. "You don't have that right!"

"But we must do it that way if we are to survive," Schechter insisted. "Don't you see? A woman over forty simply doesn't have the strength or the will to survive, and she would place the rest of us in danger."

Anna Gelbman was stunned. No, she was furious. "I want to speak!" she shouted.

"There's no need for any further discussion on this," Schechter said.

"I *will* be heard!" Anna demanded.

"Let her speak?" someone insisted.

"She has the right!" another protested.

"All right, all right," Schechter said, giving in with a sigh. He pointed to Anna. "You may speak, Mrs. Gelbman."

"Thank you," Anna said. She looked out over the faces of the others, then back at Schechter. "Two lines," Anna said. "This line, you may go; this line, you must stay. That is what you're saying, isn't it? And because I am over sixty you are telling me which line I must be in. Perhaps you will remember that the Germans also had two lines: this line, you may live; this line, you must die. Well, I did not let the Germans choose which line I would be in. . . and *I will not let you!* I escaped from Auschwitz, Mr. Schechter. My husband sneaked me onto a train, and then when I was free of the camp, I jumped from the train and I walked all night, avoiding German soldiers and SS men until I found a safe haven. I did *not* ask the Germans if I could do that. I did not *ask* a committee if I could do that. *I just did it.* And when I did it, Mr. Schechter, *I was nearly sixty years old!* I am sorry. You may have your committee, you may appoint your lines, you may say who will go in this line and who will stay in that line, but you will not say such a thing to me. I will make the choice for myself, and if you do not like it—to borrow an American expression from my late husband, may he rest in peace—you can damn well lump it."

Anna's speech was met with loud and enthusiastic applause and so many cheers that anxious crewmen signaled the passengers to be quiet lest the British guards outside the ship get wind that something was going on.

"All right, all right, Mrs. Gelbman,' Schechter relented. "You may go."

"*No!*" Anna shouted.

"What? I don't understand," Schechter replied, confused by her reaction. "I thought that was what you wanted."

"Not just me," Anna said. "Anyone who wants to may go. I don't think a person is foolish enough to try it if they really think they can't make it. But if they think they can, they will, for determination is half the battle."

Schechter was silent for a moment; then he smiled graciously in defeat. "All right," he said. "All right, anyone who wishes to go may go. But please, Mrs. Gelbman, do you mind if we organize a little?"

"Organize?" Anna smiled. "No, organizing is good. That we should do."

"Ah, good, we have Mrs. Gelbman's approval," Schechter quipped. "Then it is decided: We will organize."

The passengers laughed, then broke into excited conversation, many of them coming over to congratulate Anna for her stand.

"You are listening to a broadcast of recorded music from the British Forces Radio Service of Palestine. Our next selection is a recording of Beethoven's Overture Fidelio *as performed by the London Symphony Orchestra."*

Beethoven's music was audible all over the ship because it was being piped over the ship's loudspeakers. Those who were going to make the attempt to get ashore were ready to go at a moment's notice, and they had positioned themselves on the dock side of the ship.

Although there was actually only one connecting gangplank between the ship and the dock, other gangplanks had been fashioned, brought on deck, and hidden in places where they could be easily recovered. It had been decided that three additional gangplanks would be put in place, providing four exits for the 211 people who were going to try to leave. They had already been broken down into four groups, each group near its appointed exit.

115

Anna, Esther, and Lily had drawn the stern exit. It would be the steepest, and without ropes or handrails the most difficult to manage, but once on the dock they would be shielded from view by a stack of empty oil drums. Esther had been a little worried about the steepness of the angle, but some of the men had erected a practice gangplank, pitched at the same angle, down in the hold of the ship, and some passengers, including Anna, Esther, and Lily, had made several trial descents. Of course, the one in the hold of the ship wasn't as long as the one from the stern to the dock, and there were no British soldiers to avoid. But it had served its purpose, and now those who were waiting to use the stern gangplank did so with some degree of confidence in their ability to make it.

The hours stretched on, and the tension was increasing by the minute.

"When is something going to happen?" Lily asked. "The longer we wait, the more nervous I get."

"Have patience, little one," Anna counseled. "The plans have been made. Don't do anything to upset the apple cart now."

"It's just that I can't help but think something must have gone wrong. Surely if anything was going to happen it would have happened by now. Maybe—"

The music suddenly stopped and the announcer came back on.

"We interrupt this broadcast of recorded music to bring you the following news bulletin.

"At shortly after four o'clock this afternoon, Jewish terrorists attacked the prison fortress in Acre. According to information received here, several explosions were set off in the streets of Acre to divert attention from the prison itself. That was followed by an attack of one hundred terrorists, many of them wearing stolen British Army uniforms.

"The attackers rode in jeeps and strafed the guard towers with heavy machine-gun fire, then blew up the walls of the fortress. Several prisoners then managed to escape, although the exact number is not known at this time. A search is under way for the prisoners and the attackers, and the Army has moved quickly to regain control of the prison.

"All British Army personnel who are not currently on duty are instructed to report immediately to your company headquarters.

"And now, we return you to our program of recorded music."

"That's it!" Anna said excitedly. "That's what we've been waiting for."

"Where is Acre?" someone asked.

"I think to the north about ten miles."

"Smoke!" someone called down from the ship's superstructure. "I can see smoke in the sky to the north."

On the dock, behind the barbed wire and the British guards, someone suddenly started blowing a whistle.

"What's going on?" Esther asked.

"Look, they are gathering in the guards," Anna said, pointing. "They are going to send them up to Acre to respond to the trouble there."

116

"Our visitor was right. The guards are leaving."

Within five minutes of the announcement, a number of British trucks loaded with soldiers drove away. They left behind just four guards to watch the *Let My People Go*.

About five minutes later, there was a loud explosion at the far end of the pier, quickly followed by the rattle of machine-gun fire. The remaining guards ran toward the explosion, holding their rifles at high port.

Four trucks came barreling up to the concertina wire. At first Anna thought it was the original group returning, but a handful of men jumped down and started firing toward the British guards, and she recognized one of them as the man who, disguised as an Arab, had visited the *Let My People Go* two days earlier.

The four guards who had left to investigate the explosion now realized, too late, that they had been suckered. They tried to get back to their posts, but they were kept pinned down by the gunfire of the Irgun soldiers.

"*Now!*" Schechter shouted over the ship's loudspeaker. "*Evacuate now!*"

Quickly, the four gangplanks were put into position, and the passengers began to scurry down them to the dock. The first people down the gangplanks were young men who had volunteered to stand at the bottom and help the others. They got into position, then shouted back up to the ship.

"Come on! Come quickly! Hurry up!"

One of the British guards, realizing what was happening, stood up and sprayed a stream of machine-gun fire toward the ship. One of the two young men at the stem gangplank was hit, and he went down. A woman screamed, and those who were still on board, waiting to leave, hesitated.

"Come, Esther, Lily!" Anna shouted, climbing onto the gangplank. "We can't stay here any longer."

Anna's move seemed to galvanize the others into action because immediately after she climbed onto the makeshift exit, several others did so as well. Within a moment all four gangplanks were full as the passengers hurried down. The British guards, unwilling to fire on women and children, and under fire themselves, stayed behind cover and made no further attempt to stop the mass exodus.

"This way, this way! Into the trucks, quickly!" someone shouted.

The tailgates of the trucks were already down, and two people at the end of each truck were helping the passengers board. Within moments the trucks were loaded and under way.

They drove for about an hour, with the wind flapping the canvas tops against the bows overhead. Anna studied the faces of the other passengers. Some were still frightened and some were confused, but many were smiling broadly. Anna knew that she was in the latter category.

She was in Palestine, the fulfillment of a lifelong dream.

117

8

NOVEMBER 1947, FROM
"TRAILMARKERS" IN
EVENTS MAGAZINE:

MARRIED: Princess Elizabeth, daughter of King George VI and
Queen Elizabeth of England, and her cousin, Prince Philip, Duke of
Edinburgh. The ceremony, performed at Westminster Abbey on
November 20, was presided over by the archbishops of Canterbury
and York and the bishops of London and Norwich. The couple will
reside in London.

BORN: The United States Air Force. A separate and equal branch of
the United States military service created by Executive Order 9877,
the United States Air Force is charged with the responsibility to organize, train, and equip air forces for a variety of operations; to develop
weapons, tactics, technique, organization, and equipment of Air Force
combat and service elements; to provide missions and detachments for
foreign service; to provide means to coordinate air defense among all

services; and to assist the Army and Navy in their missions. W. Stuart Symington has assumed the position of Secretary of the Air Force.

CHOSEN: "Bookwatch" has selected the most significant books of 1947. They are: *Under the Volcano,* by Malcolm Lowry; *The Stoic,* by Theodore Dreiser; *Mother,* by Maxim Gorky; *Tales of the South Pacific,* by James Michener; *Out of the Night,* by Eric Twainbough; *Doctor Faustus,* by Thomas Mann; and *I, the Jury,* by Mickey Spillane.

BREAKTHROUGH: The *transistor,* developed by Bell Laboratories, is a new solid-state electronic component that is faster, lighter, and 1/200th the size of a vacuum tube and generates less heat and requires less than 1/100th the power of a vacuum tube. According to scientists, the miniaturization achieved by using the transistor will make possible electronic advances not yet conceived.

PROTEST: To show their disfavor of the House Committee on Un-American Activities hearings on Communists in the motion picture industry, several Hollywood stars, including Lauren Bacall, Humphrey Bogart, Demaris Hunter, Danny Kaye, and Gene Kelly, flew to Washington to protest the proceedings. Traveling separately from the group were Ronald Reagan and Robert Taylor, both of whom expressed their approval of what HUAC is doing by testifying before the committee.

WASHINGTON, D.C.

When Shaylin McKay showed her credentials to the guard at the press entrance to the HUAC hearing room, he nodded his approval and let her in. Because of the intense public interest in what was going on, tickets to the hearings were at a premium. The House Un-American Activities Committee was investigating the degree of Communist infiltration into the film industry, and a statement released by the committee promised to name "at least seventy-nine subversives" by the time the hearings were over.

Shaylin had picked up quite a large national following as a result of her wartime stories for the PNG. When she won the National Journalists Award for *Open: The Gates of Hell,* a rival magazine said in a story about her:

Shaylin McKay, an attractive woman with red hair and green eyes, does not hesitate to use any tool in her possession to get a story. Her aggressive and inventive nature has enabled her not only

119

to win a coveted National Journalists Award, but to have been nominated twice previously.

Miss McKay has never married and is best described as "free-spirited" in her social life. She has been linked romantically with some of the most newsworthy personalities of our time—often, and not necessarily coincidentally, with men who are the subjects of her stories. She is known to have been "more than just friends" with Floyd Stoner, a popular radio personality for ARN (also owned by the Petzold News Group); Sir John Paul Chetwynd-Dunleigh, Earl of Dunleigh, who was killed while serving in the British Army in Burma during the war; and best-selling novelist Eric Twainbough.

Floyd Stoner was adjusting the microphone at his assigned desk in the Senate hearing room when Shaylin took a seat beside him. Though the gallery was already full of spectators, neither the committee members nor any of the witnesses had made an appearance.

"I thought you weren't going to cover these hearings," Floyd said. "I thought you said they were nothing more than a witch-hunt."

"They *are* a witch-hunt," Shaylin replied, "but my boss sent me down here, so what can I do? I swear, it's reached the point where people are seeing Communists in every closet and under every bed. Parents are using Communists instead of the bogeyman to frighten little kids."

Floyd laughed. "Come on, Shaylin, you have enough clout to get out of any story if you want. If you really feel that way about this story, why are you here?"

"All right. It's because, whether I like it or not, this is *the* story right now," Shaylin confessed. "That's all anyone wants to hear about, even though there *are* a few other things happening in the world. Palestine is being partitioned to give the Jews a homeland, a man named Chuck Yeager has flown an airplane faster than the speed of sound. . . Ha! Imagine that, Floyd. Now if someone doesn't want to listen to you, they can run away from your voice. Oh, and Princess Elizabeth married the Duke of Edinburgh."

"Oh, my, that must've been a blow to you to let that one get away," Floyed teased.

"I met Prince Philip," Shaylin said. "I threw him back. I thought John was much more handsome."

"Well, of course you'd say that, now that Princess Elizabeth has him. But you can't fool me. I know it's just sour grapes on your part."

"All right, you've got me, it is," Shaylin said dramatically. "But no matter, if I can just get dear Philip to acknowledge the love child he and I spawned, I'll forgive him and wish the royal couple all the best."

Floyd laughed, then held up his finger for a second, signaling Shaylin to be quiet. He put on his headset and spoke into the mike. "Nick? Nick, do you read me? Okay, fine. We've already got readings on the committee mikes and the witness mikes, right? How long until broadcast? Ten minutes? Okay, I'll be ready." He flipped the switch to the off position, then removed his headset and turned back to Shaylin.

"You weren't here when Ronald Reagan and Robert Taylor testified, were you?"

"No," Shaylin replied. "But I'm sure they were both handsome and heroic. I have the background sheet here." She cleared her throat and began to read aloud:

"'Ronald Reagan, president of the Screen Actors Guild, testified that while certain undesirables were making an effort to infiltrate the entertainment business, SAG was definitely not controlled by leftists. Mr. Reagan added, "I abhor the Communist philosophy, but more than that I detest their tactics, which are the tactics of a fifth column."

"'Actor Robert Taylor was the most strident of all the witnesses. Rumors circulating before his appearance indicated that he would name names, and HUAC was very hopeful he would be a fount of information for them, but he failed to produce. Mr. Taylor said, "I personally believe the Communist party should be outlawed. If I had my way, they'd all be sent back to Russia."'

Shaylin looked up from the paper and smiled. "Now, there's a well-thought-out solution for you. Just send 'em all back to Russia." She continued to read.

"'When the Committee pressed Mr. Taylor for specific names of card-carrying Communists, he was unable to provide them. He did say that he suspected quite a few actors, though he confessed that he did not know for sure whether they were Communists or not. He added that there were some Screen Actors Guild members who, if they weren't Communists, 'were working awfully hard to be so.'"

Shaylin put the paper down. "Does that about cover it?" she asked.

"Pretty much, though several actors and actresses came to Washington to protest the activities of HUAC," Floyd replied.

"Yes, I know, and good for them," Shaylin said.

"Demaris Hunter was one of them, but of course you would expect something like that from her," Floyd continued. "Especially since Guy Colby is one of the ones the committee is looking at the hardest."

121

"Haven't you heard? Guy Colby and Demaris Hunter are no longer married," Shaylin said.

"I know, but it couldn't be good for her career to have been married to a Communist, even if they are divorced now. People will always wonder about her. And, of course, how would it look for her child to be brought up with a known Communist for a father?"

"Wait a minute, am I missing something here?" Shaylin asked. "I thought the purpose of these hearings was to determine whether or not there really was a Communist threat in the motion picture industry. I didn't know that individual guilt had already been established."

"I guess technically Colby's guilt hasn't been established. But it probably will be today. He's scheduled to appear if the other witnesses don't take too long."

It was another thirty minutes before the heavyset, white-haired representative from New Jersey, J. Parnell Thomas, the committee chairman, called the committee to order. The hearing room, which had been buzzing with scores of conversations, grew quiet. The other members of the House Un-American Activities Committee were seated at their designated positions, passing pieces of paper back and forth. A couple of them held whispered conversations as they waited to begin.

The first witness was Harrison Fleming, an independent producer. Fleming, who had been testifying the day before when the committee adjourned, sat in front of the microphones at the witness table for the continuation of his testimony. He poured himself a glass of water and took several swallows. A page delivered a document to Chairman Thomas and the chairman nodded, then began reading it.

The counsel for the committee spoke to Fleming.

"Mr. Fleming, you were sworn before your testimony yesterday, and therefore I remind you that you are still under oath."

"Yes, I am aware," Fleming responded.

"Now, you have heard the testimony given to our committee, which stated that there are very few actors who are known Communists. According to what we have been told so far, most of the known Communists in the business are writers. Do you agree with that statement?"

"I do."

"Would you elaborate, please?" the counsel asked.

Fleming cleared his throat and took another sip of water before he began to speak, leaning toward the microphone as he did so.

"Mr. Chairman and distinguished members of this committee, it should be very obvious to each of you just why Hollywood would be the focus of such intense effort on the part of the Communist fifth columnists. The motion picture industry is our nation's greatest medium of propaganda, and because of that the Communist bigwigs in Moscow would like nothing better than to use our great art for their evil purposes which, as we all know, is the overthrow of the American government and the undermining of our way of life.

"The Communists were, for the most part, unsuccessful in their attempt to convert any of the actors and failed miserably with the established stars. However, they did manage to find much more fertile ground among the writers."

"What about the producers and directors?" one of the members asked.

"Among the producers they were as unsuccessful as they were with the actors. They did enjoy a bit more success with the directors, however, especially those who were what we in the industry call writer-directors. That is to say, writers who direct their own scripts."

"And would you say that Mr. Guy Colby fits the description of writer-director?" the counsel for the committee asked.

"I would say so, yes," Fleming replied. "His last picture, *Out of the Night*, illustrates that point."

"Excuse me, Counselor, I would like to ask a question," one of the members interrupted. "Correct me if I'm wrong, Mr. Fleming, but isn't *Out of the Night* from a book? A novel by Eric Twainbough?"

"It is," Fleming agreed. "And it's a good case in point of what I am trying to tell you. You are right, it was a novel, but you must understand that in the motion picture business we can't just make a movie from a book. First the book must be converted into a screenplay. A screenwriter is hired to do that, and it's very much within that screenwriter's power to emphasize certain aspects of the story while diluting others, completely distorting the intent of the novel's author. In this way a screenwriter could make the final picture present whatever message he wanted. And if you saw *Out of the Night*, the picture is a leftist indictment against American southerners for the peculiar relationship they enjoy with their Negroes. If one had only the film to go by, one might think that relations between the races have made absolutely no advancement since the Civil War. And, of course, we all know that simply isn't true."

"Did Mr. Colby write the screenplay? I saw the movie, and I thought I read Eric Twainbough's name in the credits, not only as the author of the novel, but of the screenplay as well."

Fleming cleared his throat. "Yes, sir, Eric Twainbough is *credited* with writing the screenplay as well as the book. However, it is also a well-known fact that Eric Twainbough was Mr. Colby's house guest for several weeks during the time he was supposed to be working on the script, and most insiders are sure that if Colby didn't actually write it himself, he exercised such a heavy influence over its final content that he may as well have."

"Mr. Chairman, may I suggest that this committee subpeona Mr. Twainbough to question him as to the true authorship of this screenplay?" one of the committee members asked.

J. Parnell Thomas cleared his throat. "Uh, that won't be necessary. Mr. Twainbough has volunteered to appear before the committee, but we simply won't have time to question him. He has stated in an affidavit that he is the author of both the story and the screenplay."

"I see. And you, Mr. Fleming, still insist that it was Mr. Colby and not Mr. Twainbough who authored the script? Does that mean Mr. Twainbough lied on his affidavit?"

"I think the distinction is such a fine one that Eric Twainbough may truly believe he authored the screenplay as well as the novel. In that case, his sworn statement wouldn't be a lie. . . but it wouldn't be the truth."

"I must confess, Mr. Fleming, that that is a distinction that escapes me. However, regardless of who the screenplay author is, is it your opinion that the movie *Out of the Night* is detrimental to the United States?"

"Absolutely," Fleming replied. "If the story had been offered to me, I would have refused to produce it. It holds America up in a bad light to the rest of the world, and with the unrest in so many colored areas today—India, China, and the Middle East—such a picture has to work against us."

"Mr. Fleming, to your sure and certain knowledge, is Guy Colby a Communist?" the committee chairman asked.

"In my heart, I believe he is."

"That's not what I asked you, Mr. Fleming. Do you know for a fact, as a result of some piece of hard evidence, that Guy Colby is a Communist?"

"If it's evidence you're looking for, you need look no further than the movie he produced for the Soviet Union during the war," Fleming replied. "Surely you remember *Red Banners over Mother Russia*? And the 'Second Front Now' petition he circulated with that picture, in which he asked all Americans to request—no, to *demand*, regardless of any military considerations and regardless of any risk to our boys already fighting—that the United States open a second front to relieve the pressure against Soviet troops?"

"Mr. Fleming," one of the other committee members said, "while that may *suggest* that Mr. Colby is a Communist, or at least a Communist sympathizer, it is not really what we would call hard evidence. Hard evidence would be something like your personal knowledge that Guy Colby has admitted to being a Communist before witnesses or that he has, perhaps, tried to recruit others to join the Communist party."

"Mr. Congressman, if you are asking me if I can testify to something like that, then the answer is no, sir, I cannot."

124

One of the other members spoke up then. "Even though there is no hard evidence, do you have any doubt in your own mind that Colby is a Communist?"

"If I have any doubt, then I don't have a mind," Fleming replied.

Chairman Thomas looked up and down the length of the table. "Are there any more questions from any of the members?" he asked. When no one spoke up, he said, "This witness is excused."

"Thank you, Mr. Chairman," Fleming said. "And may I add, sir, that your efforts in these proceedings are to be commended."

"Thank you for your comment," the chairman said. "The committee now calls Mr. Richard Macaulay."

Shaylin knew that Richard Macaulay, a screenwriter, had already stated publicly that the Screenwriters Guild was Communist-controlled. He had also offered a list of people who he was "morally certain" were Communists. Guy Colby was on that list.

Shaylin stayed the rest of the day, listening to a parade of witnesses, all of whom testified that while they personally were not now and never had been Communists, they were sure that there were many in Hollywood who were.

When the committee adjourned at six o'clock that evening, Guy Colby had not yet been called.

"I'll be anxious to see what Colby has to say in response to all this tomorrow," Floyd said as he began taking down his microphone.

"Everyone did seem to pick him out as a special target today, didn't they?" Shaylin observed.

Floyd chuckled. "Well, why not? If they can throw those committee sharks something to nibble on, they might be able to save their own hides."

Shaylin adopted an expression of mock surprise. "Surely you don't mean that some of these witnesses may be Communists themselves and are merely using Guy Colby to save their own necks?" she asked sarcastically.

"Makes you wonder what's happening to the human race, doesn't it?" Floyd replied, equally sarcastically. "So, do you want to have dinner with me or what?"

Shaylin laughed. "Oh, yes, I'm sure Jean would love that."

"Ah, don't worry about Jean. We have a strong, healthy marriage," Floyd said. "We trust each other completely."

"Thanks, but no thanks," Shaylin replied. "I like to *write* the news, I don't like to *be* the news, and if we're seen together, some gossip columnist somewhere will have a field day with it."

"Yeah, you're probably right," Floyd said. "I mean it's getting to where a person can't even sneak in a little piece of ass anymore without the whole world finding out."

Shaylin snickered. "It's good to see that fame and fortune haven't changed you, Floyd Stoner. You're still the same contemptible jerk you've always been."

"Yeah, that's me. Well, where are you headed now?"

"I have an appointment to interview one of tomorrow's witnesses. So you see, I couldn't go to dinner with you tonight even if your wife came along to show the world how innocent it was."

"Who are you interviewing?"

"Come on, Floyd, I haven't asked you who you're interviewing, have I?"

"I'm not interviewing anyone," Floyd said.

"You aren't? Oh, well, then it's a good thing I didn't ask, isn't it? It's probably embarrassing to have to confess that you couldn't find someone to talk to you. Good night. I'll see you tomorrow."

Shaylin left Floyd standing there watching after her with a puzzled expression on his face, and she knew that he was wondering whether he should try to find someone to interview before the next day's session—and whether he should be embarrassed if he didn't.

Shaylin hadn't been exactly truthful when she said she had an appointment to interview one of the witnesses. She was going to try. . . but she didn't have an appointment. She had discovered, quite by accident, that she and Guy Colby were staying in the same hotel, and she felt reasonably certain that she could get to him.

Shaylin walked purposefully to her hotel, which was close by the Senate chambers. Eschewing the house phones on the reception desk—she didn't want to have any nosy hotel operator standing there, listening in she—crossed the lobby to the bank of pay phones and called the director.

"Mr. Colby?" she said when he answered the phone.

"Yeah?"

"My name is Shaylin McKay, Mr. Colby. I'm a friend of Eric Twainbough's. He suggested I give you a call."

"Is that a fact?"

"Yes."

"Just a minute."

Shaylin waited for a moment, wondering what was going on; then she heard another voice. . . a very familiar voice.

"Hello, Shaylin."

"Oh, shit," she groaned. "Eric, I didn't know you were with him."

Eric chuckled. "No, I don't suppose you did. It was a nice try, though."

"Listen, Eric, you've got to get me up there. I need to talk to Colby."

"Why?"

"Why? You know why, goddammit; it's my job. Besides, I might be able to help."

126

"I doubt that you can help," Eric said. There was a brief pause. "But let me see what I can do."

"Come on, Eric, do more than just see," Shaylin pleaded. "Get me up there. You can do it, I know you can.

"Hold on."

Shaylin held the receiver impatiently, and then Eric's voice came on again. "There's a liquor store on the corner. Bring up a bottle of bourbon."

"Sure'n wouldn't some Irish whiskey be better now?" Shaylin asked in a thick, affected brogue.

"Bourbon," Eric said flatly.

"'Tis a heathen you are, Eric Twainbough, but bourbon it will be."

Ten minutes later, with a bottle of bourbon in her hand, Shaylin knocked on the door of Guy Colby's suite. To her surprise, the door was opened by Demaris Hunter.

"Demaris!" Shaylin gasped. Demaris Hunter wasn't exactly one of Shaylin's intimate friends, but she had met the actress several times and had even done an in-depth interview on her, spending a week with her in the process. It had been an honest story, but it hadn't been one that burned the bridges between the writer and the subject. That wasn't always the outcome, and Shaylin knew that Demaris respected her for that.

"Hello, Shaylin, how are you doing?" Demaris asked, stepping back to invite her in.

"I'm doing fine," she said. "It's good to see you here."

"Are you surprised?"

"A little, yes. Though I know you came out here to protest the HUAC hearings, and I must tell you I admire you for that."

"Thanks," Demaris said. "It made a few people in the business nervous, but I wasn't alone. Thank God, I wasn't alone. . . I don't know if I would have had the courage to do it on my own."

"What are you talking about, you don't know if you'd have the courage? Didn't you get discovered by making a parachute jump onto a Hollywood set?"

"Not me. That sounds like a story some Hollywood press agent dreamed up," Demaris retorted with a laugh.

"Don't mislead the woman, Demaris. Don't forget, it was *my* set you jumped onto," Guy Colby said, coming over to join them. "Miss McKay, I'm Guy Colby. I see you brought the bourbon."

"Small enough price to pay," Shaylin replied, holding out the bottle.

"Well, after all, Eric did suggest that you drop by," Guy said with a sly grin.

"Uh, yes," Shaylin replied, smiling sheepishly. "I'm sorry about that. Where is he, by the way?"

"He's in the other room, on the phone. He'll be here in a moment," Guy answered. "I'll fix us a drink. Coke? Water? Neat?"

"Neat," Shaylin said.

"I knew you had to be my kind of girl," Guy replied, walking toward the bar.

"When's the last time you saw Kendra?" Demaris asked Shaylin, inquiring about Kendra Petzold, Shaylin's boss.

"Last week, when I was in St. Louis. I did an article about her new television station. It's going on the air in January."

Demaris chuckled. "Isn't she something, though? When Kendra and I were college roommates back at good old Jefferson, I thought I was going to be the shaker and mover, and she was going to wind up as some mousy little reporter, doing a women's page for a newspaper in Flat River, Missouri, or Pinkneyville, Illinois, or some such place. Now look at us. We're the same age, but I'm an over-the-hill star, while she's a media mogul in the middle of her prime. Next time you speak to her, tell her I asked about her, will you?"

"Of course I will," Shaylin promised.

Eric Twainbough stepped into the room. He had a way, Shaylin thought, of dominating any room he was in. He was a big man, but it wasn't just his bulk. It was his "presence," a word she couldn't exactly define.

He grinned at her. "Shaylin McKay, have you no shame, girl, lying your way into a man's room like that? If you're that desperate for some male companionship, why don't you just hang around a bar and try to look seductive? Maybe you'll get lucky."

"Time was when I could, true enough," Shaylin answered, sighing. "But I've had to develop other ways to compete with the younger, prettier girls. Besides, what's the good of being Irish if I can't roll a lie off my tongue every now and again?"

"It's grand to see you've lost none of your blarney," Eric said, coming over to kiss her. "As full of sass and shit as you ever were.

"Who were you talking to on the phone? Your new girlfriend?"

"Well, now, you might be a bit closer to the truth than you think. I was talking with Paige."

"Paige? Your granddaughter? You mean she's old enough to use the phone?"

"She can say Papa, and that's good enough for me. That's what she calls me." He added with a chuckle, "Hem would be furious. I think he feels he holds the copyright on the name."

Guy brought the drinks over and distributed them. He sat on the windowsill, the Washington Monument framed in the window behind him, and looked at Shaylin.

"Thanks," she said, holding up the drink. "And thanks for agreeing to see me."

"I'll be honest with you, Miss McKay, I didn't want to see anyone," Guy said. "And I especially didn't want to see anyone from the press. But both Eric and Demaris told me you were a square shooter, so I gave in. Now, what is it you want?"

"I want to know what you're going to say to the committee tomorrow."

Guy smiled and took a swallow of his drink. "Hell, that's easy. I'm not going to say a goddamn thing to them."

"But you can't just say nothing," she warned. "You weren't there today. You don't know what all the witnesses said about you. You were crucified!"

"I know. I heard some of it over the radio, and I already knew what Fleming was going to say."

"And you're just going to let it go? Without fighting it?"

"What do you want me to do, perjure myself?"

Shaylin was surprised and showed it. "You mean, you *are* a Communist?"

Guy smiled sadly. "See what I mean?"

"No," Shaylin said. "I don't see at all what you mean.

"All you needed was the slightest inkling that I might be a Communist, and you were ready to accept that I am. To answer your question, no, I am *not* a Communist," Guy said. "But the question won't be put that way. The way the committee puts the question is: 'Are you now, or have you ever been, a member of the Communist party?' I cannot truthfully answer no to that."

"I see."

"No, I don't think you do," Guy said. He sighed. "I joined a group in the early twenties, before I left New York. I was young and idealistic, and I thought the idea of 'From each according to his ability, to each according to his need' made sense. It didn't take long, however, before I realized that the idea was just a cruel hoax. I had already paid the first year's dues, but I never renewed."

"But surely no one could hold something like that against you," Shaylin said. "I mean, that should be a positive thing, shouldn't it? You tried it and you didn't like it."

"I think that as far as the committee is concerned, being a little Communist is like being a little pregnant. There are no degrees. You either are or you aren't. So, I'm not going to tell them anything."

"If you do that, they'll suspect the worst," Shaylin said.

"Let them. I'm not alone. I know ten others who are going to refuse to testify as well."

"Really? Who?"

Guy began naming them then, ticking them off on his fingers as he did so. "Albert Matz, Dalton Trumbo, Samuel Ornitz, John Howard Lawson, Ring Lardner, Jr., Lester Cole, Alvah Bessie, among the writers. Herbert

Beberman, a director-producer; Edward Dmytryk, a director; and Robert
Adrian Scott, a writer-producer."

"If you refuse to testify, you'll be cited for contempt of Congress,"
Shaylin cautioned.

"Yes, I'm sure we will be."

"Don't you understand? You could go to jail."

Guy finished his drink. "Yes," he finally said.

Shaylin looked at Eric. "Eric, you're his friend, aren't you? Do something."

"What do you propose that I do, Shaylin?" he asked. "Convince him to go
against his conscience?"

"Conscience? What the hell does conscience have to do with it? We're
talking about jail! You know, those uncomfortable rooms with iron bars and
exposed toilets?"

"I have a prepared statement to read before the committee," Guy said.

"Thomas won't let you read it," Shaylin said.

"I know. That's why I'd like to read it now. You can print it if you'd like."

"I'll print it for you," Shaylin said. "It won't do you any good. It won't
change the mind of the committee, and if you're cited for contempt, it won't
keep you out of jail. But I'll print it."

"Thanks," Guy said. "Darling," he said to Demaris, "you want to get it for
me? It's in my briefcase."

Demaris retrieved the paper and handed it to him. Guy put on his reading
glasses, cleared his throat, and began to read just as if he were delivering the
statement to the full committee.

"Believers in democracy—true believers—know that open debate
and the unlimited exchange of ideas are necessary to preserve freedom.
The best test of truth is its ability to stand up to competition in the
marketplace of human endeavor. Therefore, the greatest expression of
confidence and faith in democracy and the American system is the
willingness to allow the fullest possible exploration, through free
speech and thought, of all competing ideas.

"For Congress to illegally abridge its citizens' constitutional rights
of debate, speech, and thought on the grounds that such ideas may be
dangerous is not only a usurpation of our basic freedom, but an arro-
gant presumption of infallibility on the part of Congress. Such an act
stifles human rights and short-circuits those procedures of democratic
government so wisely protected by the First Amendment."

Guy looked up from the paper. "That's my opening statement."

"It's beautiful," Shaylin said.

"It is," Eric agreed. "I told him Thomas Jefferson couldn't have expressed it better."

"It's a shame no one will get to hear it," Demaris added.

Shaylin looked over at Demaris and saw that the actress had tears in her eyes. Then she realized with surprise that she had tears in her own eyes.

"Maybe they won't hear it," she said. "But they'll damn sure read it. I promise you, Mr. Colby, I will make sure that it's printed."

When the hearings reconvened the next day, the Senate chamber was more crowded than it had been at any time since the appearances of Ronald Reagan and Robert Taylor; the word was already out that the day's scheduled witnesses were going to refuse to cooperate with the committee. Nearly all of those appearing had been accused by at least one previous witness of being presently or formerly members of the Communist party or "fellow travelers," a term being used to mean Communist sympathizers.

The first witness to be summoned before the committee was Guy Colby. He was sworn in; then he took his seat behind the battery of microphones.

"Mr. Colby, you are aware of why you have been called before this body?" Congressman J. Parnell Thomas asked.

"Mr. Chairman, I would like to read a statement," Guy said, ignoring the question.

"I am not prepared to hear a statement at this time," Thomas said.

"Mr. Chairman, the statement does have a bearing on these proceedings," Guy insisted.

"I am not prepared to hear a statement at this time," Thomas repeated testily. "If you would, sir, answer the question that was put to you. Are you aware of why you have been called before this body?"

"I would like to read my statement," Guy reiterated.

A rustle of conversation spread through the spectators in the chamber, and Thomas banged his gavel on the table.

"I cannot believe that you would be unaware of why you are here, Mr. Colby," he said. "But just in case you do *not* know, I will inform you: You have been accused, both by witnesses who have given sworn testimony before this committee and in depositions taken from those people who did not appear, of either being a Communist or being sympathetic to their aims. Are you aware of these accusations?"

"I would like to read my statement," Guy said again.

This time the murmuring from the spectators was louder, and Thomas reacted with an even louder bang of his gavel.

"I have *told* you, Mr. Colby, that we are *not* going to listen to your statement. Now, I'd like to ask you a question. Are you now, or have you ever been, a member of the Communist party?"

"I refuse to answer that question."

"You refuse to answer?"

"That is correct."

"Are you invoking your rights under the Fifth Amendment?"

"No, this committee has already repealed all Constitutional protections. It would do me no good to stand on Constitutional grounds since neither I nor any other American has any Constitutional grounds anymore. I refuse to answer your question, Mr. Chairman, just because I refuse to answer."

"Mr. Colby, it would seem to me that you would want to clear up this question. You sit here before us, accused by many of your peers—and some say accused by your own actions—of being a Communist, or at least a Communist sympathizer. Surely when you made that piece of propaganda for the Russians called"—Thomas picked up a piece of paper and adjusted his glasses as he examined it—"*Red Banners over Mother Russia,* you had to know that you were being used by the Communists?"

"Did you see the film, Mr. Chairman?" Guy asked.

"No, I am very proud to say that I did not see it."

"Then what right do you have to call it propaganda?"

"Are you trying to say that the film was *not* favorable to the Russians?"

"Of course it was favorable to the Russians," Guy replied. "In case you have forgotten, Congressman, we were at war with Germany at the time, and Russia was our *ally.* Would you have preferred that the film be favorable to the Nazis?"

"I need no history lessons from the likes of you, sir!" Thomas snapped. "The point is, your film was a tribute to the Communist doctrine, was it not?"

"My film was a tribute to the courage of men and women who were then in a desperate fight for their homeland."

"Their homeland was the Soviet Union, am I right?" Thomas asked.

"It wasn't Mars."

There was a tittering of laughter from the spectators' gallery, and Thomas angrily banged his gavel.

The congressman smiled mirthlessly, triumphantly, at Guy. "Thank you, Mr. Colby. You have made my point. And since we now seem to have moved beyond your repeated requests to read your statement, I will ask again if you are now, or if you have ever been, a member of the Communist party."

"And again, Mr. Chairman, I refuse to answer that question."

"Under the Fifth Amendment?"

"No amendment," Guy said. "I'm just not going to answer."

"Mr. Colby, are there any questions you *will* answer?" one of the other members asked.

"I don't think so."

"Would you confess, for example, to being a member of any organization? The Screenwriters Guild? Are you now, or have you ever been, a member of the Screenwriters Guild?"

"No, by God, I don't think I'm going to answer that question either."

Thomas slammed the gavel down so hard that it banged like the crack of doom. "Mr. Colby, you are dismissed!"

"Before I go, Mr. Chairman, I would like to read my statement."

"Sergeants at arms, please see to it that Mr. Colby leaves this chamber at once," Thomas ordered angrily.

Two men came to the witness table then and grabbed Guy's arms from both sides. When he refused to cooperate with them, they began pulling him, so his feet dragged up the aisle. In the meantime, even as Guy was being hauled from the chamber, he started reading his statement, shouting it out so it could be heard.

"Believers in democracy—true believers—know that open debate and the unlimited exchange of ideas are necessary to preserve freedom!"

Thomas banged his gavel repeatedly in an attempt to drown out Guy's shouted words.

"The best test of truth is its ability to stand up to competition in the marketplace of human endeavor!"

Still banging his gavel, Thomas demanded, "Silence that man!"

One of the two men dragging Guy out of the committee room put his hand over Guy's mouth so that his words became nothing more than unintelligible noises. A moment later Guy was outside the room, and the door was closed.

The spectators buzzed in excitement until finally the continued banging of the chairman's gavel quieted the room.

"If there are any more reactions to these proceedings, I will have the room cleared and continue the hearing behind closed doors," Thomas warned.

Anxious to see the remaining accused Hollywood personalities wriggle out of their charges, the spectators grew quiet.

'Thank you," Thomas said. "Will the counsel for the committee please call the next witness?"

True to her promise, Shaylin did see to it that Guy Colby's statement was printed in its entirety. Unfortunately, the statement's impact was diluted by news of the action taken by the movie industry.

The leading story in the "National" section of *Events Magazine*—a story splashed on the front pages of newspapers across the country as well—stated it all:

> More than fifty leaders of the American motion picture business gathered at the Waldorf-Astoria Hotel in New York this week. They met to discuss what action to take with regard to the HUAC hearings on their industry. The industry was very well represented, with the presidents of Paramount, United Artists, Universal, Galaxy, and several independent companies in attendance.
>
> The decision was made to permanently bar the "Hollywood Eleven" from any current or future employment. The term refers to the eleven professionals of the industry who refused to testify and were thus held in contempt of Congress.
>
> The conference of the motion picture companies produced a joint document that reads in part: "We will forthwith discharge or suspend without compensation those in our employ, and we will not reemploy any of the eleven." The document goes on to say that before being reemployed, anyone who was cited must "purge himself of contempt and declare under oath that he is not a Communist."

DECEMBER 10, 1947, NEW YORK

Shaylin was disgusted by events and by the fact that Guy Colby's beautiful indictment of the committee took a poor second place to the committee's indictment of him and of the remaining Hollywood Eleven. She sat at her desk in her New York office trying to work, trying to come up with some idea for another story, but her mind was a complete blank.

This is ridiculous, she scolded herself. She had learned long ago that she couldn't work unless she could maintain a degree of professional detachment. No matter how strongly she felt about the way things had turned out, she couldn't allow herself to dwell on it. She had to put the inquisition—even that was a loaded term, she told herself, and she must quit referring to the hearings in that way—out of her mind. Finally, with a sigh of disgust over her inability to concentrate, she got up from her desk, put on her coat, and left her office. She was going for a walk.

She took the elevator down to the lobby, buttoning her coat and pulling on her gloves as she descended. She greeted the doorman, who held open the door for her, and stepped outside. It wasn't too cold, though the air was crisp enough to make her walk down Forty-fourth Street in quick steps. New York's street commerce was carrying on as usual, totally undisturbed by the injustices that plagued her. A pretzel-and-chestnut vendor was doing a lively business on one comer of Forty-fourth and Fifth, and on the opposite comer a young man was handing out leaflets, asking the world to repent before it was too late.

She kept walking briskly across town, and when she reached Times Square, she looked up at the flashing news sign racing around the *New York Times* building:

. . . . . . MOTION PICTURE INDUSTRY BANS HOLLYWOOD ELEVEN. TO WORK NO MORE . . . . . .

She continued on to the theater district, where a large sign below one marquee read:

A STREETCAR NAMED DESIRE ". . . a *must* see!" *N.Y. Times.*

Just beyond the theater she saw a sign for Rosy O'Grady's Bar and decided to go in.

It was dark inside, a warm, mahogany dark. Half a dozen people stood around a piano singing *When Irish Eyes Are Smiling,* laughing and waving their glasses in time to the music.

Shaylin started toward the bar. One of the singers, a short, white-haired, red-faced leprechaun of a man, motioned to her. Shaylin smiled and, on impulse, joined them.

Without interrupting the song, the leprechaun signaled for another glass and poured Shaylin a beer from a large pitcher. Shaylin raised her glass and waved it in time to the music, joining with the others until the song was finished. Then they all laughed and applauded the piano player and each other. The leprechaun spoke to her.

"The name is Sean O'Leary, my pretty colleen. And would you mind tellin' me what brings the likes o' you into this place?"

"Are you daft, Sean O'Leary, for askin' such a question? Where better to be than a place where there's good drink, *foine* company, and a bit of heaven's own music?" Shaylin answered, matching his Irish brogue.

Sean laughed out loud. "Sure'n I couldn't have said it better meself—'n 'tis said I've a way with words."

"But of course you do," Shaylin said. "Are you not the playwright of *An Irishman's Lament?*"

"By God, the woman's not only beautiful, but damned intelligent, too! Now, I ask you, what do you think of that?" Sean said, looking at the others. "Aye, my pretty colleen, the play was mine. 'Tis flatterin' to think you would've even heard of it. It opened and closed in one week. . . off Broadway."

135

"And t'was a pity, that. I saw it."

"Did you now? And did you like it?"

"That I did. I heard it's to be made into a movie. But if it is, I'm not sure I want to see it."

"Why not?"

"I'm not all that certain a director could capture on film the mood and tone you achieved on stage."

"Aye, 'n 'tis my worry as well," Sean said. "But I've a desperate need of funds, you see. 'Tis the curse of man that we have settled upon a system of monetary exchange in order to survive. I would like to see a cashless society. . . a society where one barters for everything."

"Sean, see if you can trade a poem for another pitcher of beer," someone suggested, and everyone laughed.

"Innkeeper, would such a barter be of interest to you, now?" Sean inquired. He looked at Shaylin. "Eyes of jade, hair of fire. . . you're a thing of beauty, a woman to desire."

There was appreciative applause for his effort, and Sean bowed to all. He looked back at the bartender. "Now, would such heartfelt sentiments be a fair exchange for a pitcher of beer?"

"I don't know, Mr. O'Leary," the bartender hedged.

"I'm willing to say it is," one of the other men of the group said, taking out some money. "Bring us another."

"Ah, such is the pity," Sean said. "I fear I've no fair barter for the cashless society. But then, who does? Those who truly barter, barter with things that should never be tendered. Things like integrity and ethics and soul." He looked at Shaylin. "Tell me, Miss McKay, if I sell my little play to Hollywood, will they ask me to give up my soul as they have asked those poor devils of the Hollywood Eleven?"

"You know who I am?" Shaylin asked—her brogue abruptly gone—surprised at the revelation.

"Aye, lass, I know who you are. You are a young lady of ambition, tempered by principle. And as the two are not always compatible, you sometimes find yourself in the wrong man's bed metaphorically speaking, that is. And that's bad, for when you are in the wrong bed, the vampire can pollute your blood. He can come to you in the silver splash of moonlight and sink his fangs sweetly, ever so sweetly, into your lovely white neck."

"I don't know what you're talking about," Shaylin said, somewhat embarrassed to be the center of attention.

Sean laughed. "Nor does anyone else, my lovely. I'm a prophet without following. . . but 'tis often the way of those of us who must sound the tocsin. Enough of this." He stood up, a bit unsteadily. "'Tis my last night in New York, for on the morrow I must be off to that great Sodom on the Pacific, Los Angeles." He pronounced "Angeles" with a hard g, as the natives did. "Come with me now, Shaylin McKay. Come with me this one night, and make it a memorable one."

Shaylin looked at him and almost laughed at the absurdity of his request. He was propositioning her—actually propositioning her right here in front of everyone. And he wasn't a handsome man by any standard. His face was red-blotched, probably from too much drink, and there were huge bags under his eyes, his hair was white and totally unruly, and he was short—at least two inches shorter than she.

But a verve for life suffused his person, and a sense of humor crackled from him, pushing through the melancholy that itself held a strange appeal for her. She opened her mouth to decline the invitation but instead heard herself laughing and saying, "Sure'n you're a silver-tongued devil, Sean O'Leary. I don't know what girl could resist such charm. Let's go."

9

MARCH 21, 1948, ST. LOUIS

"H*ey, kids, what time is it?*"
"It's Howdy Doody time!" Alicia Canfield shouted back to the TV.

> "*It's Howdy Doody time*
> *It's Howdy Doody time*
> *Bob Smith and Howdy, too,*
> *Say howdy-doo to you. . .*"

"Alicia, will you please turn that down?" Morgan Canfield complained to his younger sister. "You're eleven years old, for crying out loud. Don't you think you're a little too old for that kid stuff?"

"You're thirteen. Don't you think you're too old for *Uncle Bob's Circle Twelve Ranch?*" Alicia shot back.

"That's different. Uncle Bob shows Western movies. Everybody likes Western movies. Even Dad and Uncle Willie like Westerns."

"Well, I don't like Westerns, but I do like *Howdy Doody.*"

At that moment Clarabelle the Clown got a pie right in the face, and all the kids in the "peanut gallery" laughed. So did Alicia.

And so did Morgan.

"You laughed!" Alicia said.

"No, I didn't," Morgan insisted, but another bit of slapstick occurred, and he couldn't help but laugh at it as well. "All right, maybe I did laugh a little," he admitted, as he flopped back on the couch to watch the program. "But that doesn't mean I *like* this kid stuff."

The two of them watched the rest of *Howdy Doody,* then sat through all of *Uncle Bob's Circle 12 Ranch,* which, Faith Canfield told her husband, John, when he came home that evening, just proved her point: "People will watch anything that's put on television."

John laughed. "Oh, I hardly think television is going to revolutionize society. After all, there aren't really that many television sets out there, and I doubt there ever will be. And not just because they're expensive, either. I mean, Pop doesn't own one, and it certainly isn't because he can't afford it. Besides, how many people do you think will be willing to just sit still all night, staring at that little picture?"

"Lots of people," Faith insisted.

"I'll believe it when I see it." John looked at his watch. "It's time for the news."

Faith laughed. "See, what did I tell you? Even *you* are getting addicted to it."

"Don't start on me, Faith. That's not the same thing and you know it. It's not like I'm watching the roller derby or wrestling. I'm watching the news."

"You could listen to the radio or read the newspaper."

"I *do* listen to the radio, and I read the paper," John countered. "I just like to be well rounded, that's all. I like conflicting points of view."

She snickered. "You read *The Chronicle,* you listen to KSTL radio, and you watch KSTL-TV. Those are all owned by the same company. How are you going to get conflicting points of view?"

"Maybe it isn't conflicting points as much as subtle nuances."

"Subtle nuances?" Faith scoffed. "John Canfield, you forget I am the daughter of a former United States senator. I've been around politicians all my life, and I've developed a very good ear for hogwash. If you want to watch television, watch television. You don't have to justify it to me—and you don't have to try to snow me, either."

Laughing sheepishly, John took a beer from the refrigerator, then went into the parlor and sat down on the couch to watch the news. Smiling back at him from the television screen was a man holding a cigarette who, in stentorian tones, began addressing the viewers.

"More people are smoking Camels than ever before. Like others, I tried different brands of cigarettes, and compared them for mildness, coolness, and flavor. Camels are the choice of experience. And no wonder. Camels are made from choice tobacco, properly aged and expertly blended."

By the magic of special effects, a large letter T was superimposed over the spokesman's mouth and throat.

"Let your T zone tell you why. T for taste, T for throat. That's your proving ground for any cigarette. See if Camels don't suit your T zone to a T."

The image of the smoker disappeared, replaced for just a moment by a package of Camel cigarettes. That picture then faded and was replaced by a newsman sitting behind a desk. On the wall behind him were several clocks, each set for the different time zones of Moscow, Paris, New York, Chicago, Los Angeles, and Hong Kong and each duly identified.

"Good evening. In Berlin tonight tensions increased sharply between the Western powers and Soviet Russia when the Soviet delegates walked out of the Control Council meeting.

"There are also reports that the Russians have moved more guards to the border that separates their sector of Berlin from the American sector. It is known that the Russians are very resentful of the steady flow of refugees who have been fleeing from their control. Several German newspapers have even reported that the Russians may go so far as to attempt to stop the flow of goods into West Berlin. West Berlin can only be reached by three corridors that cut right through the Russian zone. If that happens, the citizens of West Berlin could face food shortages so serious as to bring on a famine.

"These actions taken by Russia are believed to be the direct result of anger over the fact that the Western Allies are conducting meetings to which the Russians have not been invited. Unofficial sources, however, say that the real reason for the Russian dissatisfaction is the refusal of the Allies to form a central German government that would include the Communists."

The newsman's picture was replaced by newsreel film of presidential adviser Clark Clifford. Although it was a very animated picture, with Clifford smiling and pointing to reporters who were obviously asking questions, the only sound was the continuing narration of the studio newsman.

"Clark Clifford, President Truman's adviser, told reporters today that he is absolutely positive President Truman will be reelected this fall. This assurance comes despite the fact that Phil Murray. of the CIO and PAC boss Jack Kroll are said to be exploring ways to persuade Mr. Truman to withdraw his candidacy so that the Democrats can nominate a more 'suitable' candidate. Just whom the Democrats would then turn to is uncertain, though New York City's James A. Farley has been mentioned. Mr. Farley, while not responding to questions as to whether or not he would be a presidential candidate, did state emphatically that under no circumstances would he accept a vice-presidential bid."

The picture returned to the studio, with the newsman sitting before his array of clocks.

140

"This week, the Army and Navy released motion picture film of a rocket called the Aerobee, and we have these pictures for you."

The screen was filled with footage of a rocket being launched, spewing fire and trailing a long column of smoke. The newsman's voice continued over the pictorial footage.

"The Aerobee rose to an altitude of seventy-eight miles above the White Sands, New Mexico, proving grounds and reached a speed of three thousand miles per hour.

"Although this performance was not as good as the record one hundred fourteen miles altitude and thirty-five hundred miles per hour speed of the V-2 rockets built by Germany during the war, United States military officials were pleased with the Aerobee's performance because it marks a definite improvement over any previous American rocket.

"Germany's top World War Two scientist, Werner von Braun, is now working with American scientists on the series of rocket experiments."

That evening, as John lay in bed looking over a report to be discussed at a Canfield-Puritex board meeting the next morning, Faith sat at her dressing table, brushing her hair. A radio on the bedside table was playing softly. The song was "Nature Boy."

"John, do you think the President will be reelected?" she asked, watching her husband's reflection in the mirror.

"Yes," John answered without looking up from his report.

Faith put the brush down and turned to face him. "I'm serious," she said. "Do you honestly believe he'll be reelected, or is it just something you're saying because you had to spout the party line for so long?"

John closed the report folder and laid it aside, then studied her face. "Are you really concerned?" he asked after a moment.

"Yes."

"I never knew you were that big a Truman supporter."

"I wasn't," Faith admitted. "I mean, I never could get over the impression that on the day he was sworn in as President, he still had straw in his hair and cow shit on his shoes. And I can't stand that flat, almost whiney twang of his. I'm from Missouri, too, and I don't talk like that. Neither do your parents or you or Willie or anyone else I know."

John laughed. "You need to come down to the mill and spend some time around the people who work the processing machines or load the trucks and trains. Or visit one of our farms down around Sikeston. I guarantee you, Faith, there are a lot more Missourians who sound like the President than there are Missourians who sound like us."

She smiled. "Yes, well, despite how he looks—and sounds—I wouldn't like to see him leave office prematurely. The truth is, I really believe the country needs him."

"I agree with you. And I think he *will* be reelected. The Democrats certainly have no one else to turn to. And if Tom Dewey is the best the Republicans can come up with, then they're having problems of their own."

"The Republicans may run Harold Stassen. He's got quite a following," Faith suggested.

"Stassen has a lot of popular support right now, that's true, but Dewey controls the party machinery, and you've been around politics long enough to know that that's who nominates." John grinned. "What the Republicans don't seem to realize yet is that by choosing Dewey, they'll only be selecting a candidate and not inaugurating a president. Dewey's so certain that Truman's going to lose, he doesn't think *he* has to win. He thinks all he has to do is wait for his coronation. And while he's busy appointing his dream cabinet and counting votes that haven't been cast, Harry S Truman will be out pressing the flesh. You have heard Truman's theory on how to win any election, haven't you?"

"I can't say that I have."

John chuckled. "It's a very simple theory, but given how far it's taken Truman, I'd have to say it's effective. 'Truman's law of getting elected' is: 'Two men are campaigning against each other. Each of them buys a monkey, makes a rubber mask of his own face, then puts that mask on his monkey. They train their monkeys to shake hands, then turn them loose on the electorate. The candidate whose monkey shakes the most hands will get elected.'"

"That's awful," Faith said, laughing.

"It's also very practical, and in the end it will get the President reelected."

"John, do you ever miss Washington?"

"Yes, a little," John admitted. "I miss the immediacy of things. This business with the Russians in Germany, for example. I can follow it on the news like everyone else, but if we were still in Washington, I'd know *exactly* what was going on—and before it became public knowledge. And what's more, I'd have some hand in formulating the policy we'd follow to counteract it."

"Yes, well, that part of Washington I *don't* miss," Faith said. "Your staff meetings until two or three in the morning. . . your nervous stomach when things weren't going right. . . the way we would have to sit on things when friends of ours were getting pilloried by the press, and we knew the truth but couldn't speak about it for national security reasons. . ."

She turned back to the mirror to brush her hair again. "Ah," she continued, "but the social life, the intimate gatherings with witty conversations and interesting guests. . . writers, musicians, artists, actors and actresses"—she laughed—"the ones who aren't Communists, I mean. And, of course, senators and congressmen, Republicans and Democrats who would lambaste each other on the floor of the House or Senate and in the press but would sit on

142

the same sofa, drinking together and exchanging jokes, the best of friends when they were out of the spotlight. And I miss the embassy balls, too, with all the elegant gowns and magnificent jewelry, and the foreign dignitaries with colorful ribbons and blazes of decorations on their formal attire. . . There is nothing in St. Louis to compare with all that."

"Faith, you aren't suggesting that we go back, are you?"

"Oh, no," she said quickly. "No, that wouldn't be practical. Besides, you're needed here. Your father has all but retired, and Willie is so tied up with the airline that he hardly ever attends board meetings. Someone has to run the company." She turned around again to face John directly. Smiling broadly, she said candidly, "I've grown accustomed to a certain life-style, and I certainly wouldn't want to see it jeopardized by a failing company." She nodded toward the folder he had been studying. "So, perhaps you'd better get back to work." She turned back to the mirror.

John got out of bed and walked over behind her. He slipped his arms around her and cupped her breasts in his hands, letting his fingers caress her nipples through the silk of her nightgown. They grew instantly hard under his touch.

"John, what are you doing?" she asked, her voice dropping.

"What does it look like?" John replied. He kissed her neck. "Better yet, what does it *feel* like?"

Faith put her hand on his and pulled it to her lips to kiss. "It feels good. But I thought you had work to do."

"You know what they say: All work and no play makes John a dull boy. And weren't you just complaining about how dull things are in St. Louis?"

"It's a little early, isn't it? The kids aren't even asleep."

"Why do you think they put locks on bedroom doors?"

Faith stood up and turned toward him, leaning into him as she put her arms around his neck. "My," she said. "You think of everything, don't you?"

SIKESTON, MISSOURI

Bobby Parker stood shivering in the early morning darkness as he watched his father back the red REO tractor under the silver trailer. The ten-year-old was shivering as much from excitement as from the cold, for his dad was taking him to St. Louis to pick up a load of cereal products from Canfield-Puritex for the Foster and Matthews Grocer Warehouse Company.

When Richard Edward Parker had come back from Memphis with a load of vinegar the day before, he had disconnected the cab and left the trailer at the warehouse dock to be unloaded. Now he was reconnecting the empty trailer for the trip to St. Louis.

The big, flat, heavily greased fifth wheel on the back of the tractor slid under the trailer until the two units were rejoined. Richard Edward got out of the tractor and began attaching the air hoses and electric lines.

"Bobby, you want to start cranking up the landing dolly?" Richard Edward asked, pointing to the small crank that would raise the wheels that had been supporting the front of the trailer while it was disconnected.

"Sure, Dad," Bobby answered, eager to be of some help, and he started turning the crank importantly. It was hard to turn, and the handle was cold against his hands, but he didn't complain. He had it only half raised by the time his father had finished making all the other connections, so Richard Edward came over to complete the job.

"I could've done it," Bobby said.

"I know, son, but we need to get going. Canfield-Puritex closes its loading docks at noon on Saturday. We don't want to be late."

"Is there anything else I can do?"

"You could get the chocks out," Richard Edward suggested, and Bobby ran back and pulled out the bricks that kept the rear wheels from moving.

Five minutes later they were pulling out of Sikeston, heading north on Highway 61. The heater had warmed the inside of the truck enough for Bobby to take off his coat, and he wadded it up and put it between his head and the door window. The drone of the truck engine was soothing and the heat was relaxing. Bobby closed his eyes. . . just for a moment.

St. Louis was exciting. There were trucks and cars and buses and trolley cars everywhere Bobby looked. He particularly liked the trolleys with their clanging bells, whining motors, and sparks flying from the overhead conductors. The buildings were exciting, too. They were high —many of them even higher than the Scott Country Grain elevators. When Bobby was younger, he had really believed that the grain elevators must be the tallest structures in the world.

He wanted to point out all the exciting things to his dad, but Richard Edward was working hard to move the truck through the heavy traffic, shifting up and down through the gears, braking sharply several times to avoid cars weaving in and out of the traffic without regard for how much extra work their impatience might be causing for all the truck drivers they cut off.

It wasn't long before Bobby saw a huge redbrick building with several smokestacks looming ahead. Painted on one end of the building was a giant square of alternating blue and white lines—the logo printed on every box of Corn Toasties that Bobby had ever eaten.

They turned off the road and drove up to a gate, where they were stopped by a man wearing a uniform and badge.

"Is he a policeman?" Bobby asked.

Richard Edward chuckled. "No, he's a plant guard," he explained. "He's a lot tougher than a policeman."

"Really? But he's so old."

"Haven't you ever heard that old chickens are the toughest chickens?"

Bobby studied the plant guard closely as the man took some papers from Richard Edward, glanced at them, then wrote something down on a clipboard.

The guard handed a blue card with a white number through the open window to Bobby.

"Here you go, young man," the guard said. "Put this up in the windshield on your side."

Bobby put the number in the windshield, making certain it could be seen by anyone who looked.

"Wow! You were right! He *is* tough! Did you see his eyes?" Bobby asked as Richard Edward put the truck in gear and drove away from the gate.

"His eyes? No, what about them?"

"They were steely."

Richard Edward looked over at his son, his mouth quirking. "Steely? What do you mean?"

"I'm not real sure," Bobby said. "I think it means this." He squinted tightly. "That's the way the guard's eyes were." He stared at his father, working hard to make his eyes look steely. "I read it in a story," Bobby explained. "Someone who's tough has steely eyes."

Richard Edward squinted his eyes. "How's this?" he asked. "Are *my* eyes steely?"

Bobby laughed. "It doesn't work like that. Someone who really has steely eyes keeps them that way all the time."

"Wow. That must be hard to do."

"I know. That's why anyone who can do it is really tough. Like the plant guard."

"Well, then we'd better not get on his bad side."

"Uh-uh," Bobby agreed.

He had always thought that Foster and Matthews was large, with its loading dock and the half-dozen or so trucks and trailers always parked in the lot. But as he looked at the lot of this place, he figured that ten or twenty companies the size of Foster and Matthews, including the lot and all the buildings, could be put here, and there'd still be room left over. He could see at least six loading docks, and it was possible there were more. He counted fifteen trucks backed up to one of the loading docks; he didn't even try the others. In addition, several trucks were parked out in the lot that weren't being loaded or unloaded.

There was an entire network of railroad tracks, too, and on several of them sat long strings of boxcars, all bearing the Canfield-Puritex logo.

"There's where we're going," Richard Edward said, pointing to a narrow gap between a couple of big rigs at one of the docks.

"Wow! Can you really back this thing in there?" Bobby asked.

"Sure. Watch this."

Richard Edward wheeled his truck around, shifted gears, then opened his door and leaned out as he started backing up. Bobby watched with fascination and pride as his father slipped the big trailer into the skinny space between two other large trucks. He put on the brakes with a squish of air pressure, set them, then killed the engine.

"Dad, can I walk around and have a look?"

"Sure. Watch out for trucks and trains, though, and don't get in anyone's way."

"I'll be careful," Bobby promised.

The boy began exploring, looking into open boxcars, walking between trucks, crawling through empty crates, and climbing onto the top of a large loading chute. That afforded him a great view of the entire complex, and he slowly pivoted around, getting a panoramic view of the plant and all its facilities. One building that caught his attention was a much smaller, newer one, detached from all the rest. Whereas the other buildings were surrounded by concrete and blacktop, this one had a lawn and shrubbery. A white sign on the front of the building read:

CANFIELD-PURITEX CORPORATION, ST. LOUIS
Executive Offices

The blinds were open, and from Bobby's vantage point he could look through all the windows of the office building. One window in the back gave him a glimpse of several men sitting around a long table. At first Bobby thought they might be eating; then he realized they were just talking. He was glad he wasn't in there. That had to be awfully boring.

One of the men got up and left the room, and Bobby giggled. The man was probably bored, too.

Bobby had just started to climb down off the loading chute when the man he had seen leave the room suddenly reappeared in a window several down from the meeting room. The man was standing by himself, holding his hand to his chest. He turned, as if he were going to go back to the room with the others, but after only a few steps he fell.

"Hey!" Bobby shouted. "Hey, mister, what's wrong?"

Bobby looked back at the room where everyone else was still sitting around the long table, and he realized that none of them knew about the man who had just fallen. He jumped down from the loading chute and ran as fast as he could back to his father's truck.

"Dad! Dad! He fell! I just saw him fall!" Bobby shouted.

Insurance regulations had it that the stevedores at Canfield-Puritex could only bring the product as far as the dock. Richard Edward was responsible for loading it into his truck, and that was what he was doing when Bobby climbed up onto the dock, then ran back into the trailer, which was already one-third full.

"He fell!" Bobby shouted, pointing excitedly.

Richard Edward set down a large box and looked at his son. "Who fell?"

"I don't know. A man. He's over there, in that building. He did this." Bobby put his hand over his chest and demonstrated.

Richard Edward walked to the back of the trailer and looked in the direction Bobby was pointing.

"He's in there, behind that window," Bobby explained. "Maybe you better call the doctor, Dad. Those other people don't know about it."

"Those are the executive offices," Richard Edward said. "Did you say nobody else saw him?"

"No. He was in the same room, sitting around the table with the others, but he got up and went into another room. Then he fell."

Richard Edward jumped down from the back of the truck and started running toward the executive offices. Bobby followed him.

"Hey!" one of the stevedores shouted, having just brought another two-wheeler load out onto the loading dock. "Where you goin'?"

Richard Edward didn't take the time to answer. Hurrying across the compound, he reached the executive building, pushed through the front door, ran through the reception area, and started down the corridor.

"Wait a minute!" the receptionist shouted. "Who are you? What's going on here?"

"Get an ambulance!" Richard Edward shouted back over his shoulder. "Hurry! You've got someone hurt in here!"

"What?" the receptionist answered, too shocked to react.

As Richard Edward ran down the corridor, he banged open the doors and looked into all the offices. By now the men attending the board meeting were drawn out into the hall to locate the source of the commotion.

"Who are you?" one of them shouted in anger and alarm.

"Parker. I'm a driver," Richard Edward said. With no further explanation as to what he was doing, he pushed open another door. "Here he is, in here! Get an ambulance! Hurry!"

One of the men who had just come into the hall looked into the room. "Pop!" he screamed, when he saw the man lying on the floor. "Oh, my God!"

147

Richard Edward knelt beside the prostrate man and put his hand to the side of his neck. "He's still alive," he said.

"I'm John Canfield. This is my father. How did you know about this?"

"My boy just happened to be looking through the windows and saw him come in here, grab his chest, and fall," Richard Edward explained.

The elder Canfield moaned.

"Get some water," John ordered, and one of the men hurried out to comply.

Bob Canfield started to get up, but Richard Edward put his hand gently on his shoulder.

"Mr. Canfield, maybe you'd better just lie there until the ambulance comes," he said. "Bobby, get that pillow off the sofa and bring it over here."

Bobby brought the pillow over and handed it to his father, who then placed it under Bob's head.

"Thanks," Bob murmured. Someone brought over a glass of water, and Richard Edward took it and held it to the tycoon's lips.

"How do you feel, Pop?" John asked anxiously.

Bob Canfield sipped the water, then indicated he'd had enough. Looking up at all the people standing around, looking down at him, he said calmly, "Well, as a matter of fact, I feel silly as hell. Would someone please tell me what happened? This is damn embarrassing." John explained how the boy had seen him through the window and spread the alarm.

"I'm very thankful to you and your son, sir," Bob said to Richard Edward. "Who are you? What's your name?"

The trucker smiled. "As a matter of fact, you know me, Mr. Canfield. Or at least you knew my pa. He used to work for you."

"I don't mean to sound rude, but I've got over thirty thousand people working for me," Bob said. "It's pretty hard to remember all of them."

"My pa didn't work for you up here. He used to manage your farm for you, down in Sikeston."

Bob got a startled look on his face, and he tried to rise again, but John gently pushed him back down, instructing, "No, Pop, stay there."

"Are you talking about L.E. Parker?" Bob asked.

"Yes, sir, that was my pa."

"Then you must be Richard Edward."

Richard Edward smiled. "Yes, sir, I am. I'm flattered that you remember me."

"Remember you? Why, man, there's no way I could ever forget you." Bob chuckled. "John, did I ever tell you about the baby your Uncle Billy delivered on the kitchen floor?"

John looked at Richard Edward.

"That's me, all right," Richard Edward said, grinning. "At least, that's what my sister and my mom always told me. Of course, I don't remember anything about it."

"It's a pleasure to meet you, Mr. Parker," John said, extending his hand. "I've heard that story several times, but I never was quite sure whether or not I should believe it."

"So it was your boy who saw me, huh?" Bob asked.

"Yes, sir."

"Well, get him over here. I'd like to meet that young gentleman and thank him personally."

Bobby had been standing back out of the way, partly out of shyness and partly because he was afraid the man on the floor was going to die. He had never seen anyone die before, and he didn't want to see it now.

"Come here, Bobby," Richard Edward said.

Hesitantly, the boy started forward.

A siren sounded faintly, but it was clearly a long way off.

"So Bobby is your name?"

"Yes, sir."

Bob smiled. "What a coincidence. That's my name, too. Of course, it's been a long time since anyone called me Bobby. Now everyone just calls me"—Bob paused, then smiled—"*Mister* Canfield."

"That's because you're old," Bobby said.

"Old?" Bob laughed. "Well, I guess I am getting old at that," he agreed. "It's funny, you never think of yourself as old. You just go along living your life one day at a time, and then one day you wake up an old man, just like you, remember your grandpa. I don't guess you remember your grandpa, do you, Bobby?"

"I know my grandpa that lives in Jackson, Mississippi," Bobby said. "But my other grandpa died before I was born."

The siren was very close now.

"Well, I want to tell you something so that you will always remember. I have known presidents, kings, baseball players, and movie stars. Heck, I even knew J.P. Morgan, who was perhaps the richest man in the world. But your grandfather, L.E. Parker, didn't have to take a back seat to any of them. He was one of the finest men I have ever known. Will you remember that, Bobby?"

"Yes, sir," Bobby said, suddenly feeling proud of the grandfather he had never met. . . and a little sad that he had never met him. "I'll remember that."

"Make way! Make way!" a man's voice shouted, and everyone moved to one side as two white-clad men rushed into the room, carrying a folded-up stretcher.

"You won't need that stretcher," Bob complained. "I can walk."

"It would be better if you'd let us carry you, sir," one of the ambulance drivers said.

"Do what they say, Pop," John insisted.

"Oh, all right," Bob agreed with an exaggerated sigh. "Let's do it and be done with it."

149

He was quickly loaded onto the stretcher. The ambulance workers started to leave, carrying their patient between them, when Bob called out, "Wait a minute!"

The stretcher bearers set him down.

"Come here, Bobby. I have something for you," Bob said.

Glancing up at his father for reassurance, Bobby walked over to the stretcher to see what Mr. Canfield wanted. He handed Bobby a bill.

"Here," the businessman said, a bit gruffly. "This is for you."

"This. . . this is a one-hundred-dollar bill!" Bobby gasped. He had never seen a bill that large, much less ever held one.

"Go buy yourself some bubble gum."

"Bubble gum only costs a penny," Bobby said.

Bob laughed, then coughed and wheezed. "Well, then you can buy ten thousand pieces, can't you?"

Bobby shook his head. "No, sir. If it's all the same to you, I'd rather keep the money."

Bob laughed again. "Smart lad," he called back as they carried him out.

"Thanks, Mr. Canfield," Bobby called back.

Richard Edward reached down to pat his son's shoulder.

"He won't die, will he, Dad?"

"I don't know, Bobby. I hope not."

"I hope not too."

JUNE

The old auditorium in Spengeman Hall was now far too small to accommodate the student body of Jefferson University, so it was used only for the most special occasions. As far as Bob Canfield was concerned, however, with its cherrywood paneling and the wine-colored drapes and hangings, it was still one of the most beautiful places on the entire campus. Also, it had deeply cushioned chairs, unlike the hard wooden ones in the new, much larger theater that was used for most of the school's assemblies.

The auditorium was being used that day to unveil a plaque and establish a chair in honor of David Gelbman. Bob found the honor to his friend particularly satisfying, and he thought it very fitting that the older auditorium was the setting since it had been the one in use during David's tenure at Jefferson. Because Bob was a special guest for the unveiling, he had a seat in the front row.

Connie Canfield, sitting beside him, reached over to adjust the shawl she had draped around his shoulders. "Now, keep this around you," she scolded. "You don't want to get a chill."

150

"For crying out loud, woman, I had a heart attack, not pneumonia," Bob protested.

"Yes, and you certainly don't want to get pneumonia on top of that," Connie said, unperturbed by his grumbling.

Bob took his wife's hand and squeezed it. He continued holding it while they waited for the proceedings to begin.

"I'm glad they're doing this for David," he said. "I just wish there was someone here for him."

"There is, dear," Connie said. "We are here. We remember him. . . and love him."

"That's true, isn't it?" Bob said. "It's been, what? Forty-four years? It sure doesn't seem that long since David and Terry and J.P. and I used to sit out there on the quad by the Spengeman statue, watching all the girls get off the train from Stephens."

"Watching *all* the girls?" Connie said in mock dismay. "What do you mean, watching *all* the girls? You never told me that. You always told me you were there to wait for *me*."

Bob chuckled. "Well, I *was* waiting for you. But you weren't the only girl to come to our campus from Stephens. And I had to look at all of them, didn't I, to make certain I got the right one?"

"Of course you did," Connie said, smiling.

"And now the train from St. Charles doesn't even stop here anymore," Bob said, almost wistfully. "Even the little commuter station is gone. There've been so many changes on the campus since then that I don't think David or Terry or J.P. would even recognize it now."

"They would recognize Statue Circle," Connie said. "That hasn't changed."

"No, I guess not," Bob agreed.

"Oh, here's Dr. Williams," Connie said. "We must be about to start."

There was a polite smattering of applause as university president Dr. Stacey Williams, wearing his academic robes, stepped up to the podium.

"Thank you," Williams began. "As a former member of the Quad Quad, I must say that today is particularly meaningful for me. Jefferson University, like most colleges and universities, is blessed with an excellent representation of fraternities and sororities. We also have many wonderful professional and honor organizations with national affiliation. But the most prestigious organization to which any young man attending Jefferson can belong is unique to our university. I am talking about the Quad Quad.

"As probably most of you know, the Quad Quad is made up of seniors who have demonstrated superior academic and athletic achievement, social deportment, and outstanding citizenship. Each year four of our best and brightest young men are selected for this distinction.

"The Perkins School of Journalism is named for Terry Perkins, one of the original Quad Quad. The J.P. Winthrop Scholarship Award for Fine Arts was established in honor of J.P. Winthrop, another of the original Quad Quad.

"And today we are pleased to announce the establishment of the David Gelbman Chair in the School of Business, in honor of David Gelbman, a third member of that original Quad Quad.

"It is our misfortune that these three fine men are all deceased, each taken from us before their time by tragic events. Terry Perkins succumbed to yellow fever while on a journalistic assignment in Panama during the building of the canal. J.P. Winthrop lost his life on board the *Titanic*, and David Gelbman died several years ago in a Nazi concentration camp.

"However, we are fortunate to have with us today the surviving member of that first Quad Quad, Mr. Robert Canfield."

There was another round of polite applause.

"Mr. Canfield, would you now do us the honor of unveiling the plaque commemorating David Gelbman?"

Bob got up from his seat and climbed onto the stage to a cloth-covered stand. After the unveiling the bronze plaque would be mounted on a special marble pedestal in the quad, taking its place alongside the other two bronze plaques honoring Terry Perkins and J.P. Winthrop. There was room on the pedestal for a fourth plaque, the position reserved for Bob, but as the other three had been posthumous mountings, Bob joked that he wasn't all that anxious to see his plaque go up.

He pulled on a cord and the cover fell away, revealing the plaque:

DAVID GELBMAN, CLASS OF 1904
A member of the first Quad Quad.
In respect and loving memory.

There was more applause as Bob returned to his chair and sat down.

"And now, ladies and gentlemen, if I may," Dr. Williams continued, "I would like to introduce Mr. Mike Nolan, a junior in the class of' 49 who has been selected to be a member of the Quad Quad next year. Mr. Nolan."

A handsome young man stepped up to the podium and smiled nervously at the audience. Although Bob didn't know him personally, he certainly knew of him, for Mike Nolan was the quarterback for the Jefferson University football team. There were some who believed Jefferson U. might win the conference title next year. That belief was based solely on Mike Nolan's ability.

"I have to be honest with you. . . I'm more nervous now than I am when I'm facing Ohio State's defensive line," Mike started.

The audience laughed appreciatively.

"It was a great privilege to be selected to the Quad Quad for next year," Mike said. "And it was an even greater privilege when I was asked if I would introduce our next speaker.

"Ladies and gentlemen, counting the four of us who have been selected to serve next year, one hundred and eighty men have been honored by membership in the Quad Quad. To read through a roll call of Quad Quad alumni is to read a *Who's Who* of twentieth-century American achievement. Our own Dr. W.W. Wilkerson, chairman of the Department of Physics and one of the developers of the atomic bomb, was a member of the Quad Quad, as was John Canfield, adviser to Presidents Roosevelt and Truman and current chairman of the board of the Canfield-Puritex Corporation. In its number the Quad Quad counts eminent physicians, noted philosophers, Pulitzer Prize winners, and university presidents, including our own Dr. Stacey Williams. In the field of athletics the Quad Quad produced six All-American athletes and four gold medal winners in the Olympic Games.

"Last year the executive committee of the Quad Quad Past and Present Association created the 'Compass Rose' award. The compass rose was selected because its four arms pointing to the four directions of the globe symbolize the four members of the Quad Quad spreading out to the four corners of the world.

"It was decided by the QQPPA executive committee to make an annual award of the Compass Rose to the American man or woman who best symbolizes the motto of the Quad Quad: 'Learn to grow. Grow to serve.' You may be interested to know that the nominees for this very first award included, but were not limited to: Secretary of State George C. Marshall, T.S. Eliot, Eleanor Roosevelt, and General Dwight D. Eisenhower. Against such stiff competition the winner must be special, indeed.

"And now, here to announce the name of the winner, is a Fellow in the American Academy of Science, a recipient of the Goodpasture Award for physics, a member of the President's Council on the Ethical Use of Nuclear Energy, dean of the School of Science, and a past member of the Quad Quad. Ladies and gentlemen, I give you our own Dr. W.W. Wilkerson."

The hearty applause for Dub Wilkerson was genuine. As Dean of the School of Science and head of the Jefferson University Physics Department, he was one of the university's stars. His serving on Jefferson's faculty had attracted bright young students from all over the country.

Dub had recently published a paper on "The Wilkerson Effect," a study dealing with the low-energy escape of electrons from a nucleus. Bob, through his association with the university, was aware that the paper had created a stir in the scientific world, but he didn't know enough about physics to understand what it was about.

"Thank you, Mr. Nolan," Dub Wilkerson said as he took his position behind the podium. "Ladies and gentlemen, too many times an award such as this one is given posthumously or in absentia. It is therefore a particular pleasure not only to announce the winner, but to be able to make the actual presentation, because our recipient—who incidentally received eighty-six percent of the total vote cast—is here with us today. It is my very great pleasure to announce that the Compass Rose is awarded to Mr. Robert Canfield."

The audience exploded in applause; then, when one of the members of the faculty stood, everyone did likewise for a standing ovation. Bob was shocked by the announcement. He had no idea he was going to be so honored, and he was a bit embarrassed by the unexpected praise. He glanced at Connie. It was clear that she had known about it and had been charged with making certain Bob attended the ceremony. She was indisputably thrilled as she held his hand, and she beamed proudly while the applause continued.

Dub Wilkerson waited patiently until the applause died down and the audience took their seats again. Then he smiled and continued his speech.

"Most of the time when awards like this are given, it is the speaker's responsibility to heighten the mystery by extolling the virtues of the recipient without revealing his name. But that wouldn't have worked in this case, because as soon as I started telling you about the man, you would have recognized him immediately. But that doesn't mean that his accolades won't be sung, because I intend to do just that.

"When Bob Canfield graduated in 1904 from what was then Jefferson College, he went back to the family home in southeast Missouri. Once the nation's leading producer of hardwood lumber, the region had fallen on hard times. Much of Missouri's Bootheel was swampland then, and the trees, once cut, couldn't be reharvested.

"Fifty years of timbering had left a large, ugly scar across the land. From the foothills of Benton to the state line in Arkansas, along what's called the upper Mississippi Delta, hundreds of thousands of acres of land lay under stagnant, mosquito-infested water, studded with millions of decaying tree stumps. Those without vision could see only the swamp. But Bob Canfield looked through the swamp water and saw the rich, black dirt that would make excellent farmland. . . if the swamps could only be drained.

"That was a big 'if,' ladies and gentlemen. But in a project that nearly equaled the Panama Canal in scope, Bob Canfield, alone and without any government assistance, began reclaiming the swamp. Others, inspired by his example, began to do the same thing, and today, the ten counties of Missouri's Bootheel would, if they were a state, be one of the top row-crop-producing states in America. Sikeston, Missouri, Bob Canfield's hometown, was so economically depressed that it was nearly deserted in 1904. Today, in 1948, Sikeston, Missouri, is the wealthiest town per capita in the United States.

"But Bob Canfield didn't stop there. He came to St. Louis to work his economic miracle in this city, buying a bankrupt animal-feed processing company and building it into Canfield-Puritex, the second largest corporation of its kind in America.

"Then, after making a significant impact upon not only Missouri's economy, but the economy of all of heartland America, Mr. Canfield turned his efforts to helping others by creating the Canfield Foundation. I could go through a list of hospitals, orphanages, and schools that owe their very survival to his eleemosynary activities, but it would take the rest of the time I have allotted to me just to name them all. I will, however, give you one example of a charity in which all of us have a vital interest—Jefferson University.

"Since Jefferson University was saved in 1907, largely through the efforts of Mr. Canfield, the Canfield Foundation has given our university the library—named after his late brother—the women's dormitory, and an academic hall. Most people are aware of this. What many do not know is that in addition to the aforementioned buildings, the Canfield Foundation has given the university more than one hundred million dollars."

There were gasps of surprise and admiration. Dub Wilkerson waited until the audience had finishing expressing itself and then continued.

"It is a happy coincidence that the first winner of the Compass Rose is also a former member of the Quad Quad. . . and not just a member, but one of its founders. Of course, his association with the Quad Quad was not sufficient to garner him the award; he had to earn that on his own. For when the QQPPA executive committee met to consider the first Compass Rose award, they decided that it should go to a person who will set the highest standard for others to follow. Bob Canfield, builder of empires, savior of cherished institutions, adviser to presidents, and guardian of twentieth-century America, has established a standard that some in the future may equal. . . but none will surpass. Ladies and gentlemen, Mr. Robert Canfield!"

Again, there was thunderous applause, and the university president signaled for Bob to approach the podium.

"Speech, speech!" someone shouted, and the call was taken up by others.

Hesitantly, Bob got up, waved once to the audience, which was again on its feet, then climbed the short set of stairs up to the stage. He walked up to the podium, where he was given the award, a crystal compass rose mounted on a brass stand. He shook Dub Wilkerson's hand, then President Williams's hand, then young Mike Nolan's hand. Finally he turned to face the microphone, and when he did, everyone sat down. After a few moments the shuffling and murmuring subsided, and there was absolute silence. Bob then spoke.

"There have been times over the past several years when I observed the Quad Quad and wondered how the small, casual group that Terry Perkins, J.P. Winthrop, David Gelbman, and I had started out of simple friendship ever developed into an organization of such prestige," he began. "I must be perfectly honest with you and say that none of us had held such lofty goals.

"Once, a number of years ago, I almost went to the university president and said, 'This is wrong. This is not what we had in mind at all!' But, as the roll call of former Quad Quad members grew, and as fine young men strived to be equal to the honor that had been bestowed upon them, I reconsidered my opinion.

"Friendship, stewardship, a desire to help others: Are these not honorable goals? I am being credited with founding the Quad Quad, but that isn't quite true. The Quad Quad developed of its own volition, adhering to the principles so wonderfully espoused in the motto adopted several years after it became an official institution. 'Learn to grow. Grow to serve.' If Terry, J.P., or David were here today, I believe they would be extremely proud of what our little comradely group has become. I know I am. Thank you very much."

10

MAY 14, 1948, A SETTLEMENT IN
ISRAEL

The village had not been authorized by the British and therefore had never appeared on any of their maps of Palestine. But today, on the first day of independence in the new nation of Israel, a sign was erected at the edge of the little settlement, identifying it as Hodiah. In Hebrew this meant "splendor of God."

Moshe Meir lived in a small house on the eastern edge of Hodiah, nearest the source of trouble if the Arabs decided to attack the settlement. Though at that very moment a celebration was going on in the Hodiah community center, Moshe Meir was at home, sitting at a table in his dining room, studying the numbers written on a small tablet.

Moshe wasn't avoiding the revelry because he was antisocial. He had been to several such events already, because the Jews had been celebrating their deliverance all day long. Moshe knew, however, that the Arabs were saying: "Let the Jews celebrate today. Tomorrow they will be dead." He knew also that it was not an idle threat.

So the others could celebrate; Moshe had to prepare.

From the kitchen he could hear Miriam shifting pots and pans around as she prepared their dinner. He could also smell the food cooking, and it made him hungry.

"Is dinner nearly ready?" he called. "I'm starving to death."

"Oh, and are you a little child that you are getting so anxious.?" Miriam asked, coming to the door to razz him. "Can't you wait for your dinner?"

"No. Not if you're going to stir up such delicious smells. It's cruel to make me wait so long for my meal. Besides, soon it will be the Sabbath; you'd better be finished before then."

Miriam walked over to his chair and reached down to put her arms around him.

"So," she said, "we have been married only two weeks, and already you're my boss?"

"I have *always* been your boss," Moshe laughed. "I am a captain, you are a lieutenant. That's the way it is."

"That was in the Irgun. We are a nation now. The Irgun is no more."

"But the Haganah is. The Haganah is to be the new army of Israel, incorporating the Irgun into its ranks."

Miriam pouted. "I don't want to be incorporated into their ranks. And I don't want to fight anymore. I want only to live in this village, be your wife, and raise your children."

"The time will come when we can do that," Moshe promised.

"I am thirty-six years old, Moshe. I am not a blushing young bride. We cannot put off having children much longer. Besides, I want to be young enough to enjoy our grandchildren."

Moshe chuckled. "You are talking about our grandchildren when we don't even have children."

"*Someone* should think about these things."

"You're right, and I, too, look forward to the day when there will be children—and grandchildren—to bounce on my knee. But for now, my love, we must be prepared to hold on to what is ours."

"I know," Miriam said with a sigh. "And we will—all of us—do what we must do." Suddenly her pensive mood changed, and she laughed. "But until then, what I must do is feed my husband who complains like a child and growls like a bear when he is"—she held her thumb and index finger slightly apart—"just a little hungry." She kissed him and started back to the kitchen.

Smiling to himself, Moshe returned to the figures he had been studying. Hodiah was the nearest to Jerusalem of all the settlements in Israel, and Miriam's cousin, Simon Blumberg, had asked Moshe to be ready to lead a rescue force into Jerusalem if one were needed.

"But I could raise fewer than a hundred men," Moshe had replied. "We have a sizable force in Jerusalem now. What good would another hundred do?"

"It's not new Jerusalem I am worried about," Simon had explained. "You're right, we do have many Jews there, and I don't think the Arabs can run us out. But inside the walls of the Old City our numbers are very small, and I fear for them. The defenders of new Jerusalem will have their own hands full so they won't be able to send any assistance. If our people in the Old City are to get any help at all, it must come from outside Jerusalem. It must come from you."

"I will do what I can," Moshe had promised.

Simon had nodded, satisfied. "If you do what you can, that will be enough."

Though he may have questioned how effective his efforts would be, Moshe never questioned following Simon's orders. In fact, if Simon had asked Moshe to lead a rescue force all the way to Damascus, he would have done that, too. Simon Blumberg was an inspiration, not only to Moshe Meir, but to everyone who knew him.

Simon had lost a leg during World War I, but that hadn't kept him from escaping the Nazis and taking Miriam with him. It hadn't kept him from fighting for Israel's independence. And it didn't stand in the way of his being one of the first men in Israel to be appointed to the rank of general in the new army.

Realistically, however, Moshe knew that it would take more than inspiration to mount an effective rescue operation. It would take numbers, and no matter how he worked with them, the numbers simply weren't there.

There were 1,611 Jews in Hodiah and more than 12,000 Arabs between Hodiah and Jerusalem. Of the 1,611 Jews, fewer than 200 could be counted on to bear arms—which hardly mattered since there were weapons enough for only 93. The numbers were not pleasant to contemplate.

The imbalance Moshe was facing in his immediate area was magnified on the national scale. There were just over a half million Jews in what had been Palestine and twice that number of Arabs. In addition to the Palestinian Arabs, another thirty-six million Arabs were living in the countries that surrounded the new state.

Of course, there being nearly a half million Jews in Israel didn't mean there were a half million people who could bear arms. Some were too old and some were too young. Some were physically unable to fight.

And then there were the ultraorthodox Hasidim.

Though not the only sect of ultraorthodox, the Hasidim were one example of the diversity with which the new nation had to contend. They lived in the district of Jerusalem known as Mea Shearim, a settlement built like a fortress with its windows facing inward, as if shutting out the rest of the world. The inhabitants retained the dress, customs, and speech of the seventeenth century and were theologically opposed to what they considered the blasphemy of an independent state of Israel. But such people were the problems of the leaders of the new nation. Moshe didn't waste much time worrying about them. He had problems of his own.

MAY 15, INSIDE THE WALLED CITY OF OLD JERUSALEM

To Anna Gelbman, as to most Jews, the Old City was the heart and soul of Jerusalem. Within its one square mile area twenty-five thousand people lived in four distinct religious zones. The Old City was a bewildering assortment of stone buildings built, rebuilt, and maintained down through the centuries. It was laced with intricate alleys and footpaths that had known the commerce of millennia.

Shops and stalls lined the narrow streets; handcarts and donkeys competed for the right-of-way with pedestrians. The loudest traffic sounds were the clip-clop of donkeys' hooves and the squeaking of cart wheels.

As the religious center for three of the world's great religions, the city stirred the souls of half the people on earth. For the Jews it was the City of David, where God was first revealed as a personal God who commanded the obedience of all His people. For Christians it was the scene of the Passion of Christ, and the very street down which He carried His cross was traversed and revered by the faithful. For Muslims it was the site of the Rock of Jerusalem, where Abraham prepared the sacrifice of Isaac and from which Muhammad was lifted by Gabriel to heaven.

Of the three religions, Islam was the most culturally invasive, for five times a day the muezzin called its followers to prayer. The muezzin sang their calls from minarets —mosque towers—and they had become so much a part of daily life that even the Jews and Christians were comforted by their timelessness.

In the new Jerusalem the muezzin had their calls augmented by loudspeakers, but not so the muezzin whose minaret was nearest the small apartment in the Old City where Anna lived. He was proud of his high, clear voice, and when he issued his call, he used no amplification other than the ancient method of cupping his hands around his mouth.

"La ilaha illa-llahu, Muhammad rasul allahi!"

Anna pulled her shawl about her shoulders as she hurried to prayer—not the prayers called for by the Islamic muezzin, but her own private prayers that she would give at the Wailing Wall. She walked through the narrow, twisting streets of the Old City, her feet whispering softly as they trod the same paving stones as had the sandals of King David, Jesus Christ, Omar the Friend of the Prophet, Roman centurions, Turkish soldiers, Byzantine merchants, and the knights of the Crusades.

The tops of the small domed houses of the Moroccan quarter she was passing through shimmered gold in the newly risen sun, while shadows still lingered lower down in the nooks and crannies of the walls and in recessed doorways. A vendor, squatting alongside a doorway, was selling the pre-ferred breakfast of the working Arab: flat bread, eggs, and falafel. She passed a tiny shoe-repair shop, then a juice seller who was filling his cus-tomers' cups with a long-stemmed pipette, holding his finger over the top to control the flow. On the other side of a waist-high door, with only his head showing over the top, an old man sat smoking his narghile. From the torpid expression on his face Anna knew that the tobacco in the water pipe was liberally laced with hashish.

She saw few Arab women because they tended to keep out of sight by staying within the warren of overhanging buildings and shadowed courtyards. The Arab women she did see were so wrapped in their dark veils that only a single eye stared out, and even it was averted as they passed.

And then she saw the Wailing Wall, rising like a great cliff above the small, closely built houses that crowded right down to it, leaving only a small space for those who came to worship. On the other side of the wall, and higher still so that it could clearly be seen by the Jews who came to worship, stood the shining golden Dome of the Rock, one of Islam's greatest shrines.

This, the Wailing Wall, was the most sacred site of all Jewry. According to ancient legend, Solomon had charged all classes of people with the responsi-bility of erecting the temple, and he assigned the raising of this wall of the temple to the beggars. On the day the temple was destroyed, angels hovered about the wall to protect it, singing, "This, the work of the poor, shall never be destroyed."

The Wailing Wall has had a divine presence since that day, and, the leg-end says, on dewy mornings the very stones weep for the temple's fall.

A small, woven screen stood against the wall, dividing the women's side from the men's. Anna stepped over to the women's side, then leaned her head against the stones. So massive were they that her head came no higher than the second course. The coolness, and even the roughness, of these stones suf-fused her with a feeling of oneness with every Jew who had ever lived. Here she could almost literally feel the presence of her late husband, David. She kissed the stone reverently.

As Anna stood there listening to the quiet shuffling of the faithful, she looked around. Closest to the divider was a young mother who had brought a short stool to stand on, allowing her to stretch her arm across the top of the

161

screen to reassure her young son, who was standing somewhat apprehensively just on the other side.

Through the weave in the screen, Anna could look across to the men's side, where she saw a middle-aged Hasid leaning against the wall as he prayed. An elderly man was resting his prayer book in a niche in the wall, while a young scholar who was studying his prayers bowed and bobbed continuously as he read. Further down a man and his elderly father were worshiping, sharing a prayer shawl that the son had drawn over his father's head in a gesture of reverence and devotion.

On this Sabbath day, which was the second day of Israeli independence, the worship at the wall was silent. The whirring of pigeons' wings was the loudest sound to be heard. But yesterday, when the British mandate ended and the Scottish soldiers marched out of Old Jerusalem with the high-pitched, almost otherworldly music of their bagpipes, Israel became a nation, and all day the Wailing Wall was crowded with Jews from the Old City and the new, coming to give their prayers of praise and thanksgiving. To the degree possible in the small space in front of the wall they had sung and danced in joyful celebration of the birth of their new country. And because this new country was founded upon their holy laws, they made their ancient exhortations in unison.

"For the palace that lies desolate!" a worshiper had cried.

"We sit in solitude and mourn," the others had answered.

"For the walls that are overthrown!"

"We sit in solitude and mourn."

"For our glory which is departed!"

"We sit in solitude and mourn."

"For our wise men who have perished!"

"We sit in solitude and mourn."

"For the priests who have stumbled!"

"We sit in solitude and mourn."

"For our kings who have despised Him!"

"We sit in solitude and mourn."

The leader who had exhorted the others wasn't a rabbi, only a man of particular devotion. That was the way of it at the Wailing Wall. Here the devout Jew needed no rabbi to feel the presence of God.

The wall was sacred to the Hasid and the orthodox pietist. It was equally sacred to someone like Anna, who, though born in a distant country, felt as strong a sense of connection with the Wailing Wall as did someone born right there in the Old City of Jerusalem.

After escaping from the refugee ship *Let My People Go,* Anna and Esther and Lily Stein had gone to Jerusalem to live. Jerusalem was a Jewish island in an Arab sea, surrounded on all sides by enemies. It was a particularly dangerous place for Jews now that the British mandate—and British protection—had ended.

The Jews in Jerusalem were cut off from their brethren in Palestine, but they were totally dependent upon that segment of Palestine for support. There was only one way Jerusalem could be supplied, and that was by a narrow, twisting road that ran through the hills from Tel Aviv. Unfortunately that road was perfect for ambush, and though the Haganah provided security for the supply convoys, many trucks and cars fell victim to Arab attacks. As a result, burned-out, rusting hulks were scattered along the road like sentinels, spread no more than a few hundred yards apart, for the entire distance between the two cities.

Esther and Lily lived in New Jerusalem, but Anna had chosen to live in the Jewish settlement of the Old City. As she had told Esther and Lily, she could live nowhere else. "Next year in Jerusalem" had been the watchword for her entire life.

"It isn't 'next year a modern apartment building in New Jerusalem.' It is 'next year in Jerusalem,'" she had explained, justifying her decision.

The problem with living in the Old City was that it was even more isolated than Jerusalem itself. Many more Arabs than Jews lived in the Old City, and just north of the perimeter walls was a sprawling, thickly populated Arab suburb. The nearby hills were also controlled by the Arabs, grazed upon by their livestock and covered with their ancient cemeteries, including the graves of Saladin's warriors.

Anna wasn't sure how long she had been standing at the wall when the gunshots and the stomach-shaking thump of nearby explosions began.

The gunfire and explosions were followed by screams of panic and shouts of anger from the Jews gathered near the wall. Some were shocked, as if unable to believe that anyone would defile such a holy place, especially on the Sabbath. The bullets whistled down the Roman-built Street of the Chain, ricocheting off the ground and slamming into the wall.

Anna turned away from the wall to see kaleidoscopic images of men, women, and children running, falling, bleeding, and dying. She saw the man who had been holding the prayer shawl over his elderly father, kneeling now, arms stretched out by his side and palms turned up in supplication, as he grieved for his father. The older man was lying on his back, his thick glasses dangling from one ear, his eyes open and sightless. A single bullet hole in his temple spilled blood onto the ancient paving stones.

The young mother who had so scrupulously adhered to the division of the sexes now violated the male space by darting around to the other side of the screen to scoop up her son and carry him away, while blood ran down his leg.

Not everyone was running. Incredibly, some of the more devout worshipers were so intent on their prayers that they were unaware of the commotion, unaware even that they were in danger.

It was then that Anna saw the attackers, several men wearing kaffiyehs and carrying Sten submachine guns, running down the Street of the Chain toward them. They were firing indiscriminately, waving their guns back and forth as if watering a lawn with garden hoses. It looked almost as if they were wasting their bullets—yet the bullets were striking targets with devastating effect.

Anna ran for the corner of one of the nearby Moroccan houses, knowing that it offered only temporary safety—and then only if the Moroccans who lived there didn't turn on her. The Jews who had come to worship at the Wailing Wall were all unarmed. If the Arabs wanted to, they could kill every one of them, and there would be nothing to stop them.

Then she heard two machine guns firing. These were deeper, louder pops than the nine-millimeter Sten guns the Arabs were carrying, and, to her surprise, she saw some of the Arabs grab their chest and go down. Pivoting around, she saw that there were two heavy machine guns in position to defend the Wailing Wall.

There was no way those machine guns could have been brought in and set up so quickly. They had to have been there already, and that surprised Anna, for she hadn't noticed them at all when she came to pray.

A Haganah soldier, wearing a blue beret and with a Sten gun hanging by a strap from his shoulder, ran out in front of the wall to direct the panic-stricken Jews toward a nearby reinforced building and safety.

"This way!" he shouted. "Everyone, come this way!"

Many had found temporary shelter in doorways and were too frightened to step out into the open again. Anna, who also felt a degree of security where she was, could understand their reluctance, but she didn't know how long she would be able to stay there, and if she could get to where there were Jewish soldiers to defend her, she was sure it would be safer.

The armed Jew in the blue beret sprayed a burst of fire toward the Arab attackers, who, caught unaware by the counterattack, were now beginning to fall back, leaving behind them some of their own dead and wounded.

Anna took a deep breath, then left her relative safety and ran as quickly as she could down the narrow pathway that ran in front of the wall, passing by the man in the blue beret. When she did so, she saw the telltale tattoo on his arm. Like her, he had been a prisoner in the Nazi concentration camps. And like her, he was now fighting back.

Anna and the others were directed into a building at the end of the street. She suddenly realized that it had been prepared for just such an emergency. There were sandbags around the doors and in front of the windows, and six armed men were standing outside, waving at them to hurry.

It was cool and dark inside the little fortress, and many of the worshipers Anna had seen at the wall were already there. Some were crying, some were praying, and some were sitting on the floor with their backs to the wall and a blank expression on their faces, as if they couldn't quite understand what was happening to them.

"Listen to me!" shouted the armed Jew who had run out to bring them in. "Listen to me!"

When everyone was looking at him, he continued.

"My name is Ben Weisel. I am a captain in the Israeli Army, and I ask all of you to please stay put. Do not leave this building again, for if you do, you will be putting yourselves in great danger."

"Stay here? We can't stay here," someone protested. "We must get back home. We have families at home."

"The Arabs have called for a jihad. Do you know what that is? An Islamic holy war as a religious duty. Syria and Lebanon have attacked Israel from the north, Iraq and Transjordan from the east, and Egypt from the south. Tel Aviv has been bombed. Our country is besieged on all sides, and here, in the Old City, we are surrounded and cut off," Captain Weisel said. "Only by staying here, in this place we have prepared, can we hope to fight them off long enough to survive."

"How long can we survive?" someone asked.

"And what is the good of surviving if we are separated from our families?" another challenged.

"As to how long we can survive, that all depends," Weisel admitted. "We have some food and water. But as more of our people arrive, the food and water will, of course, be used faster. And as for being separated from your families. . ." He shrugged. "We will not stop anyone who wants to leave. But I must tell you that there are only a few of us to defend the entire Jewish quarter. We can't spread ourselves out to all the corners. . . we must stay where we can be effective."

"What happens when we run out of food and water?"

Again Captain Weisel shrugged. "We were promised that a rescue party would try to get through to us," he said. "But with the fighting going on everywhere, I don't know if they'll be able to do so. If they *do* make it through, they can lead some back to safety. The rest of us. . . will be in the hands of God."

After Captain Weisel's briefing, Anna found a place in one corner where she could sit. It seemed ironic to her that she would survive the Nazis and Auschwitz only to be killed by Arabs, right there in literal sight of the Wailing Wall. And yet, she decided with resignation, if she *was* killed, what better place to die than there? What better time to die than now? She had witnessed the birth of a Jewish homeland. If she did die, she would die a happy woman.

Later that evening a young woman, also carrying a Sten gun and wearing a blue beret, came around, passing out bread; a young man followed her, doling out a measured amount of water. Anna accepted her portion from each of them.

It was hard to sleep that night. There was only the stone floor for a bed, and it grew cold and damp. She could also hear terrible sounds from outside—guns shooting, explosions, and screams of terror and pain. Some of the Jews of the Old City escaped the Arabs that night, and they began to show up at the small fortress in ones and twos and threes. Many of them were wounded, and they told of the terror taking place in the Jewish quarter as Arabs went from house to house on a killing rampage, shouting the name Deir Yasin.

Deir Yasin was a village where, in April, two hundred fifty Arabs had been massacred by Jews. Deir Yasin was proof, if Anna actually needed proof, that her people were as capable of acts of inhumanity and brutality as the Arabs.

The next day the Arabs launched two more attacks, both of which were beaten off. The next night was as busy as the previous night had been, and the stone floor was just as cold and just as damp, but Anna had no trouble sleeping. By now she was so exhausted she could have fallen asleep standing up.

By noon of the third day so many wounded had been brought or had found their way into the fortress that it had become, for all practical purposes, a hospital. Anna volunteered her services as a nurse, not because she knew anything about nursing, but because she was anxious to serve in any way she could. If she was going to die, she didn't want to die sitting moribund on the floor.

Just after dark on the third night, as Anna was changing bandages on one of the wounded, Captain Weisel came to her with his eyes shining in excitement.

"They are here," he said. "They came through Gehenna, and the Arabs didn't see them." Gehenna was a valley wasteland of thistles filled with ancient tombs and said to be the place where Judas hung himself from an olive tree.

"And we can take our homes back from the Arabs now?" Anna asked.

"No, I'm afraid not. There aren't enough of them for that. But they are strong enough to take those of you who are healthy out of the Old City."

"And the ones who aren't?" Anna asked. She motioned toward the patients lying in rows on the stone floor. Some were groaning in pain, some were numb with shock, and some were near death. "What will become of them?"

"The wounded, the weak, and the very old will have to stay here," Weisel said. "With us."

"Us? You are staying?"

"Yes. And my soldiers will stay with me."

"How long will you be able to hold off the Arabs?"

"We can expect to hold them off two more days. . . maybe three."

"And then?"

"If it were only my soldiers, we would try to fight our way out. Perhaps we would die trying, but we would try." He shrugged. "But we can't take the old, the weak, and the wounded with us, and I won't leave them behind. In the end there can only be one result. We will have to surrender."

"What will happen then?"

"I can't answer that question," Weisel admired. "We will become prisoners of war, perhaps. I know that we have captured many Arabs by now, so perhaps a prisoner exchange can be worked out." He smiled. "But that's not for you to worry about. You will be leaving with Captain Meir. Do you feel strong enough to go?"

"I feel strong enough," Anna replied. "But I think I shouldn't go. I think I should stay here with those who can't leave."

Weisel smiled. "I was afraid you would say that, but I don't want you to stay. I have been watching you for the last three days. You are a leader. On the very first day when the others were afraid to come into the fortress, you showed them the way. During the Arab attacks when there could have been panic, you were soothing with your calmness. And when we began to receive wounded, you offered your nursing skills. I have grown to depend on you, so I beg you not to let me down now. You *must* go."

"Why is it so important that I go?"

"You must consider the rescue party. They risked their lives to get through to us. That risk will mean something if they can save many tonight. If our people are calm and orderly, and if they will do exactly as they are told, they will make it. But many will be confused and most will be frightened. They will need one of their own to show them the way. They will need someone like you, Mrs. Gelbman. Please don't let the rescue party risk their lives for nothing."

Anna nodded. "All right. If you put it that way, I will go."

Captain Weisel grinned. "Good, good. Our new country will need people like you, people who temper their courage with wisdom and their strength with compassion. Now, come with me. I want to introduce you to Lieutenant Meir."

"Lieutenant Meir? I thought you said Captain Meir."

"Yes. Captain Meir led the rescue party, but his second-in-command was Lieutenant Meir, his wife. Like you, she is a brave and resourceful woman. The two of you have much in common, and I think you will like her. Ah, there she is," Weisel said, pointing to a soldier across the room. "Lieutenant Meir, I have someone I want you to meet," he called.

Miriam Meir, her back to Anna and Captain Weisel, was kneeling on the floor as she was comforting one of the wounded. She stood up and turned toward them with a smile on her face. Then the smile froze and she gasped in shock. Finally she managed to utter one word in a choked voice.

"Mama?"

11

JULY 1948, THIRTY THOUSAND FEET
ABOVE THE ATLANTIC

The stewardess set up the trays in front of the first-class seats occupied by Willie Canfield and Jimmy Blake. Realizing that she was serving both the chairman of the board and the chief operations officer of World Air Transport, she smiled prettily.

"Gentlemen, would you like coffee, tea, or milk with your breakfast?" she asked.

"Coffee," Willie replied, and Jimmy echoed the order.

A few minutes later the stewardess returned with a breakfast of eggs Benedict, English muffins, and fresh strawberries.

"Looks good," Jimmy said, putting the napkin on his lap and reaching for the silverware.

"Yes, but I miss the dining room of the old Windjammers," Willie said. "The ambience of waking up in the morning and walking through the plane to the dining room to have breakfast with the other passengers. . .

"We *are* having breakfast with the other passengers," Jimmy pointed out. "Forty of them."

"It's not the same thing."

"Maybe not, but you have to admit that it's a much better utilization of space. And better utilization of space means more profit for the company."

Willie laughed. "Hey, you don't have to sell me. Don't confuse nostalgia with idiocy. I know what the bottom line is."

Jimmy, who was sitting by the window, opened the curtain and looked out over the wing of the RM-505. The propellers on the two port engines were spinning gold threads from the early morning sun. Just over the leading edge of the wing and far below was the bright blue horizon-to-horizon spread of the Atlantic. The ocean's surface was spotted here and there with shadows from the smattering of clouds.

"It feels really strange to be riding as a passenger," Jimmy said. "Although I have to admit that the airplane is really pretty back here. I've never actually paid that much attention to the decor before, but I guess someone has."

"I hope to tell you someone has," Willie replied dryly. "It costs the company a lot of money to have these planes decorated."

"Well, I'm no artist or anything like that, but I'd say you got your money's worth. Look at the picture on the bulkhead there. That's nice; I like that."

Willie looked at the large, stylized globe on the right-hand side of the forward bulkhead that Jimmy had referred to. It was drawn as if it were made of glass so that the lines of longitude and latitude could be seen all the way around the globe. The American continents were viewed from above, whereas the Euro-Asian continent was seen from below.

On the left-hand side of the bulkhead was the moon, drawn in the same stylized way, showing the craters front and rear—though, as Willie had pointed out to his art director, no one really knew about the craters on the backside of the moon since no one had ever *seen* them. A representation of the RM-505 Moonraker was drawn flying much closer to the moon than to the earth.

The interior of the airplane was color-coordinated around the basic yellow and green colors of World Air Transport, and through the curtain separating first class from cabin class, one could get a glimpse of the same color and decorating scheme throughout the plane.

"But all this fluff is for the paying passengers. You and I should be up front, flying this damn thing."

"You, maybe, but not me," Willie said. "I've sat around on my butt too long. I don't know if I could keep up with all the new technology."

"You didn't exactly sit on your butt during the war. You flew your share of missions, as I recall."

"Only nineteen," Willie said. "That wasn't even enough to qualify for a complete tour. And on all of those I was more concerned with the conduct of the mission than I was with flying the airplane. My copilot handled everything but the actual hands on the wheel."

"Maybe so, but don't tell me you don't sometimes think about just putting on the uniform and going down to the flight line to take a trip on one of your own airliners as pilot-in-command."

Willie smiled. "Yeah," he admitted. "I do think about it sometimes."

"Well, you ought to do something about it."

"Like what?"

"Like come see me."

"Come see you? What good would that do?"

"I'm chief of operations, remember? The nice thing about being chief of operations is that I assign all the pilots' routes. And that means I have to make frequent trips myself, just to check up on things," Jimmy explained. "So if you ever get to where you'd like to do more than just think about it, come see me. I'll fix you right up."

Willie chuckled. "I might just do that. It's like I've always said: It pays to have friends in high places."

"You mean like generals in the Air Corps?" Jimmy asked. "Only what I can't figure out is, who's using whom? Are we using General Turner, or is he using us?"

"Remember, it isn't the Air Corps anymore," Willie reminded him. "It's the Air Force. They have their own branch of service now."

"They may have their own branch, but when the going gets tough, they still come to the civilians, don't they? They're trying to run an aerial trucking service into Berlin, and they aren't cutting it, so they've come to us. They want us to haul their ashes out of the fire."

"We aren't exactly being drafted, you know," Willie replied. "You didn't have to come."

"Are you kidding?" Jimmy grinned. "I wouldn't miss this for the world."

WIESBADEN, GERMANY

General William H. Turner pointed to a map on the wall in his office as he discussed the problems of "Operation Vittles," as the airlift was being called, with Willie and Jimmy.

"As you know, the Russians have sealed off all land routes into Berlin," General Turner explained. "When that happened, we were left with three choices: We could do nothing and West Berlin would soon reach a state of such desperation that the Russians would, as a"—he made a wry face—"'*humanitarian*' gesture, come to their rescue. If we took that course, Berlin would drop into Russia's lap like an overripe plum.

171

"The second course would be to try to force the routes open by a military operation. Such an action could, and probably would, quickly escalate until we found ourselves in a full-scale ground war with the Russians. And, gentlemen, I think it is no secret to anyone that the Russians have a larger army in Europe now than they did at the end of the war. In an all-out ground war they could sweep through Europe, and nothing could stop them—except the atomic bomb. I don't think anyone is ready to see us resort to that option.

"The only viable option remaining, then, is to attempt to resupply Berlin by air, and that's what we're trying to do." Turner sighed. "But it may be that the task is beyond our capabilities."

"General," Willie asked, "what does it take to keep Berlin going?"

"We figure a minimum of forty-five hundred tons a day. Right now the RAF is flying in about seven hundred fifty tons a day, and we're just about matching them. So as you can see, we have a shortfall of about three thousand tons."

"What about the French?" Jimmy asked.

"The French are in Indo-China. They've been invited to a little party that Ho Chi Minh is giving," Turner said. "They're with us morally, but they won't be able to contribute more than a small handful of planes."

"Well, hell, isn't this important enough for them to reorient their priorities?" Jimmy asked.

"Ho Chi Minh is Communist, so when you think about it, it's all part of the same grand struggle, whether the Communists are Russians or Vietnamese. We have no choice. We and the British are going to have to handle it ourselves, that's all."

"So what we need to do is bring in enough additional aircraft and fly enough additional missions to find another three thousand pounds per day," Willie said.

"That's it," Turner confirmed. He smiled at Willie. "I was organizing a little aerial mule train over the 'hump' during the war," he said, "so I didn't get a firsthand look at how you handled things here in Europe. But Curt LeMay thinks you hung the sun and the moon, and he's the one who suggested I get you in on this."

"I'm flattered by General LeMay's observation," Willie said. "I hope I can live up to his expectations."

"Would you like to take a flight into Berlin to see the operation firsthand?"

"Yes. Yes, I think I would like that."

"Good, I was hoping you would." Turner picked up the phone on his desk. "Captain Cookson, do we have a C-47 on standby? Good. Have it fueled and moved to the ready line. Who are the pilots?" General Turner looked at Willie and Jimmy with a challenging smile on his face. "The pilots will be General Canfield and Colonel Blake. By the way, they're here in mufti, so dig up a couple of flight suits for them, will you?" Turner hung up, then said to Willie and Jimmy, "Gentlemen, I hope you don't mind flying yourselves into Berlin. I'm too short of crews to spare you anyone."

"I don't mind the flying part," Jimmy said, a rueful grin on his face. "But I'm not real happy with the 'general' and 'colonel' part. I thought we were over here as civilian advisers."

"Your rank is temporary, Colonel, merely temporary," General Turner said.

"Yes, sir, that's what they said during the war. But I wound up staying for over three years."

The first thing Willie and Jimmy had to do was attend the operations briefing on how the flight would be conducted. Flights were very closely coordinated because the air routes into Berlin were extremely restrictive. Templehof, in the American sector, and Gatow, in the British sector, were only four minutes apart by air. Also, there were seven Russian airfields immediately around Berlin.

A young, very intense-looking lieutenant was waiting for them in the pilots' briefing room. He was holding a clipboard, and he remained standing after Willie and Jimmy seated themselves in the two chairs pulled up for them. The lieutenant waited until Jimmy got out his notebook and pen, then cleared his throat and began talking.

"All eastbound flights will carry the code name Easy," he explained. "Westbound flights are Willie. Your departure time will be ten forty-five plus thirty seconds. Your radio call sign will be Easy Dakota seven-one-five. The three ships immediately in front of you will be Easy Dakota seven-one-two, Easy Dakota seven-one-three, and Easy Dakota seven-one-four. The two ships behind you will be Easy Dakota seven-one-six and Easy Dakota seven-one-seven. As you can see, gentlemen, the tail numbers you will be using are *not* the tail numbers of your aircraft. They are temporarily assigned tail numbers to help in the sorting of the flight stream. It is very important that you remember that, for if you call the tower and give them any tail number other than the one you have just been assigned, it will cause mass confusion."

"Dakota seven-one-five," Jimmy said. "I've got it." In addition to writing it in his notebook, he also wrote it on the back of his hand. Willie did the same thing.

"Now, you will start engines, taxi out in time to begin your takeoff roll at *exactly* ten forty-five and thirty seconds. Climb out at five hundred feet per minute to altitude of three thousand. Maintain three thousand and takeoff heading until you cross Aschaffenberg. At 'A-berg' you will turn to and maintain a heading of zero-three-three degrees until you cross the Fulda range station. At Fulda you will say aloud the *assigned* tail number of your aircraft so that each pilot behind you can check their separation.

From Fulda you will proceed at exactly one hundred seventy miles per hour, directly to the Templehof range station. When you cross the Templehof station, turn left to the beacon at Wedding. Begin your letdown procedure on that leg. At Wedding, turn downwind, continuing a five-hundred-foot-per-minute descent to fifteen hundred feet. At fifteen hundred feet turn on final and land at pilot's discretion. *There will be no go-arounds, gentlemen.* If there is a missed approach, make an immediate turn to a heading of two-one-five degrees, climb to three thousand, and await departure control's instructions to reenter the flight stream back to Wiesbaden. Any questions, gentlemen?"

"Yeah," Jimmy said. He looked up from his notes. "Would you say again everything after 'all eastbound flights will carry the code name Easy'?"

"Sir?" the lieutenant replied, looking pained.

Willie laughed. "He's teasing you, Lieutenant. He got it all."

"Very good, sir," the lieutenant said, not responding to Jimmy's humor. "I believe you will find your aircraft at the ready spot now."

When Willie and Jimmy walked out to the C-47 they saw that it was already being loaded with sacks of flour. A two-and-a-half-ton truck was backed up to the double-sized cargo door, and a dozen men formed a chain, passing the sacks along the line like a bucket brigade fighting a fire. Inside the airplane the cargo master, holding a slide rule to compute weight and balance, supervised the loading carefully. At the same time that the flour was being put in the plane, the craft was being fueled. A truck was parked just in front, a hose stretched from the back of the tanker to the top of the wing, where a man sat, pumping fuel.

The cowling was open on the starboard engine, and a maintenance stand was pulled up alongside. A mechanic stood on the stand, applying safety wire to the mounting nuts of one of the magnetos. The crew chief saluted Willie and Jimmy, then held out a small green-plastic-covered notebook.

"Here's the logbook, sirs," the crew chief said. "The mag drop's been taken care of, but we still got a red diagonal on a seeping hydraulic seal. I've checked it, though, an' it shouldn't be a problem. We got a new seal on order."

"The FM is out," Jimmy noticed, looking at the book.

"Yes, sir, but that ain't a grounding condition. We still got the two low freqs and the VHF. About a fourth of our planes don't even have FM. By the way, I know you two don't remember me," he added, "but we was together for a little while back at Waddlesfoot. I'm Sergeant Haverkost. I was flight engineer on the *Lusty Virgin*."

"The *Lusty Virgin*?" Willie said, trying to remember the aircraft.

"I remember that one. That was Lieutenant Sarducci's plane, wasn't it?" Jimmy asked. "Didn't it go down on one of the Schweinfurt raids?"

"Yes, sir, it did," Haverkost said. "They was only three of us got out—me an' Burley an' Vargas. Burley was the tail gunner, an' Vargas was the radio operator. We was all captured together. Burley died in prison camp. Vargas went on home to Indiana, an' I ain't heard from him since."

"And you stayed in?"

"Yes, sir. Well, I wasn't gonna stay, but when I got back home, my wife. . . well, she was livin' with another man. I don't reckon I can blame her none. I guess it was pretty hard on her, me bein' a POW an' her not knowin' if I was alive or dead. 'Sides which, she already had two young uns by this fella, an' me an' her, why, we didn't have none at all, so it seemed like the sensible thing to do was get a divorce. After that, comin' back in just seemed like the best thing. We call it the Air Force now 'stead of the Army Air Corps, but there ain't no difference 'cept we changed the color of our uniforms, is all."

"Well, it's good serving with you again, Sergeant Haverkost," Jimmy said.

"Yes, sir, good bein' with you two again, too," Haverkost said. "Oh, an' sirs, if you don't mind my tellin' you, make sure we don't miss our station time. General Turner—the boys call him Willie the Whip—is pure death on those station times. You miss one, you better give your soul to Jesus, 'cause your ass is gonna belong to him. I've seen planes leave half empty so's not to piss 'im off."

"Then we'd better not miss it," Willie said, grinning. "Jimmy, you fly left seat."

Jimmy sniggered. "This is a wonderful deal. You remember, don't you, that the 'goonie bird' is all manual? How many pilots could have the president of an airline *and* a general pumping the wheels up and down for him?"

"I've handled hand-operated pumps before," Willie said. He laughed. "I've just never been paid so much for doing it."

The takeoff was smooth, and even as they were climbing to altitude, Willie turned in his seat to see another C-47 taking off behind them. They had learned, even before the briefing, that there were actually three corridors into West Berlin. The British used the north corridor, the U.S. used the south corridor, and they both exited Berlin through the central corridor.

They passed Darmstadt and Aschaffenberg, then turned toward Fulda.

"*Easy Dakota seven-one-two, over Fulda,*" an unseen pilot ahead of them broadcast.

Three minutes later they heard Easy Dakota seven-one-three, then, three minutes after that, Easy Dakota seven-one-four. It was exactly three minutes after that when the needles on their own radio finder indicated that they were over the Fulda range station. Willie picked up the microphone.

"Easy Dakota seven-one-five over Fulda," he said.

At Fulda they turned toward the Templehof range station.

175

It wasn't long after they turned toward Templehof before two fighter air-craft flashed by just in front of them, so close that the C-47 bounced rather sharply as it flew through their wake turbulence. The fighters made a wide circle about three miles in front, then started back toward them.

"Sergeant Haverkost!" Willie shouted into his mike. "Who the hell are these guys? What's their radio push? I'm going to chew some ass.

Haverkost chuckled into his mike. *"Won't do you no good, sir. Them's Ruskies,"* he said.

"Russians?"

"Yes, sir. You see, were over their territory now, an' they like to have fun with us.'

This time as the two fighter airplanes approached, Willie looked at them more closely and saw the red stars outlined in yellow on the wings and tail. And though he had thought they were Mustangs at first, he saw now that they were Yaks, the Russian fighter very similar in appearance to the American P-51 Mustang.

The Yaks continued flying toward the C-47, as if playing a game of chicken. Willie, who wasn't flying, had to just sit in his seat while his stom-ach came up to his throat. He began sweating, and he wiped his hands on his pants legs.

"Does this remind you of flying bombers during the war?" Jimmy asked, his hands steady on the wheel. "Remember how we had sort of an under-standing worked out with the German fighters? When they came toward us like this, we didn't move. If we'd tried any kind of evasive maneuver, there might have been a collision, so they had to depend on our not moving, and we had to depend on their breaking away." He nodded toward the approach-ing Yak fighter planes and added, "I hope these guys know how to play."

Evidently the Russian pilots knew what was expected of them, for when they were so close that it seemed impossible to avoid a collision, the fighters split apart, then zipped on by at lightning speed.

"Yeah, I remember those little games," Willie said. "The only difference was, then we had gunners shooting at them from the nose and top turret. And sometimes we shot them down. I sure as hell wish we could shoot one of *these* bastards down."

Ain't that the truth?" Jimmy replied.

Fortunately the Yaks didn't return, and about an hour later Berlin and the high-intensity approach lights of Templehof Airfield loomed ahead.

"Last time I saw this place I wasn't carrying flour," Jimmy commented. "I was carrying six thousand pounds of incendiaries."

"Sirs, this is Haverkost."

"Yeah, go ahead, Sergeant," Jimmy replied, keying his mike.

"Do you mind if I open the door back here? I've got a little delivery of my own to make."

"What kind of delivery?"

"*Candy bars.*"

Willie turned in his seat and looked back toward the door. Haverkost was standing alongside a big box.

"Candy bars?"

"*Yes, sir. It's for the kids. Some of them little shits haven't had a candy bar in months. So, me an' some of the other crew chiefs, we been tyin' handkerchief parachutes to candybars an' pushin' 'em out while we're on final approach. Uh, with your permission, sir.*"

"Sure, go ahead," Jimmy replied.

Willie watched while Haverkost opened the door, then dumped the contents of the box out into the slipstream. Turning to look out the window, he saw hundreds of tiny puffs of white floating down, and he smiled as he thought of all the children on the ground below, waiting anxiously for their special delivery.

"*Easy Dakota seven-one-five, Templehof Tower. We have you on radar, clear for landing. Land on runway one-eight, expedite runway departure.*"

"Templehof, Easy Dakota seven-one-five, runway one-eight," Jimmy acknowledged. "Gear down," he said to Willie, and Willie began pumping the small hand pump between the seats. "Flaps down," Jimmy added a moment later, and Willie pumped down the flaps.

They landed without incident, turned off the steel planking that served as the runway, then picked up a "Follow Me" jeep that led them to the unloading terminal. Almost before the propellers had quit ticking over a truck full of German workers was at the plane, waiting to take the precious cargo.

Even while the cargo was being off-loaded, fuel trucks were replenishing the fuel, and maintenance men were giving the plane a fast check-over. Box lunches were delivered so that the crew could eat on board the airplane, saving the time it would take for them to go to the cafeteria. Willie had been prepared to stay right where he was when he got a radio message from the tower, asking him to please report to the operations office.

"What do you think that's about?" Jimmy asked.

"There's only one way to find out," Willie replied. He put his half-eaten sandwich down and walked back through the plane, picking his way through the workers, then hopped out and walked across the tarmac to the operations building. A captain wearing the armband and white helmet of an air policeman saluted him.

"At ease, Captain," Willie said. "I'm not a really a general anymore. I'm more like a civilian adviser."

"Yes, sir," the captain replied. "Would you come with me please, sir? General Clay would like to speak with you."

Willie followed the captain into the operations building, then down a corridor and into a comfortably furnished room.

"Wait here, please," the captain said. "General Clay will be with you in a moment."

While Willie waited, he looked around the room, examining his surroundings. He saw that part of the molding over the door had been damaged, and when he looked at it more closely he realized that the damage had been deliberate, meant to remove evidence of the Nazis who once occupied this building. Despite the attempt to remove all traces of the hated symbol, however, the shadow of the eagle clutching a wreathed swastika in its talons remained.

Willie heard a door open behind him. Turning, he saw General Lucius D. Clay, the commander of U.S. forces in Europe and the military governor of the American sector in Berlin, coming into the room. General Clay was accompanied by two women, one an attractive blonde of around fifty, and the other, an exceptionally pretty young blonde in her early twenties.

"Hello, Willie. It was good of you to come," General Clay said, sticking out his hand.

Willie laughed. "Well, I'm not in the military anymore, General Clay, but when the commander of all U.S. forces in Europe asks me to come see him— let's say there's not much chance that I'll ignore that request."

General Clay chuckled. "I'm glad to see that it still works even among you feather-merchant civilians. Ladies, this is Willie Canfield, late a general in the U.S. Army and now president of one of our finest airlines."

The older woman reacted visibly to the introduction.

"Willie Canfield?" she said, pronouncing his name "Villie." "But, no, it can't be. You are much too young and besides. . . he was killed in the Great War."

Now it was Willie's turn to react. "Are you talking about *Billy* Canfield?" he asked. "He was my uncle. I'm his namesake."

"Yes, of course. I remember now, it *was* Billy. They were great friends, your uncle Billy and my husband."

Willie shot a questioning glance toward General Clay.

"Willie, this is Frau Karl Tannenhower,' General Clay said. "And her daughter, Liesl Tannenhower."

"How do you do?" Liesl asked. She stuck her hand out and Willie took it. "I am very pleased to meet the nephew of my father's dear friend."

"Uh, yes, I am pleased to meet you as well," Willie replied. He still didn't understand exactly why he was being introduced to them.

"Willie, we have a very sensitive situation here," General Clay explained. "As you know, Frau Tannenhower's husband, Karl, is a prisoner of the four powers at Spandau Prison in Nuremberg."

"Yes, sir, I am aware of that."

178

"Tannenhower has some information that could be very useful to us. He knows the names of more than three hundred Russians who are avowed anti-Communists, and who would be willing to work as undercover agents for us. We have known about this for some time, but it wasn't until this latest outbreak of trouble with the Russians that we felt any need to take advantage of his offer."

"What is his offer? Information for freedom?"

"No," General Clay said. "Since he is a prisoner of all four powers, he cannot be freed unless all four countries agree to that—and I hardly think Russia would be interested in granting him his freedom for such a purpose. But he has asked for something we *can* do." Clay nodded toward the two women. "He wants his wife and daughter to emigrate to America. He specifically requested St. Louis. Evidently he has relatives there."

"Yes," Willie said. "Tanner Morrison is his cousin, I believe."

"You know Tanner?" Frau Tannenhower asked.

Willie smiled. "Everyone knows her. She owns the Tannenhower Brewery. She's also a friend of the family."

"Oh, of course," General Clay said. "Tannenhower beer. You know, I knew that the names were the same, but somehow I just never connected an American beer with a high-ranking Nazi official. Well, then you are the perfect conduit for this, Willie. As you might understand, this entire thing is so politically and militarily sensitive, we can't afford for the slightest hint of what we are doing to get out. That's why I want you to fly them out of Berlin today, then take them on to St. Louis with you next week when you return. You understand, I have no authority to order you to do this, but I would be most appreciative."

"What happens in St. Louis? Do you want me to get in touch with Tanner Morrison?"

"That would be nice," General Clay replied. "But once they're in St. Louis they are out of the hands of the military and become the responsibility of the State Department."

"All right," Willie agreed. "I'll do it."

"Good, good. Now, until they are safely out of Berlin, they are to be known as Frau Cohen and her daughter. We will manifest them out of here as displaced Jews. The Russians are not questioning our relocating Jews."

Willie smiled wryly.

"I suppose you think that is ironic, don't you?" Liesl said. "I mean, with my father being a level-one prisoner at Spandau."

In fact, Willie was thinking that very thing, and he was somewhat taken aback by her comment. "I suppose I was," he admitted.

"Well, it's not. It's not at all," Liesl insisted. "You see, my father never was a Jew hater. And during all the months of his trial, with thousands of pages of testimony, not one time was that charge ever brought up."

179

"I have to confess, I really don't know all that much about the trials," Willie said.

"How can you say you know nothing about the trials? Were they not conducted for the entire world?"

"I suppose so, but I didn't follow them that closely."

"You should have. If you have no knowledge of such things, then you have no way of differentiating between my father and someone like Himmler or Kaltenbrunner."

"I suppose not. But then, I never really tried to make the distinction," Willie confessed. "To me all the Nazi bigwigs were pretty much the same."

"But surely you don't mean that?" Liesl gasped. "My father and your uncle—they were very good friends. Do you think your uncle could actually be friends with a monster?"

"I don't know. I don't remember my uncle that well," Willie said. He looked at his watch, then at General Clay. "General, as you know, my time on the ground here is quite limited. If you'll excuse us, we really must be getting back into the air."

"Yes, I understand," General Clay said. "And thank you, Willie."

Twenty minutes later, with Frau and Fraulein 'Cohen' as its only passengers, Willie Dakota seven-one-five lifted off for the return flight to Wiesbaden. They didn't encounter any Yak fighters on the return trip, but they encountered something worse.

Fog.

By the time they reached Wiesbaden, the fog was as thick as proverbial pea soup, and they could barely see their wing tips.

"Wiesbaden, Willie Dakota seven-one-five," Willie called. "Do we have an alternate?"

"*Negative, Willie Dakota seven-one-five. We have zero-zero conditions in the entire western sector. You'll have to land at Wiesbaden. We will bring you in by GCA.*"

Willie looked over at Jimmy. "I guess this is *not* a very good time to tell you that I've never done a ground controlled approach," he admitted with a grimace. "How about you?"

"I've done a few," Jimmy said. He smiled nervously. "They can be a little nerve-wracking."

"Well, then let's do it," Willie said. He keyed his mike. "Willie Dakota seven-one-five, ready to accept GCA."

"*Roger, contact Approach Control. Good luck to you, sir.*"

"Thank you," Willie replied. He retuned the radio, then keyed the mike. "Wiesbaden Approach Control, this is Willie Dakota seven-one-five, requesting GCA."

"*Roger, Willie Dakota seven-one-five, this is Wiesbaden Approach Control. Please make a standard turn to the right. Execute.*"

Jimmy made a two-minute turn to the right, coming back out on his original heading.

"We have you on scope, Willie Dakota seven-one-five. No futher acknowledgment is necessary unless an emergency arises. Begin left turn. Now. . . End left turn. Now. . . Begin five-hundred-foot-per-minute descent. Now."

Jimmy throttled back and started his descent. Willie stared at the cottony fog drifting by their windshield. It was a very disconcerting feeling, for they were moving through space at well over one hundred twenty miles per hour, yet they couldn't see more than ten feet in front of them.

"Come left, two degrees."

Willie looked back into the cabin of the plane and saw Frau Tannenhower and her daughter sitting calmly, as if this were a routine flight. Sergeant Haverkost was sitting on the small canvas bench across from them, biting his fingernails. On the surface it looked strange, the experienced flyer nervous and the novices sitting calmly. But Willie knew it was only because Haverkost understood the potential danger and the two women didn't.

The soundings from the GCA operator came with monotonous regularity as they descended through the thick fog.

"You are on course, on glide path.

"You are on course, on glide path.

"Your altitude is fifteen hundred feet. You are six miles from the end of the runway.

"You are on course, on glide path.

"Please check landing gear down."

"Gear down," Jimmy said, and Willie complied.

The soundings from the GCA operator continued.

"Your altitude is five hundred feet.

"You are two miles from the end of the runway.

"You are on course, on glide path."

"One minute till touchdown," Jimmy said. He called back to the cabin, "Haverkost, are the ladies fastened in?"

"Yes, sir, we're fine back here," Haverkost replied.

"Two hundred fifty feet, one mile from end of runway. You are below glide path."

Jimmy added a touch of throttle and flattened out the descent slightly.

"Two hundred fifty feet, three quarters of a mile from end of runway. You are slightly left of course."

Jimmy pressed down with his right foot and touched right aileron.

"Two hundred feet, one-half mile from end of runway. On course, on glide path."

"Flaps down full!" Jimmy ordered sharply.

"One hundred feet, one-quarter mile from end of runway. Take over and land visually."

"Land visually, my ass!" Jimmy said, though not into the microphone. "I can't see diddly shit!"

"Just let her settle," Willie said. He looked over at Jimmy. "This is more like it was in the old days before we even had radar and GCA."

"You want it?" Jimmy asked.

"No, it's your landing."

Jimmy pulled the throttles all the way back, and the engines popped and backfired in protest. The plane continued to settle down through the fog. Then ahead of them they saw the twinkling of runway lights.

"There it is!" Jimmy shouted happily, just as they passed over the fence. He pulled the wheel back, then back farther, and the airplane wheels kissed the runway so gently that it was hard to tell when the flying stopped and the taxiing began.

"*Oh, yeah!*" Jimmy shouted, laughing. "Oh, yeah! Piece o' cake!"

ONE WEEK LATER, FRANKFURT, GERMANY

Willie Canfield sat at the table in the Officers' Club at Rhein Main Air Force Base, making Olympic rings with the bottom of his glass.

"Another drink, sir?" the waiter asked. The waiter was a German, tall and slim with blond hair and steel-blue eyes. He had a dueling scar on his cheek, and Willie had learned that he had been a colonel during the war.

Willie looked at his watch. "Thank you, no. Check with the doorman for me, will you? Make certain there's no one there looking for me. A young lady."

"Certainly. I will check again, sir," the waiter said, implying even through his obsequiousness that he thought checking again was a complete waste of time.

"I can't understand what's happened to her. It's after nine, and I told her specifically to be here at seven."

A few minutes later a major, wearing the armband of an air policeman, approached Willie's table.

"Excuse me, sir. Are you Mister Canfield?"

"Yes," Willie answered.

"We have picked up an unauthorized indigenous female who claims she came to the base to meet you."

"Fraulein Cohen?"

"Yes, I believe that was the name she gave," the major said.

"Why did you pick her up? Why didn't you let her through?"

"She didn't have a pass," the major answered. "No one is allowed on the base without a pass."

"Oh. Well, I'm afraid that's my fault. I was under the impression that a pass wasn't necessary if the gate guard called to verify."

"Yes, sir, that is the case, normally," the major replied. "But not this time."

"What happened to make this an other-than-normal situation?"

"The young lady in question had no identification of any kind."

"I can identify her. Where is she? Is she just outside?"

"No, sir," the major replied. "We have her in detention."

"In detention? You mean in jail?"

"Yes, sir."

"Major, how long have you had her in jail?"

The major looked at the clipboard he was carrying. "We picked her up at eighteen fifty-six hours," he said.

"*Six fifty-six?* You've had her in jail for over two hours?"

"Yes, sir."

"Why have you just now come to inform me?"

"She is a German national," the major said, as if that explained everything.

"Of course she's a German national. What does that have to do with anything?"

"Excuse me, sir, but you are only visiting Rhein Main. You don't know how much difficulty we're having with German nationals trying to gain access to the commissary, the base exchange, the supply areas, or even the barracks, where they offer themselves as prostitutes to the enlisted men. It's a constant battle."

"Still, when the young lady identified me by name, it seems the least you could have done was check."

"All of them have someone's name, sir," the major said dryly. "We can't spend time running down every name they give us. If we did, we wouldn't have time to take care of anything else. Besides, the young lady identified you as 'General' Canfield, and, of course, there is no General Canfield on our base roster."

"It was a temporary rank I held during the war," Willie said.

"Yes, sir, so I've since been informed. That is why I'm here now, sir."

"All right, now that you've found me, I want her released at once."

"I'm sorry, sir, I can't do that. Not without authorization," the major explained.

"I'm giving you authorization."

The major shook his head. "No, sir, I'm sorry," he said. "But only Colonel Kleuver can give me authorization."

Willie saw a telephone on the Dutch door that led into the hatcheck area. He walked over to pick it up and looked back at the major.

"Colonel Kleuver, you say?" he asked as he began dialing a number.

"Yes, sir."

After two rings the number Willie dialed was answered.

"General Turner."

"Hello, General Turner. This is Willie Canfield. I'm sorry to bother you at your quarters but I have a little matter I would like you to clear up."

"Bother me? Are you kidding, Willie? The suggestions you and Colonel Blake made to improve the airlift procedures have already doubled our tonnage, and that's before we bring in the C-54's. Now, what can I do for you?"

Willie explained the problem, adding that the major was adamant about the fact that only Colonel Kleuver could authorize the girl's release.

"What's the phone number there?" General Turner asked.

Willie looked at the dial. "Two-seven-one-five, General."

"All right, thank you. Now, please hand the phone to the major."

Willie held out the phone, and the major took it.

"Major Giles, sir. I tried to explain to this civilian that only Colonel Kleuver—"

"Stand by the telephone, Major Giles," General Turner ordered so fiercely that Willie could hear him from where he stood several feet away. *"I guarantee you, your colonel will be calling you shortly."*

"Yes, sir," Major Giles said contritely.

When Liesl was released to Willie's custody some thirty minutes later, she gave a little cry of joy and ran into his arms. Spontaneously, Willie put his arms around her to comfort her.

"Oh, thank you," she said. "Thank you for getting me out of that awful place."

"Is there anything I need to sign?" Willie asked the sergeant on duty.

"No, sir. She's all yours."

"Thank you," Willie replied. "Come along, I have a car outside."

Liesl followed Willie out of the military police headquarters and down the steps. She started toward a blue Chevrolet with U.S. Air Force markings, but Willie steered her toward a yellow Packard. She looked at him in surprise.

"This is a car for the military?" she asked.

"The car belongs to World Air Transport," Willie explained as he held the door open for her. "It was easier to use one of my own cars than to fill out all the paperwork for a military car."

"It is beautiful."

Willie hurried around to the driver's side, then slipped in behind the wheel. He looked at his watch.

"Look, it's way after ten, and I'm sure the kitchen at the Officers' Club is closed by now," he said. "And even if it was open, I don't think I want to go back there. But I haven't eaten dinner yet, and I bet you haven't either."

"I had the opportunity," Liesl replied. "But 'beans and Franks' didn't appeal to me. Why do they call them Franks? Who are these men Frank?"

"Actually they're frankfurters," Willie said, laughing.

"Frankfurters? You mean, like this city? But no, why would an American food have the name of a German city?"

"Perhaps a German-American invented it," Willie suggested.

"Oh, I hope not. They were awful. I took one small bite, and I couldn't eat them."

"Then you've answered my question. If you didn't eat the beans and franks, you're still hungry, yes?"

Liesl smiled. "I am still hungry, yes."

"What do you say we find someplace where we can get something to eat?"

"I would like that."

Willie started the car, then drove away from the Officers' Club. As they passed through the main gate a few minutes later, Liesl turned in her seat to watch the base recede through the back window.

"I guess you're glad to be away from there," Willie said. "I'm sorry about the mix-up."

"Yes, I am glad to be away. But I can't help but think of my poor father being in such a place twenty-four hours a day for twenty-three more years. He cannot drive away. . . he cannot have someone come and speak for him and get his freedom for him."

"No, I—I guess not," Willie replied. The conversation had taken a turn that made him uneasy.

"I am sorry," Liesl said, sensing Willie's unease. "I have no right to be concerned about my father's discomfort. To use an American phrase, my father slept in his own bed, and now he must make it."

Willie laughed.

"What is funny?"

"Did you mean to say, 'He made his own bed, now he must lie in it'?"

Liesl thought for a moment; then she, too, laughed. "You are right," she said. "I was very dumb."

"We are carrying on this conversation in English, not German. Anyone who can converse in a tongue other than their own is *not* dumb."

"We are leaving for America tomorrow. I must learn to speak better English if I am going to live there. Will I like it in St. Louis?"

"Yes, I think so." Willie smiled. "Of course, I may be a bit prejudiced. St. Louis is my home, and I like it very much."

"I am glad you asked me to dinner tonight. It will give me a chance to ask you many questions about St. Louis."

"Ask away," Willie invited. "What do you want to know?"

"My father says that in some ways St. Louis is like Germany. Are there many in St. Louis who speak my language?"

"There are some, yes, though not as many now as there once were. At one time we even had a German-language daily newspaper. A sizable number of St. Louisians have German backgrounds, but more and more they are being assimilated into the American culture so that German isn't spoken nearly as much as it used to be."

"I suppose because of the war, our language lost much of its appeal," Liesl said.

Willie looked at her in some surprise. "That's true. You are quite astute for someone so young."

"I am not young."

"Sure you are. You're only twenty-two years old. That's very young."

"I am a survivor," Liesl said matter-of-factly. "Survivors are not young."

"No, I guess not," Willie murmured. It was all he could think to say.

They passed a *Biergarten* that also served food and decided to give it a try. Though the place was a half block from where Willie parked the car, they could hear the music pouring out of the building from the moment they opened the Packard's doors. To Willie's surprise the music wasn't the traditional "oom-pah-pah" kind of music he associated with Germans, but was strictly an American "big band" sound, and the wailing clarinet he heard could have come from any nightclub in America.

Despite the American-sounding music, there was a definite German atmosphere inside the Biergarten. Large, buxom blond waitresses carried as many as ten beer mugs as they hurried through the crowd. A dozen or so couples were gyrating on the floor to the sound of American jazz, but most were sitting around the long, wooden tables, eating prodigious amounts of wurst and kraut and hard crusted rolls, washing it all down with beer.

"Have you ever eaten bratwurst and kraut before?" Liesl asked.

Willie laughed. "I told you, St. Louis has a lot of German-Americans. They may have given up the language, but they didn't give up the food. I love bratwurst and kraut."

They found two empty places at the end of one of the tables, and though Willie was concerned that the waitresses might overlook them in the crowd, they were waited on right away.

Most of the others at the table were much younger than Willie, and they were carrying on animated conversations, thrusting their beer mugs about as if they were pointers. On a few occasions one of the young men would get so intent upon making his point that he would shout, and the other would shout back, the idea apparently being that volume was more important than logic.

Of course, whatever logic there might have been to either argument was completely lost on Willie, since they were speaking in German. He did, however, hear one Of the young men use the word *Kommunist*, which, being virtually the same in German as in English, allowed Willie to understand at least the root of the conversation.

The waitress brought their beer and dinner.

"Ah, good," Willie said. "I'm starving."

"You are English?" one of the young men abruptly asked, speaking in English.
"American."

"Ah, yes, American." He smiled and pointed to the band. "American music.
t is good."

"It's American music, but it's being played by German musicians, and *they*
are good," Willie said.

"*Ja,*" one of the other young men said, He was the one Willie had heard
say "*Kommunist.*" "American music is good. American planes are good.
American bombs are good. American bombs *are* good, are they not? They did
kill many Germans, did they not?" he asked Willie in a challenging voice.

"Look, the war was bad for everyone," Willie replied. "I don't think it's anything we need to argue about."

The young man wouldn't be placated. "Perhaps not so bad for you,
though, eh, American? You are here in our country, drinking our beer, eating
our food. You even take our women. Your fraulein is very pretty, but she is a
little young for you, isn't she, American? By about twenty years?"

Willie sighed and looked at Liesl. "Perhaps we'd better go," he suggested.

"No," Liesl replied. "We will stay. If someone is going to leave, it will be
this ill-mannered swine." Liesl glared at the young man.

"You call me ill-mannered?" the young man replied, still speaking in
English. "It is not I who have sold out to the Americans."

"You are a Communist, aren't you?" Liesl challenged. "You are a
Communist agitator, and you will not be happy until you have corrupted and
perverted everyone else into following you. Did the war teach you nothing?"

"Yes. The war taught me that a people who will not stand up for their rights
will be taken over by despots. We Communists watched with heavy hearts and
repressed rage as the Nazis betrayed our country. But we have taken a vow not
to let that happen again. In the east our comrades are building a new country—
a country based upon the teachings of Engels and Marx and Lenin, a country
for the freedom-loving peoples of the world. And when all of Germany is
socialist, we will arise and throw off the chains of economic oppression put on
us by the war-mongering capitalists of England and America."

"You sound like you are reading aloud from one of your tracts," one of the
other young men said, also speaking English. "You talk of economic oppression, but it was you Communists who destroyed our economy and let Hitler
come to power in the first place."

"It wasn't Communists, it was Jews who destroyed the economy."

"And now you are going to blame it on the Jews? Already you Communists
are sounding more and more like the Nazis."

"Enough!" Liesl shouted. "Stop this, both of you!"

The two young men looked at her, surprised at her outburst.

187

"Listen to yourselves," Liesl said when she had their attention. "You say you are a Communist." She looked at the other young man. "And you are anti-Communist. But it does not really make any difference, does it? Communist, Nazi, Royalist. . . it's all the same. You are just looking for the chance to debate your own brand of politics when the truth is you do not really care which side you defend. Have you no understanding of the problem? It is really the German people themselves who are being examined, not the relative merits of one political system over another. Through two wars and across half a century Germans have failed that exam. Please, do not put us to the test again until we are ready."

"And how did one so young develop such a philosophy?"

"I did not develop this philosophy, but I believe in it," Liesl admitted. "It is the philosophy of my father."

"Ja? And who is your father that he has such ideas?"

Liesl didn't answer right away; then, in a very quiet voice she said, "My father is Karl Tannenhower, the former Oberreichsleiter of Nazi Germany."

12

NOVEMBER 1948, FROM
"TRAILMARKERS" IN EVENTS
MAGAZINE:

AWARDED: Nobel Prize for Physics to Dr. W.W. Wilkerson of
Jefferson University in St. Louis for his work in developing the
Wilkerson Effect. The Wilkerson Effect explains the emission of radioac-
tive particles with seemingly insufficient energy to escape the force
barrier in the nucleus, as imposed by Coulomb's Law. (Coulomb's Law:
Force between charged bodies is directly proportional to the product
of quantity of charge and inversely proportional to the square of the
distance between them.)

APPOINTED: To the position of football coach for the Yale University
Football team, Levi Jackson. Coach Jackson, a Negro, is the first
member of his race ever to be appointed coach in a predominantly
white university.

SENTENCED: To hang, General Hideki Tojo, General Yamashita, and six other military and civilian leaders of wartime Japan. The prosecution proved that Tojo and his generals whipped Japan into a militaristic fervor, thus setting the stage for the war in the Pacific. In addition to the seven defendants sentenced to hang, sixteen were sent to prison for life.

NOVEMBER 13, 1948, ST. LOUIS

When Willie walked out of the General Aviation terminal at Lambert Field, he found his airplane already moved out of the hangar and parked on the flight line. Its smooth, narrow fuselage; long, thin wings; two huge engines; and tricycle gear made it stand out in sharp contrast to the Cessnas, Beechcraft, Pipers, Stinsons, and Fairchilds that composed the rest of the general aviation fleet.

Willie's airplane was a brown and yellow Douglas A-26, converted from the attack bomber it had been when it had rolled off the assembly line into a sleek, fast executive plane. Although both Canfield-Puritex and World Air Transport had executive planes Willie could have flown, he preferred this one. The A-26, its gun turrets and blisters removed and upgraded engines installed, could cruise at better than three hundred fifty miles per hour.

A line boy was standing on a small ladder, washing the windshield.

"Is she already serviced?" Willie asked.

"Yes, sir, Mr. Canfield," the line boy replied. "I did it myself. Topped off both tanks with fuel, added thirty-weight oil to both engines, pulled and checked the filters." He took a clean rag from his pocket and ran it across the graceful, sharklike nose beyond the windshield. There wasn't really anything to wipe off; he just liked to feel the curves. Willie realized that and understood it without having to comment. The need to look at and touch beautiful airplanes was a common bond shared by all who loved flying, from the line boy to the airline president.

"Boy, Mr. Canfield, you sure have one beautiful plane," the line boy said with a sigh that was somewhere between pleasure and envy. He climbed down from the ladder and moved it out of the way.

"Thanks," Willie said. He stooped under the wing and reached up between the huge engine nacelle and the fuselage to push up on the spring-loaded fuel strainer to get rid of any water that might have collected in the fuel tanks from condensation.

"Where are you flying to today?"

"Nashville. Jefferson U. plays Vanderbilt this afternoon."

"That ought to be a good game, shouldn't it?"

"I hope not," Willie laughed.

"Sir?"

"Jefferson is undefeated this year. We should beat Vandy by three or four touchdowns. If it's a good game, that means Vanderbilt is playing us tougher than we expected."

"Oh, yeah, I see what you mean."

"Listen, do me a favor, will you? I'm going to preflight now, but I have some guests coming—my brother and his wife, and a young lady and a young man. When they show up, would you ask them to just come on out here?"

"Sure thing, Mr. Canfield."

Willie walked around the airplane, moving the ailerons, the elevator, and the high-swept rudder, looking over each unit very carefully. Then he opened the air-stair door that swung down from the bottom of the fuselage and crawled inside.

The plane achieved its great speed not only because of its two powerful engines, but also because of the sleekness of its design. That meant that the interior of the cabin was best described as "compact."

Compact, however, did not mean spartan. Four deeply cushioned and fully reclining leather seats graced the passenger cabin. Extensively soundproofed, the cabin was beautifully upholstered in brown and yellow, with an additional tint coming from the amber skylight installed overhead where the dorsal gun turret once was.

Willie climbed aboard and, hunched over slightly, made his way to the front of the airplane. He slipped into the left seat and began going through his prestart checks.

"Hello," a woman's voice said a few moments later, and when Willie turned to look back through the cabin, he saw Liesl Tannenhower. She was still on the ground, but her head and shoulders were thrust up inside the plane.

"Hello, yourself," Willie called back. "Come on aboard. Are the others here?"

"No," Liesl said, climbing into the plane. "Only I am here. I hope you do not mind that I am such an early worm."

Willie laughed. "That's early bird. Early birds catch the worm."

"Yes, early bird," Liesl repeated. "I must remember that." Over the last five months, Liesl had worked hard to rid herself of her German accent and had succeeded to the point that it was now so light as to be little more than a pleasant and somewhat mysterious inflection of a few words. It was mysterious because with the obvious Germanisms removed it was hard to identify what remained.

"Where is Roger?"

"Who?"

Willie laughed again. "Roger Daigh. Isn't he your date?"

"Oh, yes, he is," Liesl said. "He wanted to come and get me, but I told him there was no need for that. We could just meet here, at the airport."

"Young lady, you need some serious instruction on dating," Willie teased. "Don't you realize that part of the dating ritual is in the man going to the girl's house to pick her up?"

"You have never come to my house to pick me up."

"We've never dated."

"We have taken meals together, we have gone to the cinema, we have gone to baseball games. Are those not dates?"

"Well, no. I mean, we've eaten in the same restaurants, we've attended the same movies, and we've sat in the same box at baseball games, but those weren't really dates."

"What were they?"

"Well, they were more on the order of a beautiful young girl being nice to someone like a kindly old uncle."

Now it was Liesl's turn to laugh. "Remind me, kindly old uncle, before we go somewhere together again, that I should bring you a. . . how do you say, a stick for walking?"

"A cane."

"Yes, a cane. And a shawl."

"Well, I'm not quite that old," Willie protested.

"Willie?" John called from the back of the plane. "Is Liesl out here already?"

"Yes," Liesl answered, sticking her head around the bulkhead opening between the cockpit and the cabin. "I am here."

"Oh, good. That's all of us, then, so I guess we're ready to go," John answered.

John, Faith, and Roger came on board through the air-stair door, and when they were all in their seats, Willie hit the button to close the door electrically.

"Hadn't you better get back there and get strapped in?" Willie asked Liesl.

Liesl got out of the right seat, but before she went back to join the others, she leaned over to kiss Willie on the cheek. "Do a good job flying the airplane, 'Uncle,'" she teased.

Once Liesl was seated and strapped in, Willie slid open the small side window and looked out at the line boy who had serviced the airplane for him. The young man was standing just in front of the engine, holding a large red wheel-mounted fire extinguisher.

"Clear!" Willie called.

The line boy nodded and made a circular motion with his finger.

The big R-2800 engines had to be started with an inertia energizer, and Willie held the left engine toggle switch down until the accelerating whine of the flywheel reached its peak, like the highest pitch of a siren. Then he flipped it up to the "engage" position to transfer the accumulated energy to the crankshaft. There was a chirping sound as the prop started to turn, then a cough and a belch of blue smoke as the engine caught, whirling the three-bladed propeller into a blur. He did the same thing for the right engine; then, with both engines running, he contacted ground control and received instructions to taxi to runway three-zero and hold.

Willie waited for a Connie and a Moonraker to land; after receiving permission from the tower to take off, he shoved both throttles full forward, and the plane began to race down the runway. He rotated a quarter of the way down the runway and, with the wheels drawing up into the belly, pitched the nose up sharply and climbed out of Lambert Field like a rocket.

Ten minutes later the plane was at twelve thousand feet, and St. Louis was falling away behind. Willie glanced down at the eight-day clock on the instrument panel. When Jimmy Blake had heard they were going to Nashville, he had suggested a restaurant for them to try. It looked as if they were going to be there in plenty of time to have lunch before going out to the stadium.

Willie looked back into the cabin at his passengers. Liesl and Faith were sitting in the forward-facing seats, one on either side of the aisle, while Roger and John were sitting in the corresponding rear-facing ones.

On the right side of the plane, Roger and Liesl were engaged in conversation. Liesl was laughing at something Roger had just said, and she was looking at him with that way she had. She could capture a person with her eyes and make them think they were the most important person in the world to her, Willie told himself.

She brushed back a fall of blond hair, then cocked her head and looked at Roger again, hanging on his every word.

Honey, I was wrong. You don't need any instruction at all from me, Willie thought. *You know how to reach out and grab a man—any man—and wrap him right around your little finger. And that's not something you learn; that's something you're born with, like blue eyes, blond hair, or a good singing voice.*

Liesl laughed again, showing perfect white teeth and sparkling eyes. Again she touched her hair as she leaned forward to hear what Roger had to say. Willie couldn't help but wonder what Roger was saying that was so funny. He knew Roger. He was a good man, a stockbroker who everyone said was going to go far in the business. But Willie had never thought of Roger Daigh as being particularly funny.

He turned his attention to his sister-in-law, sitting on the left side of the plane. Faith was leaning forward, looking out the window. Looking out the window wasn't all that easy to do in this plane since there was only one small window on each side of the fuselage, and it was positioned halfway between facing seats so that both passengers shared it.

193

Willie didn't know how she did it, but at thirty-six Faith had retained all the beauty of her youth; Willie had first met her in 1933, when she was twenty-one. Men of all ages were immediately aware of her when she entered a room. She was conscious of her beauty, and she knew how to project it, but she wasn't vain, and there was an easy grace to her that added immeasurably to her charm. She turned on that charm in full measure when, apparently sensing Willie's gaze, she looked away from the window and caught his eyes, then smiled and waved. Willie smiled back.

He was about to turn his attention back to his duties when he noticed that John was reading *Events Magazine*. The cover picture featured a smiling President Truman holding up a copy of the *Chicago Tribune*, the headline of which read: DEWEY DEFEATS TRUMAN.

President Truman was smiling because he had not only made a liar out of the *Tribune*, he had left egg smeared on the faces of practically every political expert in America, including several in his own party. Truman's reelection was somewhat of a victory for John as well, because John had told everyone who'd listen that Truman was going to win. Most people thought he was letting loyalty color his perception. After all, John had once worked for Truman, so he could be forgiven for such bias.

Willie had to admit that even he hadn't given Truman much of a chance. Maybe that was why John was the politician of the family and he was the. . . what? *Yeah, that's a good question*, he thought. *What exactly am I?*

Well, for one thing, he was the unmarried younger brother, the fifth wheel at any social function—though he was always good to team up with the unmarried woman guest-of-the-day. And he was a kindly old uncle.

Kindly old uncle?

Yes. He was Morgan and Alicia's Uncle Willie. And Liesl. He mustn't forget Liesl.

Of course, he wasn't really Liesl's uncle, but he might as well have been, the way she was constantly coming to him for advice. Why hadn't so-and-so called back after their last date? And what about her hair? Did American men like women's hair to be long or short? And bathing suits. What about this new bathing suit called a bikini? It was a two-piece bathing suit named, for some unfathomable reason, after the island where the atomic bomb tests had been conducted. Liesl wanted to know if Willie thought she should wear such a bathing suit. Would men like it?

Yes, of course men would like it.

Well, of course they would like it, but was it too scandalous?

To get his honest opinion, Liesl had purchased one and modeled it for him, standing alongside his swimming pool, posing this way and that, pushing one hip out, holding her legs together the way models did in the fashion magazines.

194

He had laughed at her because she made such a big thing about pouting, insisting that real models always pout because they can never smile.

She depended on his advice and help, she said, because he was absolutely her very best friend. And Willie could understand why Liesl might think of him in such a proprietary way, because for the first couple of months after she and her mother had arrived in St. Louis, his was the only familiar face in an unfamiliar crowd.

But that wasn't the case anymore. The Tannenhower women—mother and daughter—had now made quite a few acquaintances. Right after they had arrived there was a flurry of interest because of *who* they were. After all, Oberreiehsleiter Karl Tannenhower had been a world figure, a name in the newspapers and magazines, on the radio, and in the movie newsreels. He had been one of the principals in the Nazi war-crime trials, and fame, even infamy, was very seductive to a lot of people. Uta and Liesl had learned to identify such people and avoid them.

Fortunately, they had soon developed a circle of acquaintances as a result of their economic position. Though they had been on the edge of destitution when they had left Germany, once they'd reached the States, they had discovered that all their financial needs had been seen to.

That was the happy result of the Old World sense of honor of Ludwig and Rudolph Tannenhower. Their father had started Tannenhower Brewery many years before on money he had borrowed from his brother, who had chosen to remain in Germany. And although the loan had long since been repaid, when their father died, the two sons had felt enough of a familial obligation to grant four percent of their stock in the company (two percent from each brother) to the son of the man who had loaned their father the money to get started—their young cousin, Karl Tannenhower.

Rudolph and Ludwig had also since died, but Karl's special stock account survived. As the company grew and increased in value, so did Karl's stock. When Uta and Liesl Tannenhower came to St. Louis to live, the company lawyer had advised them of their share in the company and, more importantly, in the company profits, which by now were quite substantial. He had drawn up a power-of-attorney for Karl to sign, authorizing Uta and Liesl to benefit from the accumulated and future stock earnings. It was now sustaining them quite nicely.

"*Havoc 720, contact Nashville Approach Control.*"

The message brought Willie out of his reverie, and he focused his attention on the task of flying. After he keyed in to Nashville Approach Control he was turned over to the tower, and because of his ability to "expedite the descent and approach," he was moved up in the landing queue. A cooperative controller slipped him in between a United DC-3 and a Delta Martin-

195

202. He lowered his flaps and dropped his gear, then greased the A-26 in on the runway, reversing props with a roar. The big brakes and the reversed props slowed the plane quickly, allowing him to exit the active runway at the first turnoff.

By the time he parked at the general aviation terminal, at least a dozen people were standing around, waiting to see the airplane that had come in so hot. The line boy who guided them into their parking place and then signaled with a cutting motion across his throat to cut engines was smiling broadly at the opportunity to service—and more importantly get a good look at—the craft.

Though World Air Transport had cars available at the airport, the group decided that rather than worry about parking, they would just take a taxi. Willie told the driver to take them to The Chatterbox in Printers Alley, which was the restaurant Jimmy had recommended.

When they arrived at their destination a few minutes later, they all stared out the window in dismay. The Chatterbox was a narrow-fronted building with chipped paint and cracked windows. A dozen or more signs decorated the front of the place, most of them for products that were no longer in existence.

"Are you sure about this place, little brother?" John asked as they got out of the car. "It looks a bit questionable to me."

"According to Jimmy Blake, this place makes the best barbecue sandwiches in the entire country. And Jimmy Blake is a barbecue aficionado."

"You know Jimmy better than any of us, Willie—and you also know he never met a restaurant he didn't like," John said wryly.

"Now, John, where's that old Jefferson U. spirit of 'Go boldly forward.' It'll be fun," Faith insisted. "Nothing ventured, nothing gained."

"Well, all right. Never let it be said that I, John Canfield, did not go boldly forward." John laughed. "Lead on, Macduff."

A waitress met them as soon as they stepped through the door and escorted them to a table near the rear wall. Like all the other tables in the place, this one had no tablecloth, and the unpainted wooden top was scarred with dozens of cigarette burns, carved initials and hearts, and countless water rings. The walls of the restaurant were plastered with more ancient advertising signs for Pears Soap, Lydia Pinkham's Pills, and Mitchell "Little Six" Automobiles as well as mule harness, saw blades, washing boards, and shelves full of patent medicine bottles.

"I can't believe you'd really want to eat in a place like this," Roger said distastefully. He took out his handkerchief and made an elaborate point of dusting the chair before sitting.

"Come on, Roger, where's your sense of adventure?" John challenged. "Faith is right. It could be fun."

"It could also be dangerous," Roger said. "I seriously doubt that any of the kitchen workers here has the slightest concept of sanitation. This place is a veritable petri dish of germs."

"You don't have to eat if you don't want to," Liesl said as she sat down. "But I certainly intend to enjoy myself."

Shamed into submission, Roger didn't say anything else until the waitress came to take their order, and he ordered along with the others: barbecue sandwiches, cole slaw, and baked beans.

The sandwiches lived up to Jimmy's praises, and they had just finished eating when a skinny, sharp-featured young man wearing blue jeans, a red flannel shirt, and a cowboy hat approached their table. >From a distance he looked very young, but as he came closer he looked older, especially in and around the eyes.

"Excuse me, sir," the man said hesitantly to Willie, "I don't mean to bother you, but are you General Canfield?"

"Yes," Willie answered. He wiped the corner of his mouth with a napkin and started to stand, but the man held his hand out quickly.

"No, sir, don't you get up now," he said. "It wouldn't be fittin' for a general to stand up for a sergeant."

Willie smiled. "Well, I'm not really a general anymore, Sergeant."

The man smiled back. "No, sir, I don't reckon you are. An' I sure as hell ain't no sergeant no more."

"Wait a minute," Willie said, pointing, "I know you, don't I? Yes, of course! You were a waist gunner on the *Stand and Deliver*, Colonel Blake's ship."

The man's smile broadened. "Yes, sir, that's me all right. Name's Buck Campbell. I know Colonel Blake was your real good friend, an' you sometimes flew in our ship, which is how come you remember me. But I gotta tell ya, I'm real flattered by that."

The two men shook hands, and then Willie said, "Buck, I'd like to introduce my brother, John, and his wife, Faith. And this is Roger Daigh and Liesl Tannenhower."

"Tannenhower? You one of them folks that makes the beer?" Buck said.

"Yes," Liesl answered without elaboration.

"Well, you make a mighty good beer, ma'am," Buck said. He laughed. "But then beer is like women. I ain't never had none bad." He looked at Willie again. "Listen, General, I'm goin' to be doin' a little pickin' an' singin' here in a bit. You're gonna hang around long enough to listen, ain'tcha?"

"Gee, I'd like to, Buck, but I'm afraid not," Willie replied. "We were just about to leave to see the ball game."

"What ball game's that?"

"The football game," Roger interjected. "Between Jefferson and Vanderbilt. I can't believe you aren't aware of it."

"Oh. Those are college football teams, ain't they?"

"Yes, of course they're college football teams. Jefferson just happens to be ranked number three in the country right now," Roger boasted.

"Is that good? I guess I don't pay much attention," Buck said, "bein' as I never went to no college." He pushed his cowboy hat back on his head. "Well sir, it sure was good seein' you again, General. I hope you folks enjoy the game an' all, but if you'll excuse me, I reckon I'd better get on into the back there and tune up my guitar. I'm gettin' paid five dollars for the set. That's pretty good money for a half hour's work, an' I imagine the folks will be wantin' to get their money's worth."

"I'm sure you'll give it to them," Willie said. "Best of luck to you."

"Thank you, General. Nice to have met all you folks," he said to the others, touching the brim of his hat.

"'Bein' as I never went to no college,'" Roger mimicked after Buck left. "To tell the truth, I'm surprised he even recognized Jefferson and Vanderbilt as colleges."

Willie looked at Roger. After a moment he said, "You played against Vanderbilt, didn't you, Roger?"

"I sure did," Roger said. "As a matter of fact, I played the last time these two teams met."

"And when was that?"

"October of '43. We beat Vandy thirty-five to seven. I don't mean to be immodest, but I got three touchdowns in that game."

"Don't apologize, Roger. I've never been one for believing that justifiable pride was immodest. Now, you take Buck Campbell, for example. He might not have gone to college, but, like you, he has a right to be proud of what *he* was doing in the fall of '43. You see, he was standing on the aluminum floor of a B-17 at twenty-five thousand feet in thirty-five-below-zero cold, fighting off Messerschmitts and Focke-wulfs. While you were hearing cheers from the crowd, he was hearing screams from the men who were dying all around. Of course, with the roar of engines and wind, the hammer of machine-gun fire, and the thump of antiaircraft shells, the screams weren't really audible. But that didn't mean you didn't hear them. Believe me, Roger, when I tell you that you could hear every scream from every man in every plane. You could even hear the screams of the people on the ground."

Roger cleared his throat. "Well I . . . I don't know anything about all that," he mumbled.

"No, I guess not. You were here in Nashville playing football, scoring touchdowns whenever the quarterback called your number. Men like Buck were dying when I called their numbers. It might interest you to know that I killed over sixteen hundred of them just by calling their numbers."

"You didn't kill them, Willie," Faith said quickly. "How can you say such a thing?"

"I guess I just got to thinking about why there were so many men like Buck Campbell who 'never went to no college.'" He looked pointedly at Roger.

"Listen, Willie, I didn't mean anything by that college remark," Roger said. "I hope you don't get the wrong idea. I mean, I realize how lucky I was to be in college while men like Buck were risking their lives."

Willie stared at him for an uncomfortable moment; then he sighed. "Ah, don't pay any attention to me. One of these days I'll learn to keep my mouth shut. Why don't the four of you go on to the ball game?"

"What?" John asked. "Willie, what are talking about, go to the ball game? Aren't you coming?"

"Yeah, I guess I'll be along later. But since Buck is one of the ones I *didn't* kill, if he wants me to hear him sing, then it seems to me that's the least I could do for him."

"Are you sure you'll come to the game after you've heard him sing?"

"Yeah, I'll come. We have reserved seats, so there won't be any problem with my joining you. I'll be down there before the first quarter ends. Listen, don't worry about me." He laughed. "Just pretend that I went for hot dogs."

"Why don't we all stay and listen?" Faith suggested.

John chuckled. "Since when did you become a fan of shit-kicking music?"

"'Shit-kicking music'?" Liesl asked, looking puzzled.

"Hillbilly music," Roger offered.

Liesl smiled. "Oh, yes, hillbilly. I have heard hillbilly music." She tried to sing in a country twang "I'm walkin' the floor over you," but realizing what a poor job she was doing, she stopped and laughed in embarrassment.

"I'm not a fan," Faith admitted. "But it wouldn't hurt us to stay around long enough to listen to the young man sing. What if we *are* late for the game? So what?"

"There's no need for you to stay," Willie said. "Thank you for offering, Faith, but I want you four to go on. I'll be along later, I promise."

"Okay, if you insist," John said, pushing back his chair and standing. "Come on, folks. Let's grab a cab and get on down to the stadium. I'd like to watch a little of the warm-ups."

They headed out of the restaurant, and John managed to hail a passing cab almost the moment the foursome stepped outside. Liesl started to get in, but at the last moment she changed her mind and slipped back outside, closing the door on the others.

"Liesl? What is it?" John asked, sticking his hand out the window toward her.

"You three go on," she said. "I will come to the game with Willie."

"Now, wait a minute here," Roger said loudly, almost shouting. "Liesl, just what do you think you are doing?"

"Please go on, and don't mind me," she said. She turned and started back toward the restaurant, and the cab driver immediately pulled away.

Liesl wasn't exactly sure why she was going back into the restaurant, but she felt compelled to do so. She knew that Willie's war memories were painful to him, and since she had painful memories of her own, she understood.

The "screams on the ground" that Willie had talked about hearing could very well have been *her* screams. Willie's, Buck's, and Liesl's memories were exactly the same; only their perspectives were different.

That common bond was a phenomenon shared by all warriors, ancient and modern. The experience of battle brought its participants into an exclusive fraternity that could be entered only by those who had faced the same peril. Because Liesl had faced those dangers she was as much a member of that ancient fraternity as the American bomber pilot, the German U-boat crewman, the English paratrooper, or the Japanese soldier. She went back inside because she *had* to go back.

Willie had turned his chair around and was facing the small stage, so he didn't notice that Liesl had returned until she pulled a chair out and sat down beside him.

"Liesl? What are you doing here?" he asked in surprise. He looked beyond her toward the door.

"I wanted to come back," Liesl replied. Noticing the direction of his gaze, she laughed quietly. "No, I am the only one. They went on without me."

"You should have gone with them."

"Why?"

"What do you think Roger is feeling right now?" Willie asked. "You can't just go somewhere with somebody, then desert them. It isn't right."

"Roger will get over it," Liesl said with a shrug. "You need me now."

"What makes you think that?"

"Because I understand. I was there, too, remember?"

Willie looked at her for a moment. Sighing, he reached for her hand, raised it to his lips, and kissed it. "I guess you were at that, kid." Then he smiled. "Well, I hope you do like shit-kickin' music, because here it comes."

Fewer than thirty other people were in the restaurant, and they applauded politely as Buck came through the small door that opened onto the makeshift stage. A guitar hung by a wide strap from his shoulder, and its cherry-red-fading-to-soft-yellow color flashed once in the pin light that shone down on the tiny stage.

Buck leaned forward and rumbled into the mike, "Thank you, folks, thank you." He strummed a couple of chords. "My name is Buck Campbell, and I'm a picker an' singer an' songwriter. What I'd like to do for you here today is sing a few little numbers I wrote myself."

He hung his head for just a moment, then started singing. He had a voice that was much bigger than he was, a low, gravelly sound that seemed to come from all over.

Buck's first song was called "Dirt Poor Country Boy." The next was "If Teardrops Were Nickels, I Could Call You on the Phone." He followed up the two songs he had written with a couple of "covers," songs written by other artists and already popular among country music fans. He did "Move It on Over" by Hank Williams and "Alabama Tornado" by Goebel Reeves.

"And now, folks, I'd like to change the pace just a bit, if you don't mind, an' play a song I wrote a few years ago when I was in a different line of work. There's another fella here who also happened to be in that same line of work, an' I'm doin' this for him—only I ain't gonna embarrass him by callin' him out or sayin' his name or nothin' like that. I just want to tell you folks what a fine fella he is, an' I'm real honored that he's here listenin' to me right now. I call this song 'Do You Hear Me Lord?'"

Buck started to sing. As he had been doing, he started out with a rumbling voice that sounded as if he had just gargled with glass. But then his voice became amazingly gentle and poignant.

> "Lord, are you there?
> Do you really care?
> O'er the sound of the engine's roar
> Can you hear my prayer?
> I don't want to die
> In this cold an' lonely sky.
>
> "Do other men pray?
> Are they scared, too?
> Or is it just me, oh, Lord,
> Comin' to you?
> I don't want to die
> In this cold an' lonely sky."

The tune, which was interspersed with haunting minor chords, continued for three more verses, touching the soul of anyone who had ever cried out in the night or felt the cold fingers of fear wrap around their heart.

When the song was over, Liesl looked over at Willie and saw that he was drenched with sweat, even though it wasn't at all warm in the restaurant. It was several seconds before she realized that the patrons in the restaurant, who had cheered and applauded each previous song with lusty appreciation, were now absolutely silent. At first she wondered if this was a rejection by them, but then one of the men at a table near the front of the room stood up and hung his head as if in prayer, tears in his eyes. He was joined by another, then another, until the entire restaurant was standing in a silent ovation, many unabashedly crying

Buck nodded once in a somewhat self-conscious acknowledgment; then he turned and walked out through the door at the back of the stage. It was only after he was gone that people began talking again, and they spoke in whispers, as if they were in church. Gradually the conversation grew louder increasing like the measured acceleration of falling rain. They hummed snatches of "Dirt Poor Country Boy," or sang "Move It on Over," but they avoided all reference to the song just completed, as if embarrassed by having a stranger so easily penetrate the defenses they had erected around their souls. And they tried, by the energy of their conversations, to pretend it had n't actually happened.

But they all knew it had.

13

FEBRUARY 1949, FROM
"TRAILMARKERS" IN EVENTS
MAGAZINE:

RECORD SET: Major Russel Schleech, piloting a six-engined XB-47 jet bomber, established a new coast-to-coast speed record by flying from Moses Lake Air Base in Washington to Andrews Field in Maryland in 3 hours 46 minutes, averaging 607.2 miles per hour.

RECORD SET: At the White Sands proving grounds in New Mexico, a WAC-Corporal two-stage rocket (it lifts off the ground with one rocket motor, discards it, then continues the flight with a second rocket motor) attained a record speed of 5,000 miles per hour on its way to a record height of 250 miles above the surface of the earth. At such altitude, scientists say, the rocket completely escaped Earth's atmosphere and entered "space."

MILESTONE ACHIEVED: The Berlin airlift reached a milestone this week when a transport plane of the Royal Air Force landed at Gatow

Airfield in the British sector with seven and one half tons of potatoes and other food. This brought the total amount of cargo delivered to the beleaguered citizens of the besieged city to one million tons. As has frequently been the case, the pilot had to land his plane while being talked down by ground controllers because visibility was severely limited by heavy fog.

AWARD GIVEN: Ezra Pound, 63, under indictment for treason and a patient in a mental hospital in Washington, received the Bollingen Prize for Poetry for his book *The Pisan Cantos*, written while Pound was a prisoner in an American Army prison camp. Pound is accused of broadcasting propaganda from Italy during the war.

AWARD GIVEN: The Heisman Trophy, college football's most coveted award, went to Mike Nolan, bazooka-armed quarterback for Jefferson University, St. Louis. Nolan led his Bears to a Big Ten Conference championship and a 20-14 Rose Bowl victory over the Golden Bears of the University of California—a contest quickly dubbed by sportswriters a "Bear fight." First runner-up in the Heisman Trophy balloting was Doak Walker of Southern Methodist University.

SENTENCED: In Budapest, to life in prison, Joseph Cardinal Mindszenty. Cardinal Mindszenty, an outspoken critic of the Communist regime in Hungary, confessed to most of the charges, though many believe he was drugged. President Truman called the verdict "infamous," and Pope Pius XII said that the Church was "crushed with most bitter grief."

RELEASED: Guy Colby, from Danbury Federal Prison, where he served one year for contempt of Congress during the HUAC hearings. Colby, a writer-director (*King of the Sand, Red Banners over Mother Russia, Out of the Night*), was one of the "Hollywood Eleven," who, when accused of Communist activities, declined to testify. When the Supreme Court refused to hear their appeal, all eleven were sentenced to jail terms. Two received six months and nine received a year. An irony of the case is that one of Colby's fellow prisoners in Danbury was J. Parnell Thomas, the New Jersey congressman who headed the committee. Thomas was convicted of violating his congressional seat by receiving kickbacks.

DIVORCED: Lennie "Swampwater" Puckett, 43, one-time pitcher for the St. Louis Grays ("Toughest pitcher I ever faced," said Babe Ruth) and currently the announcer for the Grays' televised games, by his third wife, Jane Mason Puckett, 27, after three years of marriage, no children. (Her complaint: "Swampwater Puckett is incapable of fathering children. I am still a young woman. I want a family.")

DIED: Samuel Hamilton, 65, president and associate publisher of Pendarrow House and discoverer of Eric Twainbough, among others. Hamilton was born in New York in 1884. A graduate of Columbia, he first worked as a journalist for *The New York Herald*. He was hired by Pendarrow House in 1906 and was working there when he died. Often compared to the late Maxwell Perkins, with whom he was very good friends, Sam Hamilton was thought by many to be the last of the old-time editors.

NEW YORK CITY

E ric Twainbough stood at the window of Sam Hamilton's office on West Forty-fourth Street, looking out through the gray winter drizzle at the grimacing gargoyle perched on the corner of the building directly across the street. Eric knew that Sam had named the gargoyle Mr. Melchoir. He knew, also, that Sam had sometimes talked to Mr. Melchoir. Sam had once explained to Eric that he tried to pick only the most private times for such irrational conversations, but someone always seemed to overhear him. As a result, his peculiarity and the gargoyle's name were well known to every employee of the company, from the most senior editor to the newest assistant.

It was fairly late in the afternoon, and the hour plus the gray drizzle made it quite dim in the office. But Eric didn't turn on the lights. The moody light gave Sam's office a somber tone, and considering that Sam's funeral had taken place only an hour earlier, that was the way it should be, Eric thought.

He shifted his gaze. On the wall to the right of the desk were the framed jacket covers of just over a dozen books that Sam had felt a particular affinity for. Across the top row, in positions of special honor, were all the books Eric had written. It still made him feel prouder than just about any award he'd ever received.

During Sam's career at Pendarrow House he had personally edited, or had supervised the editing of, several hundred books, but only these few had made it to his "Wall of Fame." It wasn't that they were the best-selling of all the books Pendarrow had published—in fact several Pendarrow books that weren't on the wall had sold much better, and one of the books that *did* occupy a position of honor hadn't even sold enough to pay for itself. But by Sam's exacting standards, these books were those he had taken the greatest pride in.

A long narrow table against the wall was piled high with dusty manuscripts. Eric knew that at any given time as many as forty or fifty were on that table. In fact, he was almost convinced that these were the same manuscripts he had seen when he had first come to Pendarrow House over twenty years before.

Eric suddenly had the strangest sensation that time was standing still in this office, and that the authors who'd written and mailed all those scripts had materialized just long enough to write the books, then had dematerialized after putting the manuscripts in the mail. At that precise moment those writers didn't even exist, and they would not exist again until their scripts were either purchased or returned.

Such manuscripts were unsolicited, or "over the transom," submissions, and practically every other publishing house in New York assigned its most junior assistant editors to the task of moving the slush pile through. Until the day he died, however, Sam had insisted on personally seeing each one. He didn't actually read all of them, but he did glance through them, and though unable to judge the whole of the manuscript by such a brief perusal, he felt that within one or two paragraphs he could judge whether or not the writing itself had merit. Whenever he found good writing, he'd lay that manuscript aside and give it to one of the junior editors to read, with instructions to make a recommendation as to whether or not Sam should take the time to read the whole thing. One of the books on his wall had come to him that way.

One manuscript on the table was separated from the others, several pages lying facedown. The number on the top page on the faceup pile was twenty-four. Eric picked it up and read the first paragraph.

It was Geoffrey's mouth which set him apart from the other men in Lucinda's life. This full-lipped, remarkably facile slash was a clue to the sharp mind housed in a square-jawed, angular face. It was a face which, with its facile mouth and flashing black eyes, was capable of running the gamut of emotions from gentle sadness to blissful joy. Now it was set in a small sneer of vicious contempt which struck fear in Lucinda's heart while at the same time generating, almost without her awareness, a small gnawing of desire.

"Boy, I don't blame you for stopping here, Sam," Eric said to the empty room. "If you read something like that aloud, you could stun a mule." He grinned. "I hope you didn't actually take the time to read the other twenty-three pages."

He put the page down, then looked back at the gargoyle. "Well, Mr. Melchoir," he said softly, "we're going to miss him. Maybe you more than I. You got to talk to him every day."

"My God," a woman's voice said from behind Eric, "I knew Sam *talked* to the damned beast. I never knew *you* did. . . though I must say, I'm not surprised." Eric turned to see Shaylin McKay standing in the door. He held out his arms, and she came into them. He held her close for a long moment.

"I was hoping I'd see you while I was in the city," he said.

"I figured you'd be here," Shaylin replied. She moved out of his arms and walked over to the window to look over at Mr. Melchoir. "You know, sometimes I think Sam actually believed that cement beast talked to him. One time I sat on that very sofa over there and listened to a two-way discussion between them on the relative merits of a manuscript."

"A *two-way* discussion?" Eric asked, raising his eyebrow.

"Well, I heard his side of it, anyway," Shaylin said, chuckling. "Was it a lovely funeral?"

"It was at St. Thomas Episcopal. A very high-church funeral mass. . . smells and bells. Why didn't you go?"

"I don't know. Sam and I were friends, not coworkers. I had no professional obligation to go, and I don't do well at the funerals of friends—or weddings, either, for that matter. All the pomp and circumstance gets in the way of real life."

"There were a lot of people there who weren't there because of a professional obligation."

"Oh, I know, and I didn't mean that the way it sounded. You were his star writer, but I know he was much more than your editor. It's just"—Shaylin sighed—"I couldn't bring myself to go. He wasn't there anyway." She waved her hand around the room. "There's a hell of a lot more of Sam Hamilton here in this room—now—than there was at the funeral."

"Yeah, well, you're not going to get an argument from me," Eric said.

"So, tell me," Shaylin asked, "I've heard talk that you may pull your next book away from Pendarrow House. Any truth to it?"

Eric chuckled. "Damn, woman, don't you ever stop working? What do you want, the scoop?"

"No, I never stop working, and yes, I do want the scoop. But you know me, Eric. I'm curious enough to want to know what's going on, even if I have to be sworn to secrecy. What's the name of your next book, anyway?"

"*Tea on the Veranda.*"

"*Tea on the Veranda?* What's it about?"

"Dark family secrets in a decaying southern town."

"Like *Out of the Night?*"

"No," Eric said. "Nothing at all like that. *Out of the Night* had a rape and a lynching and a confrontation between the good guy and the bad, like gunfighters meeting at high noon. *Tea on the Veranda* is much more subtle, with textures and introspective analysis. The line between good and evil isn't as clearly drawn."

"What are you doing writing something like that? That sounds more like a play by Tennessee Williams or a Faulkner novel or maybe something by that new young southern writer, Truman Capote. It sure doesn't sound like any thing you would write."

"That's good," Eric said. "I don't want it to sound like me."

"Why not? Books that sound like Eric Twainbough have been awfully suc cessful. Why would you turn your back on a winning formula?"

Eric snapped his fingers. "Because of *that*," he said.

"What?"

"Formula. Don't you see, Shaylin? I've been nailed into a box by success and that box has very precisely defined limits. All my books have a lot of action and drama and solid characters with height and width but no depth And I'll be honest with you, I don't think I've ever written a believable— mean a *really* believable—female character."

"Neither has Hemingway," Shaylin said, "but that hasn't blunted *his* success.

"That's all the more reason I should write something different. People have been comparing me with Hemingway since the early days in Paris. Maybe *Tea on the Veranda* will put some distance between us."

"What did Sam think of it?"

"Sam?" Eric stroked his beard for a moment, wanting to come up with an acceptable answer. "Sam recognized my need to try something else. He was going along with me."

Shaylin shook her head. "'Going along,' you say. But he wasn't that enthu siastic about it, was he?"

"Well, you know Sam. He was the president of a publishing company. The most important thing to him was whether or not the book would make money.

"Come on, Eric, don't hand me that bullshit. This is Shaylin, remember You know damn well Sam would get behind a book he thought had real qual ity, whether it had big sales potential or not."

"Yeah, I know," Eric muttered. "All right, I'll admit Sam didn't really like it all that much. But I think that's because he was having a difficult time associating me with something like that. He, too, had me slotted in a certain mold, and when wrote something that didn't quite fit that mold, he didn't fully understand it. sincerely believe that in time he would've come around to appreciate it."

"Now that Sam is gone, what does Pendarrow House say about your new book?"

"Nathan Loeb has taken over for Sam, and he's already trying to talk me into moving up the schedule for *Trespass of the Damned* so that both books will be released at the same time."

"*Trespass of the Damned?* That one sounds exciting," Shaylin said.

"Oh, I'm quite sure you'd like it. It's about a boatload of Jews risking their lives to run the British blockade before Israel's independence. There's danger on the high seas, sex under the sweltering sun—everything to make the heart throb. But I'm not going to release it at the same time as *Tea on the Veranda*, because I want *Tea* to be given a fair chance to stand on its own. And if Pendarrow House won't do it that way, then I'll go to Richard Toban over at Argus and Collier. He'll do it."

"Sure, of course he will, for the chance to get you at Argus and Collier. But you'd better believe that he's after *Trespass of the Damned* and not *Tea on the Veranda*. I don't know, I guess you have to ask, is this best for you? You don't deal with the public the same way I do, Eric. You just sit in your beach house down there on your island, writing your books and looking at the ocean, isolated from the rest of the world. Well, let me tell you, mister, the public is fickle. They like you now, but if they don't like the new you, you may not get them back."

"Maybe not, but I've got to try. You understand that, don't you, Shaylin? I've got to try."

Shaylin shook her head in resignation, then grasped Eric's beard and pulled him toward her. She kissed him on the lips and said, "Then you try, Eric. You'll get no more static from me."

"That's my girl," Eric replied. He returned her kiss.

"Hey," Shaylin said, leaning back from him, "you'd better watch out there. You keep this up, I might send a spark into that old, dry, burned-out timber that used to flame in your heart for me."

"Darlin', that timber is neither dry nor burned out. I keep a coal glowing there all the time."

"Do you now?"

"That is a fact, darlin'. That is truly a fact."

"And when is it you're going back to your island?"

"Not for a few days yet. I'll be in New York the better part of the week."

"It's awfully cold in New York this time of year," Shaylin warned.

"Do you have any suggestions on how a person might keep himself warm?"

"Oh, one or two," she answered, putting her arms around his neck and leaning into him. Feeling him stirring, she pulled away and looked down at the front of his pants. "Oh, my," she said, shaking her head. "Look at that. And in Sam's office, too. Whatever would he think?"

Eric laughed. "Hell, darlin', I'm fifty-eight years old. I think he'd be envious as hell and proud as punch!"

MARCH 1948, HOLLYWOOD

The office for Export Pictures was located at the end of a warehouse complex. From where he stood by the window, Guy Colby watched several trucks

being loaded and unloaded with produce. Not all the produce was fresh, a fac
Guy was able to discern the moment he'd gotten out of his car.

Hurrying inside the squat, featureless building, he had introduced himself a
George Carson to the receptionist presiding over the waiting room and asked if h
could speak with Leo Gillis, the president of Export Pictures. He had chosen th
name George Carson because he'd once read that people who use aliases are les
likely to slip up if they use pseudonyms with the same initials as their real name.

"Mr. Carson?"

"Yes?" Guy turned toward the receptionist, a short, mousy-looking youn
woman who wore wire-rimmed glasses and her dull brown hair pulled into
severe bun.

"Mr. Gillis will see you now."

"Thank you," Guy said, walking by her toward Gillis's office. It wasn't nec
essary to point the way because except for the exit and the bathroom, Gillis
office was the only other door in the place.

Gillis was about five foot five and nearly as big around. He was completel
bald, and rolls of flesh curled over his shirt collar, which he wore open. H
reached out to shake Guy's hand, and Guy noticed that he was wearing ring
on two of his sausagelike fingers.

"Ah, sit down, Mr.. . ."—Gillis looked at the little piece of paper, the
looked up again—"Carson."

Guy sat down, then glanced at the wall. It was covered with framed black
and-white photographs of women, all provocatively dressed and posed i
ways to display as much flesh as possible. When Gillis saw where Guy wa
looking, he chuckled.

"Those are the publicity photos of the stars in our business," he explained
"They've all made movies for me. That one"—he pointed to one on the end—
"is Vera Fontaine. She's my leading star. She actually gets fan mail, if you ca
believe that," he added with a laugh.

"Well, I'm sure there are movie fans for these films, just as there are fo
westerns or detective pictures," Guy said.

"Yeah, well, right, right," Gillis said. "You know, I can't get over thinkin
I've met you before. We ever work together?"

"Not to my knowledge."

"No? Well, I guess not. But you look so damn familiar to me. So, listen
you ever work around film before?"

"Yes."

When Guy didn't elaborate, Gillis motioned for him to continue. "Well
come on. Where? I mean, you've gotta tell me what kind of experience yo
have. It costs me good money to make a picture, and I don't intend to have i
screwed up by someone who doesn't know what he's doing."

"I know what I'm doing," Guy said. "You can quiz me if you want. Ask some echnical questions."

Gillis was quiet for a long moment, scratching his fleshy jowl as he looked cross his desk at Guy. Finally he chuckled.

"Hell, I don't need to ask you any questions," he said. "I don't figure any-ne would have the balls to come in here and say he had experience if he did-'t. And anyway, if you don't know what you're doing, I'll find out before it osts me too much, and I'll throw you off the set —after I've made it pretty ncomfortable for you. Now, you still want to work?"

"Yes."

"Fine. How soon can you clear your table of other things and go to work or me?"

"I have nothing else on my table," Guy said. He snorted. "I don't even have table. I can start as soon as you want."

"Good, good, how about tonight?"

"Tonight's fine."

"We're shooting a picture over at Pacific Media. You know the place?"

"Yes," Guy said. "They do mostly industrial and training films, don't they?"

"Yeah, well, they also rent their soundstage and equipment," Gillis said. But we have to shoot at night 'cause they use their equipment in the daytime. Works out better anyway; there's a lot less chance of someone that we don't vant coming onto the set, you know what I mean? By the way, you ever see ny of my pictures?"

Guy remembered a huge Hollywood party he had attended in the wenties. Several of the biggest stars in the industry were there, men and vomen whose faces and names were known by every motion picture fan n America. A lot of bootleg booze had been consumed, along with mar-uana and cocaine. Sometime after midnight, when the numbers had windled, those who were still awake enough and sober enough had athered in the house's projection room and watched the flickering nages on the screen.

It was a strange audience, composed of actors and actresses watching a novie in which not one person who was there had a role. The movie was a ne-reeler, euphemistically known as a "stag" movie. Fifteen minutes into it here had been more action off the screen than there was on.

"I don't know that I've seen any of *your* movies, exactly," Guy said. "But I ave seen movies like the ones you do."

"There *are* no movies like mine!" Gillis said, slamming his fist down. "If you re going to work here, you have to believe that. . . *feel* that! The pictures this ompany makes are works of art. Did you know that in Hong Kong and angkok, Ecstasy Pictures are shown in the finest theaters? The finest the-

211

aters, mind you, with crystal chandeliers in the lobby, carpeting on the floo
and upholstered chairs for the patrons."

"Ecstasy Pictures?"

"Here, we call them Export Pictures," Gillis explained. "But overseas the
are distributed as Ecstasy Pictures. It gives them more class."

"Oh, I quite agree," Guy said.

"It's a fine thing," Gillis went on. "Here, in America, we're supposed to hav
freedom of expression. Yet, anyone who shows my pictures in this countr
could get arrested and go to jail on obscenity charges. But overseas, in place
where they don't have our freedoms, they can show the pictures right out i
the open. Gents can bring their girlfriends—their wives even—and enjoy
good evening's entertainment. I mean, these pictures are art, for crying ou
loud. They're no different from a nude painting. I mean, what if the Haye
Office or some of these prude censors and do-gooder judges went to a museur
and saw a nude by Rubens? Would they say Rubens was a dirty old man?"

"Are you a fan of Rubens?" Guy asked.

"I have to confess that I've never met the man," Gillis said. "I just read tha
in an article one time, and I thought the person who wrote it had a prett
good idea, so I use it."

"It's a good point," Guy said.

"So, you'll be there tonight?"

"I'll be there."

"And we've never worked together before, you and me?"

"Never."

"Well, no matter." Gillis smiled and stood up, then stuck his hand across hi
desk. "Welcome to the team, George," he said. "I think you're going to like it wit
us. You'll find that we do some damn good work. In our field, we're the best."

Guy was living in Long Beach—in a small apartment that was a far cr
from the beach house he'd had especially built with wings and porches an
decks, all designed to take advantage of its prime ocean location. Arrivin
home from his meeting with Gillis, he parked in the driveway under a flow
ering mimosa tree, then walked up to peek through the window of the garag
door to see if Henry Patterson's Hudson was there. It was, which meant tha
Mr. Patterson was already home from the plant.

Guy looked at the living room window and saw the flickering glow of th
television screen. He smiled. This was, of course, Milton Berle night, an
Henry Patterson wouldn't miss Milton Berle if an entire troupe of naked danc
ing girls decided to give a command performance on his front lawn. Wit
Patterson in for the night, Guy could leave his car in the driveway for as lon
as he wanted, without having to take any guff from his landlord.

He climbed the outside stairs to the apartment that had been built over
ne garage. It consisted of three small rooms: a bedroom, a living room, and
kitchen-dining room. It was furnished in a mixture of styles that had been
elected not for attractiveness, but for availability—at a low cost.

The living room featured a hide-a-bed sofa that was boxy, stern, and util-
arian. There was also an overstuffed chair covered with a flowered-print
material, and though the big chair was out of place in the tiny room, it was
ctually Guy's favorite piece of furniture in the entire apartment. The bed-
oom held an old iron bedstead with the mattress sitting high on a set of
orings. The dresser was made of blond ash, and the bedside table was a plas-
c version of some undefinable dark wood.

It was already after seven, and Guy realized that he hadn't eaten since
reakfast, so he went into the kitchen, opened the cupboard, and took out a
an of chicken noodle soup. Opening it, he dumped it into a pot, then filled
ne red and white can with water. Standing at the sink he could see just a
iver of the ocean—"ocean view," the ad had said.

He sighed. Nope, this place sure wasn't anything like the large, rambling
ouse he'd lived in and been forced to sell before he went to prison. But on
ne other hand, it wasn't like his prison cell, either.

He had tried to go back to work after his release, but he had run into a
one wall everywhere he looked. The others of the Hollywood Eleven who'd
otten out of prison before him had warned him that he wouldn't be able to
nd work, but Guy had been determined to try.

"I'd like to have you working for me, Guy, I really would," the producers
ad all said. "You have enormous talent, more than just about anyone I know.
ut I can't use you. You've been blackballed by the entire community, and if I
ired you, I'd be blackballed, too. I'd be ruined."

"I could change my name, like Fatty Arbuckle did," Guy had offered. "I
ould work behind the scenes—editing, writing, *anything*. I just need the work."

"I'm sorry. If anyone found out. . ." The producers always shrugged their
noulders. "It's your own fault, you know. All you needed to do was testify."

"Yes, well, thank you," Guy had replied time and time again as first the stu-
ios and then the independent producers turned him down.

Guy's bank account had been used up in "the appeal that never was." The
noney he had gotten from the sale of his house was running out fast, and he'd
een on the edge of desperation when a cameraman who used to work for him
old him that Leo Gillis was looking for someone to produce and direct his
xport Films.

"The pay's not all that good," Guy had been told, "but it beats digging
itches." The cameraman who had given Guy the tip had then grinned
wdly and elbowed Guy in the ribs. "And there are some terrific side bene-

fits, if you know what I mean. I've handled the camera for him a couple o
times to pick up a few extra bucks, so I know what I'm talking about. Th
only reason I quit is because the Guild put out the word that they'd yan
anybody's card they caught working on those kinds of pictures. And I can
afford to have my card pulled."

Guy had resisted going to see Gillis for as long as he could. For a while h
had considered contacting his friends to ask for a loan. He knew without
doubt that Eric Twainbough would lend him money. So would Demaris. H
could probably even get money from his first wife, Greta Gaynor, but he did
n't want to do that. In the first place it would be too humiliating to go to an
of them. In the second, what if he did get the money? He still wouldn't hav
a job. And when the borrowed money ran out, what would he do then? As
for more?

There had been only one thing left to do and that was find work whereve
he could. So, reluctantly, he had decided to go to Export Pictures to ask Le
Gillis for a job.

What if he did get caught and was blackballed by the business? Hell, h
was already blackballed. Could a double blackball be any worse?

Nope.

It was already dark when Guy drove up to the main gate of the studio lot
The guard came over to the car, and Guy rolled down the window.

"My name is Guy. . . uh, George," he corrected. "George Carson. I'n
supposed to—"

"Yeah, I know who you are," the guard answered. He made no effort t
move away from the car.

"Well, can I go in or what?"

"For ten dollars."

"What?"

"You want to get through here, it'll cost you ten dollars."

"Nobody told me anything about that," Guy said. "I don't have ten dollars.

The guard looked incredulous, then stepped back and made a long, care
ful examination of the yellow Buick convertible.

"You're drivin' a car like this, and you tell me you ain't got ten bucks?"

"You will no doubt notice that this is a 'forty-six model," Guy said. "
bought it when I had money. I don't have any money now."

"You got no money, you don't get through."

"All right by me," Guy said, slipping the car into reverse.

"Hey, wait a minute! Hold it!" the guard called in a panicky voice. He
looked at Guy a moment longer, then sighed. "If you don't get in, there won
be no picture, and I'll lose the money from all the rest of 'em." He pointed a

214

Guy. "All right, I'm goin' to let you in, but don't you tell no one you got by me without payin' nothin'."

"That's a pretty neat little gimmick you've got going there, mister," Guy said as he shifted into first. "How would it be if I told Gillis about it?"

The guard grinned. "Why don't you just tell him and find out?"

"Never mind," Guy said, letting out the clutch and driving off. He realized then that Gillis was leaving no stone unturned. The son of a bitch was getting a kickback from the guard who was shaking down his own people!

Two cars were parked outside the soundstage. Guy parked alongside them, then went inside. The lights had already been set up, and a bare bed had been placed conspicuously under the lights. A camera technician was taking a light reading. There were no other props.

A young, heavily made-up woman was sitting crosslegged on top of one of the big boxes the lights were stored in. She was wearing blue jeans and a pullover shirt. From the way the shirt lay against her breasts, Guy knew that she was wearing nothing underneath it. A cigarette dangled from her lips.

"No outsiders on the set," the young woman said in a flat, almost bored voice.

"I'm here to work."

"Are you now?" she replied. "Honey, you're a little old to be in a picture like this, aren't you? Even if you could get it up, which I doubt, I'd have you whittled back down in nothin' flat." She held her arms up and wriggled her shoulders so that her breasts bounced and rolled suggestively under the thin shirt. Everyone laughed.

"I'm the director."

"The director?" the young woman said. She laughed. "Hey, Al, come 'ere," she called out.

A young man ambled over to the box. Guy hadn't noticed him until then, and he wondered now how he had managed to miss him. The young man was totally naked, and his qualification for pictures like this was very apparent.

Guy didn't mean to stare, but he had never seen a penis as enormous as the one hanging between the young man's legs. It was so large it looked almost deformed.

"Whaddya want?" Al asked.

The girl pointed to Guy. "He's going to direct us."

"That right?" Al asked. "You going to give me an' Tammy an' ol' Snake here"—he grabbed himself proudly and without shame—"directions on how to fuck?"

Guy smiled wryly. "Nope. I'm going to give you and Tammy and old Snake here"—he pointed to Al's penis—"directions on how to act."

14

EARLY SUMMER, 1949, DELTA,
MISSISSIPPI

The first person Colonel James Royal saw after his U.S. Air Force staff
car passed by the city limit sign of Delta, Mississippi, was a Negro
woman. She was doing her family's laundry with the wringer washer
and rinse tubs set up on the front porch of her house. Playing in the
grassless front yard under her watchful eye were six shirtless and shoeless children. The children looked up as the car passed, and one of them waved. His
pink palm was bright against ebony skin.

Smiling at the children, Colonel Royal waved back.

In front of the house next door a woman was sweeping the dirt yard as dili-
gently as if it had been her living room. The staff car, a four-door Chevrolet
painted Air Force blue, passed several more houses that fit the same general
description as the first two: unpainted, patched, and leaning, with washing
machines and/or iceboxes sitting on the front porch and barren front yards.

As the car left the black section of town and rode into the white section
there was little immediate change except for the playing children. They were

ill shirtless and shoeless, but they were white. Like the houses in the black
rea, these homes were unpainted, patched, and leaning and had the same
ppliances on the front porch. The yards were still grassless, though many did
ave cars sitting in them. Most of the cars, though ancient and battered,
poked as if they would run. More than a few, however, were up on blocks in
ne middle of a big patch of oil-soaked dirt, with the wheels off, the hoods
p, and pieces of the engine spread out and rusting in the sun.

As the Air Force car continued toward the center of town, there was a
radual improvement in the condition of the homes. Then in the last few
locks it passed large, well-kept lawns filled with towering pecan and flower-
g magnolia trees. The houses were big, two-story homes, surrounded by
erandas, porte cocheres, and Grecian columns. In most cases the owners' cars
ere discreetly parked in the garage at the rear of the estate. But here and
here Cadillacs, Lincolns, Packards, or Chryslers sat on flower-bordered,
rick-paved driveways that circled fountains or well-tended planters in front
f the house. More than once Colonel Royal saw a black man wearing a
hauffeur's hat polishing a car as proudly as if it were his own.

"This part of town sure is different from the part we just came through,
n't it, Colonel?" the driver, Sergeant Al Reeves, asked.

"Yes," Royal answered.

"Do you know where you want to go?"

"I'm not sure, exactly. The only address we have is Delta, Mississippi. Why
on't you try the police station, if you can find it?"

The town was laid out around a small, parklike square. Right in the mid-
le of a large X formed by the sidewalks that diagonally traversed the park
as a high, marble pedestal. Upon that pedestal, facing north, stood a bronze
oldier. As it so happened, the soldier was looking right toward a building that
ad a sign identifying it as the Delta police station. Two black-and-white
ords were parked in front of the station, each with a shield on the door and
red light mounted on the left front fender. The Fords were from before the
9 design change. Colonel Royal wasn't exactly sure what year they were, but
hey could have been anything from '46 to '48. He indicated that his driver
hould park alongside the police cars.

"You wait here, Sergeant," Royal said as he got out of the car. "I'll go inside
nd talk to the police chief."

"Yes, sir."

Royal crossed the sidewalk and pushed the door open, then paused in the
oorway. Just inside was a waist-high rail that separated the small entry foyer
om the two desks and one table of the "office" area. The windows were
pen to let in the outside breeze, and two oscillating fans sat on shelves on
he wall. The fans hummed quietly as they worked back and forth, ruffling

217

papers gently as the column of forced air passed across the desks and tab
At first the colonel thought no one was there; then he saw an overweig
policeman standing at the back of the room, looking through the top draw
of a filing cabinet. The policeman's back was turned to him, and Royal cou
see the inverted triangle of sweat that had soaked through the back of h
khaki uniform shirt.

"Excuse me, Officer," Royal called.

The policeman turned. Taking in the military uniform replete with ri
bons, wings, and eagles, his eyes opened wide.

"Yes, sir? What can I do for you?"

"My name is Colonel James Royal, of the U.S. Air Force. Are you the ch
of police here?"

The policeman laughed nervously. "No, sir," he said. "I'm just a patro
man. Billy Ray Hawkins is my name. Stump Pollard's chief. Would you li
to see him?"

"If you don't mind."

"Could you tell me what this here's about?"

"Yes. I'm looking for someone who lives here."

"What's the matter, Colonel? Did one of our boys go AWOL? If so, i
news to me. We generally keep up with our boys that's in the service."

"No, he isn't AWOL," Colonel Royal said. "In fact, he isn't even in the A
Force anymore. But I would like to find him, nevertheless."

"What's this here fella's name?"

"Jackson," Colonel Royal said. "Travis W. Jackson."

Patrolman Hawkins's eyes narrowed. "Is that a fact? We got us a nigra liv
here by that name."

"Yes, that would be the same man. The Travis Jackson I'm looking f
is Negro."

"Whatcha want him for, Colonel?" Hawkins asked. "I mean, the reason
ask is, our chief, he gets along with most of the local nigras pretty good. A
he seems to get along kinda special with Travis. If you're wantin' Travis f
somethin', I'm afraid you're goin' to have to go through the chief."

"Yes," Royal said, exasperated by the conversation. "If you recall, I did a
to speak to the chief."

"Well, you'll find him over to Little Man's for lunch."

"Little Man's?"

The patrolman walked up to the front window and pointed across th
square. "You see that there café on the corner? That's Little Man Lambert's.

Royal nodded. "Thank you."

He exited the building and started across the square toward Little Mar
stopping for a moment to read the inscription on the base of the statue.

In service, he found honor.
In defeat, he preserved dignity.
THE CONFEDERATE SOLDIER
1861 — 1865

When James Royal stepped through the door of the café, he was nveloped by the mixed aromas of broiled pork chops, grilled hamburgers, ied onions, fried chicken, fresh tomatoes, and a melange of other smells he ouldn't identify. He glanced around. A man in a khaki policeman's uniform as just hanging up the telephone at the far end of the room. He was a big an, with powerful arms and shoulders, and, grinning, he walked toward Colonel Royal with his hand extended.

"Colonel Royal, I'm Stump Pollard." He gestured back to the phone. "That as Billy Ray over at the station. He said you wanted to talk to me about ravis Jackson."

"Yes, if you don't mind."

"I don't mind at all," Stump said. "You had your lunch?"

"No, as a matter of fact, I haven't."

"Well, then, why don't you just sit down and have a bite?"

"My sergeant is over in the car waiting for me. He hasn't eaten either."

Pollard turned to the heavyset woman behind the cash register. "Emma ou, call Billy Ray back and tell him I said go out to that Air Force car and tell e sergeant to come on over here and have his lunch."

"Be glad to, Stump," she replied.

"And bring the colonel here some of your chicken 'n' dumplin's. Better ake it two. . . one for the sergeant." Stump smiled at the colonel. "Most of e time you can't get good chicken 'n' dumplin's in a café. But what they fix ere is about as good as any you ever put in your mouth. Hell, I wish my Cora lay could make 'em as good. You want ice tea or Co' Cola?"

"Coffee," the colonel said.

"Mighta known it," Stump said with a snicker. "Coffee, Emma Lou."

"Comin' right up," she called back.

There were nearly two dozen other diners in the café. Some were wearing usiness suits, though most were wearing coveralls. The men in suits and the en in coveralls were sitting together, engaged in animated conversations at apparently crossed any class lines their dress might have represented.

Colonel Royal's driver came in just as they were sitting down, and the offi-er held up his hand. "Back here, Sergeant Reeves."

The dumplings were brought over and put before the two Air Force men. Colonel Royal looked with ill-concealed apprehension at the pale pile of eaming pastry on his plate.

219

Stump laughed. "First thing you got to learn, Colonel, is how to eat 'em
he said. "You need to pepper 'em up real good." He demonstrated by apply
ing a liberal amount of pepper to his own plate. "I mean, you have to turn 'er
nearly black."

Hesitantly, first Royal and then Reeves followed Stump's suggestion.

'Then all you do is dig in," Stump said, transferring a generous forkload t
his mouth.

Cautiously, Al Reeves took a bite. He chewed thoughtfully for a momen
then smiled broadly.

"Hey, this shit's all right," he said. Quickly, he covered his mouth with h
hand. "Beg pardon, sir."

Stump laughed. "Don't apologize, Sergeant. Hell, that's the kind of reac
tion we *like* to get."

Colonel Royal tried the dumpling, and though his reaction wasn't quit
as enthusiastic as Reeves's, he found, to his pleasant surprise, that it was a
least palatable.

"Now," Stump said, raking a biscuit through the thick gravy that sur
rounded the dumplings, "what is it you want Travis Jackson for?"

"I'd rather take that up with him, if you don't mind," Royal said.

"Is he in any trouble?"

"Why do you ask? Is he the kind who's likely to be in trouble?"

"No, sir, not at all," Stump replied. "In fact, if you're here to tell me he *is* i
trouble, you'll get two reactions from me. My first would be that I don
believe it. And the second would be to tell you that whatever I can do to hel
Travis out, I'll do it."

"You'll excuse me for saying so, Chief, but your attitude isn't exactly typ
cal of the South, is it? I mean, most Mississippi law officers are portrayed a
men who just cruise around town, looking for Negro heads to bash in."

Stump sniffed wryly. "That's not too far from the truth, I reckon," he saic
"But you have to realize that there are a hell of a lot of niggers who *need* the
heads bashed in. Hell, I've done my own share of bashing."

"Isn't your attitude toward 'niggers' a little inconsistent with your attitud
toward Travis Jackson?"

"Not at all," Stump insisted. "In the first place, Travis isn't a nigger."

"What? But I thought—"

"Oh, he's colored all right. But there's a big difference between a colore
man and a nigger. Just like there's a big difference between a white man an
white trash."

"I must confess that the difference escapes me," Royal said. "But then, I'r
an outsider."

"Yes, sir, you are," Stump said matter-of-factly.

"Be that as it may, do you know where Mr. Jackson is right now?"

"Wait a minute and I'll find out." Stump looked toward one of the other tables. "Swain? Isn't Travis workin' on your cotton today?"

"Yesterday, today, and tomorrow," the farmer answered.

"Where d'you think he'd be right about now?"

"Well, if he hasn't run into any trouble, he ought to be down below the Dumey silos. You know the field, Stump. It's the bottomland I bought from Elmer Green's widow."

"Yeah, I know where it is," Stump said. He pushed away from the table, then glanced at Colonel Royal's plate. About half the dumplings remained uneaten. "Soon as you're finished, I'll run you down there."

"We can go now," Royal said, standing. "I'm quite full."

Sergeant Reeves started to stand as well, but Royal held his hand out. "Why don't you stay in town, Sergeant? I'll ride out with the chief."

"Yes, sir," Al Reeves said. "Oh, and Colonel, if you aren't gonna finish your dumplin's, mind if I finish 'em for you?"

"Help yourself," Royal said, sliding his plate over onto Reeves's completely cleaned one.

"Hey, that sergeant of yours is all right," Stump said as they started for the door. "The way that boy eats, we could make a southerner out of him in no time. Emma Lou," he called back, "when the sergeant is through with the dumplin's, bring him a piece of pecan pie, then put everything on my bill."

"Hey, Stump, you pickin' up *ever'one's* bill?" the farmer named Swain called, and when Stump shook his head and dismissed the rest of the patrons with a wave of his hand, they all laughed.

"Is Jackson a farm worker?" Colonel Royal asked a few moments later as he slipped into the front seat of the police car beside Stump.

"A farm worker? You mean like a field hand?" Stump shook his head. "No. What makes you think that?"

"You asked that farmer what field he was working in."

"Oh, that." Stump pulled away from the station. "Well, when I asked if he was working Swain's field, I meant was he dusting it. Jackson flies a crop-dusting plane."

Colonel Royal looked at Stump in surprise. "He does? That's a little unusual, isn't it?"

Stump laughed. "Unusual? Colonel, in these parts it's unheard of. Nevertheless, Travis is out there doing it, bigger 'n life."

"What do the farmers think of a Negro crop duster?"

"Well, there's four different opinions on that. There are those who absolutely won't use him because he's colored. They'll get someone to come over from someplace like Starkville or down from Memphis before they'd use

Travis. But the ones that do that are paying more money and they aren't getting as good a job done. Then there are those who will hire Travis just because he *is* colored. They say crop dusting is a dangerous job, and if someone's goin' to get killed doin' it, they'd just as soon it be a colored man. Then there's those who say that dustin' crops is no different from planting crops, and if they can hire a colored man to drive their tractor or a team of mules through their field, then they can hire a colored man to fly an airplane over their field."

"You said there were four opinions."

"Yeah," Stump said. "I belong to the fourth group."

"What group is that?"

"That's the group that enjoys watching a good show. I'd just as soon go out to the field and watch Travis fly that old biplane of his as see a good football game. Tell you the truth, Colonel, we've had lots of crop dusters in here, especially since the war. But none of them do it quite like Travis. He's one crackerjack of a pilot. He takes that damned plane of his over the wires, under the wires, around the trees, through the trees, anywhere he wants, and then he stands it up on its tail and makes it dance. And low? That boy gets down so low that if you were to tie a strand of barbed wire between his wheels, he could pick cotton. Oh, there he is."

Royal looked in the direction Stump was pointing and saw a yellow Stearman biplane pop up just above the treeline. It flipped around, then disappeared again.

"Quinisha should be around here somewhere," Stump said.

"Quinisha?"

"She's Travis's wife. Pretty girl, graduated from Jackson State, then came up here to teach in Travis's daddy's school. Professor Jackson is the principal of our colored school." Stump chuckled. "She wasn't up here anytime at all before Travis took up with her. They've only been married a couple of months. She quit teaching and started driving Travis's service truck for him. Ah, there she is. See that red truck over there by that line of trees? It holds all the chemicals that he needs. Quinisha has to be here all the time because Travis can't get more than halfway through a field before he has to land and refill his hopper.

Stump turned off the road and drove out across a field, his car bumping roughly across every furrow. When he reached the red truck, a young and pretty black woman came toward his car, smiling.

"Hello, Chief," she said. "What brings you out here?"

At that moment the Stearman roared by overhead, the growl of its R-985 engine beating down on them with a noise that was so loud it made the body vibrate. Colonel Royal looked up just as the airplane passed by and saw the helmeted and goggled pilot looking back at him and at Stump, no doubt curi-

s as to why they were there. The pilot pulled the plane up after its pass,
ood it on its tail, then let the nose fall over in a hammerhead stall as it
arted back across the field in the opposite direction. When the airplane
ached the edge of the field, a white spray began spewing out from the noz-
es along the trailing edges of the lower wing. As the plane flew across the
eld, the engine noise receded enough for Stump to answer Quinisha
ckson's question.

"Quinisha, this is Colonel James Royal of the U.S. Air Force," Stump said
nportantly. "He's here to talk to Travis."

"Oh, my," Quinisha said anxiously. "Has Travis done something wrong? Is
e violating a flying law or something that you have to enforce?"

Royal chuckled. "No, ma'am. Actually, the Air Force doesn't enforce flying
les against civilians."

"You don't? That's strange. I would've thought you did."

The Stearman roared by again. Again it pulled up sharply, fell off into a
ammerhead stall, then started back across the field in the opposite direction.

"I'm here to make an offer to your husband," Colonel Royal said. "And I
ope he sees fit to accept."

"Well," Quinisha said, smiling, "get your offer ready, because when he
omes back this time he's going to have to land."

True to Quinisha's word, when the Stearman reappeared, it lined up on its
nal approach for the edge of the field, with its furrowed rows. Colonel Royal
atched the plane settle down, its engine ticking over quietly now, its wheels
aching out. It touched down lightly, then bumped and bounced over the
even ground as it taxied up to the truck. The pilot climbed down from the
ane and stretched, put his helmet and goggles carefully on the lower wing,
en started toward Stump and Royal. He looked somewhat older than his
venty-eight years—no doubt due to his wartime experiences, Royal decided.
uinisha immediately climbed up onto the plane and poked a hose down into
hat had been the front seat well but was now a chemical hopper.

"Hi, Chief," Travis said, sticking his hand out and smiling. "Hello, Colonel.
nything wrong?"

"No," Stump answered. "This fella wants to talk to you, is all."

"Oh?" Travis asked. "What's this about, Colonel?"

"It's about the military, Mr. Jackson. You are aware, are you not, that what
sed to be the old Army Air Corps is now the U.S. Air Force, our own branch
f service?"

"Yes, sir, I read about it."

"Are you aware, also, that President Truman has issued an executive order
nding segregation in the armed forces?"

"Yes, sir, I read about that, too."

"What does that mean, exactly?" Stump asked.

"It means that there aren't any more all-Negro units," the color explained. "The way it is now, when a Negro enters the service, he goes rig into the same company as white men. Negroes and whites live together, wc together, and if another war comes, they'll fight together."

"How's it working out?" Travis asked.

"There are some problems, as you might expect," Royal admitte "Prejudices and myths die hard. But in the long run it will work, and when does, the armed forces will be a model for the rest of the country to follov

"That would be nice," Travis agreed.

"Which brings us to you, Mr. Jackson. You could be a great help to t desegregation efforts in the Air Force."

"How?"

"One of the problems we're having at the moment is a shortage of Negro m in leadership positions, people whom our younger Negro men down in the rar can respect and emulate. You see, they're exposed for the most part only to wh officers. We've brought in some Negro chaplains, and we've managed to get a f Negro supply and transportation corps officers to switch over from the Army. I we have a serious shortage of the officer who's the most prominent representati of the Air Force: the pilot. So what I'm here for, Mr. Jackson, is to ask you if y would be willing to rejoin the U.S. Army Air Corps in its new incarnation t United States Air Force. We would, of course, offer you a commission."

"What rank?"

"First lieutenant."

"First lieutenant? Shit," Travis scoffed, "I was a captain during the war."

"Yes, I know. But the needs of the service were greatly extended during t war. You would be amazed, Mr. Jackson, at how many enlisted men there a on active duty right now who were officers during the war."

"What happened to them?"

"They were reserve officers on active duty, and when, in the language the military, 'the needs of the service no longer required them,' their reser commission was deactivated."

"What would keep something like that from happening to me?" Tra asked. "I mean, suppose I said yes and took the commission. Then, suppo I decided I wanted to stay, but ten years from now the Air Force sudden decided that it had enough Negro officers. . . or enough officers of *any* kir What would keep the Air Force from deactivating my commission?"

"Nothing," Royal admitted.

"Yes, well, I'd like to help you, Colonel, but I've got a pretty good thir going here. I'm making a good income—probably more than I'd make in tl Air Force, frankly—and I enjoy the work."

"Can you fly all year long?"

"There are some slack months," Travis said, shrugging.

Royal pointed over to the Stearman. Quinisha had just finished servic-
g the hopper and was climbing down from the wing. She walked over to
in them.

"You flew P-51's during the war, didn't you, Mr. Jackson? Mustangs?"

"I sure did."

"It was a pretty hot ship. Now you're back to flying the same thing you
w when you took your primary training. Don't you ever miss getting into
e cockpit of something that's really hot?"

Grinning, Travis said, "Yes, sir, I don't mind admitting that I do miss it
ery now and then."

"Have you ever heard of the F-86 Saberjet?"

Travis shook his head. "No, sir, I don't think I have."

"Let me describe it to you. It's about the size of the P-51 Mustang. It's a jet,
course, so no propeller. But the wings, Mr. Jackson, the wings of this jet are
ept back, like so." He demonstrated with his hands. "It not only looks like
rocket, it takes off like one. The climbing time from rotation to thirty thou-
nd feet is six minutes."

"*Six minutes?*"

"Six minutes. And it cruises—not top speed, mind you, but *cruises*—at over
x hundred fifty miles per hour."

"Holy shit!" Travis said, clearly impressed. "That's moving."

"That's *nothing*. In the next couple of years we'll have planes faster than the
eed of sound. I'm not talking about the experimental rocket planes that are
ping it now, but front-line fighter airplanes. Are you sure you want to pass
at up?"

"Travis, what's going on here?" Quinisha asked, not having heard Colonel
oyal's initial pitch.

"I'm trying to talk your husband into coming back into the Air Force," Royal
id. "And by the way, Mrs. Jackson, I wish you could see the married officers'
using at our air bases. Most of the houses are new, what's called 'ranch style.'
hey're brick, with living room, kitchen, dining room, two bathrooms, and two,
ree, or four bedrooms, depending on how many children you have. They have
rports, patios, and large lawns. I think you would really enjoy living there."

"Baby, I didn't know you were thinking about going back into the Air
orce," Quinisha said, touching Travis on the arm.

"I wasn't thinking about it. . . until now. Listen, Quinisha, what would you
ink if I did?"

"I told you when I married you, Travis Jackson, that wherever you go, I go.
you want to go into the Air Force, and they—" She looked at Colonel

Royal. "What you were saying about the houses and all, that means I could g
with Travis?"

"Yes, ma'am," Royal said, smiling, "that's exactly what it means. More tha
half of our officers are married."

"Well, then," she said to Travis, "if you want to go into the Air Force,
won't say anything to stop you. Just as long as I can go with you."

"What about it, Mr. Jackson?"

"I need to think about it, Colonel."

"All right, I can understand that." Royal took out a business card an
handed it to him. "If you make up your mind that you'd like to come back i
give me a call and I'll get everything set up for you. Oh. . . and maybe there
one little thing I could do to sweeten the pot."

"What's that?"

"I think I can get you a regular commission. That way you couldn't b
eased out by a reduction in forces. You could stay on active duty until yc
retired, if you wanted to."

Travis nodded. "I would appreciate that, Colonel. Because if I go back i
that's the only way I'd do it."

Colonal Royal turned to Stump Pollard. "Well, Chief, if you'll take me back t
town, I guess my job's done." He looked back at Travis. "Oh, and Lieutenant. .

Travis smiled and held up his finger. "Not yet," he said.

Royal returned the smile. "I have a feeling you will be. But I was about t
say don't wait too long. The Department of the Air Force is only keeping th
offer open for thirty days."

LOS ANGELES

When Anton Delecourt stepped out the front door of his house at six A.M
his driver had the car waiting for him. It was a soft, summer morning, an
beams from the rising sun picked up the dew drops on the lawn, creatin
thousands of flashing prisms of color. Birds were singing and palm fronds ra
tled quietly in the gentle morning breeze. From the beach behind the hous
Anton could hear the crashing roll of surf from a pearl-gray ocean tinted b
the early morning sun to a pale rose.

Anton's chauffeur was standing by the Cadillac, holding the rear door ope
With scarcely a nod, Anton stepped into the back of the car, then slid across th
red leather seat to the far side. Ignoring the coffee and the orange juice nestle
securely in a pull-down compartment on the front seat-back, Anton cupped h
chin in his hand and stared morosely through the window as the car pulled awa

Today was the first day of shooting for *Priscilla*. The clock was already rur
ning on the production. An exact replica of the *Mayflower* had been built;

ll-scale Plymouth colony had been constructed; soundstages had been
served and sets built; lights, cameras, and recording equipment had been
athered; production crews had been assembled; and the roles of John Alden
nd Miles Standish had been cast, as had most of the other principal charac-
rs. According to Anton's accountant, production costs were piling up at sev-
al thousand dollars per day—yet there was no one to play the title role.

It wasn't supposed to be that way. Anton had planned to use Elizabeth
aylor. To those who suggested that she might be a bit young for the part,
e pointed out that though she was only seventeen, she had just com-
eted *Conspirator*, in which she played steamy love scenes opposite Robert
aylor. He was certain she could handle, and handle brilliantly, the role of
riscilla Mullens.

But no matter how perfect she might be for the part, he wasn't able to use
er. The reason given by the studio Elizabeth Taylor was under contract to
as a conflict between the terms of her contract and the terms proposed by
nton Delecourt. Anton didn't believe the studio's response. He was sure the
tual reason was that Elizabeth had no real desire to play any role while she
as in the midst of a much-publicized romance with former Army football
ar Glen Davis. But regardless of why she couldn't or wouldn't do it, Anton
ow found himself in full production of *Priscilla* with no Priscilla.

Some had suggested that Anton do what David O. Selznick had done
hen searching for a Scarlett O'Hara a decade earlier: Begin production by
ooting around the title role while at the same time conducting a nationwide
lent search for his star. The publicity of such a search, they reasoned, would
nerate as much public interest in this picture as it had for *Gone With the Wind*.

Anton had refused to do that. In the first place he believed that the
uality of the picture would be all that was necessary to interest the pub-
. And in the second place he didn't want the public to be involved in his
arch process. Casting the movie was very much his prerogative, and he
d no intention of turning it over to anyone, let alone to millions of movie
ns—most of whom, he pointed out, would be disappointed if their choice
asn't selected.

But he was down to the wire now. He was going to have to start shooting
at day, and he had no choice but to film around his title character. He had
sted four girls the week before, and he'd be looking at the results of those
sts that morning. *Who knows?* he thought. *Maybe I'll get lucky.* But having
atched the tests while they were being filmed, he had little confidence in
at outcome.

The Cadillac glided through the studio gates, and the chauffeur parked in
e private lot behind the studio building. A yellow Buick convertible was
rked there as well, and though it looked exceptionally well-maintained, it

was four years old. No car that old would belong to any of the executive
authorized to use the lot, which meant that it probably belonged to a janito
or perhaps one of the groundskeepers. Whomever it belonged to, the drive
certainly had no business parking it there, and Anton made a mental note t
speak with security about it. They should be more diligent in keeping unau
thorized cars out of the private parking area.

Anton unlocked the back door to the building, then stepped into the narrov
shadowed hallway. Using the back-hall entrance allowed him to get into his offic
without having to pass by anyone who might be waiting out front. Since wor
had gotten out that the role of Priscilla hadn't yet been cast, agents, actresse
would-be actresses, and would-be actresses' pushy mothers had been camping o
in the waiting room. That left Anton's receptionists to deal with them.

Some of the job seekers, not willing to believe that "Mr. Delecourt isn't i
and won't be in today," would come to the studio before Anton's office sta
arrived in the morning and stay there until the office staff left in the evenin;
Anton knew it was unpleasant for his staff to have to put up with that, but h
paid them well enough that they didn't complain.

The back door to his private office opened off the hallway, requiring
second key. Anton let himself in, then walked through the shadowy roor
over to the window, where he opened the blinds. Bars of sunlight spilled ont
the white Persian rug and brightened up the mahogany, glass, and brass offic
that had more floor space than many apartments.

When Anton turned away from the window, he was so badly startled b
the sight of a man sitting on his leather sofa that he gasped and put his hand
to his chest. "Holy shit!" he yelped.

"Good morning, Anton," Guy Colby said easily. "I'm sorry if I frightened you

"What. . . what the hell are you doing here?" Anton gasped.

Guy chuckled. "Well, obviously I came to see you."

"But how did you get in here? Who let you in?"

"I let myself in. After all, this *was* my office. You haven't forgotten, ha
you? My office was here, and yours was the smaller one at the other end <
the hall."

"But the locks. They were all changed."

"Oh, heavens, Anton, of course they were. But remember how we used t
have to change the locks every time someone left? I just got so tired of hav
ing to get new keys that I finally had masters made. I can get into any offic
or any room in the entire studio."

Anton walked over to his desk and reached for the telephone. "I think
had better call security."

"Anton, do you remember that script boy that I hired and made an assi
tant director? The one who, because no one would give him a chance, wa

out to go back home to his father's grocery store in Indiana? The one who
id, and I quote, 'If there's ever anything I can do for you—anything in the
orld, no matter how difficult or what the inconvenience—I'll do it.' Do you
member that man, Anton? Oh, but of course you do. It was you, wasn't it?"

Anton sighed and put the receiver back down.

"You have no right to do this, Guy," he said. "Nobody with class holds
other to such a statement."

"Well, I wouldn't know about that, Anton," Guy said with a smirk. "You
e, I have no class."

"What do you want, Guy?" Anton asked impatiently as he opened a silver
garette case, took out a cigarette, and lit it. "You know I can't use you—not
nile you're still blackballed by the industry."

"All I want is a moment of your time. I think it will be profitable for you."

Guy exhaled audibly. "Profitable for me? In what way?"

"I have found your Priscilla."

Suddenly Anton laughed. "Don't tell me, Guy. Don't tell me you've gone
to the agenting business."

"I'm not an agent," Guy said. "And if you use this girl, I want no percent-
e, I want no finder's fee. I don't want anything. I'm only trying to bring the
o of you together."

"Then I don't understand. *Why* are you doing it?"

"Someday this boycott against me is going to be lifted. Someday I'm going
be able to work again. But when that day does come, it means I'm going to
ve to start all over. There will be other directors, producers, writers, actors,
d actresses who will have come along since my time, and I'm going to have
be able to find a toehold somewhere." Guy smiled. "I intend to keep a few
you beholden to me."

Anton ground out the cigarette. "I see. And you think that bringing this
rl to me will make me beholden to you?"

"Oh, you *and* the girl will be beholden to me," Guy said. "You see, once
e's a star, she'll be as valuable a contact as anyone else."

"You seem pretty sure she's going to be a star."

"She will be."

"Do I know her? Have I ever seen any of her work?"

"No one has ever seen her," Guy said. "She's only done one film, and every-
ing she did in that film was cut out. I cut it out."

"*You* cut it out? Why would you do that if she's as good as you say?" Anton
ked, perplexed.

"I did it *because* she's as good as I say," Guy replied. He held up a gray film
n. "I've got the film here. When you take a look at it, you'll understand why
ut this away from the rest of the film."

"Okay, you talked me into it. I'll have a look at her. Leave the film on n desk and—"

"No," Guy interrupted. "We'll go back to the moviola and look at it rig now, together. I am the only one who has ever seen this film. No one else b you will *ever* see it."

"Guy, I must say I don't understand all this secrecy," Anton said, shakir his head. "If the girl has anything at all that interests me, you know I'm goir to want to let a few others see her."

"Make a screen test," Guy said. "Show *that* to as many people as you war But no one else will ever see this film. Now, do you want to take a look at or not?"

"All right, I'll look at it," Anton said. He chuckled nervously. "I'll say th for you. You've certainly piqued my interest if for no other reason than just see what's so mysterious about this piece of film."

Anton and Guy walked back to the lab, with Anton leading the w through the familiar turns and twists of the building. Opening the door to tl lab, he reached up in the darkness and immediately located the light switc He flicked it and flooded the room with light. Sitting side by side in a lc row on a workbench along a back wall were a number of moviolas, the devi used by film editors to get their first glimpse of the finished product. The were actually little different from the old dawn-of-the-century peep-shc machines, where motion pictures could be viewed by moving the film str through a magnifying glass over a light source with a hand crank. Of cours such a method had no sound, but for this, no sound was needed.

Guy threaded the film through the two reels, then backed away from tl moviola and, with outstretched hand, offered it to Anton. Anton put his ey to the viewer and began cranking. After only a couple of cranks he pulled l head away and fixed Guy with an angry glare.

"What the hell is this?" he demanded. "Is this some kind of joke? This is goddamn stag film!"

"It's no joke. Look at the girl, Anton," Guy said, pointing to the moviol "Look at the girl, not at what she's doing."

Anton went back to the moviola and began turning the crank. This tin he kept his eyes glued to the viewer. It took him five minutes to go throuç the entire film.

When he was finished, his hands were shaking and his palms were swea ing. He looked at Guy with an expression of awe on his face.

"That is the most erotically stimulating film I have ever seen," he said qu etly. "And I'm not talking about the sex."

"I know," Guy answered.

"It's the girl."

"I know," Guy said again.

"There is something about her. . . an innocence that comes through in even the most debasing scenes. Goddamn, even in the fellatio she came across like she was a sweet little schoolgirl."

"That's because she wants you to *believe* she's a sweet little schoolgirl," Guy said. "Don't you see, Anton? If she can make you suspend belief in what you *see* her doing and believe instead in what you *don't* see simply by the art of her projection, then she has as powerful a screen presence as anyone who's ever been in the business."

"Who. . . who is she? Where did this girl come from?"

"Well, if you haven't guessed by now," Guy said, "this is one of Leo Gillis's films."

"Leo Gillis? The porn film maker? How did you get it?"

"I work for him," Guy said simply.

"You *work* for him?" Anton looked at Guy in disbelief. "My God, Guy. You work for that louse? How could you do that? You've won two Oscars!"

"Oscars are pretty, but they aren't edible."

Anton shook his head angrily. "This isn't right. You shouldn't be—" He stopped in midsentence and sighed in frustration. "I guess we haven't left you much choice, have we?"

"What about the girl?" Guy asked. "Will you test her?"

"Why bother? If she was Bette Davis and Katharine Hepburn and Ingrid Bergman all rolled into one, I couldn't use her. You know that, Guy, as well as I do. If one of these films ever came to light. . ."

Guy grinned broadly. "It won't," he said. He pointed to the strip of film on the moviola. "You just looked at the only thing she ever did, and, as I told you, I took every bit of it out from the rest of the film. When *A Secretary's Vacation* went to Hong Kong, it went five minutes short."

"What about Leo Gillis? Where does he figure in all this? I can't see him just letting this girl go without so much as a whimper."

"Leo Gillis doesn't even know this girl exists," Guy replied. "She showed up two weeks ago with one of the other girls, looking for work. Anton, the girl is a natural. I've been around the business long enough. I know. My God, man, I can sense it in my gut the way a dowser can sense water. Whatever the mysterious quality is that makes someone a star, this girl has it in spades. Test her. I promise you, you won't be sorry."

"But what kind of girl is she?" Anton asked. "I mean, what kind of girl would do something like this?"

"Are you asking me to pass judgment on her, Anton? Because if you are, I can't do that. I've already seen that a person will do whatever a person has to do. But I will say this: This girl still has a chance. Two years or three years from now with ten or twenty of these movies behind her, I wouldn't give her a second look. The talent would still be there, that amazing aura would still be there, but it would be too dangerous to use her. You have to do it now, Anton, while the door is open. Don't let her get away."

"Suppose I wanted to give her a test. How will I find her?"

"Don't worry about that; I'll find her for you. You just set up the test."

"All right, how about nine this morning?"

"Obviously I can't bring her here," Guy said. "But I'll see to it that she's here by nine. You see to it that she gets by your Praetorian guard."

"Come back to the office," Anton said, motioning Guy out of the lab. 'I'll write out a pass for her. Have her at soundstage three." He locked the door and headed back down the hall.

"Soundstage three," Guy repeated as he followed Anton back to his office. He smiled. "That's a lucky soundstage for me. That's where we shot most of *The Corruptible Dead.*"

They entered Anton's office, and the producer reached for a sheet of stationery. "Oh, by the way, what's the girl's name?" he asked as he scribbled out the pass.

"I have no idea what her real name is," Guy said. He laughed. "She was using the name Lolly Popp."

"Ouch," Anton replied, wincing.

"Well, given the role she was playing, you have to admit that the name was not only creative. . . it was also thematic."

"Marcella," Anton said, handing the note to Guy.

"I beg your pardon?"

"The girl's name will be Marcella. Marcella Mills."

15

ULY 1949, FROM "TRAILMARKERS"
N EVENTS MAGAZINE:

TESTED: The world's first jet airliner, England's de Havilland Comet, in a debut flight at Hatfield, England. The Comet, powered by four jet engines, will immediately make all other airliners obsolete. The Comet is designed to carry 36 passengers in an all-pressurized cabin at an altitude of 40,000 feet and at speeds of 500 miles per hour. This is nearly twice as fast as the average airliner now in service.

DISCOVERED: By Linus Pauling, the molecular flaw responsible for sickle-cell anemia. The disease, which afflicts Negroes, gets its name from the shape the blood cells assume when they are infected. Because of their sickle shape, the cells have difficulty passing through the small blood vessels. Dr. Pauling's research has determined that the problem lies in the hemoglobin, an oxygen-carrying protein that consists of many subunits. The disease is caused by change in a single subunit.

MARRIED: Eric Twainbough, novelist (*A Stillness in the Line*, *The Corruptible Dead*, and the disastrous—see "Books" in this issue—*Tea on the Veranda*) to Shaylin McKay, a senior editor for *Events* and winner (in 1945) of the National Journalists Award for her series *Open: The Gates of Hell*. This is Mr. Twainbough's second marriage, Miss McKay's first. The couple will reside in Mr. Twainbough's home on Bimini.

ENGAGED: Liesl Tannenhower, daughter of Nazi Germany's wartime Oberreichsleiter Karl Tannenhower and great-grandniece of Aldophus Tannenhower, founder of St. Louis's Tannenhower Brewery, to Roger Tremain Daigh, an account manager in the St. Louis brokerage firm of Barry, Patmore, and Daigh.

From "Books" in Events Magazine: *Tea on the Veranda*. By Eric Twainbough. 248 pages. Argus and Collier. $3.

Tea on the Veranda is Eric Twainbough's first effort with his new publisher, Argus and Collier. It is not a good effort. Twainbough is at his best when he gives us action played against a well-drawn story line. He is at his worst when he tries to explore all the subtle nuances of his characters.

Tea on the Veranda abandons his best and embraces his worst. It has practically no story line and depends for its appeal upon the complex and somewhat baffling study of the psyche of seventy-year-old Miss Emma Flowers.

In a series of conversations held during "tea on the veranda" the reader learns through the first-person narrator that Miss Flowers is still pining for her onetime swain, whom she always refers to as "Mr. Ely." Mr. Ely, it seems, was a "fine figure of a man, an officer and a gentleman who graduated from West Point, then fought the Spanish at the side of the Colonel."

The Colonel, presumably, is Theodore Roosevelt, though neither Miss Flowers nor the narrator ever quite makes that point clear. Some cataclysmic event occurred during the war, psychically scarring Mr. Ely so badly that he resigns his commission and disappears "somewhere out West." Miss Flowers, who before he left for the war promised that she would wait until he returned, does wait. . . for fifty-five years.

The reader never learns just what event caused Mr. Ely to abandon his career and his "one true love" to wander aimlessly through the West. Neither does the reader ever find out what happened to Mr. Ely.

As a result, by the end of the book the reader comes away as frustrated as the old-maid protagonist herself.

It is through Miss Flowers's observations on life, love, loyalty, and the changing conditions of the Old South that Twainbough attempts to project his message, though whatever that message may be has escaped this reviewer. For example:

"Things aren't the way they used to be," she laments. "Why, I can sit right here on this very veranda and watch all the young men call on the young ladies. They sit in their automobiles and make a fearsome racket with those awful horns, and the young ladies come running out from their houses like a summoned dog without the slightest thought of delicacy or propriety."

The book abounds with such awkward prose, and one cannot read it without feeling a sense of embarrassment for the author. It is especially dissatisfying when one realizes that Eric Twainbough is capable of so much more.

Twainbough's next book, *Trespass of the Damned*, is to be published (also by Argus and Collier) in January of 1950. One can only hope that it will mark a return to that which the author does best, thus satisfying his many fans—all of whom cannot help but be intensely disappointed by this unsuccessful effort.

ST. LOUIS

"All right, pull the throttle back," Willie Canfield said.

"How far back?" Liesl Tannenhower asked, reaching for the knob in the center of the instrument panel.

"All the way back," Willie replied.

She pulled it back, and it grew quieter inside the small Cessna.

"Now pull the wheel back."

With the wheel back, the nose came up so high that nothing was visible through the windshield except blue sky through the black bars of the slowly spinning propeller.

"Now look at your airspeed."

Liesl checked the airspeed indicator. "It's coming down," she said. "Way down."

"When it gets low enough, we're going to stop being an airplane and become a rock," Willie said. "Now, do you feel it getting mushy?"

"Yes."

"Remember that feeling. That's not a feeling you ever want to have when you're too close to the ground."

Suddenly the nose pitched down, and Liesl squealed with excitement. Willie shoved the throttle forward, using the drop and the increased thrust to recover flying speed.

"That was fun!" Liesl said.

"Now you do it."

She pulled the throttle back, raised the nose, held it until it lost flying speed, then recovered just as Willie had by shoving the throttle forward.

"Very good," Willie said. "Now, let's go over into Illinois and find us a quiet little airport somewhere where we can do some touch-and-go's without getting in the way of any big boys."

"Willie, I can't tell you how much I appreciate your teaching me to fly," Liesl said. "I could take lessons from one of the instructors, but I have more confidence learning from you."

Willie chuckled. "Just because I've got quite a few hours doesn't mean I'm a good instructor. It takes a special skill to be an instructor pilot."

"Yes. Kindness. I tried one of the instructor pilots; he wasn't very kind. Every time I would make the mistake" —she stopped and corrected herself— "*a* mistake, he would shout at me."

"He was just trying to save your life," Willie said.

Liesl laughed.

"What is it?"

"I thought perhaps he was trying to save his *own* life."

Willie laughed with her. "Well, yes. That, too."

Several minutes later he pointed through the windshield. "Okay, there's the airport up ahead. It's an uncontrolled airfield, so we'll fly a left-hand pattern, entering the downwind leg at a forty-five-degree angle."

Under Willie's tutelage, Liesl flew the landing pattern—downwind base, and final—touching down with a slight bounce about a quarter of the way down the runway. As soon as the airplane was squarely on the runway she shoved the throttle all the way forward and took off, only to enter the landing pattern again. She repeated the procedure for nearly an hour, and by the end of the lesson she was putting the airplane down gently and without a bounce.

They flew back to Lambert Field, Liesl feeling confident in her newly found ability. When they landed there, however, she discovered that she hadn't quite mastered the game, for she bounced rather severely when she touched down.

"Oh!" she cried, disgusted with herself. "I was doing so well before."

Willie grinned. "Of course you were," he said. "There was no one over there to see you. That's one of Murphy's laws."

"Murphy's laws?"

"There are a lot of Murphy's laws, and all pilots should be familiar with them," Willie explained. "The one you just proved was: 'You always do your best when no one is watching and your worst when everyone is.'"

Liesl laughed. "What are some of the others?"

They turned off the runway then, and Willie held up his hand, signaling her to wait, then he took down the microphone and called Lambert Ground Control.

"Lambert Ground, Cessna three-one-four, request permission to taxi to general aviation area."

"Cessna three-one-four, taxi at pilot's discretion."

"Three-one-four," Willie said. Then, hanging the mike up again, he continued his discourse. "Well, another of Murphy's laws says: 'If something can go wrong, it will.' That's an important one. And of course, there's: 'An engine always runs rougher at night or over water than it does during the day or over land.'"

"Is that true?"

"There are people who swear that it is." Willie followed a line boy's directions into a parking spot, then cut the engine. As the prop spun to a stop, he looked over toward the parking lot and saw a red Mercury convertible sitting next to his light-blue Cadillac. Roger Daigh was leaning against the front of the Mercury. "Roger's here."

"Yes, I see him," Liesl said. She waved through the window at him, and, smiling, he waved back.

Unfastening their seat belts, Liesl and Willie climbed down from the small airplane and walked together toward the parking lot. Roger stepped across the knee-high wire cable fence that separated the parking lot from the airport apron and kissed Liesl.

"Hello," he said. "How did the flying lesson go?"

"It went very well," Willie answered. "She'll be soloing by the end of the week."

"Soloing?" Roger looked at Liesl. "You mean you would go up alone?"

"Yes, of course," Liesl replied.

"Oh, I don't know. . . ."

"You don't know what?"

"I don't know if that's such a good idea. Willie, do you think that's a good idea?"

Willie smirked. "Hell, Roger, I thought that *was* the idea. That's why people learn to fly."

"Yes, but with the wedding coming on and all, I just don't know. She's bound to have so much on her mind that it might be dangerous for her."

"I wouldn't let her do it if I didn't think she could," Willie said. "Don't worry about her. She's a natural-born flyer."

"It's easy for you to say don't worry about her," Roger replied. "You aren't marrying her, I am. I'm the one who'll worry."

"Don't be silly, Roger," Liesl said. "There is nothing to worry about."

"Nevertheless, I don't think you should do it. Now is not a good time. No, just forget about the solo. You have too many other things to do."

"Roger, when we are married you will be able to tell me what I can and what I cannot do," Liesl said testily. "But until we are married, I will make up my own mind. If Willie tells me I am ready to fly solo, than I will do so."

"We'll discuss this some other time," Roger said. "I don't want to argue about it now, in front of others."

Liesl laughed and took hold of Willie's arm. "Who are you calling others? Uncle Willie?"

"Please," Roger said. "Let's not discuss it now."

"All right, Roger, if you say so." Liesl walked around and opened the door on the passenger side of the Mercury. "Oh, my goodness, look at the time! If I am going to go to the 'surprise' shower your sister is throwing for me, I really must get home in time to do something with my hair."

"You know about the shower?" Roger asked.

"Of course I know," Liesl said. "Women don't really surprise each other. It would be a disaster if they did." She looked at Willie and smiled. "There may even be a Murphy's law about it," she said.

Willie laughed.

"Murphy's law?" Roger asked in confusion.

"Drive, Roger, drive," Liesl said. "*Schnell, schnell.*"

RANDOLPH AIR FORCE BASE, TEXAS

"And I thought Mississippi was hot," Quinisha Jackson said. Although al four windows were down in the Chevy, the wind that blew through the ca felt as if it were coming off a blast furnace. "How much farther is it?"

"I just saw a sign that said 'Welcome to Schertz, Texas,'" Travis answered "According to the map we should be there, but I haven't seen anything tha looks like an air base."

At that very moment three jet airplanes passed low over the highwa directly in front of them. They had evidently just taken off because wit streaks of fire streaming from their tails, they lifted their noses and began a incredibly steep, incredibly fast climb.

"*Whoowee!*" Travis shouted. "I guess we are here, all right! Did you see that

"What *were* those things?" Quinisha asked. "I've never seen airplanes lik that. They looked like. . . like arrowheads!"

"Yeah, didn't they?" Travis replied, grinning. "They were Saber jets, baby, F-86 Saber jets. And you'd better get a really good look at them, because my orders say I'm going to Saber Jet Transition School. I'm going to be flying one pretty damn soon."

Quinisha smiled. "I think I'm almost as excited for you as you are." She squeezed Travis's arm. "Oh, look. There's the main gate to the base just ahead."

"Open the glove compartment and get that brown envelope," Travis said. "It has my orders. Take a set out. I'll need it at the gate."

"I hope we don't have any trouble getting in," Quinisha said as she pulled out his orders.

"Baby, we're already in," Travis chuckled. "What do you think this uniform I'm wearing means?"

As they approached the gate an airman walked out of the small guard-house, holding his hand up to stop the car. The armband on his left arm was emblazoned with the large white letters AP, which Travis knew was the Air Force version of the Army's MP.

"You want to hold it right there, buddy," the air patrolman said. "This car don't have a base sticker."

"I'm just reporting in," Travis said. "Here are my orders."

The AP took the mimeographed sheet of paper from Travis and looked at t, then at Travis. Noticing the lieutenant's bars on Travis's uniform, he came o attention slowly, almost insolently, and saluted halfheartedly.

"Sorry, Lieutenant. You bein' a colored man, I didn't notice that you vas an officer," he said. "We don't have too many colored officers in the ir Force."

"How many would be 'too many'?"

The AP looked confused. "Beg pardon, sir?"

"Never mind. Would you tell me where to report, please?"

Travis was a little irritated by the AP's behavior, but he held the irritation n check. He was pretty sure there were many more irritating moments ahead, nd he didn't want to start out angry.

"Yes, sir," the AP said. "Well, you just go straight ahead to the Taj Mahal—"

"The Taj Mahal?"

"Yes, sir, the big white building right in the middle of the base. Don't you member the Taj Mahal?"

"This is the first time I've ever been to Randolph."

"It is? Well, sir, if you don't mind my askin', where'd you get your wings? I ought everyone had to come through here."

"Tuskegee," Travis said.

"Tuskegee?" Suddenly the AP pulled his pistol. "You just hold it right ere, buddy."

"Travis!" Quinisha shouted in fright, grabbing her husband's arm.

"What's going on here, private?" Travis demanded angrily.

"I ain't no private. I'm an airman, which you would know if you was real, which I don't think you are," the airman said, holding his pistol leveled toward the car. By now there was another car behind them and one across the way, leaving. The occupants of the other two cars were watching the drama unfold with open curiosity. "Sergeant! Sergeant, you want to come out here?" the airman shouted toward the guardhouse.

Another AP, this one wearing sergeant's stripes, hurried out of the tiny guardhouse. "What is it, Murphy? Whatcha got here?"

"I'm not sure," Murphy replied. "This here colored man's dressed up like an officer. And he's wearin' wings. Only he says he's never been here before, and he don't even know what my rank is. If you ask me, he's an imposter."

"Do you have an ID Card?" the sergeant asked Travis.

"No, Sergeant, not a military ID card. Not yet, anyway. I'm just coming back to active duty, and all I have are my orders. I gave them to the. . . *airman.*" He took pains to give the man's proper rank.

"Murphy, let me see those orders," the sergeant said.

"This is them right here," Murphy said, handing them over. "When asked him where he got his wings, he said Tuskegee. We ain't got no air base named Tuskegee."

The sergeant sighed. "Murphy, you don't have the sense God gave goose," he retorted. He came to attention and saluted sharply. "Welcome to Randolph, Lieutenant Jackson," he said. "I'm sorry about the mix-up."

Airman Murphy, seeing his sergeant come to attention, quickly put away his pistol and came to attention himself, his right hand quivering just above his right eyebrow in a stiff salute.

Travis thought about the situation for a moment. By now four other car were waiting, and any more disturbance at the gate would just cause furthe trouble. Finally he returned the salute and chuckled.

"That's all right, Sergeant," he said. "It fills me with confidence to know that no Russians will be able to get through this gate. Especially if they cam through Tuskegee."

"Where the hell is Tuskegee?" Travis heard Murphy ask as he starte through the gate.

"It's where the colored pilots trained during the war, you dumb shit, an they were all aces, every last damn one of 'em," the sergeant growled.

Travis smiled to himself. They hadn't all been aces, of course, but wh could it hurt to have a few people thinking that they were?

Driving onto the base, Travis quickly located the Taj Mahal. It was a bi, white, very unmilitary-looking building, and it was easy to see how it had go ten its name, looking as it did something like the real Taj Mahal. When Travis inquired about it, he was told that a former base commander had asked for funds to build a headquarters building but was turned down. He then asked if he could build a water tower, and that request was approved. The commander had his base engineer draw up a plan for a water tower that would incorporate in its design rooms to "monitor the water level, pressure, pump operation, and *other such rooms as may be necessary to maintain overall water efficiency.*" Those other rooms became the base headquarters.

After Travis completed his "in-processing," he was given the keys and the address to a set of junior officers' quarters. The housing officer explained that since the Jacksons had no children, they were only authorized two bedrooms.

When they stopped in the driveway in front of the house that was to be theirs, Quinisha gasped. "Oh, Travis!"

The house was actually half of a duplex unit. Made of brick, with forest-green shutters and trim, it had a carport, a patio, and a spacious lawn filled with shrubs and flowers.

Travis started opening his door to get out, but Quinisha grabbed him by the arm and held on tight.

"Baby, what's wrong?" Travis asked.

"No," she said, "don't get out! I'm sure there's been a mistake."

Travis looked at the housing assignment orders he had just been given and checked that address with the address on the front of the house. "No, there wasn't. This is it. See? Three-eleven on the orders, three-eleven on the house."

"I'm afraid," she said.

"What are you afraid of?"

"Look around at the other people here. They're all so. . . so. . ."

"So what?"

"White."

Travis laughed. "No, they aren't white, baby. They're officers. Junior officers. And we're junior officers, too. And the President, and the Congress, and the United States Air Force says that you and I are going to live right here, at number three-eleven. Now, let's go in and have a look around our house."

Travis and Quinisha got out of the car and walked up to the front door. Quinisha hung on to his arm the entire time, wanting desperately to look around the neighborhood but frightened to do so. She was aware, but only peripherally, of eyes staring through the slits of drawn venetian blinds in some of the other houses.

Once inside, she looked at the house with barely contained joy. It was, she claimed, the most beautiful house she had ever seen, and every time she noticed one of its features, she let out a little whoop of glee and ran to point it out to Travis.

Travis was also impressed and pleased with the house, but more than that, he was enjoying Quinisha's excitement. He stood in the middle of the living room as she ran across the shiny hardwood floors, going from empty room to empty room to shout out yet another discovery.

"Travis, it has heat grates in *every* room. I mean, I know it's hot now, and you probably aren't even thinking about winter, but you've got to think about it and, well, look! There won't be a cold room in the whole house!

"Oh, and Travis, it has *two* bathrooms. Two! Why, that's a bathroom apiece! Can you imagine that?

"And look at the kitchen! At all this counter and cabinet space! And an electric range! Oh, the meals I'll cook for you on that stove!" She laughed. "You think our white neighbors will get used to the smell of chitterlings?"

Quinisha then ran into the master bedroom, coming back to the living room with yet another joyful report.

"Travis, wait until you see the bedroom closet! Why, it's as big as a bedroom itself!"

"I might as well start getting the car unloaded," Travis said. "There's no telling how long it'll be until our furniture gets here."

"Oh," Quinisha said, embracing herself and looking around at the house with eyes shining bright with excitement, "our things are going to look so nice in here."

Travis decided they would eat at the officers' club that evening. Quinisha found the thought a bit intimidating, but she didn't express her anxiety to Travis, because she didn't want him to know—as if he couldn't already tell by the way she was acting.

She changed dresses three times while she was getting ready, thinking the first was not dressy enough and the second was perhaps a bit too dressy. Until their furniture arrived, the only mirrors were those fronting the medicine cabinets in the bathrooms, and that made it difficult for her to check herself out before they left.

"How do I look?" she asked Travis.

"Beautiful."

"No, now be serious," she said. "This is important. We can't go to the officers' club looking like we've never been before."

"We haven't."

"Well, I haven't, yes, but *you* have. You were an officer during the war."

Travis shook his head. "I was a colored officer in a colored wing during the war," he said. "We had a little bitty colored officers' club where we could get a drink and a sandwich, but baby, when we go into that place tonight, it'll be as new for me as it is for you."

"Oh!" Quinisha said in alarm. "I wish you hadn't told me that."

Travis laughed. "Listen, we won't be any different from some second lieu-tenant going in there for the first time," he said. "Except that I outrank every second lieutenant in the entire U.S. Air Force. Now, you just hold your head up and remember that we have as much right to be in there as anybody else."

"It isn't just the officers' club, Travis," Quinisha said in a quiet voice. "I'm a little old colored girl from Jackson, Mississippi. I've never been *anywhere* nice."

Quinisha was quiet during the short drive to the club. Stepping from the car, Travis took her arm and led her inside. As they waited to be seated in the dining room, he felt her move a bit closer to him. This time he didn't blame her for being somewhat intimidated; he was nearly so himself.

He looked around at the place. The deep-pile carpet was dark blue, and the chairs around the tables were upholstered in a rich velour of the same shade. The tables were all covered with crisp, white linen and set with sparkling silverware and glistening crystal. About half the tables were filled, and though a few of the diners interrupted their conversation for a moment when Travis and Quinisha came into the dining room, it appeared to be out of nothing more than simple curiosity. There might have been a few people looking at them with more than a normal amount of curiosity, but if so, they weren't so obvious about it as to make the Jacksons uncomfortable. In fact, the most noticeable stare came from the Negro piano player. Perhaps the Negro man slapping the bass might have stared, too, had he not been so lost in the music that he hadn't opened his eyes since they came in.

They were shown to their table, then given menus. The menus were dark blue, with silver lettering on the outside, while the writing inside was in big, bold script. Travis had never seen a menu as large—if he had stood it on end on the floor, it would have come up to his knee—but despite the numerous choices, they both ordered steak.

Whether the food was actually that good or if it was made so by the set-ting and the excitement of the occasion they couldn't be sure, but they both agreed that it was the most delicious meal either of them had ever eaten. Talking quietly across the table, they relaxed to the point where it felt per-fectly natural for them to be there. Their prerogative was underscored a short while later when a Negro major came in. The major nodded at them, and Travis nodded back.

At just about the time they were getting ready to leave, four officers entered the club, talking and laughing. Their conversation wasn't really bois-terous, but given the low-keyed atmosphere of the room, it was quite notice-able. Two of the officers were captains, one was a major, and one was a lieutenant colonel. Spotting Travis and Quinisha, the lieutenant colonel came straight toward their table with the other officers following close behind. Travis, seeing him approach, started to stand.

"No, no, Lieutenant, you stay right where you are," the colonel said. "I just wanted to get a good close look at you."

"I beg your pardon?" Travis replied.

"You *are* Travis Jackson, aren't you?"

"Yes, sir," Travis said, wondering where this was going.

"When you finish T-school, you're going to be assigned to my squadron. When I got your orders, I thought that name was familiar, so I went back and looked it up."

"I'm sorry, sir, do we know each other?" Travis asked.

"Of course we do, watermelon man!" the colonel said.

Travis was beginning to grow very uncomfortable. Why would a senior officer want to make a racial slur in public?

"That *is* what you had painted on the side of your airplane, wasn't it? The P-51 you flew in Europe? One watermelon for every German you shot down?"

Travis relaxed, feeling the tension drain from his face. It wasn't a racial slur after all; it was a legitimate question. He smiled. "Yes, sir, that's what I had painted on my ship."

"Good, I'm glad you're the same person. Did you get the bourbon all right?"

"The bourbon, sir?"

"Damn, Lieutenant, did you save that many B-17 pilots during the war who *all* gave you a case of bourbon as a way of saying thanks? I'm Colonel Overstreet. I was copilot on the *Stand and Deliver*. You may not remember the name, but you might remember the incident."

Travis smiled broadly. "You had just thrown a propeller when you were jumped by German fighters," he said.

"That's it." Colonel Overstreet looked at the other officers with him. "We only had three fans turning and a sky full of Germans. Fellas, I don't want to embarrass the lieutenant and his missus here—" He suddenly interrupted himself to look at Quinisha. "Oops, I haven't already embarrassed him, have I? You *are* his missus?"

"Yes, sir," Quinisha replied.

"You don't have to say 'sir' to me, Mrs. Jackson. That's your husband's problem"—he looked back at the other officers who were with him—"and these bums," he added. "Anyway, as I was saying, I don't want to embarrass Lieutenant Jackson, but I saw a lot of hot fighter pilots during that little fracas in Europe and I never saw one who was better than this man. He flew that Mustang like he had it strapped to his ass. Excuse my language, Mrs. Jackson, but you see, we just completed a Command Readiness Inspection today, and we've been in the bar celebrating. Those things are rough, but we managed to pull a superior. After you're checked out in the Saber jet, Lieutenant, and report to the squadron, you'll see what I mean. If we get another superior, *you'll* be celebrating with us."

"Yes, sir," Travis said.

"I'll be looking foward to having you in the squadron, Jackson," Colonel Overstreet said. "I'm glad to have anyone around who can fly like you. Well, you folks go ahead and finish your dinner and pardon me for interrupting."

That night Quinisha spread out quilts and blankets on the floor of the empty bedroom to use as a sleeping pad until their bed arrived. As they lay together in the darkness, her head on Travis's shoulder, she thought about the events of the day. . . how exciting everything had been and how nice Colonel Overstreet and the other officers had been. They had related to Travis as an aviator and fellow officer, not as white men relating to a colored man. She had never felt that same sense of equality before—not even around Stump Pollard, whom she truly liked.

Quinisha thought she heard Travis sniff. Rising on one elbow to investigate, she saw, in the ambient light from outside, something shining on his face and in the comers of his eyes. Tears!

"Travis, honey?" Quinisha asked, shocked and dismayed. "Travis, are you all right?"

"I'm all right," he said in a choked voice.

"What is it? Why are you. . ." She couldn't bring herself to say "crying" even though that's what he was doing.

Travis tightened his arm around her and pulled her closer to him.

"I'm home, baby," he murmured. "I'm home."

AUGUST 1949, FROM
"TRAILMARKERS" IN EVENTS
MAGAZINE:

DIED: Loomis Booker, 68, retired president of Lincoln University, of a stroke. While a janitor at St. Louis's Jefferson University around the turn of the century, this self-educated Negro salvaged discarded textbooks, then mastered the school's entire curriculum. In 1907, in an unprecedented move, the university awarded him a Doctor of Humanities degree, even though Negroes were not then granted admission to Jefferson. (Three Negroes are now enrolled.)

Dr. Booker, who leaves his wife and two grandchildren, was the father of Andrew Booker, a research physician who helped in the development of blood plasma. Ironically and tragically, Andrew Booker died from injuries suffered in an automobile accident when a supply of plasma that would have saved his life was denied him because it had been reserved for white use only.

245

ON THE CAMPUS OF LINCOLN
UNIVERSITY, JEFFERSON CITY,
MISSOURI

The auditorium in Memorial Hall wasn't big enough to hold all the mourn-ers, so chairs were set up on the lawn outside the hall. When those chairs were full, others coming to the funeral sat on the ground in small solemn groups or stood quietly behind the seated mourners, listening to the service over the bat-tery of loudspeakers that had been placed on stands outside.

Loomis Booker's coffin sat on a catafalque at the front of the hall. The entire hall as well as much of the area outside was banked with flowers of every hue and description. At the head of the coffin a large spray of red roses was prominently displayed. The inscription read: PRESIDENT AND MRS. HARRY S TRUMAN. Nearly as prominent were the flowers from General Dwight D. Eisenhower. There were also sprays from the governor of Missouri and from the presidents or chancellors of every other college and university in Missouri as well as several out-of-state universities, including Hampton Institute Howard University, Tufts, Harvard, Notre Dame, and even one from Oxford University in England.

Eric Twainbough was sitting in the front row between Shaylin and Loomis's widow, Delia. He held Della's hands throughout the service, letting go only when she found it necessary to hold her handkerchief to her eyes.

On the other side of Della sat her two grandsons, Artemus and Deon fourteen and thirteen respectively. They were trying hard to be manly, trying hard not to cry, but despite their best efforts, the cheeks of both boys were streaked with tears.

Bob and Connie Canfield also had seats in the front row. White-haired now and puffy-eyed from crying, throughout the service Bob recalled those days so many years past when he and Loomis Booker would hold long philo-sophical discussions at the head of the steps that led down into Loomis dreary apartment in the basement of Spengeman Hall.

The Men's Glee Club sang a few selections, including Loomis's person favorite, the spiritual "Going Home," whose music was from Anton Dvorak *Sinfonie No. 9, Aus der Neuen Welt*. The lead was sung by a golden-toned bar tone, who, though tears streamed down his face for the entire song, manage to keep his voice strong and resonant. There wasn't a dry eye in the hous after that song.

Following numerous eulogies, the front doors of Memorial Hall we thrown open, and Loomis's coffin was borne by the student-body presiden from the last six years, one of whom had lost an arm during the war. Just front of the hall was an old, weathered, and obviously well-used farm wago draped with black crepe and pulled by a matched team of Missouri mules. The mouners outside the hall gave way, forming a pathway for the funeral cortege to climb the hill where Loomis Booker would be laid to rest.

First to come through the path were drummers, playing a slow cadence on muffled drums. They were followed by the wagon, led by a weeping young man dressed in the uniform of a drum major in the Lincoln University band. Behind the wagon walked Della, Eric, Artemus, and Deon. Behind them came Shaylin, Bob, and Connie, then all the remaining mourners.

Loomis was being buried on the university grounds at a location he had often said was his favorite spot on campus: atop a hill overlooking the state capitol. The grave was between two large maple trees that in the fall would be ablaze with color. Already plans were under way to erect a statue to his memory.

The solemn cortege reached the gravesite. Alongside the grave, under a canopy, chairs were set in place for the "family," which included, in addition to Della and the two grandsons, Eric and Shaylin and Bob and Connie.

The coffin was taken from the wagon, then slowly lowered by ropes into the ground. The minister, wearing a long, flowing black cassock with a white surplice and a purple stole, stepped to the head of the grave.

"Unto Almighty God we commend the soul of our brother departed, Loomis Booker, and we commit his body to the ground; earth to earth, ashes to ashes, dust to dust; in sure and certain hope of the Resurrection until eternal life through our Lord Jesus Christ; at whose coming in glorious majesty to judge the world, the earth and the sea shall give up their dead; and the corruptible bodies of those who sleep in him shall be changed and made like unto his own glorious body; according to the mighty working whereby he is able to subdue all things unto himself."

16

SEPTEMBER 4, 1949, ST. LOUIS,
MISSOURI

E ric Twainbough and his son, Hamilton—named for Sam Hamilto
and known virtually since his birth twenty-seven years before a
Ham—sat in the living room of Ham's house, watching the baseba
game on television. Actually, since the game hadn't yet started, the
were watching the two announcers, for the camera was now on them.

"*Swampwater Puckett here, along with my old sidekick Gabby Kincaid, bringing y*
today's matchup between our own St. Louis Grays and the Boston Red Sox. It's a beautif
day for baseball, don't you think, Gabby?"

The camera moved from a "two shot" to a "one shot" of Gabby Kincai
Gabby switched a large wad of chewing tobacco from the right to the le
side of his mouth, then reached down to get a tighter grip on the micr
phone. He leaned toward the mike, and though he'd been announcir
games for quite some time and had been told repeatedly that it wasn't ne
essary to get closer to the mike every time he talked, he did just that a
raised his voice.

"You're absolutely right, Swampwater, and, of course, the day bein' pretty an' all, well, this is just exactly the kind of day a batter like the great Red Sox slugger Ted Williams likes or even Stan Musial who, if we had someone like him, maybe we'd be sittin' in first place now or at least fightin' for first place like the Cardinals are fightin' for first place over in the National League with the Dodgers, while over here in the American League the Graybies are stuck down here in fourth or fifth place, ten or twelve games behind or maybe even fifteen or twenty, I don't remember which, but the season is over for us."

Eric laughed and pointed to the TV screen. "I can see you didn't hire Mr. Kincaid for his succinctness."

Ham laughed with him. "He does go four ways to make every point," he said. "Just in case you didn't manage to wade through all that, he was trying to tell me I need to get a long-ball hitter."

"Why don't you?"

"If I could find one, I would. Believe me, I've shopped around. I've talked to the Red Sox about Ted Williams, the Dodgers about Duke Snyder, the Pirates about Ralph Kiner. . . I've even tried to buy Stan Musial from the Cardinals, but no one wants to give up their big guns."

"Anyone coming up from the minors?" Eric asked.

Ham shook his head. "No. No one promising. But we do have our scouts out. We'll find someone somewhere."

"Papa," Eric's granddaughter, Paige, said, walking over to his chair and holding up her arms to show him a piece of paper. "Do you like the picture colored?"

"Like it? Why, I love it," Eric said, smiling and picking her up to hold on his knee. "That is a beautiful picture. Perhaps the most beautiful picture I have ever seen.

"It's the most beautiful picture I've ever seen, too," Paige said, admiring her handiwork. She hopped back down. "I'm going to do *another* one that's the most beautiful you've ever seen. Come watch. I want you to see how I can stay in the lines."

"I've never been able to stay in the lines. Maybe I'd better watch so I can learn."

"It's real easy, see?" Paige said as she picked up a purple crayon and began coloring. "That's the line and you. . . Oops!"

"Ah, that's just a little mistake," Eric said. "It won't hurt anything."

"No, it won't hurt anything," Paige agreed. With her tongue sticking out between her lips, she concentrated on her coloring.

The baseball game got under way, and Eric looked up when he heard the increased volume of Swampwater's voice.

"He tagged it good, folks! It's up, up, and out of here for Ted Williams. A home run with two men on and one man out, so the Red Sox go up by three in the top of the first inning!"

"Damn!" Ham said.

"*Of course, it was like I was saying,*" Gabby Kincaid put in, in his rather mush-mouthed delivery, "*you give a hitter like Ted Williams or Johnny Mize or Joe DiMaggio—or anyone like what we* don't *have—a good inside fast ball, which as you know Swampwater, being a pitcher yourself Howie Simmons ought never to have throwed in the first place, but he did, and you saw what happened.*"

Ham turned off the TV and the picture diminished into a small, brightly glowing dot in the middle of the black screen. After a moment even the dot was gone.

"Daddy, if you aren't going to watch the baseball game can I watch *Howdy Doody?*" Paige asked, looking up from her prone position on the floor.

"Honey, he's not on right now. But as soon as he does come on, you can watch."

"Do you feel guilty about not being out at the park?" Eric asked his son as he settled back in the big leather armchair.

"That's where the owner *should* be," Ham admitted. He chuckled. On the other hand, being the owner also means being the boss, and if I want to take off to visit you while you're in town, I don't have to ask anyone. Besides, as that mush-mouthed Gabby Kincaid likes to remind me every chance he gets it isn't as if we were fighting for the pennant."

"Why do you keep him?"

Ham gave his father an ironic smile. "Why? Because we've taken polls of our fans, and for some reason they like him. So, if we can't give them a winning team, we can at least give them announcers they like."

"Is that important? Giving them what they like?"

"Of course it is. At least I think so. Don't you? I mean, it's just good business, isn't it?"

Eric leaned his head against the back of the chair and drummed his fingers for a moment on the leather-covered arms. "Yeah, I suppose," he finally said. He sighed. "Maybe I could learn a lesson from you. If I had had any sense, I never have let them publish *Tea on the Veranda*. Sam tried to talk me out of before he died; Shaylin tried to talk me out of it; even Richard Toban confessed to me that he was just letting me publish the book as payment for agreeing to come over to Argus and Collier. Somewhere in all that the message should have gotten through to me."

"I read some of the reviews, Pop. Is the book really as bad as all the critics are saying, or did a few not like it and everyone else just jumped on the bandwagon?"

Eric sighed. "I wish I could answer that question for you, son," he said. "But the truth is, I'm afraid I've lost all objectivity. At one time I thought *Tea on Veranda* might be the best writing I'd ever done. But"—he shrugged—"who knows now?" He snorted. "Listen, why don't we talk about something else for a while? Nobody likes to talk about failures, and that's all we've been talking about. . . my book and your baseball team."

Ham laughed. "Thanks a lot, Pop. Now you've grouped my baseball team in the same category as your sorry-assed book."

"My sorry-assed book?" Erie reached over, grabbed a pillow off the sofa, and threw it at his son just as Shaylin and Amy came into the living room.

"Here, here, what is this?" Amy Twainbough called. "I leave you two boys alone just for a moment and this is what happens? If we can't trust you while we're here, how are we ever going to be able to leave you while we go shopping?"

"Shopping? What are you going to buy?" Eric asked his daughter-in-law.

It was Shaylin who answered. "I want to get a wedding present for Liesl and Roger. Have you any ideas?"

"We could give her an autographed copy of *Tea on the Veranda*," Eric suggested sarcastically. "We could give her *fifty* autographed copies. There are probably a few left around."

"Come on, Eric, we do want to give her something we can be *proud* of, don't we?" Shaylin teased.

"Ouch!" Eric said, making an exaggerated reach behind his back. "Somebody take the knife out."

"Papa, you don't have a knife in your back," Paige chimed in, looking at her grandfather with grave concern.

"Are you sure?"

Paige looked pointedly, then shook her head. "I'm sure," she said. "I don't see a knife."

"Funny. I could have sworn I had one there," he said, smiling at Shaylin.

"Listen, Paige, honey, why don't you come with us?" Amy said. "We're going to need your help to find something nice."

"I'll help," Paige promised. She put the crayon down on the coloring book. "Papa, you won't let anyone finish coloring that for me, will you? I want to do myself."

"I promise, darlin', I'll guard that book with my life," Eric said, holding up his right hand as if taking an oath.

After a few minutes of getting-ready-to-leave fussing, the "womenfolk," as Eric called them, left on their shopping trip. Turning back to his son, Eric asked, "You want to check the game again?"

"I guess I could turn it on without sound," Ham replied. "Watching us lose bad enough; I don't need to be told about it with every breath." He walked over to turn the TV set back on. "I was really sorry to hear about Dr. Booker's death," he said as he waited for the picture to come up. "I know what a good friend he was to you."

"He was a lot more than a friend," Eric said. "He was a surrogate father. I have to confess that over the last several years I didn't keep in touch with him as well as I should have. I just got too busy with my own life. But I really liked knowing that he was around, and I'm going to miss him." He paused, then added more softly, "I'm going to miss him more than I can say."

"I know what you mean about not keeping in touch," Ham said. "You and I are that way with each other."

"Yeah, I'm sorry about—"

"No, don't apologize," Ham said, raising his hand. "Listen, I'm a big boy now, and this is a two-way street. You're busy with your life, and I get busy with mine. I follow you pretty closely, through your books and the articles written about you. And, as you said about Dr. Booker, I like knowing you're there." He laughed. "And I'm glad Liesl and Roger are getting married tomorrow, keeping you in St. Louis a day longer than you'd planned."

"I've never cared much for big weddings," Eric said. "That's why both of mine have been small. But I know they're important to some people, so if that's what they want, good for them." He smiled. "So you're going to be Roger Daigh's best man. I didn't realize you and he were such good friends."

Ham chuckled. "I didn't either," he confessed. "I must admit I was surprised when he asked me."

"Maybe he's just trying to brownnose the family," Eric suggested with grin. "Did you even know him before he started seeing Liesl?"

"I knew him when we were both at JU, though he was a couple of classe behind me. We were in the same fraternity, and he was my backup on th football team."

"What do you think of him?"

"He played hard. He's a good man. He wasn't in the war, and I think he fee guilty about that—though why he should, I don't know. As far as I'm concerned anyone who missed the war should thank God for his good fortune."

"Yes, but you have to have actually been in war to be able to arrive at that perspective," Eric said. "You can't tell someone who's never been in war what war is like. It's like trying to describe the taste of artichokes. It ju can't be done."

"I guess you're right. Anyway, you asked what I think of Roger. I think he a good man, and I think Liesl is a fine woman, but frankly the two of the together strike me as a most unlikely pair."

"Why?"

"Well, I'm not sure it'll make sense to you, but Liesl is so much old than Roger."

"Older?"

"Chronologically, of course, Roger is older. But Liesl. . ." Ham shook his head. "I don't know, Pop, maybe it's everything that she's been through. It's as if she's a forty-five-year-old in a twenty-three-year-old's body."

Eric grinned. "It could be worse. She could be a twenty-three-year-old in a forty-five-year-old's body."

At that same moment, across the city at the executive offices of World Air Transport, Willie Canfield stood at the window of his office, looking out at the planes landing and taking off from Lambert Field. He saw a Trans World Airlines Constellation settling down on the runway while an American Airlines DC-4, an Ozark Airlines DC-3, a World Air Transport Moonraker, and another TWA Connie waited in line to take off. The DC-4 moved out onto the runway, then started accelerating until, with all four engines roaring, it left the runway and started its long, slow climb. In the meantime, a Delta landed just behind it.

Willie turned away from the window and went back to his desk, where he had been examining the publicity on the Galaxie, a new four-engine turbo-prop aircraft being proposed for the airline industry by Rockwell-McPheeters. He read some of the copy:

> In marrying the speed and power of the jet turbine engine to the proven efficiency and reliability of the propeller-driven craft, the Galaxie will blaze boldly forth into the next generation of commercial airliners.

The artist's conception of the plane showed a long, fat body held aloft by graceful wings and a swept-back empennage. The four engine nacelles, however, were the most distinctive feature. They were long and thin, only about half the diameter of normal reciprocating engines.

According to the design specifications, the airplane would be able to fly at four hundred miles per hour and carry one hundred passengers. That made the "seat cost," by which operating expenses were computed, just about half that of the Moonraker.

By comparison, the seat cost of the de Havilland Comet, the all-jet airliner being built for British Overseas Airways, would be six times that of the Moonraker. There was no doubt that the Comet was going to greatly enhance the prestige of BOAC, but Willie knew that the British airline company could depend on government subsidies. World Air Transport, on the other hand, would have to pay its own way.

Willie looked at the picture of the all-jet Comet and sighed. He had once read an article in which the writer discussed the three most beautiful vehicles ever built by man. One was the Roman chariot, one was the China clipper ship (Donald McKay's sailing ships, not Pan American's airplanes, the writer was quick to point out), and one was the 1941 Lincoln Continental. Surely, Willie thought, to that list must be added the de Havilland Comet, with its long, sleek body, its swept-back wings, and the four engines nestled in streamlined pods in the wing roots. The Galaxie as envisioned by the artist was a beautiful airplane, but not nearly as beautiful as the Comet.

From outside his window came the roar of a jet plane, and Willie looked through the window just in time to see it take off. It was one of the Rockwell-McPheeters jet fighters, called the Ghost, painted in the dark blue of the U.S. Navy. As soon as it rotated, it pulled the nose up sharply, then shot up like a rocket, riding a pillar of flame.

Willie closed the prospectus and set it aside. No matter how beautiful the Comet was, and no matter how exciting the concept of jet aircraft might be there was no question what World Air Transport's next move would be. The jet airliner would have to wait a while longer. The next generation airliner would be turboprop aircraft, and Willie had already authorized the ordering of fourteen Galaxies.

"Willie?" The female voice was quiet, hesitant, almost pained.

Willie looked up from his desk and saw Liesl standing just inside his doorway

"Liesl? How did you get in? I mean, my secretary didn't buzz me. Well never mind that. Here, come in, come in." He stood and walked toward her

"Don't be angry with your secretary," Liesl said. "I waited outside the office until she stepped away from her desk, and then I came in without being seen.

"Why did you do that? You know she would have let you in."

"I didn't want anyone to know I was here."

Willie chuckled. "Why all the secrecy?"

Another four-engined airliner took off outside, and for a moment the roar of its engines made Liesl's response impossible. She waited until it grew relatively quiet again.

"I don't want anyone to find me for a while. Willie, we must talk, you and I

"Okay." Willie led her over to the white-leather sofa and sat her down then sat beside her. He took her hands in his. "What is it, Liesl? Why so serious? Are you nervous about tomorrow? It's quite common, you know, prewedding jitters."

"How can you do it, Willie?"

Willie was completely mystified by her question. "How can I do what?"

"How can you give me away?"

"You *asked* me to give you away."

"But is it what you want to do? I mean, do you *really* want to give me away

"Well, of course I do, if that's what you want," Willie replied.

"Oh, Willie, you are *impossible!*" Liesl said angrily. She pulled her hands away from his and got up to walk over to the window. She stood there with her back to him for a long moment, looking out at the airfield—though Willie was certain that she didn't even see the DC-3 taking off.

"Come on, Liesl, tell your Uncle Willie. . ."

"*No!*" she said sharply. She spun around to face him, and her eyes were flashing. Tears streamed down both cheeks. "You are *not* my *uncle!*"

"Well, no, of course I'm not," Willie said, "but I've always felt—"

"What you have always felt, yes, that's what I want to talk to you about," Liesl interrupted. "*How* have you felt? Willie, what do you think about me? What do you *feel* about me?"

Willie cleared his throat and shook his head. He had a tightening in his chest and a queasy feeling in his stomach, but he refused to acknowledge the cause of it. "I don't know what you're getting at, but if you ask me, we may be getting on shaky ground here. I think we'd better talk about something else."

Liesl came quickly back to the sofa and sat down beside him again. She reached for his hands and held both of them in hers.

"No, I don't want to talk about something else. Don't you see, Willie? I am already on shaky ground, and you must come out to rescue me."

"What's all this about, Liesl?" Willie asked quietly. "What's brought all this on?"

"I want to know. . . no, I *must* know how you feel about me," Liesl said.

"But you already know how I feel."

"No, I do not know. I asked you to give me away at my wedding, and you agreed to do so. Do you really want to give me away?"

"I considered it an honor to be asked."

Liesl grimaced with frustration. "Willie, listen to the question. Do you *want* to give me to another man?"

Willie sighed and shook his head. "No," he said quietly. "I don't want to give you to another man."

Liesl raised her hand to Willie's cheek. "Do you love me, Willie?"

Willie reached up to take her hand in his. He held it for a moment, then moved it to his lips and kissed the tips of her fingers.

"Of course I love you," he said easily, almost flippantly.

"That is not the kind of love I mean. Are you in love with me?"

He looked away from her probing blue-eyed stare. "I am trying hard not to be," he admitted.

"Why are you trying so hard? Am I so unlovable?"

"No, no, of course not!" Willie said quickly. "But you are so young."

"I make no apology for my age, Willie. We are all as old as we are, and we can be no older."

"You are so vulnerable."

"Anyone with a heart is vulnerable."

"Liesl, what do you want from me?"

"I want to know that I am not crazy. I want to know that I have not just imagined that you are in love with me. I want to hear you say the words."

"Why?"

"Don't you understand? I *must* hear them."

"All right, you can hear the words. Yes, God help me, *I do* love you," Willie sighed. "I've loved you almost from the moment I met you. There, I said it. Are you happy now?"

"No," Liesl sobbed. "I am miserable. I am more miserable now than I have ever been in my life."

"Why? Isn't that what you wanted to hear?"

"Not now, Willie. Not now! I wanted to hear it long ago. Now it is too late. Don't you understand? I am going to marry Roger tomorrow."

Willie tightened his grip on her hands. "But you aren't still going to do that, are you?"

"Yes."

"Why? If you love me and I love you, why are you going to marry Roger?"

"Because I have no choice. I must marry him now. It has gone too far."

"Liesl, are you pregnant? Because if you are, I want you to know that it doesn't matter one whit to me."

Liesl's eyes opened wide in surprise at the question; then they softened and she laughed. She put her hand to his cheek again. "Oh, my *liebchen.* Now know that you really do love me. But no, I am not pregnant."

"If you aren't pregnant then there's no need at all for you to marry Roger."

"If I don't marry him now, I will break the heart of many, many people Liesl sighed. "And if I do marry him, I will break only my own."

"And mine," Willie said.

"Yes, and yours," Liesl agreed. "But, Willie, if you have loved me for so long, why did you let this get so far? I prayed that you would stop me before it was too late."

"But how could I have known how you felt?" Willie lamented. "You never said anything."

Liesl shook her head sadly. "It was not my place to do so. I was a young foolish, immigrant girl. How could I have come to you and told you that loved you? Such things are simply not done. That was for you to do, not me There are times when the man simply must take charge of things." With a sad smile, she got up from the sofa and walked to the door, opening it. Just before she left she turned and looked back toward him. "You should have taken charge, Willie."

Liesl wasn't sure how many times the phone rang before she was able to come out of a troubled sleep and reach for it. According to the luminous clockface it was going on four A.M., and she was more curious as to who would be calling her at this hour than why she was being called.

"Hello?" she asked.

"Do you want to go flying?" an exuberant voice asked.

Liesl ran her hand through her hair as if by that action she could brush away some of the grogginess still clogging her mind. "Willie? Is this you?"

"Yes." Willie chuckled. "Who else would ask you to go flying with them at four in the morning?"

"Are you drunk?"

"Come on, Liesl, you know better than that. Have you ever known me to take a drink before I went flying? Now, do you want to come flying with me or not? I mean, this is your wedding day. You'll never have this opportunity again."

"But there are so many things I must do today," she protested. "I have breakfast with the maids of honor, a final dress fitting. There are many, many things I must do."

"What time were you going to get up?"

"Nine."

"You've got five hours," Willie reasoned.

"I don't know," she hedged.

"Look. . ." Willie said, his tone flattening. He sighed. "You're the one who opened Pandora's box. If you hadn't come by my office yesterday and said all that you did, I would've put on my tux this afternoon and gone down to the church to give you away, just as planned. It would have torn my heart out to do it. . . but I was prepared to do it. But you started me thinking, and now I have a few things I want to say to you. Will you go flying with me or not?"

"I'll meet you at the airport in half an hour," she said. "Get the Cessna. If I'm going with you, I intend to do the flying."

Willie laughed. "Of course. I already have the Cessna out."

"Look at that," Willie said above the sound of the Cessna's engine. He pointed out the left side of the airplane, just under the wing, toward the Mississippi River. In the early-morning sun the river was a bright, thick, winding thread of molten gold that stretched its serpentine form southward until it disappeared on the horizon far ahead. "Isn't that pretty?"

"It's beautiful," Liesl agreed. She steered the plane a bit more toward the river. When they had left St. Louis, it was still dark, but now the sun was half a disk above the eastern horizon, and the dark had been pushed away.

"Do you see that little town up there?" Willie said, pointing just to the right of the nose. "The diamond shape, formed by all the trees?"

"Yes."

"That's Sikeston, Missouri. That's where I was born."

"It's a pretty town."

Willie laughed. "How do you know? All you can see from up here is trees."

"Well, then the *trees* are pretty," Liesl said stubbornly. She glanced at the clock on the instrument panel. "Say, don't you think we should be starting back?"

"Aren't you hungry?" Willie asked.

"Hungry? No, not really."

"I am. I'm as hungry as a bear." He pointed south. "I thought we'd just cross the line over into Arkansas and have breakfast there, if you don't mind."

"I'm supposed to have breakfast with my bridesmaids, remember?"

"Oh, right. Well, you can have a cup of coffee with me. We still have plenty of time. Come right about ten degrees."

Liesl steered ten degrees to the right. She smiled at the plane's response to her control.

"You love flying, don't you?" Willie remarked, reading her expression.

"Yes. I'm going to miss it terribly after I'm married."

"Maybe you won't have to. I'll continue the lessons with you."

Liesl shook her head. "No, Roger has already made it clear that he won't approve. Besides, after what we, um, said to each other yesterday, I think it would not be a good idea for us to fly together anymore. Do you agree?"

"Let's don't talk about it now," Willie said.

"But I thought that was why you invited me to go flying with you this morning, so we *could* talk about it."

"I've changed my mind. I don't want to talk about it now. Let's just enjoy the moment."

"All right," Liesl said.

Neither of them said anything more until a short while later another small town began sliding toward them from the south. Willie pointed to it and said, "That's where we're going. See the little airport over there?"

"Yes," Liesl replied.

"Put us down there."

Liesl got the wind direction from some smoke she saw drifting up from the ground; then she set up her downwind leg. Willie kept his arms crossed, showing her that it was all hers as she maneuvered the airplane through all the legs of the landing pattern, then descended through the final approach, finally flaring out just a few feet above the short sod strip. She touched down smoothly.

"Hey, that's damn good," Willie said. "I've got guys flying my airliners who don't make prettier landings."

His compliment was rewarded by a pleased smile.

They taxied up to a small white hangar, then killed the engine. A Stearman biplane was sitting in front of the hangar, and a man wearing coveralls and perched on a yellow maintenance stand was working on the Stearman's engine.

"Howdy," Willie said, as he and Liesl stepped out of the Cessna. "You're getting started early this morning."

"Promised the owner I'd have it done for him by this afternoon," the man said. He pointed to the Cessna. "Need gas?"

"Yes, if you don't mind," Willie replied. "We thought we'd run into town and get breakfast. Is there a phone we can use to call a cab?"

"Hell, you don't need a cab. Take my pickup," the man offered, pointing to a red Chevrolet truck.

"Thanks," Willie said. "Keys in it?"

The mechanic chuckled. "You don't need no key. Just turn the switch and start her up. 'Pologize for the dirt."

"Don't apologize. We thank you for the loan."

The bed of the truck was filled with various aircraft parts: spark plugs, magnetos, brake disks, an inner tube, bell cranks, and a badly twisted propeller. The smell of stale cigar smoke permeated the cab of the truck. The ashtray was full of crushed stogies, some of which had fallen onto the rubber floormat, where they lay alongside piston rings, more spark plugs, and a couple of dirty filters. The upholstery was in very bad shape, but the seat was covered with an old army blanket, and that kept some of the stuffing from spilling out. The glass over the speedometer was cracked, and the window crank on the passenger door was broken, though the window could still be raised or lowered with some effort.

Willie waved at the mechanic, then drove away from the airport and headed toward the little town.

"Do you know where to go for breakfast?" Liesl asked as they drove down quiet, still-sleeping residential street.

"I think we can find a place," Willie answered. "But we have something else to do before breakfast."

Liesl looked at him curiously. "What?"

"We need to get married," Willie said matter-of-factly.

"*What?*" Liesl gasped, staring at him in shock.

Willie pulled the truck over to the side of the road in front of a small, neat house. He killed the engine, then turned to look at her.

"I want to marry you," he said. "Right here. Right now."

"Willie, don't be ridiculous. I'm getting married to Roger in a few hours. Besides, we couldn't get married just like that. You have to have blood tests and license and you have to post banns and wait at least three days and—"

Willie held up his hand to stop her. "You're talking about getting married in Missouri in a church," he said. "There is no *civil* requirement to post banns. And we're in Arkansas now; a blood test isn't required. Also, the man who marries you can issue the marriage license. And there's no mandatory three-day waiting period. So what about it, Liesl? Will you marry me?"

Liesl grew very still. "Willie, are you serious?" she asked in a barely audible voice.

"I'm quite serious. In fact, I have never been more serious in my life," Willie replied. "You said something yesterday that opened my eyes."

"I told you I loved you, and I do, but—"

"No, not just that. You said there were times when a man must take charge Well, I'm taking charge of things right now. I brought you down here, where we can get the job done in half an hour. The rest is up to you. I've done all can do, but I can't drag you up to the altar by your hair."

Liesl's eyes filled with tears. "But what about my obligations? My socia responsibilities? How would I ever face everyone if I did something as. . . a *irrational* as this?"

"You won't have to face them." Willie kissed her cheek. "At least, you won' have to face them alone. I'll be right there, right beside you, as your husband You do love me, don't you?"

"Oh, yes, I love you. I love you so much that I—"

"So much that you'll forget about 'social' responsibilities, and conside only what's important? So much that you'll marry me?"

The tears spilled over. "Oh, Willie, I want to. I want to so much!"

"Then do it," he said. He looked at his watch. "Thirty minutes from no you can be Mrs. William Canfield, and none of these issues you've raised wi amount to a hill of beans. This is the last time I'm going to ask you, Liesl. W you marry me?"

Liesl put one hand over her heart and the other on his arm. She took sharp breath and nodded. "Yes. Yes, I'll marry you—but please, let's do quickly before I get too frightened and change my mind."

Willie opened the door of the truck. It groaned and creaked in protest.

"What are you doing?" Liesl asked.

"You said let's do it quickly," Willie replied. "This is where we're going do it."

Liesl looked around. "Here?"

"That's right," Willie said, pointing to the house they were parked in fro of. "This is Orr Street, and that house is number one-ninety-one, the home

Judge Manley Lester, who, according to the ad I saw in the Yellow Pages of the Piggott telephone directory, will perform marriages."

"But the house is completely dark. It doesn't even look as if anyone is awake. Don't you think we're a little early?"

"No," Willie replied. "I don't think we're early. I think we're about six months late."

Liesl smiled and nodded. "You are right," she said. "Okay, let's go."

Arm in arm they walked up the front walk to the small bungalow-style house covered in slate-gray asbestos shingles. Willie knocked on the door. When there was no answer, he knocked again, banging louder this time.

"Just a minute!" someone called irritably from inside. "Just a minute! Hold your horses, I'm comin'!"

Liesl shivered, and Willie put his arm around her and drew her to him. "Cold?"

"No."

"Nervous?"

"Happy."

Willie pulled her to him to kiss her, and they were still kissing when the door opened. The man who opened it was a short man wearing a nightshirt and a nightcap. Willie had never seen anyone wear a nightcap outside of old movies, and he almost laughed. The judge looked at the two of them, then yawned and scratched himself.

"What is it?" he asked. "What do you want at this hour of the morning?"

"Are you Judge Lester?"

"Yes."

"Well, sir, we'd like to get married."

The judge looked at Willie, then at Liesl, then at the sky. He frowned. "What time is it?" he demanded.

Willie looked at his watch. "It's a bit before seven."

"Do you mean to tell me that you're here knockin' on my door before seven o'clock in the mornin'? Don't you realize that decent people are still in their beds at this hour? Come back at nine." The judge started to close the door, but Willie reached out to stop it.

"Do you have any idea where we might find someone who would marry us now?" he asked.

"Before seven?" The judge shook his head. "Mister, I don't think you're goin' to find anyone." Again, he started to close the door.

"Surely there's someone in this town willing to start their day slightly earlier for one hundred dollars," Willie suggested, waving the bill.

The judge stopped and looked at Willie with a questioning expression on his face. "Did you say one hundred dollars?"

"Yes. *This* one hundred dollars," Willie said pointedly.

Judge Lester smiled broadly, took the bill, then pulled the door all the way open and stepped back to invite them in.

"You two nice folks come on inside here," he said. "Listen, have you had your breakfast yet? I can get my missus to fix breakfast for you. It'll only cost you—" He stopped and laughed, then examined the one-hundred-dollar bill he was holding. "Truth is, for you nice folks it won't cost you nothin' more a'tall. Martha could fix somethin' up for you right away. And I promise you it'll be ever' bit as good as anythin' you might get over at the City Pig. 'Specially Martha's red-eye gravy."

"Thank you," Willie said. "We may just take you up on that."

"Good, good." Lester pointed toward the living room. "Now, you two jes wait in there till I get dressed and—"

"You don't need to get dressed on our account," Willie said quickly.

"I'll be gettin' dressed, thank you," the judge retorted huffily. "They's go to be *some* dignity to a marriage, no matter how much of a hurry a body migh get in. And as long as I'm duly empowered to perform weddin's, I'm gonna be performin' 'em with dignity—and with my pants on."

When Willie and Liesl returned to St. Louis, John and Faith Canfield wer waiting for them at the general aviation terminal, standing in the parking lo in front of John's car. Faith was wearing a worried smile, but John's face wa totally unfathomable. Willie and Liesl walked toward them from the Cessna hand in hand.

Willie's brother and sister-in-law knew about the marriage because he ha called from Piggott and told John the whole story. Although Willie didn't as him to do it, John volunteered to break the news to everyone else.

"How do they look to you?" Liesl asked Willie under her breath as the approached. "Do they look angry?"

"You never can tell about John. He spent too much time around politi cians. He's very good at hiding what he feels."

"Oh, Willie, what if they hate us?"

"They'll get over it."

When they reached the car, John said, "Well, little brother, I'd say you' had quite an active day."

"I stayed busy," Willie said dryly. "How about you?"

"Oh, no busier than a one-legged man in an ass-kicking contest," Jol replied. "If you recall, I had quite a few people to inform about your impet ous decision." Suddenly John laughed and stuck out his hand. "*You old son o gun!*" he roared. "I never would've guessed that you had anything like this you! Congratulations!"

"You aren't angry?" Liesl asked in a plaintive voice.

"Angry? Hell no! My God, we're both as happy as we can be about this, aren't we, darling?"

"I'll say we are," Faith said, smiling as broadly as her husband. She looked at Liesl. "Come here and let me hug you," she said. "I've always wanted a little sister, and now I have one."

"Well," Willie said with a huge sigh, "I must say, I'm relieved that everyone is taking it so well."

"Hold on there, little brother, don't go getting too complacent," John said. "Who said *everyone* is taking it well?" He chuckled. "The fact is, you and your new bride have pissed off a lot of people."

"Who?"

"Who? I think a better question would be who did you *not* piss off? You've got everyone howling, from the jilted bridegroom to all the bridesmaids to the guests who came from out of town and all the way down to the parking-lot attendants who are going to lose out on the tips they would've collected at a large and prominent wedding."

"What about Mom and Pop?"

"Ah, don't worry about them; they'll be okay," John said, dismissing the notion with a wave of his hand. "Same with Liesl's mother. I think they're all a bit embarrassed by everything, but when it comes right down to it, all they want is for you two to be happy." He peered at them. "Are you happy?"

Willie put his arm around Liesl. "I've never been happier."

"Nor have I," Liesl added.

"Well, then, hey," John said, laughing, "what else counts?"

Willie looked thoughtfully at John. Recollections of the past few years flashed through his mind like movie highlights—the triumphs and tragedies of the war, the changes in his life in the years since. . ."Nothing, big brother," he answered quietly, his heart filled with contentment. "Nothing at all."

About the Author

Writing under his own name and 25 pen names, **ROBERT VAUGHAN** has authored over 200 books in every genre but Science Fiction. He won the 1977 Porgie Award (Best Paperback Original) for *The Power and the Pride*. In 1973 *The Valkyrie Mandate* was nominated by its publisher, Simon & Schuster, for the Pulitzer Prize. Vaughan is a frequent speaker at seminars and at high schools and colleges. He has also hosted three television talk shows: *Eyewitness Magazine*, on WAVY TV in Portsmouth, Virginia, *Tidewater* A.M., on WHBQ TV in Hampton, Virginia, and *This Week* in Books on the TEMPO Cable Television Network. In addition, he hosted a cooking show at *Phoenix at Mid-day* on KHPO TV in Phoenix, Arizona. Vaughan is a retired Army Warrant Officer (CW-3) with three tours in Vietnam where he was awarded the Distinguished Flying Cross, the Air Medal with the V for valor, the Bronze Star, the Distinguished Service Medal, and the Purple Heart. He was a helicopter pilot and a maintenance and supply officer. He was also an instructor and Chief of the Aviation Maintenance Officers' Course at Fort Eustis, Virginia. During his military career, Vaughan was a participant in many of the 20th century's most significant events.

Printed in the United States
63993LVS00002B/282

9 781585 86638